Sarah Grazebrook was born in Guildford. After drama school she worked in repertory theatre, at the Old Vic and in television, appearing in many programmes including *The Brothers* and *The Onedin Line*. After having her second child she wrote her first novel, *Not Waving*, which won the *Cosmopolitan* Fiction Award. She lives in Kent with her partner, David Donachie, who writes naval crime fiction, and their two children. *A Cameo Role* is her third novel.

This book belongs to

Marijke Westerhuys

York 18 October 1996

SCEPTRE

Also by Sarah Grazebrook

Not Waving
The Circle Dance

A Cameo Role

SARAH GRAZEBROOK

SCEPTRE

First published in 1996 by Hodder and Stoughton
A division of Hodder Headline PLC
A Sceptre Paperback Original

10 9 8 7 6 5 4 3 2 1

British Library Cataloguing in Publication Data

Grazebrook, Sarah
  A cameo role
  1. English fiction – 20th century
  I. Title
  823.9'14 [F]

ISBN 0 340 67514 4

Typeset by Hewer Text Composition Services, Edinburgh
Printed and bound in Great Britain by
Cox & Wyman Ltd, Reading, Berkshire

Hodder and Stoughton
A division of Hodder Headline PLC
338 Euston Road
London NW1 3BH

For my mother

Acknowledgements

Thanks to the estate of W H Davies and to Jonathan Cape for permission to quote from 'Leisure', from *Collected Poems* by W H Davies.

1

Michael Snelcott, theatrical agent, pressed his fingers lightly together. 'It's a cameo role – the secretary . . . René saw your picture in *Spotlight*. Very impressed.'

Sally Grosvenor rolled her eyes. 'It's an awful photo.'

'Well, yes it is rather,' Snelcott conceded. 'But they wanted someone a bit . . .'

'Downtrodden?' It had got her two parts as battered wives already.

'Not downtrodden exactly.' He sought to convey the director's intentions. 'Someone with a bit of . . . you know . . . experience . . . of life. On the downside.'

Sally smiled. 'Eleven o'clock?'

Snelcott nodded. 'On the dot. René hates people to be late.'

She stood up. 'When was I ever late for an audition?'

Her agent rose and helped her fussily into her coat. 'Oh, not you, darling. Never. But you know what some of them are like. Think it helps to go swanning in half an hour late and screaming about the bloody traffic. Take a word from one who knows,' he leant forward conspiratorially, 'it doesn't. Especially with someone like René. A real professional. He hasn't got time for airs and graces. That's why I suggested you for the part. "You'll like Sally Grosvenor," I said to him. "She's a real little trooper. Never late. Never dries. What more could a director ask?"'

Equity minimum, thought Sally ruefully, aware that the only work Snelcott ever found for his clients was based on his ability to undercut their rivals financially.

Still an audition was an audition. Times were hard and, despite his protestations that the new series would sweep all but *Blind Date* before it, it would probably only mean a few weeks' work if she did get the part. Then she could go back to Resting Pieces, a co-operative of thirty-something actors who mounted classical productions in the hall of a Greenwich Baptist church, at present doubling as a venue for Adult Literacy classes.

Unfortunately the audiences in the Baptist church tended to be those who had come to learn to read, and thus were not entirely ready for the metaphysical debate that made up much of Resting Pieces' productions. They were even less prepared for the unsolicited lurches into song and dance which peppered the dramatic repertoire – a legacy from Colin Manx, company producer and one-time member of Pan's People.

Sally, too, found the combination a bit of a strain but she clung on, mainly from the hope that somewhere in the audience lurked a scout from the RSC who would sweep her away from all this with promises of Beatrice and Portia and tours of the USA. Till such time she filed documents, made occasional commercials and even more occasional sorties to the provinces to play repressed spinsters or badly-treated mistresses who never got to take their clothes off.

Sally didn't desperately want to take her clothes off before an audience; she had no small problem in taking them off in front of a married lover (the only kind, it appeared, available to women in their thirties without a regular income), but she would dearly have liked to be asked. The assorted casting directors, however, to whom

Michael Snelcott occasionally gained her access, had a very clear idea of how to cast Sally Grosvenor. She was what was known as a 'useful' actress. Neither tarty nor posh, gross nor ethereal, she fell neatly into that blob of middle Englanders that people the police stations, hospitals and staff common rooms of British television, offering advice, hot drinks and platitudes, occasionally on the receiving end of the protagonists' pent-up frustration, but never of the audience's sympathy.

Although this provided work in a profession where employment was scarce, it had also bound her, hand and foot, to mediocrity – requiring her only to do what she could not reasonably mess up, rather than stretching her to new and unpredictable heights of theatrical achievement. She was a face without a name, and as such a godsend to her agent, but Sally had not become an actress to be invisible. She had been that all her life. Acting was to be her way out. Only she knew that.

A reputation for reliability had followed her into her private life, or perhaps it was the other way round. Either way she was considered a 'useful' shoulder to cry on and had unknowingly come to enjoy her role as confessor/comforter, though the advice she dispensed was frequently spiked with acid and very rarely acted upon. She lived alone, if not estranged from her family, then certainly divided from it by more than distance.

The theatre had been a world as alien to her elderly parents as Mars, and peopled, they had been prone to believe, by creatures of considerably less integrity. Scientists of some repute, Leonard and Eunice Grosvenor had mistrusted all forms of invention unless backed up by appropriate proofs. Thus Sally and her brother, John, had never been allowed to visit pantomimes as children for fear that Jack's magic beanstalk or Cinderella's coach would encourage a belief in the illogical. This made perfect sense to John who was more stonily rational than either parent, but seemed to Sally a cruelty beyond redemption, only serving to confirm her in the suspicion that she had been stolen at birth for the purposes of genetic experimentation. Dark hints to her schoolfriends (duly passed on to their horrified mothers), had resulted in a trip to an educational psychologist.

Sally had been pronounced sane but 'over-imaginative', leading to the removal of the television set and its rapid replacement with fifteen volumes of *A Child's Guide to Natural History*.

Despite this or more probably because of it, she had plunged headlong into a world of fantasy and make believe which no amount of ecological summer schools or family outings to Dungeness had managed to erase.

In adulthood her alienation had become more marked, with John following his father into chemical research, marrying his sponsor's daughter, and settling down to rear the next generation of sceptics. Sally had tried to show proper interest, particularly after her parents died, but John was too much his father's clone to let the legacy fade, and her efforts to seduce her plummy little nieces with gifts of conjuring sets and fairy tale cassettes had met with hooting derision from the infant purists.

Contact had inevitably lessened and Sally, though disappointed at first, now found that she preferred her freedom and the occasional company of those she liked to regular visits from those she ought to like. It was, however, a state not reached without a certain amount of heart-searching, for whatever their views on its chemical properties, her parents had always insisted that blood was thicker than water.

She let herself into her flat. The answerphone was resolutely unblinking, the second post had brought nothing but circulars. She opened the fridge and extracted a bottle of wine. The phone rang.

'Sally?' It was Colin Manx.

'Colin. Yes. Hello.'

'I can't take no for an answer.'

'I'm afraid you'll have to, Colin. I'm not right for the part.'

'A true artiste accepts no limitations.'

'Well this one does. I cannot do the can-can. I have never been able to do the can-can and, short of a miracle, I never will be able to do the can-can. What's more to be perfectly frank, Colin, I'm not at all sure it's right for *Iphigenia in Aulis*.'

There was a silence as Colin debated whether to wheedle or sulk.

'There's a very good part for you in *Volpone*.'

Sally sighed. 'I don't mind being in the chorus. I have absolutely no objection to that. It's just that I have passed the age where I can split my body into three pieces for the sake of welcoming someone else's son back to Thebes.'

'Maria's had to pull out.'

'Oh?'

'Yes, she finally got her date for her abortion. If you can't do it we may have to cancel.'

'Poor Maria. Is she all right?'

'As far as I know. I'd've asked Kirsty but she'd never learn the lines in time.'

'She was all right in *Pericles*.'

'Yes, but that's because no one else knows them. Anyway she wasn't all right, she was making it up as she went along.'

What do you expect on four days' rehearsal, reflected Sally. 'She's a very good dancer,' she reminded him.

Colin pondered this fact. 'Yes, well, if you're really sure . . .'

'I am. Absolutely. Much as I'd love to have been in it. Anyway . . . there's just the chance . . .'

'What?'

'I don't expect anything will come of it . . . but I've got an interview tomorrow.'

'What sort of interview?'

'Oh, nothing spectacular. Some television series Majestic is trying to get off the ground. About a stationery factory. Sounds dire.'

'It sounds fascinating,' said Sally, having waited forty-five minutes to meet the stickler for punctuality. René Havers thought so too. It had been created by a man from Wardrobe who had moved sideways into Video Audio and hence upwards to Assistant Producer and then down again to Writer.

'It' was *The Firm*, a thirteen-part serial revolving round a small family-run stationery factory in the West Midlands. The script, according to its director, was quite seminal in its ability to unite passion, ambition, loyalty and betrayal with sound working practices and ethnic integration, and all this within Majestic's generous yet limited budget strictures. Havers counted himself lucky to be involved in such a project.

The love interest would be provided by the self-educated young foreman locked in a loveless marriage with the nymphomaniac niece of the chief shareholder. 'We're hoping to get Sean Bean,' he confided sotto voce, 'otherwise we'll probably make him black.'

Havers' dissertation was brought to a halt by the arrival, unannounced (if slamming doors, raised voices and the doleful wail of receptionists could be so counted), of a tall dark-haired woman swinging a Gucci handbag with the vigour of someone about to launch a ship. 'Bloody traffic!' she complained. 'Christ knows how anyone gets anywhere in this bloody town. Do you know how long it's taken me to get from Regent Street in that taxi? I mean, Christ!' The bag struck the desk as she rummaged for cigarettes and lighter.

A pale girl appeared in the doorway. She looked very junior and as the most expendable member of staff had clearly been allocated the task of removing the invader. René leapt to his feet. 'What the hell's going on?' he demanded. 'Ermm,' said the girl and stuck. René turned a simpering smile on the newcomer while endeavouring to maintain his frown in the girl's direction. The effect was of someone recovering from a stroke and Sally made a mental note to practice it in front of the mirror, as it was the kind of part she might well be asked to play.

The woman deposited herself on the corner of the desk and drew heavily on her cigarette. The girl remained in the doorway, while Havers displayed the indecision which had kept him a staff director all his life.

'Stephy, darling. Poor you. Never mind. No probs. Thing here will get you a coffee. I'm nearly through with . . .' he studied his notes, 'Sally, then we can catch up on old times. Just give me a teeny moment, OK?'

Stephy uncrossed her legs, which Sally observed had undergone a certain amount of surgery, and allowed herself to be led by the crimson-faced Thing in the direction of the vending machine. She allowed herself a moment's blissful reflection on the diseases to be caught from them, before being dragged back to reality by Havers' request that they get a move on as time was pressing.

The secretary, it seemed, was a very small part, her main duties consisting of summoning people to the phone and making restaurant bookings for the various members of the family who, despite the threat of imminent liquidation hanging over the company, were never to be seen with less than a four course meal in front of them.

Havers asked her about her acting experience, humphing enigmatically as she recited her CV and only coming to life when she mentioned a recent commercial for crème fraîche. 'The one with the baked salmon cutlets?' he demanded energetically. 'Yes, that's right. I'm the woman who tries to get to the last pot before Felicity . . .'

'Yes, yes, I know. Now tell me – who directed you, by the way?' Sally groped around for the name. Havers' lower lip curled contemptuously. 'No wonder. Do you know the whole of the front of the dish is completely overshadowed by the wine bottle? Anyway, what I need to know is how much dill do you use if you're doing a whole salmon?' Sally stared at him. This was presumably a joke. Instinct told her not to treat it as such. 'I suppose,' she faltered, all her improvisational skills deserting her, 'it would depend on the size of the salmon.'

René Havers gazed at her critically. 'A salmon's a salmon,' he said coldly.

Sally watched her mortgage payments flying out of the window, 'but the recommended amount is two tablespoons,' she blustered. 'Dried, that is.'

Havers narrowed his eyes slightly as though trying to gauge the level of her mendacity. 'That seems an awful lot.'

'It's a very delicate herb.'

'You've tried this dish, have you?'

'Oh, yes. We had it at my brother's wedding. It was a great success.'

Havers humphed again and scribbled something on his pad. Then he looked at his watch, groaned and blew his nose. 'Well, thanks for coming in. It's been most interesting. I've got a lot of people to see, you understand. By the way, can you type?'

'Yes,' Sally lied again, praying he would not ask for a demonstration.

'And all that other secretary stuff?'

'Oh yes. I've worked in a lot of offices in between . . . well, you know.'

'Yup, yup, yup,' said René Havers. 'Thanks a lot.' Sally made for the door.

'By the way I might as well tell you, we're looking for someone black.'

It was three weeks before Michael Snelcott phoned to tell Sally that she had got the part. She had been working in a civil engineer's office, having fought a running battle with Colin over the can-can chorus in *Iphigenia*. Kirsty had proved to be more than usually dyslexic when it came to learning her lines, which wouldn't have mattered particularly if she hadn't had to speak in unison with the others. Colin had even offered Sally the title of Co-director if she would take over, but she had seen this more as a threat than a temptation and refused to budge. She had been to see the production and thought it possibly the worst experience of her theatrical life, returning home with the renewed conviction that Kirsty would be more at home in the Adult Literacy class than ever she would be on the open stage.

The news that she had got the role of Laura Barnes was almost too much for her. Her contract was for all thirteen episodes with an option to renew. Michael Snelcott had arranged a Special Low fee for her, indicating that she didn't normally work for this kind of money (which was perfectly true), but that she was prepared to accept it on this occasion, owing to the length of the contract. Sally would have been prepared to be dyed black if it meant she could buy a new Hoover and some insulation for her bathroom window.

Her news was not greeted at Resting Pieces with the exhilaration she had expected. When she had arrived loaded with wine boxes and peanuts at the read-through for *Volpone* (in which, contrary to promises, she had been cast as a serving wench), she had been told in no uncertain terms that, in accepting the role ('soap opera, for God's sake, and anyway it won't run') she was not only betraying her colleagues but also her calling. 'Not much Shakespeare in a paper factory, duckie.'

She went home disappointed, because she had thought they would be pleased. She had entertained grandiose dreams of refusing to sign a second contract if each and every one of them were not given a part in the series. She had planned the refurbishment of the Baptist Hall, right up to the inclusion of an audiovisual room for the Adult Literacy class. The Sally Grosvenor Theatre – no – Studios. A haven of culture and excellence. So much for that.

Her spirits were immediately lifted by the sight of a thick brown envelope lying on her doormat. It was stamped 'Majestic' and contained scripts for the first four episodes of *The Firm*, dates, recording details, and a map of how to get to the church hall in Cricklewood where the first rehearsal would take place the following week.

Sally hugged the envelope to her, waltzed unsuccessfully round her tiny kitchen and made herself a plate of beans on toast then, curling her feet beneath her in true personality-relaxing-at-home style, she settled to read the treasured document.

René Havers had not lied about the size of her part. Laura Barnes came in on page sixty-one in the first episode, and departed at the top of page sixty-two, having delivered two telephone messages and a cup of black coffee to John Christie who, a quick flip through revealed, had just received the news of his father's tragic death. Episode two was not noticeably much better since most of it took place in the cemetery.

She began to see hints of character development in number three, when she was called upon to offer a handkerchief to a weeping Errant Daughter and remark that 'life could be very strange sometimes'. Since this was the longest speech she had come across so far she made herself a cup of coffee and set to to practice it. After about ten minutes it became clear to her that not only Life, but the words themselves were becoming incomprehensible as she toyed with stress, intonation and accent in an effort to find the perfect interpretation.

The phone rang. It was Make-up to ask what colour her hair was and, on hearing that it was brown, whether she would have any objection to wearing a wig? Sally made none, although she wondered with some alarm whether it would be Afro-Caribbean, and contemplated rethinking her line in terms of a West Indian lilt.

In episode four things really took off. The family was by now enthralled in suit and counter-suit; the factory was threatened with an all-out strike, and Solley Sedgewick, the foreman, had just discovered that his wife, the nymphomaniac niece of the shareholder, was engaged in a lesbian affair with the mother of his nine-year-old illegitimate son. The shareholder, on hearing this had threatened to withdraw his offer to bale out the company and had promptly suffered a minor stroke over Laura Barnes' typewriter. Laura had managed to get him sitting up with a cup of tea and a slice of the sponge cake regularly made for her by the deaf and dumb woman she visited every Tuesday on her way home from work.

Sally made a note to contact the voluntary services to see if they could put her in touch with a friendly local mute.

She saw Laura Barnes as a resourceful woman, albeit practically mute herself. She had inner strengths, deep dark passages just waiting to be explored, a secret life more fascinating than the superficial crises affecting the Christie family. After all, series like *The Firm* often ran for years and years and the scriptwriter seemed to have covered most of the potential plots in the first fortnight. How on earth was he going to maintain the momentum? At this rate there'd

be none of the family left by episode six. Then they would
have to turn to the secondary characters. Sally felt a shrill
sharp stab of panic and delight. Then she would come into
her own.

Someone was moving in. Sally had been woken by the clank of a ramp being lowered, and had been shocked to see a large transit van parked outside her home and three men humping furniture up the path towards the front door.

Five, Marchbank Gardens comprised three flats; her own on the first floor which stretched from front to back, and two on the ground running parallel to each other. All three were similar in size with bedroom, living room, kitchen, and broom cupboard bathroom. The area opposite Sally was part of next door's loft.

Till recently the flat below had been owned by an elderly widow but she had died the previous spring and since then it had been empty. Sally had been nervous at first at the prospect of new neighbours or worse still, squatters, but as time had elapsed and it had remained unoccupied she had stopped thinking about it. Mr Davenport in Flat Two, though well into his eighties, was harmless in every respect but one and Sally had taught herself to live with the inconvenience, reflecting that 'better the devil you knew'. He reminded her vaguely of her father, but in a softer, kinder form, and she had come to feel slightly responsible for him, particularly since the death of his wife. She refused, however, to let her fondness for him spill over into accountability. Neighbourliness was one thing, involvement was another.

She shivered and hugged her dressing gown tighter. It seemed awfully early to be moving anywhere. She looked at her watch. Eight o'clock. And it was Saturday. The fact that in her job no calendrical distinctions existed had never stopped Sally considering the weekend sacred. She wondered if she should go back to bed, but they were making such a noise she'd never be able to sleep anyway. She went to make herself some coffee. Perhaps she should offer the men some? But that would entail getting dressed. No, let them get on with it. Serve them right for waking her up. She peered again round the curtain. One of the men, fair and horribly tanned, looked up and waved. She withdrew hastily and went to run a bath.

By the time she had finished they had disappeared. Can't have much furniture, thought Sally, pleased because it couldn't be a whole family and annoyed because they needn't have started so early and woken her up.

She had arranged to meet Colin at lunch time. He had been a little distant with her since she had got the part in *The Firm* and was obviously feeling guilty because he had rung up at half past eleven the previous evening to say he was going to let her buy him a margarita in the Black Dragon 'to make up for everything'. Whether the onus of making-up was on her or Colin, Sally didn't know, but she was pleased to have somewhere to go at lunch time because, despite its sanctity, Saturday was usually a rather empty day for her, though not so empty as Sunday.

On her way out she peered casually into the ground floor flat. There were a number of cardboard boxes and tea chests dotted around and she could see a mattress leaning against the wall. It looked awfully big. A couple, she thought and sighed resentfully.

Colin was unusually perky, insisting on not only his margarita, which the barman had no idea how to make, but a large steak pie and mashed potato. 'I'm letting you treat me,' he informed Sally between mouthfuls, 'because I know it's been getting you down a bit.'

'What has?' asked Sally, extracting raw onion from her sandwich.

'Oh, this grim little part you've got yourself. But you mustn't worry about it, darling. No one thinks the worse of you for taking it. I mean, we all have to live. But obviously you're missing out – first the *Volpone* role and then if you're going to be stuck in some studio for months on end you're going to lose the *Chester Miracles* as well. Not to mention if we do get *Le Cid* off the ground.'

'*Le Cid*?'

'Yes. A friend of Matthew's got a livery and he says we can have all the horses we need. A whole army if we like.'

'Do you think the Baptist Hall's up to a whole army of horses?'

'Ever the pessimist,' cheeped Colin pinching her cheek. 'And you must try not to be bitter, Sally my love, because at your age it begins to tell. Have you been doing those exercises I gave you?'

'Yes,' lied Sally. 'Every morning.'

'Good. Well keep at it. 'Ooh ee ooh ah ah.' Twenty-four times before breakfast. I never miss and look at my crow's feet. I haven't got any.'

Sally returned to her sandwich. 'I've got a new neighbour.'

'Oh. What's he like? Is it a "he" or a "she"? Or a "they" even?'

'I don't know. Three men turned up this morning. The crack of dawn, and started unloading a van into Mrs Davies'. I assume it must be one of them.'

'Or all three. Goodness, how exciting. I must pop round with a cup of sugar. What are they like?'

'Not your type,' said Sally quickly. 'All bowler hats and brollies.'

'To unload a furniture van? Sounds kinky. I'll walk back with you. I need to borrow your microwave anyway.'

'You what? Whatever for? Anyway you can't.'

'Sally, Sally, Sally ... What have I just said to you? Remember, "every frown is a wrinkle's crown" at your age. Of course you must lend it to me. It's for *Clytemnestra*. We're doing a Benefit Night for Maria.'

'When?' asked Sally, thinking a play about a woman who cooked children was hardly the best possible choice for someone recovering from an abortion.

'On Wednesday week.'

'Well you can borrow it on Wednesday week, then. For the evening.'

'I see. So now you're a television star you've forgotten all your old friends?'

'That's not fair, Colin, and you know it isn't. How am I meant to manage for two weeks without my microwave?'

'You've got an oven. You'll have to learn to cook.'

'I don't want to learn to cook,' grumbled Sally.

'Well, in that case you might as well let me take the cooker as well,' suggested Colin. 'As a stand-by.'

'You can't. It's all piped in. Anyway, I'm keeping it for when I want to gas myself.'

'I shouldn't leave it too long, duckie. Prices are going up again in April. Come on, buy me another drink and stop feeling sorry for yourself.'

Despite her objections Colin insisted on accompanying Sally home. She made him carry her shopping which he did with very ill grace, setting up a liturgy about his sciatica, his bruised forefinger and his stress-related breathing difficulties. Sally suggested that his respiratory problems might be eased if he stopped twittering, and Colin lapsed into a wounded silence which was only broken by the sight of two of Sally's removal men staggering up the path with a large gilt-framed mirror.

'Goodness, is that them? But they're enormous. I wonder if they need any help.'

'What about your sciatica?' snarled Sally as Colin dropped her shopping on the pavement and went bounding after them with the vivacity of a spring lamb.

'Do you need a hand with that?' She turned to see the third man, the one who had waved to her that morning, climbing out of the van. 'Oh . . . Thank you. I can manage. Thanks all the same.'

'Give me the one with the bottles,' he insisted, taking it from her before she had time to object. 'I'm your new neighbour, by the way. Dan Chamberlain. I hope we didn't wake you up this morning. We did make a bit of a racket.'

'Oh no,' declared Sally. 'I'm always up at that time. It was no problem at all.'

They had reached the front door and through it she could see Colin on tiptoes, fingers clinging wildly to the top of the mirror. 'Just giving Keith and Charlie here a hand,' he wheezed as they carried it and him into the flat. 'Back in a mo.' Sally and Dan stood in the hall grinning foolishly.

'I live upstairs,' said Sally.

'I know. I saw you this morning. I waved.'

'Oh. Yes. Well, if there's anything you need . . . cup of sugar . . .'

'Thank you. I suppose it's rude to ask your name?' Sally blushed. 'Oh. Sorry. Sally Grosvenor. I forgot. And that's Colin in there. Colin Manx. He's a friend. Let me know if you want anything.' She hurried up the stairs to be followed shortly by Colin who had promised to make tea for everyone.

'Not those,' pleaded Sally, as he emptied her shortbread on to a plate. 'Why can't you give them the Rich Tea?'

Colin clucked disparagingly. 'The trouble with you, Sally Grosvenor, is that you've got Scottish blood.'

'I haven't at all,' said Sally defensively. 'It's just it won't make any difference to them and I won't have any left.'

'Bread and butter saves the clutter,' said Colin.

The three men sat awkwardly on the edge of her sagging couch while Colin fluttered round them with cups and milk jugs and teaspoons. Sally knew instinctively that they would have preferred mugs and the tea chests below and so would she. They talked about the weather, the parking problems, Sally told Dan the day the dustmen came, and Colin produced a picture of himself as Methuselah which killed all conversation stone dead.

Dan tried to revive it by asking what Mr Davenport was like, but now was not the time to go into details so Sally said he was 'very nice'.

'I'm a director,' said Colin into the vacuum.

'What sort?' asked Keith, struggling with a splinter in his thumb.

'A theatre director,' said Colin as if surprised to learn there was another kind.

'Plays and that?' asked Charlie, trying to show a proper interest.

'Plays and that,' confirmed Colin. 'And Sally's an actress.'

'Go on!' Keith forgot all about his splinter and turned a critical eye on her. 'An actress?'

Sally smiled awkwardly. 'Yes, that's right.'

'What you been in?' he demanded. 'Oh not all that much. *Casualty*. I played a battered wife.'

'Go on!' said Keith again, plainly impressed. 'That's my missus' favourite. That and *Noel's House Party*. What else?'

Sally sought around for programmes he might have seen. 'I was in a Sainsbury's commercial. The one about baked salmon.'

'I can't stand fish,' declared Charlie.

'And I've done some Alan Ayckbourn plays – on tour, not in the West End.'

'They're good,' enthused Keith. 'My missus did the costumes for one of them.'

'Really?' asked Sally and Colin together. 'Yep. Whitby Players. Something about a garden. It was quite funny, some of it.'

'Do you know Joanna Lumley?' asked Charlie, fixing Sally with an advocate's gaze.

'No,' she admitted. 'I was once in a charity show she was hosting.'

Charlie nodded disappointedly. 'Dan here's a teacher.'

'Really?' said Sally again. She was beginning to sound like the Queen.

Dan shook his head. 'I'm just doing some instructing down at the Training Centre.'

'That's teaching,' insisted Charlie.

'What do you teach?' asked Sally.

Dan shrugged. 'Construction, plastering, bit of bricklaying.'

'Plumbing?' Sally interjected. Her overflow had been leaking for weeks.

'He does the lot,' said Keith. 'We're his students. That's why we're giving him a hand. So's we get a good pass at the end.' They all laughed.

'So,' said Colin, 'it's just you, is it, Dan, moving in below?'

There was an awkward pause. The men shifted in their seats. 'That's right,' said Dan eventually, staring fixedly into his teacup. Even Colin could sense he had intruded. 'They're nice flats,' he gabbled. 'Everyone's very friendly. I'm just round the corner, so if there's anything you need . . . cup of sugar . . .'

'I don't take sugar,' said Dan rather sharply. Keith got up. 'Better be getting that van back,' he said. 'Otherwise the bleeders'll be charging you for a second day.' Dan nodded. He and Charlie rose. 'Thanks for the tea.' They left.

'He's nice,' said Colin.

'Who?'

'Who! Dan, of course. Lovely eyes, I don't suppose you noticed.'

'No,' said Sally, who had.

'That's the trouble with you, young Sally.'

'What is?'

'You don't open your heart to love.'

'How's Matthew?' Sally responded primly. Colin sighed and for a moment the mask slipped. 'He's fine. Gone up to look at those horses I was telling you about. He needed a break. The country air'll do him good.' Sally nodded, ashamed of her cruelty. Matthew Rayner, as everyone but Colin knew, was a self-seeking promiscuous parasite of indefinable talent whose hold over Colin had seen him rise from Prompt to Co-Director to Star in the Resting Pieces' productions and, as such, was no small contributor to the company's continuing lack of success.

After Colin had gone, tottering down the path with her microwave clutched to him like Sisyphus' rock, Sally cleared away the cups and thought about her new neighbour.

He didn't look like a teacher, albeit of bricklaying, but nor did he look particularly like a builder. He didn't seem very talkative, but who would with Colin in the room? It would be nice if he could fix her overflow.

Having thus consigned him to the 'possibly useful in a practical way' pigeonhole of her acquaintances Sally turned her thoughts to *The Firm* and all that it might mean for her in terms of her career. She had seen the look of glazed politeness on the three men's faces when she had mentioned her provincial tours. It was a look she had seen a million times before. Television was what counted. Television meant status and status meant clout and clout, sufficient clout, might one day mean the phone call from the RSC. 'We're wondering if you'd be interested in playing Portia.'

3

The rehearsal room in Cricklewood was, if anything, less prepossessing than the Baptist Hall in Greenwich.

Despite the sunshine it smelled of damp and mildew and what natural light there was was effectively obliterated by the heavy green drapes, covering all but the grimy skylights. The butterflies in Sally's stomach took a perceptible plunge as she crossed the threshold.

Several people were sitting on slatted wooden chairs against the wall as a white blonde girl rushed to and fro with a metal tape measure and marking tape. Her movements were dictated by a thin young man in cycling shorts half hidden behind the folds of a ground plan.

At the far end of the hall was a stage on which a trestle table had been erected. Behind this stood René Havers, deep in conversation with a large red-faced man smoking a pipe. The pipe was obviously causing Havers some discomfort for he had periodically to turn his head aside and gulp in air before returning to his discussion. Watching him Sally was reminded of a singing exercise which required you to take in a deep breath and then expel the air in a series of eight small puffs. She herself had never got beyond six and that only by turning purple and sinking slowly to her knees.

'Are you Sally?' A tall girl with curly hair was standing beside her, clipboard in hand. Sally nodded. 'Yes. Sally

Grosvenor.' The girl smiled. 'I'm Mary Jennings, Assistant Floor Manager. Do you know anyone here?'

Sally looked around. The man in the corner seemed familiar.

'That's Patrick Crichton,' said Mary, following her gaze. 'He's playing John Christie, the older son.'

Sally frowned in an effort to place him.

'I believe he was in a series called *Dr Merryweather*,' the girl murmured. 'I don't remember it myself.'

'*Dr Merryweather*?' echoed Sally, rather louder than she had intended. Several people including Crichton himself turned and stared at her. She reddened. 'I do remember it,' she whispered apologetically. She had watched it in her childhood on her grandmother's black and white set. Crichton had been the idealistic young locum who had set so many pulses racing with his piercing dark eyes and arrogant disregard for the conventions of a small Highland practice. That must have been twenty years ago. Where, she wondered, had he been since?

Closer inspection came down heavily on the side of 'in mothballs' for, though Crichton's eyes were still dark, they now watered rather than pierced, and the black soft waves of his once abundant hair had given way to a scattering of salt and pepper, though not without some evidence of a fight, Sally noted, seeing the inky tips to his sideburns.

'Patrick, this is Sally Grosvenor. She's playing Laura Barnes.'

Patrick Crichton turned on her a ravishing smile. 'Sally, how lovely to meet you.' He seized her outstretched hand and pressed it greedily to his lips. Sally swallowed and said she was glad to meet him too.

Mary turned to an elderly woman whom Sally instantly recognised since she was never off the screen. 'This is Marley Webb. She's playing Rebecca Christie, the founder's widow.' Marley Webb beamed and squeezed Sally's hand. 'Lovely to meet you, dear. I'm sure we're all going to have a lot of fun.'

Sally would look back on this day and remember Marley's words.

'Hello, everyone.' René Havers had managed to dispose of the red-faced man who was now suffocating the blonde floor assistant. 'Welcome. I'm afraid it's a little bit make do at the moment. Poor Rolo has only just got hold of the ground plan, but we hope to be up and running after the read-through, so if everyone's ready?' There was nervous laughter and much remarking that it was 'now or never', and 'always darkest before the dawn', making Sally wonder if the cast had had a hand in writing the script, which was certainly laden with similar forebodings.

Chairs were drawn up, cigarettes produced, objected to and finally consigned to the far end of the table where the two female culprits, one very young and the other whom Sally recognised as the formidable Stephy, puffed angrily and ostentatiously into the already hazy air.

René Havers sat at the opposite end bordered by Crichton who had protested most strongly against the smokers, and Marley Webb who continued to beam and chat to all around her with the insouciance of a baby at a church service.

Havers cleared his throat. 'Right. Let me say once again how glad I am to see you all here. We had a tough time casting, believe me, but I'm confident we've got together the very best team that money could buy.' There was strained laughter as the actors eyed each other surreptitiously and tried to calculate their category of fee.

'Not that money was a criterion,' Havers assured them hastily. 'Quality is what counts with Majestic. I'm sure no one can have any doubts about that. Now, before we begin, just a few points about the scripts. I know we're only up to ep. four, but I'm sure you've already begun to get a feel for the way the thing's going.' Affirmative grunts. 'I mean this guy, Wellard Kenning, can WRITE.' He looked around as if daring anyone to challenge the assumption. Sally kept her eyes firmly glued to the table. 'And although it's only early days, I think I can safely say that we are on to a WINNER here.'

'Hear, hear,' said a man of about thirty with a protruding Adam's apple.

'Oh, yes,' enthused Marley, handing round marshmallows. 'Very good indeed.'

This seemed to satisfy Havers who relaxed slightly. 'We're on a tight turnaround. I don't have to tell you that. One day off a fortnight if we're lucky. Worse than a munitions factory.' There was muted laughter. Plainly not everyone's agent had explained the minutiae of the contract. Sally began to think one line an episode might not be so bad after all. 'Anyway,' the director rubbed his hands together, 'what are we worrying about? With a script like this the thing will act itself.'

Patrick Crichton unfurled a paisley handkerchief and blew his nose noiselessly. 'With all due deference to the author,' he murmured, raising his eyes above half-moon reading glasses, 'I think even the Bard acknowledged the need for actors.'

There was a silence. René Havers laughed a little hysterically. 'And that's just what I was coming to. We have the ideal combination. Scripts that are second to none, artistes of international repute,' nobody disputed this, 'and an A1 producer in Jeff Wilkins.' The red-faced man, on hearing his name, sent acknowledging plumes of smoke in their direction.

'Before we begin, I'd just like to make sure we all know each other and, more importantly, who everyone's playing. Could get a bit confusing otherwise.' They were back on firmer ground now. There was an expectant shuffling as the actors took each other in.

'Ladies first.' Havers turned to Marley. 'This, as I'm sure you all know, is Marley Webb. She needs no introduction from me except to say that she is playing Rebecca Christie, mother to John and Richard who have inherited Christie Paper Inc. on the untimely death of their father, Robert.'

'And me,' came a croaky voice from the end of the table. The younger of the smokers was glaring petulantly at Havers' receding hairline.

'And you, of course, Veeney, my pet. Veeney Rogers is playing Solange, the boys' sister.' Glancing at the trio Sally estimated that there must have been at least thirty years between Rebecca's confinements.

'Next to Veeney is Stephanie. Stephanie Baxter is playing Cariola, our anti-hero Solley Sedgewick's wife. Speaking of which I'm afraid Drewe Atkins, who plays Solley, can't be with us till lunch time.'

'Why's that?' barked Crichton.

Havers' mouth creased with minute irritation. 'I really can't say, Paddy. Anyway we won't get to him before this afternoon so it's not a prob. Next to Steph we have Simon Peyter who is playing John's brother, Richard.'

'Playboy of the Western Midlands,' broke in Peyter, his Adam's apple bobbing like a yo-yo.

'Right,' said Havers without a flicker of amusement, 'and next to Si is Dilys Lewis who is John's wife, Lesley,' Dilys Lewis was a very thin woman with raven black hair. She looked terminally depressed. 'On Dil's left we have Hazel Macintosh who is Richard's better half, Trish.'

'Couldn't be much worse,' interjected Simon and rocked with laughter.

'Right,' said Havers again, 'next to Haze is George – George Bennett who plays Alderman Bradley, Cariola's uncle and chief shareholder in the company. Here on my right is our leading man, Patrick Crichton who plays John Christie.' He consulted his list. 'And last but not least, we have Honeytree Jalullah.'

Sally felt the eyes of the assembly upon her. 'Er,' she began. Havers looked across at her then slapped his hand to his head.

'Idiot,' he cried, not indicating to which of them he referred. 'Not Honeytree at all. She was unavailable. It's,' his eyes raked the paper in front of him. 'Sally Grosvenor,' said Sally, unable to bear the tension.

'Sally Grosvenor,' Havers echoed with relief. 'And she's playing Laura Barnes, John's secretary and, I think it might be safe to say, the linchpin of the series.' There was generous laughter at this statement since no one in any way believed it.

A wheezing sound heralded the return of Jeff Wilkins. 'Good morning, everyone.' He removed his pipe from his mouth and gazed round at them thoughtfully, as though trying to remember why they were there. 'Glad to see you all here. Jolly good. I won't be around for a couple of weeks. Spot of fishing. Can't get out of it. But I'll be down to see you at the Producer's Run. Looking forward to it. Jolly good.' With a final belch from his pipe he made his way back down the stairs and pottered off across the hall, giving the blonde girl a friendly pat on the buttocks as he passed.

'Good old Jeff,' said René Havers as the front door swung shut. 'Rolo, get these windows open, will you, before we all choke. This is Rolo Dempsey, by the way, PA. Best there is. And down there's young Penny. All right, Pen?' The blonde went a deep red and avowed that she was.

'Righto, everyone. Any questions?' Veeney wanted to know why she was limping in scene eight and not in scene twelve. Havers seemed genuinely surprised by the question. 'Scene twelve is the next day. You've got better.'

'It says in my script that I had a bicycle accident as a child and have had trouble walking ever since.'

'Yes, well, trouble . . . "trouble",' flustered the director. 'That doesn't mean you go everywhere on one leg. Come on, darling, use your imagination. It's like the curse. Some days you feel lousy, some days you feel fine.'

'I always feel lousy with the curse,' growled Veeney, looking very much as though she might have it at the moment.

'Yes,' wheedled Havers, 'but you only have it one week in four. It's the same with Solange's leg. OK?' Veeney said nothing, but she threw him a very sharp look. 'Right,' said Havers, 'if there are no more questions I really think we'd better get a move on.'

'What I'm wondering,' said Patrick Crichton, 'on page forty-seven . . .'

'I think we'll leave it till we get there, Paddy old love,' interrupted Havers. 'These things are better sorted out as we get to them.'

'Please yourself,' said Crichton, his nose burrowing deep in his handkerchief.

'Penny,' called Havers. 'Where's Penny?'

'She's making coffee,' said Rolo who had drawn up a chair and was waiting, pencil poised.

'So who's on the book?'

'I am,' said Rolo.

'Ah. OK. Begin.'

'*The Firm*,' intoned Rolo like a speak your weight machine. 'Scene One. Interior John Christie's office. Morning. Phone rings. John answers. Christie Paper Inc. Who? What? When?'

There was a whinnying from the paisley handkerchief as Patrick Crichton prepared to wrest his part back from Rolo. 'I think we'd better go again,' said Havers wearily. 'Rolo, stick to the directions, there's a love. I know you're burning to act but so are all these other lovely people.' Rolo went a brilliant red and muttered about having brought the wrong glasses.

They began again, Crichton reading with a mixture of Irish and west country accents which plainly confused his siblings who countered with a careful blend of Brummie and Glaswegian. Only Marley Webb as his mother stuck resolutely to the Home Counties.

Sally delivered her own lines in her normal voice as the only dialect she was proficient in was Australian and it hardly seemed the moment to try it out.

Rolo Dempsey, whether because of his glasses or because his thoughts were elsewhere, continued to snatch everyone's best lines. Patrick bore with considerable patience the filching of his scene in bed with his wife, and the greater part of his confrontation with his younger brother over the price they should pay for carbon paper, but when it came to raining down curses on his father, his sister and the company itself, he was not prepared to delegate the task to Rolo. 'D. him. D. her. D. the whole d. company,' he roared, hardly flinching at this nod towards the watershed, 'I'd rather see him dead at my feet.' Rolo, who could not see the full stops, mumbled mantra-like beside him till he came to the bit about Christie's whole world being torn apart like paper. This reminded him that he had forgotten to phone Props about the printing presses so, abandoning the script, he rushed away to sort it out. Crichton could hardly believe his luck as he continued his tirade unaccompanied and, pulling out all the stops that twenty years of provincial touring had welded shut, he treated them to a soaring sobbing rendition of the Christie firm's latest set of accounts.

Unfortunately this decision to 'seize the moment' had a rather deleterious effect on the next scene which involved the news that his father had indeed dropped dead, not at his son's feet, but at those of the his mistress, Melanie Rinseworth, a role so far uncast. More than a little out of breath the actor was reduced to a few panting monosyllables. 'What? Dead? My father? Dead? OH. Oh.' At which point

Sally made one of her few entrances to ask if her employer would like a cup of coffee.

If John Christie would not, it was clear that the rest of the cast was getting pretty desperate for one and René Havers, sensing that this might be an appropriate place to pause, brought forward the coffee break, which annoyed his principle actor greatly since he suspected that by the time they resumed Rolo might well be back in situ. Havers, however, had made the sensible decision of replacing Rolo with Penny when they began again, and by lunch time they had managed to get through the bulk of episode one.

The atmosphere was easing as they trickled out in search of the nearest pub. Only Stephanie Baxter had declined to join them and was last seen gliding towards a trattoria in a haze of cigarette smoke.

Crichton, having made his mark, seemed less tetchy and insisted on buying everyone a drink. Observing him again, Sally thought she detected some of the old allure in his crinkly crooked smile and sudden barks of laughter.

Marley Webb had been set upon by autograph hunters and sat beaming like a May Queen as they crowded round her. Veeney Rogers was playing pool with Penny and Simon Peyter. They all drank a toast to the success of *The Firm*, much to the excitement of the regulars who nudged each other and gazed critically at the women's legs.

Marley escaped her fans and came and sat beside Sally, seizing the menu and examining it in detail. 'What are we going to have?' she asked. 'What are you having, Patrick? Are you going to try the pie?'

'I'm having goujons of cod in batter,' said Patrick. 'With chips.'

Marley appealed to Sally. 'Do you think you'll have the pie, dear?' Sally considered. She'd been planning to make do with a sandwich in case she had to buy a round. 'It's chicken and leek,' urged Marley enthusiastically. 'I do love chicken.'

'It does sound very nice,' Sally agreed. Marley's face lit up. 'Two chicken and leeks, please, dear,' she called to the barmaid.

'Chips or boiled?' asked the barmaid. Marley's face contorted. 'I'm supposed to stick to boiled,' she confessed, casting a wary eye at René Havers who was making disgusting noises with a hot dog. 'Yes, boiled please, dear. Twice?' Sally nodded. Marley's voice dropped. 'Blood pressure. I'm not allowed fried food.' Sally nodded sympathetically. Marley's voice sank even lower. 'It's in my contract.'

'What? They've actually told you what to eat?' Marley smiled deprecatingly. 'Well it's thirteen episodes, isn't it, dear? With an option of twenty-six to follow.'

'But you could get anything you wanted. You're never out of work.'

Marley smiled again. 'I'm also seventy-four. There comes a time when you don't want to fly to Barbados and tell someone how good their credit cards are. Or catch the five thirty train to Edinburgh to be someone's grandmother. You want to turn up at ten in the morning and know you'll be home by half past six. And you want to know you can turn your heating on and have a couple of brandies if you fancy it.' She rested her hand lightly on Sally's arm. 'And most of all you want a few friendly faces round you while you're working. A family. That's what a serial gives you. Ah, here come our pies.'

4

After lunch they reassembled and were joined by an effete young man who introduced himself as Drewe Atkins. Sally was disappointed, though not surprised, to see that he bore small resemblance to Sean Bean and even less to a black man. The newcomer explained that he had spent the morning filming a commercial for British Telecom and that the money had been 'telephone numbers, darling'. This he clearly thought too witty to be repeated less than five times in as many minutes, before going on to inform them that he would be away for most of next week as well, 'doing a titchy Bacardi ad in Barbados'. Sally watched the colour draining from René Havers' face as he received this news, but he said nothing beyond welcoming Drewe to the production and suggesting that, since time was at a premium, they should complete the read-through with all speed and proceed to plotting the moves.

'This your first?' Simon Peyter had plonked himself down beside Sally and was gazing raptly at Penny's bouncing breasts as she rushed around the hall setting props.

'First what?' asked Sally. 'Serial – long-runner.'

He turned his attention to her. 'Chance, I suppose I mean.'

Sally nodded. 'Yes, I suppose it is. If you can call it that. It's not exactly a big part. How about you?'

Simon sucked in his cheekbones. 'God, yes. If I screw this up I'll kill myself.'

Sally smiled uncertainly. 'Let's hope it doesn't come to that.'

Simon opened his eyes very wide. 'Don't you believe me? I'm perfectly serious, I assure you.' Sally shrugged. 'I can't think it would be a good career move.' Simon peered at her as though she were completely mad then burst into hiccups of laughter. 'I like you,' he chortled. 'You're all right.'

'Sssh!' hissed René furiously. He was trying to coax Drewe Atkins into something like a display of passion, which was proving very hard given his obvious distaste for women and Stephanie's habit of staring at him as though he had just crawled out of a dung heap.

Sally now began to observe her fellow actors in more detail. Apart from Marley Webb none of them were 'names', if you discounted the fact that Patrick Crichton had been once. George Bennett she recognised because he was one of those actors who turned up in everything, always playing themselves. George's particular line was brusque no-nonsense businessmen which he trotted out to order, Alderman Bradley being no exception.

Young Veeney Rogers looked less like an actress than anyone Sally had ever seen. In fact she looked ill. She was pale and spotty and wore no make-up beneath her clump of crimson hair. She was also alarmingly thin, with blue-veined arms and long shapeless legs extending from tartan Doc Martens. She complained of the cold incessantly. Marley was clearly worried about her and had tried to get her to share her chicken pie at lunch time, but it had transpired that Veeney was a vegan and lived almost entirely on bread and Marmite which probably accounted for the state of her t-shirt, if not her health. She seemed to have no respect at all for René which, though understandable, struck Sally as a little reckless, given the power he held over her career.

Hazel McIntosh reminded Sally of her pack leader in the Fifth Limebridge Brownies. She was kind, capable and breathtakingly competent. Sally watched with admiration as her fingers twisted and turned the wool of the shawl she was crocheting, in between delivering her lines, fixing the zip on Simon's jacket and covering her own script with an exquisite sheet of William Morris wrapping paper. The other Christie wife, Dilys Lewis, was decidedly less active. Sally was not sure if she had seen her move all day. Instead she sat, gazing into the middle distance, apparently impervious to all that was happening around her.

Of them all Sally thought probably only Marley and George Bennett had any idea of what was expected of them. They managed to sail through the author's clichés without overtly flinching, whereas Patrick Crichton tended to dwell on the terrible prose as though trying to make sense of it.

The potpourri of accents was now reaching epidemic proportions with Stephanie branching out into mid-Atlantic and Drewe countering with a sort of farmyard stutter, not made any clearer by his tendency to lisp. Sally was struck with the thought that anyone turning on their set in the middle of the first episode would be justified in thinking it was a programme on speech impediments.

Simon had wandered away and could be seen turning the same wide-eyed expression on Penny who was looking suitably alarmed.

Marley took his place. 'It's going very well, isn't it?' she murmured contentedly. Before Sally could answer she pressed her arm conspiratorially. 'Do you like sponge droplets?'

'I'm not absolutely sure what they are.'

'Oh, they're delicious. Little sponge cakes with jam and a tiny splodge of cream.'

'Sssh!' René threw them a savage look.

'They sound very nice,' Sally whispered. Marley beamed. 'I shall make some and bring them in,' she mouthed back. 'Poor little Veeney needs feeding up a bit. Such a pretty little thing but there's nothing of her.' She pottered off to admire Hazel's crochet.

René Havers had his eyes shut, palms pressed to his temples. Looking at him, Sally felt a wave of pity. It couldn't be an easy task to weld this disparate group of people into a unit. Especially with so little time. True, the programme would not start broadcasting till October, but an awful lot must hang on the success of these first few episodes.

Over on the far side of the hall the action was gathering pace. 'You may be my husband, Solly Sedgewick,' barked Stephanie, struggling with the incongruity, 'but I know a lie when I see one.'

'And you may be my wife, Cariola Thedgewick,' retaliated Drewe, showering her with spittal, 'but you're a Chrithtie, too, and blood'th thicker than water, tho they thay.'

'Right,' snapped René, his hands clenching and unclenching at his sides. 'That was excellent. PENNY.' Penny came hurtling from the kitchen. 'Is tea ready yet?'

'Yes, René. Practically. I'm just boiling the kettle.' Penny dipped her eyes as though confessing to an unwanted pregnancy. 'Right. Break everyone. Ten minutes. There's a lot to get through.'

'René's such a pro,' Simon confided, dunking his biscuit in Sally's tea.

'Have you worked with him before?' she asked, wondering on what the observation was based. Simon sucked in his cheeks. 'Me? No. But you can tell, can't you? He sort of exudes confidence.'

'I expect you're right,' Sally agreed, watching as their director poured a handful of Valium down his throat.

* * *

After the break rehearsals began in earnest. Obviously the intimacy of television imposed its own restrictions, but nevertheless Sally was a little surprised to find that the only person allowed to walk across the office in both directions seemed to be John Christie. His mother came in and sat, his brother came in and hovered, and she herself never got any further than the filing cabinet, despite the difficulty of having to hand her employer his coffee over a distance rarely equalled in the long jump.

The brothers' wives never got to the office at all. Dilys was confined to an ironing board, and Hazel to a hall phone. Poor Veeney spent most of her time sobbing in the corridor outside the print room. This was denoted by two very narrow black lines into which her various abusers and comforters had to squeeze at sundry points in the drama. It was fine for Veeney herself who was slim to the point of emaciation, but not so easy for Marley who, despite the strictures of her contract, still came down firmly on the side of 'cuddly'. Sally wondered fleetingly if the forbidding of fried food to her had more to do with *The Firm*'s budgetry constraints than any real anxiety for her health.

By six o'clock the episode had been set. Havers released them with the instruction that they should have the words by tomorrow morning and that they would start a full run as soon as Costume and Make-up had done their rounds.

Marley walked with her as far as the Underground. 'I think it's all going to be an enormous success, don't you, dear?' she asked.

'I hope so. I really do,' said Sally. It was the best she could manage.

Marley chuckled. 'See you in the morning, dear. Word perfect.'

Sally hesitated. 'Does René really expect everyone to know all their lines by tomorrow?'

Marley nodded. 'Oh yes. This is a budget show, remember.

He wasn't joking about the munitions factory. I've worked with René before. He's pretty tough under all that boyish charm. Goodnight, dear. Safe home.'

There was another message from Make-up when she got home, slightly higher-pitched than the first, demanding to know what size shoes she took. This seemed an odd request unless they were planning to give her a club foot, which would possibly account for her inability to cross the office. She rang back but there was no reply so she made herself some supper and settled to the daunting task of learning her lines for the morning.

Shortly after nine there was a knock on the door. Sally had given up on her script and was watching a programme about Spanish donkeys who seemed, on the whole, to have a worse deal than Spanish bulls. She made a note to write to her MP and then another to find out who her MP was.

Opening the door she found Dan Chamberlain clasping a monkey wrench and covered in a fine coating of plaster dust. 'Hullo,' she said amicably. 'I don't suppose you know who our MP is?'

Dan's eyes registered confusion. 'Not offhand. I've only just moved in. My other one had to resign. Is that any help?'

'Not really,' said Sally. 'What can I do for you?'

Chamberlain hovered uncertainly. 'It's a bit awkward.'

'How awkward? Do you want to come in? I'm watching a programme about donkeys. Those Spaniards are absolute bastards when it comes to animal welfare.'

'Their child care facilities are second to none,' Dan informed her self-consciously, staring at a point on the ceiling.

'Really?' said Sally, raising an eyebrow. 'Still that's not much consolation for the donkeys, is it?'

'No,' Dan admitted, seemingly unwilling to pursue his argument.

'Is that why you came?'

'Sorry?'

'To tell me about child care in Spain?'

'No of course not,' said her neighbour with a hint of irritation. 'You mentioned it. I just wanted to paint a fairer picture.'

'I see.'

'There is a small problem.'

'What sort of problem?'

'Well, two really.'

Sally waited. Dan heaved a sigh. 'The first is the old boy downstairs. I went over to introduce myself and that and we got chatting. And it seems he thinks he's an Alsatian or something. I thought you ought to know.'

Sally burst out laughing. 'I do know. I've known for months. Actually it's a Dalmatian. I was wondering how I was going to tell you.'

Dan looked relieved. 'But the thing is he . . . last thing at night, I don't know whether you've noticed . . .'

'He pees all over the bannisters.'

'He doesn't do it every night, does he?'

'Of course he does. Dogs are very regular.'

'And you don't mind?'

'I'd prefer it if he didn't, if that's what you mean. But apart from that he's a very sweet old man.'

'Dog.'

Sally smiled. 'What was the other thing?'

'I've cut your water off.'

'You've what?'

'I've cut your water off. I was plumbing in my shower and it seems we're on the same system and there was a small problem and now I can't get your water back on.'

'What do you mean, you can't get it back on? You just turn it, don't you?'

Chamberlain looked harassed. 'Well, yes you do normally . . .'

'But . . .?'

'But you see your pipes are imperial and mine are metric.'

'So?'

'So I need a gauge link to make sure there's no link between the two. And I haven't got one. Till tomorrow.'

Sally stared at him incredulously. 'Are you telling me you turned my water off without my permission and now you can't get it back on?'

'I thought I'd be able to.'

'Well, that's very helpful. You're saying I've got no water till tomorrow?'

'Yes. No. You haven't.'

Sally was seized with a wave of panic. 'But I've got Costume and Make-up coming tomorrow. I can't turn up unwashed. What am I going to do? Look at my hair, for God's sake.'

Chamberlain took a step back, plainly alarmed by the force of the outburst. 'I didn't mean to,' he repeated. 'I'll have it back on by tomorrow.'

'That's no good to me.' Sally began to pace the floor with the anguish of Patrick reciting the company accounts.

'You can use mine if you want,' suggested Dan. 'The bathroom's nearly finished.'

'Oh, well that's good news,' snapped Sally. 'And it has the added attraction of running water.'

'I don't know what else to suggest,' Dan pointed out. 'These things happen.'

'I thought you were supposed to know about "these things". I thought you were meant to be teaching people. God help the building trade if your students are being set loose on it.'

'I think you're over-reacting a bit,' said Dan sullenly. He

took a breath, 'I realise that for women these things are more important than for men.'

Sally stared at him. 'Like child care in Spain, you mean?'

Dan's eyes darkened. 'I was only trying to see it from your point of view. Isn't that what men are supposed to do nowadays?'

'I'd be interested to see how it looks from your point of view. Move in crack of dawn. Three days in the house. Right, time to cut the woman upstairs' water off. What's next? Lead lining off the roof? How about the lights? They still seem to be working.' She flicked the light switch angrily on and off.

Dan watched her sulkily. 'Has anyone ever told you you overact?' he asked.

'What do you know about acting?' demanded Sally, stung.

'Only what I've seen.'

'Oh, yes, of course. *Noel's House Party*. They're all straight from the Moscow Arts, aren't they?'

Dan shrugged and turned back down the stairs. 'My shower's there if you want it.'

'I don't.'

'Good.'

There was a click as Mr Davenport opened the door of his flat and came tottering out. 'Thought I heard voices,' he said affably. 'Settling in all right, young man?'

'Yes thank you,' said Dan.

'Young Sally'll see you're all right,' said Mr Davenport. 'She's an absolute treasure. Been like a daughter to me. That's how neighbours ought to be, don't you think?'

'Oh yes,' said Dan energetically. 'I couldn't agree with you more, Mr Davenport.'

'Just call me Spot,' said Mr Davenport. 'I'll have some

potatoes for you at the weekend, Sally.' He turned and shuffled back into his flat.

'I wouldn't have called no door "nearly finished",' Sally grumbled as Dan tacked the blanket over the gap. 'I would have thought as a building expert the very first thing you'd want in a bathroom is a door.'

Dan swivelled his hammer longingly in his hand. 'I could brick you in if you like. It'd be no trouble.' He stood back. Sally pulled at the blanket critically. 'It doesn't stretch.'

'Who's looking?'

'Yes, well . . . don't,' she retorted, feeling she had rather overstated her attractions.

Dan went into the kitchen. 'Do you want a beer?' he called.

'No thank you,' said Sally primly, dragging a chair in front of the slit. 'I shall be about five minutes.'

'Right,' came the reply. 'I'll just get my clothes off.'

5

'Is that your normal style?' Wendy, Costume, was staring with professional disdain at the halo of frizz surrounding Sally's face. Sally knew she shouldn't have gone to bed without drying it, but the strain of even washing it with her odious neighbour lurking feet away from her blanket had been such that she'd gone straight to bed when she got back.

She ran her fingers through the crackling tendrils. 'I wear it up sometimes.'

Wendy sighed, something she did a lot, and whipped a skein of hairpieces from her holdall. Deftly she held them against Sally's head. 'Is that your natural colour?' she demanded briskly.

'Yes,' said Sally.

Wendy sighed again and wrote something beside her name. They were joined by Make-up, a square woman in corduroy slacks and a bomber jacket. 'Jean, this is Laura,' said Wendy without looking up.

'Sally,' said Sally.

Neither of them took any notice. 'I'm wondering if she could wear glasses,' Wendy continued. 'Who else has got them?' Jean looked at her list. 'Only Rebecca for reading. We were wondering about Richard. He needs ageing up a bit.' Wendy clucked in frustration. 'What do they think I am? A miracle worker?'

Sally thought this unlikely on the available evidence, but Jean roared with delighted laughter. 'Of course they do, darling. That's why they gave you the job.' This appeared to mollify Wendy who permitted herself a girlish trill. 'Does she have any scenes OB?'

'No,' said Jean, 'not so far.'

'Thank God for that,' said Wendy. 'No coat, then. How old's she meant to be?' Jean consulted her list.

'Twenty-nine to thirty-five,' she said doubtfully. They both looked at Sally.

'I see her in a skirt and blouse,' said Wendy.

Jean nodded. 'Not a suit?'

'No, not a suit. Lesley's in a suit, and Cariola. Laura's not an important character. We don't want her to stand out. Something navy, I think, with a little blouse, quite plain. She can wear her own shoes.'

Sally wondered if the other members of the cast were faring any better. Looking across the hall she could see Patrick standing with both his arms outstretched while a man with a tape measure pirouetted round him. His face bore an expression of saintly resignation. Marley and Simon were drinking coffee and running through their lines while a dwarf female skinhead flapped an identical card of switches at their heads. She looked as though she was trying to swat a fly.

Veeney was arguing with René and Drewe had not yet arrived.

'The thing is,' Wendy was saying, 'do we want her older or younger?'

'Younger?' suggested Jean.

'Older. John's only thirty-seven, remember. The older the secretary looks, the younger he'll look.' Sally had visions of herself crossing the office on a zimmer frame. That would certainly explain her inability to get as far as the fax machine. The two women had wandered off, still discussing ways of rendering her hideous and wondering whether the budget could run to a course of suntan treatments for Patrick.

'Any sign of Drewe yet?' René Havers' restrained tone hinted at storms to come. It was already a quarter to eleven.

'I'm sorry, I simply cannot have that.' Stephanie Baxter's voice cut fiercely across the hum of conversation. 'No, I'm sorry, but that is absolutely impossible. René, love, can you come over here a minute please?' Sally noted Wendy's twitching face as René reluctantly left his pacing to see what the matter was.

'René, darling, am I totally mad or did we not decide that Cariola was THE glamour factor in this series?'

'She is certainly one of the more – exotic members of the family.'

'Exotic. Precisely. Now can you explain to me or, for that matter, to these two dear ladies how I am supposed to look exotic in a Mix and Match tweed ensemble from Marks and Spencers? I mean, PLEASE.'

René's cheeks flapped in and out as he glared at Costume and Make-up. 'What is this?' he asked.

'It was only a suggestion,' said Jean, coming to the aid of her colleague who seemed to have lost all use of her vocal cords. 'Stephanie didn't understand what Wendy meant.'

'I understood Marks and Spencer's Ladies Wear,' said Stephanie icily.

'I was going on to say,' squeaked Wendy, but had to pause for breath, 'that if Stephanie didn't like the idea of that, we could perhaps have a look in South Molton Street.' Her voice had now hit top C so she had to stop again and resume lower down. 'I think Cariola might shop at Brown's.'

The faintest glimmer of triumph flickered across the actress' face. 'I tend to agree.'

'Unless, perhaps Peter Jones?'

'I like Brown's.'

The humiliation now being complete Stephanie was all graciousness. 'When would you like us to go shopping?'

'Oh, well, I'll fit in with you.' Wendy was not to be outdone in the consideration stakes.

'Darling, you must be rushed off your feet. Just tell me when you want me. I'm yours to command.'

'Oh, well in that case . . .' Wendy shot frantic looks at René. 'Perhaps after rehearsal tomorrow? It's late night in the West End.'

'Perfect,' agreed Stephanie. 'Oh, hang on, though. I'm meeting Frank. We're going to see that thing at the National that everyone's raving about.'

'I wonder if I could "borrow" Stephanie for a couple of hours on Saturday morning, then, René?'

'Nope,' said René. 'We're doing a full run.'

It was finally decided that Wendy would cancel her trip to the V & A and come in on her day off when René was almost sure he would be able to spare Stephanie. Further discussion was curtailed by the arrival of Drewe who had been to the dentist and then got stuck in a traffic jam in Kilburn High Street. Nobody believed him, with justification as it turned out, for he later confided to Veeney that he had spent two hours being photographed in his bathing trunks for a possible part in a film version of *Timon of Athens*, to be directed in Italian with English subtitles.

Wendy and her helpers departed, leaving the cast to discuss amongst themselves the various iniquities of their lot. Veeney had been promised pink streaks and some new Doc Martens so was in relatively good mood. Patrick had been threatened with blond streaks and was absolutely livid, although he was not averse to the projected sunbed sessions. Simon, who did not have a lot of hair at all, was to be fitted for a toupé. Sally was still unclear what they had in store for her, but an educated guess led her to suspect a blue rinse at best, and possible alopecia if the streaks didn't work on Patrick.

'Right, everybody. Scripts away. Ready for a run.' The words rang round the hall like a knell. Sally's mind went completely blank.

She need not have worried. It soon became clear that whatever effort had been put in to the learning of episode one of *The Firm* had been largely wasted.

Patrick was particularly at fault, extending the writer's protracted pauses into silent retreats as he paced his chalked-out office, chin in hand, brow furrowed in furious contemplation. Marley knew her lines, but since they were almost entirely addressed to her elder son, she had nowhere to put them till Patrick emerged from his mutism with a demand for a prompt, followed almost immediately by 'I know that, I know that. What comes after?'

Poor Penny on the book was reduced to a quivering wreck by coffee break, having had to read out everybody's part and then suffer their inexorable wrath for coming in just as they were 'about to remember'. Sally did better than most since very little hung on whether she offered coffee or lunch, and therefore was not responsible, (as Simon had been), for bringing forward Robert Christie's funeral to three hours before his death, or, in the case of Veeney, for demanding her right to an abortion before the results of her pregnancy test were made known.

René Havers crept around the hall in soft-soled shoes looking like a trapped rat. Thin lips pursed, he wrote copiously in a fine-lined notebook, periodically picking at a wart on his knuckle.

The afternoon was devoted to 'tricky bits'. To her immense relief, Sally was not required for any of them. She sneaked into the loo and spent twenty minutes trying to mould her hair back to its normal shape, then sat in a corner and ran through her lines again. Marley came and plied her with butterscotch. 'I hope he doesn't keep us all day Saturday.'

'I bet he does,' said Sally.

'I expect you're right. He's really got the bit between his teeth, hasn't he? To be perfectly honest,' Marley glanced stealthily around, 'I don't think he's completely happy with his casting.'

'Oh?' Sally felt an icy chill run down her spine. 'Is that your natural colour?' echoed through her mind.

'Not a word to anyone,' whispered Marley, who had already told three people, 'but it's Drewe.'

'Drewe?' repeated Sally, turning it into an elongated snort as Marley signalled her to silence. 'He's a bit . . . young. Don't you think?'

'I suppose he is,' said Sally, reflecting that that was the least of his problems. 'I think René's been a little hasty. Obviously the boy's got talent, but really Solley, well, Solley needs someone with a bit more . . .' Marley sought around for something that would not denigrate whatever qualities she had managed to spy in Drewe Atkins.

'Bulk?' suggested Sally.

'Yes, bulk. What a clever little thing you are, dear. Have another butterscotch. There's nothing of you. I like your new hairstyle, by the way. You look like Barbara Stanwyck. When she was young, that is. Is Gwenda giving you something nice to wear?'

'A blouse and skirt, I think. She wasn't very specific.'

'No, well they never are, are they? Such sweet things, though. I always like the Wardrobe. What are you laughing at?'

Sally smiled. 'I was just wondering if there's anyone you don't like.'

Marley considered. 'I'm not very fond of that man in charge of the police force,' she said finally. 'I think he's got some very mistaken ideas. Still, dear, politicians. It's not a job I'd like. It can't be easy for them.'

'Tea,' came the director's wrathful voice. 'Back at a quarter to.'

There was a palpable sense of dejection amongst the cast when René dismissed them that afternoon. Not because they had forgotten their lines, but because of a growing feeling that most of their lines were best forgotten. The initial excitement at being part of a brand new peak time programme, at being a leading character – or even, as in Sally's case, at being in work – could not disguise the fact that *The Firm* was a pretty imperfect proposition. The tantalising prospect of several months' work stretching into years, should the options be taken up, was looking more and more like an invitation to sit in the stocks.

Sally shuddered, squashed on the tube amongst the anonymous commuters, to think that in only a few weeks' time she might not be able to travel on the Underground without people nudging each other and whispering her name. Where two days ago this had seemed like a glorious dream, now it was looking ever more like a nightmare.

She wondered if Dan Chamberlain had got her water back on yet. He'd better have. It was his fault she was probably going to have to wear a wig. She also wondered if she would have to wear the same navy skirt and plain little blouse throughout the series or whether, in the interests of general hygiene, she might be permitted a spare set.

There were signs of heavy activity in the hall as she opened the front door. Several planks of timber were stacked against the wall. She struggled past hoping, in spite of herself, that Mr Davenport would not choose now to mark out his territory. There was no sign of Dan, although his front door was wide open. She made straight for the kitchen and turned both taps full on. There was a stuttering sound followed by several gurgles as the water made its way down the pipes, flowing freely into the sink. 'Thank God for that,' she muttered and went to try the bathroom. That, too, was functional again. She wondered if she ought to go and thank the man but decided not. After all it had been his fault in the first place. Still if she said nothing he might think he could do it again with impunity. A quick glimpse at her hair convinced her that this would not be a viable situation. She went to the top of the stairs. 'Mr Chamberlain.' There was no reply. Grudgingly she descended. Someone was hammering. 'Mr Chamberlain,' she took a tentative step. The hammering continued. She followed the sound to the kitchen. Chamberlain was bent over a worktop smacking nails into a cabinet. Sally coughed. He turned. 'I just wanted to say thank you for putting my water back on again.' Dan took a nail out of his mouth. 'All right, is it?'

'It seems to be. I've only just got back.' Dan nodded. 'I'm sorry about all that.'

'Yes, well . . .' Sally strove to combine reproof with magnanimity. 'If you could just let me know if you're planning any major works in future?'

'Yes, of course. I should have thought.'

At half past eight the lights went out. Sally, in the process of frying herself an egg, screeched with fury as the invisible fat shot up at her. Typical bloody PowerGen. Weren't they supposed to let you know if they were cutting you off? Unless it was an emergency. She went to the window. The lights across the street were still on. Come to that, so were the ones next door. A hideous thought gripped her. Fumbling for some matches she prodded her way to the front door and opened it. She felt for the landing light. It was working. I don't believe this, she thought. I do not believe this. I'm going to kill him. If he comes out of that door in the next ten seconds, I'm going to kill him.

She waited, breathless with intent, for Dan Chamberlain

to appear. She knew now what drove Lady Macbeth to her unseemly acts of violence. It was nothing to do with regal ambition, it was having to live without basic utilities. Yesterday the water, today the lights, presumably tomorrow he would be filling her flat with carbon monoxide. The man was a liability. Worse than that, he was a maniac. He shouldn't be allowed to wander free. The thought of him actually passing on his skills to innocent young trainees defied belief.

The door opened. Dan emerged, looking sooty and bemused. He nodded to Sally. 'Whoever dreamt that lot up must have been off their flaming rocker. The whole lot blew just as I touched it. There's no cutout on any of them. I've never seen anything like it. Absolute death trap.' He wiped a grimy arm across his face.

'Then how come you're still alive?' demanded Sally with glacial restraint.

'Because I knew what I was doing,' replied Chamberlain cheerfully. 'I was coming to see if you could spare me a couple of candles till I've sorted it out.'

'I haven't got any candles,' said Sally with horrible calm, 'but if I had I should be making effigies of you with them. How dare you stand there asking me for candles when you've just cut off my electricity? I admire your cheek, I do really.'

Dan Chamberlain looked mildly annoyed. 'It's only for a minute or two. I'll have them back on as soon as I've found the right fuse.'

Sally shook her head. 'I don't believe this. It's not two hours since I was standing in your flat while you swore blind you'd ask me before you did anything like this again. Two hours. And all the time you were planning to cut me off. You've no right to keep doing this you know. It's harassment. I suppose the next thing is you'll be trying to burn me out. Oh my God.' She turned and fled back to the kitchen where her wizened egg was spattering its last. She turned off the gas and was plunged into total darkness.

In her yoga class they stared for hours at imaginary sources of light. It was accounted very restful and an aid to serenity of mind. Sally pictured her imaginary gas flame, then her imaginary table lamp, then her imaginary three-bar spotlight. Having thought of all these she took a deep and soothing breath and screamed at the top of her voice. After that she felt a great deal better.

As if on the cue the lights came on again.

6

The days passed quickly with rehearsals, fittings, rewrites, re-plotting, rumours about who would play Melanie Rinseworth, more rewrites, and what were euphemistically defined as 'technical hitches'. These could range from the wrong coloured envelopes to the threat of a total walk out by Props if their lunch breaks were further disrupted. Throughout it all the actors remained stoic, with the exception of Stephanie who clearly felt less than one tantrum a day was the equivalent to missing a cue.

Hazel had nearly finished her cot cover and had been commissioned by Marley to make a poncho. Sally was a little surprised by the dimensions till the old lady drew her aside and confided that the poncho was really a present for Veeney because, 'she's always so cold, poor lamb'. Sally hadn't the heart to say that the green and orange which would have looked quite cheerful on Marley would make Veeney look like a carrot.

Simon Peyter had worked his way round the entire cast professing his intention of killing himself if *The Firm* was not a success. His plan had received a mixed reaction, George insisting that 'no bleeding job was worth it', Drewe immediately phoning his agent to see if his own part could be enlarged to accommodate a leading character's demise, Dilys not batting an eyelid and Hazel assuring him that his feelings were 'perfectly natural under the circumstances'. Patrick and Stephanie were united for perhaps the only time in their lives in attesting they would personally finish him off if anything he did were to interfere with their own chances of fame and fortune.

Only young Penny, paler than ever and weak with adoration, had crawled into the back of Simon's Ford Sierra and offered her body in token sacrifice. Sally had spotted them emerging as she hurried back to rehearsal one afternoon. They hadn't seen her for which she was grateful, because along with his other confessions Simon had let it be known that he was married to an 'absolute angel', the 'backbone of his life' without whom his career would never even have got off the ground. Sally, who had come across his type more times than she cared to remember, felt sorry for Penny, but she lacked Hazel's expertise or Marley's curiosity and so let the matter wash over her.

No further disasters had befallen her at home so far, though the planks remained piled in the hall, irritating her more each time she saw them. She thought of speaking to Dan Chamberlain about them but she hadn't seen him since the electricity fiasco and really she had too many other things to think about without getting into another row with him.

Colin Manx had turned up late one night just as she was going to bed, and had spent a full two hours sobbing into her cushion covers because Matthew had yet again been seen cavorting with the owner of a local Greek restaurant, when he was meant to be rehearsing his role of Orestes for Maria's benefit night. Colin had confronted him on his return only to be fobbed off with some tale of 'researching the true Greek psyche' which, as Colin rightly pointed out, should not entail mutual masturbation.

Sally, exhausted and uncharacteristically depressed by Colin's determination to find an excuse for his lover's behaviour, had been on the brink of telling him exactly what she thought of Matthew and all his ilk, but the sight of the ageing harrowed face, unhelped by any amount of ooh ee ooh ah ah's, had dredged up the usual Mary Renault stand-bys, and she had seen him off in a taxi at a quarter past two with the last of her Belgian chocolates and the firm conviction that if she fluffed her 'would some coffee help, Mr Christie?' just once more she might well be reduced to servicing Greek restaurateurs herself before too long.

She washed the hall floor, as was her habit. Poor Mr Davenport. He was such a gentle old man. It was hard to understand how someone like him should be reduced to peeing in the hall, albeit in the guise of a Dalmatian. Why couldn't he have been a cat, or better still, a goldfish?

Colin had remonstrated with her more than once on her lack of tolerance. 'You're cold,' he often remarked when she had been impatient with him. 'You don't know how to give.'

'And you don't know how to stop giving,' she would retort aggrievedly.

'I know which I prefer.'

'So do I.'

Lying in bed too tired to sleep she thought about his accusation. Insomnia gave it a significance it would not normally have deserved. How could anyone say she didn't know how to give? She was always giving, particularly to Colin. Look at the lunch she had bought him only last Saturday. When had he last paid for his own meals, let alone anyone else's, setting aside the odious Matthew who didn't count? And it wasn't just Colin. She gave to charities – she was quite incapable of passing a tin shaker in the street. She shopped in Oxfam, she used recycled notepaper, she had even once taken part in a sponsored three-legged race. She shuddered as she remembered how it had brought about the end of her last enduring love affair. 'Enduring' as in 'six months, on and off'. Pretty good by her standards, but she could never have lived with a man who complained about her speed in a three-legged race.

Could she have lived with anyone? It was difficult to envisage. She had shared digs with people at various times, but that was different. The thought of giving up her hard won independence for the privilege of picking up someone else's socks was not one which tempted her greatly. Of course it would have been nice to have someone around to cheer her up when she felt low but that would have been counterbalanced by their need for her to do the same for them, and her experience with Colin had taught her that commiseration was nothing if not addictive.

No, she was better off as she was – free, unencumbered, self-sufficient. What more could anyone wish for?

She woke at a quarter to eight, panicking that she had missed the alarm and was dismayed to find she had done herself out of half an hour.

Arriving early at rehearsal she found a distraught Penny weeping pitifully into the cast's biscuits. 'Penny, whatever's the matter?' she asked, trying to forget her own pounding head. Penny looked up aghast. 'Oh nothing,' she choked. 'Nothing at all. Really.' She fled in search of props to set.

Sally sat down. What a mess people made of their lives. Penny, young and pathetically innocent, wasting herself on a balding married man who would be out of her life in six months' time. His own, too, very likely, if he stuck to his promises and the script stuck to its present standards. But Penny was young. She would recover. What about Colin? Nearing fifty and throwing away everything on a promiscuous prat whose legacy to him would probably be Aids?

And what about poor Mr Davenport? Widowed, batty, how much responsibility did she bear for him? 'Like a daughter to me,' he had said to Dan, but she wasn't his daughter. She was only a neighbour. She couldn't get involved or where would it all end? She shook her herself. It's not my fault, she thought. People have to take charge of their own lives. It's not for me to try to sort them out.

'Morning, Miss Mouse.' Patrick, newly coiffured and looking unnaturally brown, came sweeping into the kitchen. 'I don't suppose you could be an absolute angel and make me a cup of that delicious coffee I so adore?' Sally said nothing and Patrick, noting the silence, turned to examine her more closely. 'On second thoughts, why don't I make you a cup? Heavens, girl, what have you been up to? You look like death warmed up.'

'I feel like it,' she admitted. 'I had a bit of a late night, that's all. I supposed I'm not used to them.'

Patrick clattered ineptly around with the kettle. 'Do you think this is enough water? Where shall I plug it in? I don't suppose you know where young Pen keeps the coffee?' In the end Sally made it as she knew he intended her to.

Simon arrived just as she was pouring the water. 'Oh smashing. Any chance of a cup for me? I've had a shitty journey. Burst water main in Highgate. Diversions everywhere.' Sally debated informing him that he had a burst water main of his own in the shape of Penny to worry about, but other people were now arriving, and really it was none of her business. Best not to get involved.

Penny had pulled herself together by the time the rehearsal got going, though Sally could not help noticing how her pale eyes followed Simon longingly around the room whenever she was not occupied elsewhere.

More rewrites appeared. Closer examination revealed that they were actually the original text but it was now so long since anyone had seen it that they were greeted as new and innovative by the majority of those concerned.

It was becoming abundantly clear that certain scenes, particularly those involving the elusive Drewe, were not going to be ready for studio the following week. What's more, Stephanie had still not got her costumes, and there seemed to be some problem about who would insure the location buildings.

Meetings were held. Jeff Wilkins had been contacted in his Highland retreat. Faxes flew, timetables were re-arranged. Sally found herself staying later every evening, mainly because she and Marley were the only people who signally failed to come up with a reason why they should not. Stephanie had dinner parties, Patrick ex-wives to console, Simon was doing voice-overs, and Veeney sang with a grunge band called the Haemorrhoids the other side of town. Drewe was never there anyway, and Hazel and Dilys had no scenes that didn't involve the others so there was no point in detaining them.

It was on her way home after one of these late sessions that she bumped into Dan Chamberlain. He was coming out of the Adult Education Centre, a tatty leather folder under his arm. She was too close to pretend not to have seen him. The two of them gazed at each other in mutual apprehension.

'Hullo,' said Sally briskly, preparing to cross the road.

'Hullo,' responded Dan, delving in his pocket. 'Oh no,' he exclaimed with theatrical despair. 'Left my keys inside. See you.' He hurried back into the building. Pathetic, thought Sally. I wasn't going his way anyway. She had decided to call in at the Baptist Hall, ostensibly to see how rehearsals were going, but really to check on her microwave. She wished she hadn't as she saw it perched precariously on a plywood bench, its plug amongst several sprouting like fungi from the adaptor. 'That's dangerous,' she said to Kelly who was stage managing. 'You could have a fire. The wiring's very old in here, you know.' Kelly grunted in acknowledgement and lit a cigarette. 'How's it going?' Sally asked, afraid she had sounded too censorious.

'It's fine,' said Kelly. 'Col's doing a marvellous job.' As if to test the truth of this remark Colin appeared on the opposite side of the stage and sank balletically down before burying his head in his arms and beginning to sob hysterically.

'Which part is he playing?' whispered Sally.

Kelly shook her head. 'He's not. He's directing it. I think Matthew's just walked out again. He's been a bit funny all week.'

Matthew's habit of walking out, either on Colin or the production or both, was now so regular as to have become an unofficial part of the rehearsal schedule. What the more tactful stage managers referred to as 'afternoon free', the less patient among them had taken to calling 'Matthew's flip'. Neither reference had the slightest effect on the young man's neurosis which peaked with the predictability of PMT two days before the technical rehearsal and subsided again within twenty-four hours amid much weeping and hugging and swearing of eternal devotion. Sally had more than once wondered why Matthew seemed unable to reproduce these fountains of emotion in any of the roles allotted to him, which had so far ranged from Hamlet to Al Capone and back again via the Count of Monte Cristo.

'I'd better go,' she whispered again to Kelly.

Kelly nodded. 'You coming to the show?'

'If I can. Is it still Wednesday?'

'Not sure. Might be Thursday. If Bob's back.'

'Where's Bob gone?' Bob never got any work.

'Hospital. His hernia job came up. Col was furious. Said he'd done it on purpose.'

'Oh surely not? I mean Bob's been waiting eighteen months, hasn't he?'

'That's the point. Why pick now when he's got a decent part? Col said he should've belonged to BUPA. He's thinking of making it a condition of joining the company.'

'Is that wise?' asked Sally. The image of Colin touring

the private wards in search of unemployed actors with a penchant for sado-masochism was not a pretty thought.

'Sally, my love. Thank God you've come.' Colin, bored with crying to no audience, had spied her through his fingers and was now making his way delicately between the latex molehills covering the forestage. 'Darling,' he seized her hands and squeezed them helplessly between his own. 'You look worn out. I'm going to let you take me for a drink. I'm all washed up here. In fact I think this production will be my last. I can't take it any more. I'm drained. Completely drained. Still let's not talk about me. I want to hear all about what's been happening to you.' He led her, chattering nonstop about the trials *Clytemnestra* was causing him, the perfidiousness of Bob (though not Matthew), and the inferiority of her own microwave, out of the side door and across the road to the Black Dragon.

Sally dutifully purchased their drinks and a Cornish pasty for Colin who hadn't eaten for weeks and was not sure if he ever would again. Cornish pasties obviously didn't count, she reflected, watching it bobbing down his throat.

'Oh, look,' Colin gargled, pointing an ethereal hand in the direction of the door. 'Isn't that your friend?' Sally followed his gaze. Dan was standing at the bar, his back half turned to them.

'Not my friend,' she said quickly. 'He's just a neighbour, Colin.'

'Call him over,' insisted Colin, his eyes alight.

'No,' said Sally firmly. 'Anyway he's probably with someone.'

'It doesn't matter. If you don't I will.' Colin was away, bouncing through the chairs to the bar. Sally saw the look of surprise on Dan's face as Colin tapped him on the arm and gestured to where they were sitting. She also saw the reluctance with which he followed him across the room, Colin prancing ahead like a winning poodle at Crufts. Really some of her friends were appalling, she reflected wretchedly. Perhaps she should start looking for some more normal acquaintances now her career was taking off. She gazed around the bar and thought how totally normal everyone else looked.

'Here we are.' Colin squeezed himself affectedly into the chair in the corner and gestured Chamberlain to the one opposite. Sally sat between them feeling less like a gooseberry than a malignant tumour, her face set in fury with them both. 'I can't stop,' began Dan. 'No,' Sally cut in, 'neither can I.' The three of them sipped their drinks.

'Tell me,' said Colin, oblivious to the annoyance he was causing, 'you are going to come to our next little offering, aren't you?'

Dan grunted politely. 'I'm not much of a one for the theatre.'

Colin gave a tinkling laugh. 'That's what a lot of people say until they've seen one of our productions. Don't they, Sally?' Sally stared hard at her nails. 'But they come out feeling completely different,' continued Colin. 'Now take next week's production for instance. *Clytemnestra*. Now to a lot of people that might sound like just some boring old Greek tragedy where the woman kills her husband and serves her sister her own children cooked in a pie. And they might think "that's not for me".'

Dan was visibly shocked. 'I think I might be one of them,' he muttered.

'Ah, but that's just the point,' Colin leaned forward in his enthusiasm and clasped Chamberlain's forearm. 'We've managed to get over all that. Oh, we've got the murder and the infanticide and all that but we've got MORE. So much more. We get right to the heart of the tragedy, and we do it in a way that is – immediate, if you see what I mean.' He gazed poignantly into Dan's flecked hazel eyes then abruptly released his grip and turned to Sally. 'I really think you have to bring Dan with you.'

'I'm not absolutely sure I can make it myself, Colin.'

'Nonsense, of course you can make it. It's Maria's benefit. You have to make it.'

'I thought Bob was in hospital.'

Colin clicked his tongue dismissively. 'Don't mention that apostate's name to me, if you don't mind. Anyway, he'll be out by then. They only keep them in for twenty-four hours these days. And that's for heart transplants.'

Sally made a last ditch attempt. 'I think Dan's pretty busy, Colin. He might not have time.'

'Aaah.' Colin flung a hand to his head in mock despair. 'The Philistines are among us. Of course he has time. "What is this life if, full of care, we have no time to stand and stare?" He must make time. And I know you will, Dan. You have such a sensitive face. You must not close those brilliant eyes to the light that art can shine in them.' Any further homilies were cut short by the arrival of Kelly to say that Matthew had returned and was now sitting on stage crying his eyes out and threatening to throw himself under a train if Colin didn't come back and forgive him for being a selfish cow.

Had Sally been less anxious to curtail the discussion she would have been tempted to tie Colin to his chair, in the hope that Matthew might break the habit of a lifetime and keep his word. The matter was taken out of her hands, however, by Colin who immediately leapt to his feet and ran choking from the pub in order to restrain his loved one from anything so likely to further jeopardise the opening night.

Dan and Sally remained seated. 'I'm, er, sorry about that,' said Sally finally, setting her glass down and preparing to leave.

'No,' said Dan. 'Nothing to be sorry for. He's quite lively, isn't he? Colin?'

Sally grimaced. 'You could say that. He's very kind, though, under it all.'

Dan nodded. 'I'd never have guessed you were an actress.'

'Thanks.'

Dan frowned. 'I didn't mean it like that. It's just that you're not exactly the way you expect actresses to be, if you see what I mean.'

Sally steeled herself. 'How do you expect actresses to be?'

Dan considered. 'I don't know really. More actressy, I suppose.'

Sally laughed. 'Like Colin, you mean?'

Dan grinned. 'I suppose I do a bit. I mean it's not hard to imagine him working in the theatre. In fact it's a bit hard to think of him working anywhere else.'

Sally sighed. 'I sometimes think I might have done better if I had been more neurotic.' There was a spluttering noise from Dan. Sally looked up in alarm. 'Are your all right?' Dan nodded, wiping his eyes vigorously.

'You're well-balanced, are you, for an actress?'

Sally eyed him curiously. 'I think I'm pretty well-balanced on anyone's terms,' she said mildly.

Dan smiled. 'When's your serial coming out?' he asked.

'The middle of October. October the fifteenth it starts. We'll still be filming then. It'll be awful if the critics pan it. Imagine having to turn up at work and carry on knowing everyone thinks you're rubbish.'

Dan drained the last of his beer. 'I'd've thought that happened all the time to actors.'

Sally was inexplicably annoyed that an outsider should speak so cavalierly of her profession. 'It doesn't make it any easier.'

'I suppose not. At least with my job if you screw anything up you can go back and do it again.'

'If you can get the parts,' said Sally drily.

Dan laughed. 'You're never going to forgive me for that, are you?'

Sally shrugged. 'I doubt it. I'm not the forgiving type.'

'Why not?'

'I can't see the point. Why forgive someone for something they're probably not sorry for anyway, and will more than likely do again the minute they get the chance?'

Dan was watching her curiously. 'Don't you ever do things you regret?'

'Of course I do.'

'But don't you want people to forgive you?'

Sally gathered up the beer mats and started to make a house with them. 'Up to a point. I don't give it much thought, to be honest. If it's something small it usually gets brushed over anyway, doesn't it?'

'What about the big things?'

Sally lowered the final mat on to her house. 'There are no big things,' she said steadily.

Dan gave a low whistle. 'Lucky you.'

'Yes. Lucky me.' She looked at her watch. 'I must be going. I've got a load of new lines to learn before tomorrow.'

Dan nodded. 'I've got an early start. We're doing a practical in the morning.' Sally's eyebrows rose.

Dan smiled. 'Don't worry. It all takes place in a secure environment.'

'I'm glad to hear it,' she responded. 'What are you teaching them tomorrow?'

'Sewerage.'

'They keep you late at the college, don't they?' Sally remarked as they turned into Marchbank Gardens.

'Not really. Ten till five. Not too bad for a loafer.'

'But it was half past eight when I met you . . .'

'Oh that,' Dan looked away. Sally could have sworn he

was blushing. 'I do an evening class, a couple of nights a week.'

'"How To Stay Ahead in Sewerage"?'

Dan stared ahead angrily. 'Nothing like that.'

'What?' probed Sally, her curiosity aroused. 'French? Upholstery? Sugarcraft for Christmas? I once did a Musical Appreciation class, but I got a job when we got to baroque and by the time I came back it had closed.' Dan said nothing. They had reached the gate. Crossly he fumbled for his keys. Sally noted they were in a different pocket to the one he had pretended to search when she met him. 'It doesn't matter,' she said airily, producing her own. 'You don't have to tell me if you don't want to.'

'Thanks. If you must know, it's psychology.'

'I didn't know they did classes in that,' said Sally, genuinely surprised. 'I've never seen it in the brochure at the Baptist Hall.'

'Yes you have,' said Chamberlain stiffly. 'It's called "Understanding the Modern Woman. For Men".' He opened the front door and disappeared into his flat.

Twenty minutes later there was a knock on Sally's door. It was Dan. 'Oh. Hullo. Again.' said Sally.

'Hullo,' said Dan formally. 'Again. That is . . .'

'Yes.'

Dan took a breath. 'Erm . . . you know what your friend was saying . . .?'

'What?'

'About going to his play . . .'

'Oh, Colin. Yes?'

'Well . . . I mean, could you get tickets?'

'How many?' asked Sally, trying to sound as though it was probably sold out.

'Two.'

'I should think I could arrange that.' She hesitated. 'If

you don't mind me saying, Colin's productions . . . they're a bit . . .'

'Over my head?'

Sally recoiled. 'No. I didn't mean that at all. Why do you say that?'

Dan looked at her ironically. 'Because I'm a labourer. I'm not artistic, am I? I watch *Casualty* and *Match of the Day*.'

'Oh for God's sake,' retorted Sally, 'spare me the "coals in the bath" saga. Anyway for a labourer you make a jolly good artiste. I was only going to say that most of Colin's productions are rather long . . .'

'How long?'

'Very.'

'And?'

'A bit complicated.'

'You don't think I'd understand them?'

'I don't think Colin understands them. Will that do?' She had the idea that he was laughing.

'And you'll come with me?' The request took her by surprise.

'Me?'

'As interpreter.'

'I'm not sure. I may not be free.'

'If you are?'

'All right.'

'Promise?'

'I don't make promises.'

7

Monday being the last official day of rehearsal barring the filming and the Producer's Run, Sally had expected a greater sense of urgency when she arrived.

Patrick was nursing a hangover, the result of a supper with one of his ex-wives which has started off well but rapidly degenerated into the ritual slanging match that had driven them apart in the first place. He had resorted to a pub, then a wine bar and finally the buffet on Charing Cross station before finishing the night off in a club renowned for its clientele of out-of-work actors. Here he had got into a fight with an ageing contemporary who, it appeared, had also been up for the part of John Christie. The fact that the two of them had both been too drunk to make contact did not lessen the dramatic relish with which Patrick recounted his evening, in between screeching at Penny to bring him more aspirins and pleading with Marley to crunch her boiled sweets more quietly.

Veeney too looked as though she had passed more restful nights. Her normally pale skin was almost luminous, the only colour coming from the treacly circles under her eyes and the matching purple of her lipstick. It was hard to imagine her in anything but a Hammer Horror, although, Sally reminded herself, *The Firm* had all the ingredients for a very passable imitation. She was arguing yet again with

René, not, so far as Sally could gather, about anything to do with the show, the word 'clinic' being uttered several times by both of them. René finally stalked away and left his young protegée slumped against a radiator gnawing furiously at her fingernails and spitting the offcuts into a paper cup.

Wendy Costume had taken Stephanie shopping as arranged, but this did not stop their director making some very caustic comments about actors who cared more about clothes than performances. His annoyance could possibly be traced to the fact that Drewe had arrived on time for the first time since rehearsals began and was now busily engaged on Rolo's mobile phone trying to bring forward his interview for the Next catalogue.

George Bennett had a dental appointment at a quarter to twelve and was anxious to have his stroke before coffee. He had drawn up a book on potential Melanie Rinseworths, and was trying to persuade Hazel Macintosh to run it for him while he was away. Poor Hazel, who had completed the poncho and was now two thirds of the way through a tablecloth, protested that she was a befriender for Gamblers Anonymous and as such could not be expected to take over.

Dilys Lewis was having trouble focusing. Twice she had crashed into the table, the second time knocking all René's notes flying. 'Oh for God's sake, Dilly,' Havers had begun, then checked himself. 'Got out of bed the wrong side this morning,' he apologised feebly, avoiding Dilys' wavering eye as she edged herself stiffly towards a chair.

At lunch time Stephanie re-appeared looking very pleased with herself, trailed by a harassed Wendy, arms piled high with carrier bags. 'Did you manage to sort anything out?' snapped René, who had just been informed by Drewe that he would have to get away early as Stephen Spielberg had expressed a particular desire to meet him. 'Yes, thank you, darling,' drawled Stephanie. 'Not everything, of course, because we were in such a rush, but enough to get us past studio this week, I should say.' Wendy was seen to blanch at this, since she had already exceeded her budget by forty per cent and could well envisage Majestic Production Company deciding to lop the excess from her fee.

The afternoon crawled on. George was back with a frozen jaw which proved so effective as he stuttered and sank into unconsciousness over Sally's typewriter that it was generally felt he should have another jab before recording to maintain the quality of performance.

Patrick was heard to mutter that the same treatment for Drewe might lift his acting into the realms of the merely brain dead but Marley came strongly to the young man's defence, declaring that it was 'only nerves, dear. We all get them'. Patrick asked wearily why no one else felt the need to shout on one note with their head slanting sideways like a ski slope, but Marley simply smiled and pressed a melting sherbet lemon into his hand.

Filming schedules were handed out and mulled over gloomily. Everyone expect Patrick had been called at six in the morning. He was not required until eight due entirely to the superior pull of his agent, a power that had regrettably not been reflected in his fee.

They said good night. 'Want a lift?' Simon Peyter was just manoeuvring out of his parking space. Sally hesitated. 'I'm only going as far as the tube.'

'Get in. Where do you want to be? I've got to go into town.'

'Charing Cross, for Greenwich.' There was a furious honking behind from a van that Simon was blocking. 'F. off,' called Simon cheerfully. Sally got in, fastidiously avoiding any glances at the back seat which had reverted to upright and was now covered in tins of cat food.

'I've played Greenwich,' said Simon as he cut in on a foreign driver. There was a hideous screech of brakes and

Sally closed her eyes. 'Ever heard of wing mirrors?' bellowed Simon. 'Nice little theatre. You done much there?'

'No,' said Sally, hoping she would not have to mention Resting Pieces.

'Always the same,' sighed Simon, leaning on his horn as an elderly woman put her foot on a zebra crossing. 'Look at them. Hopeless. "Care in the Community"! I don't know. No, I come from Salisbury. Could I get into the rep there? Could I heck.'

'"A prophet is not without honour, save in his own country",' said Sally.

'*Richard the Second*,' said Simon.

'I thought it was the Bible.'

'Nope,' Simon shot through an amber light, '*Richard the Second*. Stake my life on it.' Sally smiled nervously, thinking Simon's life was not something he rated very highly. Perhaps the cat food had something to do with it.

'How do you think it's going?' he asked as they rocketed down Edgware Road.

'The car?'

'The show. *The Firm*. How do you think it's shaping up?'

Sally considered. She didn't know Simon well enough to be frank, and anyway there was always the possibility that an adverse comment would drive him to kill himself immediately, and her with him. She pictured the headlines, 'Unknown actor and actress killed in car crash'. It was not in the realms of a 'Gotcha'.

'I think it's coming together very well.'

Simon turned on her an inquisitor's eye. 'Really?'

'Yes. I think you're very good. The scenes between you and Marley are excellent.'

'You're not just saying that?'

'No. SIMON. There's a BUS.'

'Stupid idiot,' muttered Simon, flashing his lights as he swerved round it. Sally had a brief image of the lower deck full of terrified faces. 'René's such a pro,' he continued, giving the V sign to the bus driver. 'All right if I drop you at Piccadilly?'

'Oh yes, anywhere. Here if you like.' Simon laughed. 'Piccadilly's fine for me.'

'Are you going to see a show?' asked Sally, trying to take her mind off the traffic.

'Nope. Bit of post-synching. Keeps the wolf from the door.'

He dropped her outside the Café Royale.

'Thanks very much,' she murmured, feeling as if she were being rescued from a shipwreck. 'Any time,' called Simon and shot off, narrowly avoiding a crowd of Japanese tourists who were hovering on the edge of the pavement.

'Unknown actor kills thousands' came to Sally's mind as she made gratefully for the asylum of the Underground.

Mr Davenport was standing in the hall when she opened the front door, a carrier bag in his hand. 'Ah,' he said when he saw her. 'I've been waiting for you, young Valerie.'

'Sally,' said Sally.

'Yes. Got a few lettuces I thought you might like.' He reached in his bag and pulled out two earthy Webb's Wonderful.

'Oh thank you, Mr Davenport. What beauties.' She took them, wishing she had not been wearing a cream jacket. 'Thank you very much. I shall enjoy these.'

'My wife used to make soup with them,' said Mr Davenport. 'I might have the recipe somewhere. I think you need an onion.'

'That sounds delicious,' said Sally whose own way with lettuces was half a tomato and salad cream.

'I'll ask her when she comes in,' nodded Mr Davenport. 'You could make some for your young man. He could do with feeding up a bit.' He chuckled and went back into his flat.

Dan was some time coming to the door. When he did he looked anything but pleased. 'Yes?'

'I've brought you a lettuce,' said Sally. 'Mr Davenport gave me two and they're a bit big so I thought you might like one.' She proffered the muddier of the two like a missionary trying to tempt a tribesman. Dan reacted with appropriate suspicion. 'Why's he given you a lettuce?'

'He grows them. Down the garden. Surely you must have noticed?'

Dan continued to stare at it with revulsion. 'Can't say I have.'

'Well do you want it or don't you?'

Her neighbour shook himself and took it from her. 'Yes. Thank you very much. I'm sorry, I was thinking about something else. Thank you. It's very nice. Of you. And him. Thank you.'

'Don't mention it,' said Sally, relieved to be rid of it. Dan continued to clutch the lettuce as though it were an unexploded mine. 'Apparently you can make soup with them,' she told him helpfully. 'I think you need an onion.'

'Right,' said Dan and carried it through to his kitchen.

Sally happened to be looking out of her window when the lettuce shot past. It landed in a small redcurrant bush about halfway down the garden and lodged there for several seconds before thudding to the ground and rolling into a pile of grass cuttings. She stared for several seconds registering the evidence of her eyes then, seized with an insurmountable fury, put down the tin of sardines she had been endeavouring to open and marched down the stairs.

Dan was clearly surprised to see her again so soon. 'Yes?' he said, less aggressively than before.

'There was no need for that,' said Sally, struggling to retain her temper.

'I'm sorry?'

'Are you just? I bet you are. You didn't think I'd notice, I suppose? Not that it matters to me. It's him I'm thinking of. How's he going to feel? I don't know how you could. I think it's the meanest thing I've ever seen.' Dan gazed at her as though she had gone completely mad. 'Eh?' he said finally.

'You know what I'm talking about,' said Sally savagely.

'I only wish I did.'

'Oh ha ha. I suppose you didn't just throw the lettuce I gave you down the garden?'

Dan took a step back, his face reddening slightly. 'You saw?'

'Yes I did.'

'I'm sorry. It was a reflex. I couldn't help it.'

'Why couldn't you just have said you didn't like lettuces? Surely that would have been simpler?'

'I didn't want to hurt your feelings.'

'My feelings? What on earth has it got to do with *my* feelings? What about Mr Davenport's feelings? What's he going to think when he goes down the garden and sees his present lying on top of a manure heap?'

'You're right. I should have thought. It's just . . .' He wove his fingers in and out each other. 'What do you think I should do?'

'I should have thought it was obvious. Go down the garden and fetch it back. Surely you can put it in your rubbish bin? He's hardly likely to go through that.'

Dan looked wretched. 'I don't suppose you could do it, could you?'

Sally stared at him incredulously. 'I most certainly could not. I'm not your personal servant, you know. If you want someone to pick lettuces up for you I suggest you get in touch with the Job Centre.' She turned on her heels.

'I didn't mean it like that.'

Sally glanced back. 'How did you mean it?'

Dan was staring hard at his nails. 'It's got a slug on it. I can't stand slugs.'

'A slug?'

'Yes.'

'You're afraid of slugs?'

'Not afraid,' said Dan unconvincingly. 'I just don't like them very much.'

Sally nodded. 'I can't say I'm all that fond of them.'

'But you don't mind them?' Dan pleaded. Sally sighed. 'I'll get my rubber gloves.'

Dan did not refer to the incident as he handed Sally a glass of beer. 'How's your part going?'

'Fine,' said Sally guardedly. 'We record the first episode this week.'

Dan nodded. 'Did you have any luck with those tickets?'

Sally frowned. 'What tickets?'

'For Colin's play. You were going to try and get a couple.'

'Oh yes. To be honest it had rather slipped my mind.'

'Do you think it's too late?'

Sally put her glass down. 'Are you really sure you want to go?'

'Yes I do, actually. I've been reading up about it. Clytemnestra was a matriarch out of her time. We see similarities in women like Imelda Marcos and Jackie Kennedy.'

'Do we?' asked Sally.

'Yes. When power is within a person's grasp yet seemingly unattainable they either succumb to despair or sublimate their urges by redirecting them through other channels. It's particularly true for women, of course.'

'Of course,' Sally agreed, thinking she had never heard such rubbish in her life.

'We were talking about it the other night,' said Dan awkwardly. 'At my class.'

'Ah.'

'I've learnt a lot from that class.'

'I can see that.'

'We could have something to eat afterwards.'

'If we still feel like it.'

Dan grinned. 'I always feel like eating. We could discuss the play.'

'I'll look forward to that,' said Sally.

8

It was with a decidedly sinking feeling that Sally took her place beside Dan Chamberlain in the auditorium of the Baptists' Hall the following Wednesday.

He had rung her the previous evening to confirm that she had got the tickets and though she had not, neither had she the nerve to swear that the play was fully booked. These sort of lies always caught up with her, and she could think of nothing more awful than bumping into Colin in the pub and Dan launching into a spiel about how sorry he was it had been sold out. Nothing more awful, that was, except sitting there beside him, waiting for it to begin.

They were in the fourth row, next to the centre aisle. There was no one in front of them, beside them, or so far, behind them. They were the only people there.

'I think we're a bit early,' Sally whispered apologetically, glaring at her watch which clearly showed twenty-five past seven. Dan nodded and studied his programme. Glancing across Sally saw that it was not one of Colin's more informative efforts. In fact it consisted of a two-page fold-out containing a photocopy of a venison pie, a list of the players and a small essay by Colin on the role of the torturer in modern day society. He should know, she thought bitterly.

A side door opened and the Adult Literacy class filed

dutifully in and settled themselves round the walls. As veterans of Resting Pieces' productions they knew better than to position themselves within the actors' sight lines. Sally should have known better, too, but it was difficult to explain to her guest that there was an odds-on chance he would be called upon to thrust his hand down someone's throat or be the recipient of a glass of foaming offal before the night was out. He had chosen the seats. He must pay the price.

From behind the makeshift curtain came the sound of someone crying. Matthew, thought Sally wearily. A few more people had arrived. She recognised most of them as friends of the cast. 'Sally, Angel . . .' a podgy man in check bow tie and dinner jacket came bounding across to clasp her hand, his eyes roaming predatorily over Dan as he spoke.

'Hullo, Stephen,' said Sally brusquely. Stephen was one of the more constant causes of Colin and Matthew's break-ups.

'And who is this?' demanded the newcomer.

'This is my next door neighbour,' she replied dimissively, making no effort to introduce them.

'Hulloooo,' said Stephen winsomely. Dan nodded and returned to his programme. Stephen sighed. 'I just must pop backstage and wish them all luck.' He waddled across to the pass door.

The lights went out and music began to crackle from the speakers. 'Carmina Burana' again, Sally noted, wondering if Colin owned any other tapes.

There was a creak as the doors at the back swung open and a cold blast of air swept through the hall. Heads swivelled curiously to see what was going on. Three women and the luckless Bob, plainly not fully recovered from his hernia operation, came swaying down the aisle, their hips encased in Batik tablecloths and the upper parts of their bodies entirely enveloped in huge latex breasts which hung from halters round their necks.

'I'll have a choc ice and a bag of popcorn, came a voice from the side. Sally recognised it as the centre's resident alcoholic who came to all the productions and seemed to have a greater grasp of dramatic timing than any of the participants.

Oooohoooohoooohoooooooh,' responded the four actors, groping their way through the gloom and hauling themselves unceremoniously on to the stage where they struggled to hog the wavering spotlight. Sally caught a glimpse of a thick white bandage beneath Bob's tablecloth as he staggered to his feet endeavouring to look queenly and omnipotent. 'Ooooohooooohoooh,' went the handmaidens. 'OoooohooooohoooOOH.' Bob had caught his bosom on a tripod and was having trouble detaching it from the spikes. 'Bring me my cup,' he bellowed. 'Make haste and bring me my cup.'

'He needs two,' came the voice from the side. 'Double D with wire.' Sally could feel Dan shaking in the seat beside her. She stared grimly at the stage, concentrating on her gas bill and the condensation in her bathroom.

The evening lurched on. Twice Matthew, who had been too busy not throwing himself under trains to learn his lines properly, threatened the whole production by drying so completely that not even the 'Ooohoooohoooh'-ing of the chorus could cover the fact.

Bob did well as Clytemnestra, given that he had given up accountancy to become an actor and was really better suited to playing Home Counties' magistrates than cannibalistic matriarchs with a penchant for microwaving children.

The performance lasted three hours, by which time Sally's stomach was rumbling louder than the backstage drums. She felt sure Dan could hear, but by then he probably considered it part of the sound effects.

The night had turned chilly. 'Drink?' said Dan with an air of desperation. Sally nodded. They crossed the road to the Black Dragon. 'Well?' she said, when they were settled in a corner. Dan took a deep swig of his beer. 'They were good seats,' he said. They both began to laugh uncontrollably.

'We'd better get out of here before Colin and the rest come over,' said Sally when they had got their breath back. Dan looked genuinely nervous. 'Do you think they will?'

'They might. If they do come you'll have to say something nice about it.'

'I did.'

Sally shook her head. 'You'll have to do better than that. Otherwise they'll all start crying.'

'You're kidding?'

'I'm not. Oh no . . .'

'Darlings . . . why didn't you come round?' Colin, dressed entirely in black save a jaunty little lilac neckerchief, was slipping through the tables towards them. 'Matthew spotted you in the audience, at least he did you, Sal, but he couldn't place your lovely friend. He thinks that's what made him dry.' Colin turned to Dan, 'Nothing like that has ever happened before. Poor darling, he was absolutely distraught. There was meant to be a man from the *Daily Telegraph* in. He's so afraid it may have blighted his whole career. Did either of you see anyone who might have been from the *Telegraph*?' The two affirmed that they had not. Colin looked relieved. 'Anyway, we're not stopping off here. Stephen – you remember Stephen, don't you, Sally?'

'I certainly do.'

'Well, he's treating us to a Greek at that little place by the station. I'd ask you to join us but Stephen's so horribly shy. I'm sure you understand.' They assured him that they did. Colin beamed. 'I just came over for some plonk for the cast. I meant to get it before the show but what with one thing and another . . . What did you think of Bob, by the way?'

'Very good,' said Sally swiftly. 'I didn't know he had it in him.'

Colin nodded critically, 'To be perfectly honest, I don't think he has. All direction, that performance. One doesn't like to brag, but there it is. See you, my sweets.' He flitted away.

Dan and Sally sat back in relief. 'I'm starving,' said Dan.

'So am I.'

'I don't suppose there's much open at this time. Unless you fancy a Greek?'

Sally laughed. 'I'd rather starve.'

They found an Italian restaurant where they were shown to a table by the kitchen and swooped on by the waiters who had no intention of missing their last buses for the sake of a solitary couple.

'What did you really think of it?' asked Sally, when they had ordered.

Dan stared hard at the wine bottle as though willing it to provide him with an answer. 'It wasn't what I'd expected quite.'

'Colin's productions hardly ever are. What were you expecting, anyway?'

Dan continued to stare at the bottle. 'I thought it would be a bit more straightforward, I suppose. You know, reveal a few inner truths. Be a bit more symbolic. I don't know. Clear a few things up for me.'

'What sort of things?'

Dan shrugged. 'I don't know. The bloke who's teaching our class lent me a book. It said the way to understanding all human behaviour was to study the Greek philosophers, so I thought if I went and saw a play by one of them it might help.'

'And did it?'

'No. I suppose it's all a bit too clever for me. I didn't

understand why those women kept ooohing and aahing all the time.'

'Greek choruses always do that.'

'Yes, but why?'

Sally thought. The most obvious, and probably most truthful answer was that they could none of them remember their lines, but she sensed that Dan was searching for something more from her. 'I think it's to sort of herald approaching disaster,' she suggested. Dan was silent.

Their food arrived. 'If you don't mind my asking, why do you go to your class?' asked Sally when she could bear the silence no longer. Dan looked up sharply. 'You think I'm a prat, don't you?'

'No,' she protested, unnerved by the attack. 'There's no need to be so defensive about it. I was only asking a question.'

Dan shook his head. 'I'm sorry. You're right. I don't know why I go. At least I know why I started going, but that reason's gone now, so I don't know why I keep it up. Specially as I don't agree with a word the bloke says.' He caught Sally's eye. 'And it's not funny.'

Sally shook her head vigorously. 'I know it's not. I'm not laughing at you. Honestly I'm not.'

'Yes you are.'

'Yes I am.'

Dan glared at her then slowly his face softened and he began to chuckle. 'I was trying to be a New Man,' he said ruefully. 'But I left it too late.'

'What was wrong with the way you were?'

'Everything, it seems. My attitude was wrong. I was selfish, insensitive, blinkered – what was the other thing? – repressive.'

Sally sipped her wine. 'That's quite a catalogue.'

'Those were my good points.'

'And the class has changed all that?'

Dan nodded. 'Oh yes. Now I'm all of that and I've got a bloody bad temper as well.'

Sally shrugged. 'Sounds like every New Man I ever met.'

Dan was strangling the pepper mill. 'You don't think much of men, do you?'

'Not enough to go on a course about understanding them.'

'Because they're not worth understanding?'

'Because I think it's the height of arrogance to think you can learn how to understand people from two hours a week at an evening class.'

Dan looked palpably shocked. 'I go to try and improve myself,' he explained. 'Suzanne kept telling me I didn't understand her, and she was right. I didn't. She was growing further away from me every day.'

'Who's Suzanne?' asked Sally, sensing she was on thin ice.

Dan ground more pepper. 'My wife. Soon to be ex.'

Although it was not a complete surprise to her she felt unaccountably disturbed by the revelation. 'I see. So you joined this class to try and find out what was going on in her head?'

'Something like.'

'Did it not strike you as strange that a class supposed to be about understanding women was run by a man?'

Dan looked confused. 'Not at the time. I've wondered once or twice since, but he's got all sorts of letters after his name so presumably he knows what he's talking about.'

'Don't you believe it,' said Sally angrily, remembering all the Oxbridge graduates who had sat in judgement over her auditions.

Dan's food was disappearing under a hill of black pepper. 'Will you be able to eat that?' she asked anxiously. Dan glanced at his plate. 'A bit of pepper's not going to kill me,' he grunted aggressively and dug his fork into the midst.

The waiter brought more water as Sally alternatively slapped Dan on the back and dabbed at his face with a napkin. 'I thought you were overdoing it,' she told him once his breathing had reverted to normal.

'I thought you said you'd been in *Casualty*,' retaliated Dan, fending off the thumps. 'You ought to know what to do when someone chokes.'

'I was a battered wife,' Sally objected. 'I can't be expected to deal with emergencies.'

'Perhaps you should pick your parts more carefully.'

'Perhaps you should pick your wives more carefully if they have this effect on you,' snapped Sally, incensed that anyone could imagine she'd had a choice. Dan looked chastened and she immediately felt guilty for making light of his problems. 'How did you get into teaching?' she asked to change the subject.

Dan shrugged. 'It was a friend of Suzanne's, said they needed people to help with the bricklaying course down at the tech. Work's been pretty scarce in the building trade of late so I said I'd give it a go. Then, when I knew I was moving here I made a few enquiries locally and they came up with this. It's a bit more advanced than I'd bargained for . . .' Sally kept her eyes resolutely on her plate. 'I quite like it, actually,' he continued cautiously.

Sally nodded. 'I did a bit once. Drama for Second Years. An introduction to Shakespeare.'

'How did you get on?'

'It was murder. Thirty-five twelve-year-olds all wanting to play Bottom. Chaos from start to finish. God knows what they were telling their parents. The headmistress got a letter from one saying she didn't want her child to take part in a pornographic play. I was asked to leave at half-term. If they hadn't sacked me I'd've gone anyway. Teaching's a gift. One which I absolutely do not have.'

Dan nodded. 'Suzanne's training to be a teacher. Part-time. She always wanted to do it but she gets migraines. They interfere with a lot of things.'

'I shouldn't think thirty-five twelve-year-olds would help,' said Sally a trifle spitefully.

'Oh not children. She doesn't want to teach kids. Evening classes, that's what she wants to do.'

'What's she going to teach them?' asked Sally.

Dan's face was a blank. 'She hasn't decided. At the moment she's just learning how to teach.'

The waiter brought coffee. He had his coat on. In the background the staff were saying noisy farewells to each other and the owner had come out from the back and was totting up the day's receipts on the table opposite.

'I think they want us to go,' Sally whispered. Dan looked around indifferently. 'When we're ready,' he said. The waiters lifted chairs and arranged them in neat cubes on top of the tables till Dan and Sally were surrounded by a stockade. 'I feel like Sleeping Beauty,' Sally giggled. Dan, who had been looking increasingly irritated, burst out laughing.

'What are you laughing at?'

'You. If this had been Suzanne she'd have been in hysterics by now. Calling for the manager, the police, the lot.'

'But why? They've got to go home sometime, poor things. So ought we, if it comes to that. I've got a rehearsal in the morning.'

Dan felt for his wallet. 'I've got the real thing.'

He refused to let Sally contribute which unsettled her since she was used to paying for herself. 'You got the tickets,' he explained.

'Yes, but they were free.'

Dan looked surprised. 'I didn't mean him to give them

to us. I wasn't trying to cadge them,' he murmured with an air of embarrassment.

Sally laughed. 'Of course you weren't. They're nearly always free. It's the only way they can get an audience for most of the shows. Anyway Resting Pieces gets a grant from the council. He'd lose it the moment we went into profit.'

'Now I feel bad for not liking it.'

'You'd feel a lot worse if you had. I don't actually think Colin wants anyone to like his productions.'

'Oh, come on.'

'No, really. It would mean that someone else understood them, don't you see? I don't think he could cope with that.'

Dan took her arm. 'I don't think I'll ever understand actors.'

'Or women?'

'Women, perhaps. Actors, never.'

Mr Davenport had obviously done his round. The end to a perfect evening, thought Sally wrily as she closed the front door. Well, if not perfect, a lot better than she had anticipated. She turned to Dan.

'Good night. Thank you for dinner.'

Dan grinned. 'My pleasure.' Sally smiled, feeling she ought to say something more but since she couldn't think of anything, she merely nodded and went upstairs in search of a mop. She felt suddenly very weary.

While she was filling the bucket there was a tap at the door. Dan was standing there. 'Oh,' said Sally. 'Yes?'

Dan shifted awkwardly. 'I forgot,' he said, thrusting a box of expensive chocolates towards her. 'I got them for the theatre but then I left them at home by mistake. They were for you.'

'Oh. Thank you,' said Sally, embarrassed. 'Thank you very much,' their earlier rapport dissolving in the banality of the gesture.

Dan hesitated. 'By the way, I've er . . . seen to . . . you know, the old man.'

Sally felt a wave of gratitude. 'Thanks. I appreciate that.'

'Well . . . You know . . . neighbours . . .'

'Yes.'

9

The producer's run for all the ominous finality of its title was a downbeat affair. Jeff Wilkins was late, having caught a sleeper from Oban which didn't get in till ten. Sally noted a look of complete confusion, wrestling with boredom, as he listened to Rolo's muted explanations of the scenes now played out before him.

Only once did he raise a query, when Solly Sedgewick, allegedly fresh from the ravages of his wife's intemperate passion, launched into a long debate on the quality of photocopying templates from Taiwan. 'I say, René,' Wilkins ventured, puffing vigorously into the director's face, 'would he? I mean, how much time does he have after . . . You know . . . all that?' René smiled forgivingly. 'Don't worry, Jeff. Perhaps I didn't make it clear. *That* was on Tuesday. *This* is on Thursday. We've got all the scenes at the graveside in between.'

'Ah,' Wilkins nodded sagely. 'Where'll you be doing those?' René looked increasingly smug. 'Penny's found a lovely little spot, just off the M2. Actually it's a crematorium but they've got a bit of spare ground round at the back they're happy to let us use.'

'Jolly good,' said the producer and was silent for the rest of the run.

After lunch René gave them notes, his own rather than

Jeff Wilkins', although he made a very fair effort at sounding as though their producer both cared about the production, and was sorry to have to be returning to his fishing holiday when he would so much rather have come on location to the crematorium and the disused industrial estate the following day.

After that he said he would like to run through a couple of scenes, looking fiercely in the direction of Drewe who already had his coat on, and let those who were not involved, including Sally, go.

To her deep surprise there was a cheque waiting for her when she got home. It was not large – a payment for Costume Fitting, but considering she had not been for one it seemed remarkably generous. She decided to spend it on some new clothes in token. Stephanie's return from South Molton Street had irked her, not only because the woman was a pain in the neck, but because she could very well have pictured herself in some of the ensembles Stephanie had badgered Wendy into buying for her.

Laying her purchases on the bed the next evening she blushed at her extravagance. The sage culottes would have paid this quarter's electricity, and the wine silk shirt dress would have kept her newly sponsored donkey in hay for the next three years. She pulled herself together. The donkey must not suffer. As soon as her fee for episode one came through she would send him a Carrot Voucher. These were available in multiples of five up to the sum of seventy-five pounds, by which time any right-thinking donkey would presumably have expired from exploding eyeballs.

Lovingly she hung the new clothes in her wardrobe. She wondered what she should wear to Studio on Friday. Nothing too elaborate. Either the culottes with the corn silk jersey or the wine with the linen jacket.

*　　*　　*

'Sally Grosvenor?' The receptionist scanned her list. 'Basement. Room twenty-nine. Blue. If you follow the corridor round you'll come to some stairs just past the coffee machine. That's your quickest way. Sign here, please.'

That she was in the basement did not come as any surprise to Sally since all her dressing rooms had been in the basement for any television part she had ever played. What did come as a surprise was that she did not have to share it with anyone else. It seemed inconceivable to her that the door of B29 Blue should have revealed not the line of metal coat hangers, each dripping an identical serge skirt and lumpy jacket, but a small (very small) room with cupboard, armchair, table and full-length mirror. She scrutinised the door. 'Sally Grosvenor' said the tag.

'Oh, there you are.' Jean Make-up was bearing down on her. 'Wendy's been awfully worried.'

'Why?' asked Sally although she could think of a thousand reasons.

'Haven't you heard? Oh no, of course, you weren't at the filming, were you?'

'No,' said Sally. 'Has something happened?'

Jean rolled her eyes in a way that should have put her in line for Black Beauty. 'It certainly has. We only lost the fork lift. Anyway Rolo'll be over to talk to you. What have you got on?' She started to probe under Sally's coat with an intimacy that made her nervous. Hastily she undid the buttons. Jean stared at her ominously. 'Denims,' she intoned. 'The shirt might be all right. Ah, here's Rols. She's here, Rolo, but she's got denims on.' Sally stood between them feeling naked and exposed as Rolo, with equally tragic face, reviewed her attire. Eventually he nodded, sucked in his cheeks and, casting a quick glance along the corridor, murmured 'Do you think we could step into your dressing room for a moment, Sally, please?'

Sally obeyed, wondering rather sickly what he had in

mind. Rolo gestured her to a chair and kicking the door to, perched himself on the edge of the table. 'I don't know if you've heard? We lost the fork lift.'

'Jean did mention it just now,' said Sally, sensing the inadequacy of this response.

'Yes, it's worse than that.' Rolo had taken a notepad from his pocket and was flipping through the pages. Sally was struck by his potential as a doctor. 'In fact, Sally, we lost four scenes. Eight minutes of filming, that's what it amounts to.'

'Eight minutes?' How on earth could anyone film a fork lift truck for eight minutes? That was nearly a fifth of the air time. Was this a show about fork lift trucks and the drama merely a background? No wonder everyone was looking so grim.

'That's over the two episodes, of course,' Rolo continued. 'Approximately four from each.'

'What happened?' asked Sally, trying to show concern. Rolo shrugged. 'It wasn't Simon's fault. No one told him about the reverse. The first take went like a dream but René wanted another, just for luck. He's such a professional. Anyway, poor old Si got a bit confused and flicked the wrong button. Whole thing landed up in the ditch. Curtains.'

'For Simon?' screeched Sally, the blood draining from her face.

'No, no. Simon's fine. Bit shaken. The fork lift's a goner, though. Christ knows what that's going to slice off the budget. The insurance company's bound to kick up stink. Should've been someone with him, you see. It's a condition.' He fell silent.

'Will you be able to get another?' asked Sally at last, wondering why she had been singled out for Rolo's confidences. Rolo roused himself. He, too, was a professional. 'I daresay,' he said. 'But the filming's done for one and two. And that's where you come in.'

'I do?' Sally had a fleeting image of herself in a cardboard fork lift truck costume, crawling between the office and the stationery depot.

'Yes. We've had to add some padding. Wellard's been wonderful. He's given Veeney another scene where she has a premonition of her father's death. It's a nightmare but she wakes up just before she sees his face.' One less actor to pay, thought Sally. 'But the rest is pure wallpaper, and that's where you come in.'

'Me?'

'Yes, he's penning you a couple of phone conversations. Nothing too elaborate, but they take place after the funeral. We were rather hoping you'd be wearing the right sort of thing . . . Still, not your fault.' He gave her a quick smile. 'So, that's all clear, is it? Penny'll be round with the new pages just as soon as Wilkie's given them the thumbs up.'

'I've got other clothes,' murmured Sally, thinking how she would have loved to swan around the office in her sage culottes. Rolo gave her a kindly smile. 'Yes. Still . . . You know . . .' His eyes strayed wretchedly over her. 'Never mind. It'll be fine. Not a thing to worry about. We'll focus on the receiver. The GBP will never know.' He backed out of the dressing room and Sally heard his anxious voice seeking to reassure George Bennett, who was next door, that he would certainly be free in time to phone his bookie before lunch.

Penny arrived shortly afterwards with the new scenes. Their resemblance to the old ones was so uncanny as to make Sally wonder whether they were indeed the progeny of Wellard Kenning's fertile brain or merely a reprint of pages sixty-one and sixty-two. Why anyone should need a change of clothes to repeat themself so completely was beyond her. Surely it would be cheaper just to run the same scenes twice? She half thought of suggesting it, but checked herself rapidly with the reminder that extra scenes might mean extra loot and anyway, she was an actress. It was up to her what she made of the script. Look what Patrick had managed with 'What? No! Oh.' It had reminded her of King Lear when she saw it on Monday. And conversely, look what a hash Drewe made of his rhetorical speeches about life and love and photocopying templates.

This was her chance and she must seize it with both hands. Proudly she retreated to her armchair and set about studying the new lines.

This being the Technical Run there were the usual delays and frustrations. There was also a problem with Simon's nose which had suffered a considerable blow during his entanglement with the fork lift truck. Despite heroic efforts on the part of Make-up and the Wig Department, which had dropped his toupé several inches and added a tousled lock, it still came through purple and brown in close-up.

René re-plotted his moves to allow him to play his part in profile but this then left the actor with the task of conveying grief, despair, rage, horror and confusion through the undeniably limited offices of his left eye and one nostril. He looked extremely depressed when they broke for lunch and Sally caught sight of Penny tapping timidly on the door of his dressing room as the rest of them made their way up to the canteen.

They finally got to Laura Barnes' scenes just before tea. There had been something of a hold-up when Dilys Lewis failed to return from lunch. Mary Jennings was dispatched first to her dressing room and then to the restaurant and finally to the bar, where it appeared she had been seen earlier. Mary returned looking extremely agitated to report that Dilys would be with them in two ticks. The ticks were plainly of unspecified length for there was still no sign of her twenty minutes later by which time, after due consultation, they had moved on to Veeney and Marley in the corridor.

Time was now pressing and it was decided to set all of Sally's scenes at once, rather than shift the cameras.

The original ones went smoothly enough owing to René's foresight in forbidding her the right to move, but the new stuff, though conducted entirely on the telephone and, as far as Sally could tell, equally motionless, caused deep groans and cries of 'Sorry, love, we'll have to do it again,' till she seriously began to fear it was not too late for Laura Barnes to be dropped from the series entirely.

Rolo stood on the edge of the set, his arms outstretched like a prophet, receiving directions from René through his headphones. Sally watched admiringly as he translated what was clearly an apoplectic fit into 'Could you just try to hold the phone a little bit nearer your chin, Sally? We're getting the teeniest shadow.'

By half past nine sweat was beginning to glimmer on the faces of all but the technicians. Studio time finished at ten thirty and the cost of running into overtime was so prohibitive that they might as well have cancelled the last four episodes. There were nine scenes to go, including two of Dilys'. She had disappeared to the bar again during the supper break and now seemed to be having trouble understanding where she was, let alone why she was there.

On René's orders they had turned off the iron which she had twice scorched holes in a shirt with and she was now leaning blearily against the set while René and Rolo debated whether to slip her scenes altogether, and trust to luck that she would get through them tomorrow. It was finally decided that they should move on and the technical was completed, minus Dilys' contribution, with seventeen seconds left on the clock.

Simon gave Sally a lift to the Underground. She had been unable to think of a decent excuse, apart from a desire to live, which she knew would carry no weight at all.

'That was a bit hairy,' he commented as they screeched out of the car park. 'Talk about cutting it fine. Old René's going to end up with a carry over if he's not careful. Mind you, it's his own fault. All those fiddling extra scenes. I mean what a time to bring in new pages. They'll all be edited out in the cutting room. You'll see.'

'Do you think so?' asked Sally, feeling more than a little deflated.

'Bound to be. René always shoots more than he can use. He's right to do it, mind. Such a pro, that guy, but I ask you – nightmare sequences. Poor old Veeney. She didn't even have a bed. What a load of rubbish. No, it'll be out come the day, you see. And the rest of them. What was the point, anyway? God, my nose hurts.' He rubbed it cautiously. Sally looked out of the window.

'Pity about old Dilys,' said Simon after a while.

'She did seem a bit . . .'

'Out of it,' Simon declared. 'Absolutely out of it. God knows what they're going to do tomorrow. Unless they shoot all her scenes first. That's their only hope, I should think. Get to her before she gets to It. When I think of all the actresses out of work.' He thumped the steering wheel in frustration. 'Jenny could have played that part. Off the top of her head. Bloody nepotism, that's all it is. You know she's married to the Chief Exec.?'

'No!'

'She bloody is. Penny told me when we . . . the other day . . . in rehearsal.'

'Is that why . . .?'

Simon threw her an ironic glance. 'What do you think? Yep. Jobs for the boys. Keep it in the family. Never mind she's flaming blotto half the time. Jenny would have been ideal for that. Makes you sick.' He lapsed into silence. Sally had never seen him so rattled. It must be the pain in his nose.

'Who's Jenny?' she enquired, hoping to show solidarity.

'Jenny?' Simon gazed at her curiously.

'The one you thought would be good at Dilys' part.'

'Oh, Jenny . . .' Simon sighed and gave his nose a sorrowful rub. 'She's my wife,' he said. 'Here we are.' Sally got out of the car.

10

'I've got a little surprise for you all after the recording.' Jeff Wilkins, whose actual arrival was something of a surprise to most of them, had poked his head round the door of Make-up to wish them all luck. 'Jolly good,' said Patrick in grim imitation as he disappeared. 'I daresay we'll have a few for him before the day's out.'

René came round with 'one or two notes'. These consisted mainly of ordering everyone to stay near the set in case there were any 'last minute changes'. The more seasoned members of the cast exchanged wary glances.

The recording started reasonably well. There had been a hiatus at the end of the Solley Sedgewicks' first scene when Drewe, with an unprecedented surge of adrenalin, had grabbed hold of Stephanie by her halter neck and nearly throttled her. This caused panic in Wendy Costume, who had the dress on loan from Moss Bros and could see the five hundred pound deposit disappearing before her eyes. Jean Make-up was also concerned since it has taken forty minutes to tease Stephanie's complexion into something resembling a young woman's, and it was disconcerting to see it turning blue then purple in the space of as any seconds. Fortunately Drewe's stamina was of the limited variety and the two of them were soon back on form, lisping, spitting and pouting.

Sally sat in her dressing room and waited to be called. Her hair had been wrenched up into a French roll and sprayed with enough lacquer to petrify a wheat field. It itched. All her lines had disappeared from her memory, her skirt felt too tight and her shoes had developed an unaccountable tendency to clop like carthorses every time she moved. Her stomach felt as though it had been lined with coiled springs timed to shoot open if she so much as shifted in her chair. She tried breathing deeply. It just made her skirt feel tighter. She stood up, stretched and heard the ping of a button flying across the room. Aghast she searched for it. There was a knock and Mary Jennings opened the door, looking if anything more nervous than Sally. 'Are you all right?' she asked, seeing Sally scrabbling about the floor.

'Yes. No. I've lost the button off my skirt.'

Mary smiled in genuine relief. 'Is that all? I'll send Wardrobe round to fix it. I don't suppose,' she hesitated, 'you've seen Dilys at all?'

'She was in Make-up when I first went in. That was about ten o'clock.' Mary nodded. 'Yes I think she's in her dressing room. It's just she doesn't answer when I knock . . . I expect she's having a little zizz.' Her voice trailed away.

'I expect so,' said Sally brightly. How's it going?'

'Oh, fine. We should get to you in about twenty minutes.'

'Really?' A wave of ice crashed over her. 'Which scene?' Not that it mattered because she couldn't remember any of them.

'The first one,' said Mary in some surprise.

'Oh, yes. That's what I meant,' burbled Sally. 'I meant which scene comes before it?' Mary's smile faded. 'Umm, it's the one with Dilys ironing. There's just the tiniest possibility that we might skip that one and come back to it later, so if you'd like to start making your way up to studio.'

'Oh. Right. Yes. What about my button?'

'I'll tell Wardrobe.'

'Right. Yes. Thank you.'

Mary went off to tap on Dilys' door again. Sally threw one last feverish look round the room then, clasping the back of her skirt made her way despairingly up to the studio. She didn't know why she was so nervous. She had done television before and never felt this bad. She supposed it was because so much depended on it. Not her, but the serial itself. She didn't want to be the one to let them all down. She shook herself. This was ridiculous. How could she possibly make any difference? Nothing she did or didn't do could seriously affect the outcome of *The Firm*. She was NOT IMPORTANT. How many times had they told her this? René, Costume, Make-up, even her own agent, had been at pains to point out the insignificance of her contribution. Now she was panicking as though the whole thing stood or fell by her. It was absurd. Think positive. She was a professional. She had been given the role because she was the best possible person to play it (Honeytree Jallulah aside), and that was that. All she had to do now was get on and play it.

'Ah, Sally,' Rolo put a kindly but purposeful hand on her shoulder and propelled her towards the Office set. 'Here's Sally,' he informed the Viewing Room. 'We've decided to bring your scenes forward.' Sally nodded submissively. 'So if we could just have you over behind the door.' On the way she passed Dilys' ironing board. It had been folded up.

They did three takes. One in which Sally spilt Patrick's coffee, another in which the phone fell off the table, and a third which René, via Rolo, pronounced 'perfection'. Sally, though knowing full well this was rubbish, felt unaccountably encouraged.

The rest of her scenes went fairly smoothly despite her skirt's tendency to creep a little further down her hips with every entrance made. They broke for lunch. Sally found a safety pin and hoisted her skirt back to a more manageable length. 'Well done, our Sal,' said Patrick in a broad Yorkshire accent. 'Thou's done reet fine, dost know?' Marley too was warm in her enthusiasm. 'You put so much into it, dear,' she told her. 'It's not an easy part, you know. I don't think I could do it. I'd get in such a muddle.'

Towards the end of lunch Rolo came hunting for her. 'I've had a word with René. I'm afraid we can't give you a clear just yet.' He hesitated. 'There's just the chance we may have to do a bit of . . . jigging around later on.' Patrick's eyebrows appeared over the top of his newspaper. 'I hope you're not two-timing me, Rolo dear boy,' he remarked. Rolo went beetroot-coloured. 'Not like that. It's just that . . . You know . . . Well, there it is. Sorry, Sally.' He hurried off.

'What do you suppose that was about?' asked Simon as Penny set a slice of gâteau before him. Marley leant forward conspiratorially. 'I'm afraid it's to do with poor Dilys.'

Simon frowned. 'She's never at it again, is she? When I think of all the actresses . . .' He never got to the end for at that moment George came rushing into the canteen to tell them there was a horse called Firm Ground in the four-thirty at Folkestone and that they must all put something on it.

Returning to her dressing room after lunch Sally found a peevish note pinned to her door saying that Wardrobe had been looking for her everywhere and would she please report to Wendy the moment she got back. She duly made her way up to the Wardrobe room which was empty except for one of the male dressers who was making himself Pot Noodles with the water from the steam iron.

When she got back to her dressing room there was another peevish note from Rolo saying she was needed on set IMMEDIATELY. She hurried up the stairs again to be confronted by Jean with a tin of navy blue buttons which she insisted on trying to match to the colour of Sally's skirt.

'I'm sorry, Jean,' she protested, 'but Rolo wants me on set straight away.'

'You can't go without a skirt,' snapped Jean, grabbing at it proprietorially.

The studio doors swung open. Mary Jennings, looking as though she might burst into tears, came rushing through. 'Oh, there you are. Can you come, please, Sally? René's getting a bit worked up.' Even Jean could not gainsay the requirements of the director and Sally was hurried across the snaking cables to the illuminated set.

'I've got her,' Mary called as they went, taking Sally's arm and waving it in evidence towards the little group of people clustered round the props table. She was immediately leapt upon by an angry mob, one girl dabbing her nose while another re-sprayed her hair, Props, who wanted to make sure she used the phone on the left of the desk as the other one was on the blink, and Rolo, who tried to explain to her that she didn't have to say anything, merely nod from time to time and possibly scribble something on the desk pad. Jean, meanwhile, had crept up behind her and was fumbling unashamedly with her waist band.

By six o'clock she had still not been given a clear. The silent shots had taken nearly as long as her speaking scenes and she still had no idea what they were for, unless René was planning to superimpose her face over the shattered carcase of the fork lift truck.

By ten o'clock, with thirty minutes till finish, only Dilys' scenes remained. Mary Jennings was sent once more to try and rouse her, Wendy Costume in tow.

She had been spotted briefly at lunch time when she had emerged to request a tuna sandwich, and again before supper ostensibly in search of paracetamol. Nothing had been seen of her illustrious husband, the Chief Exec., who was allegedly conducting a heated affair with a woman researcher from Wildlife and was very rarely to be found on the premises.

Patrick had been called and was pacing irritably up and down in a pair of psychedelic nylon pyjamas which Costume had decided would further increase his sex appeal. Sally saw the cameraman wince as he struggled to adjust his lens. René was running the titles along with the theme music which owed quite a bit to 'Rhapsody in Blue' and even more to 'Land of Hope and Glory.' She felt a sudden buzz of excitement as her name flashed by. 'Laura Barnes . . . Sally Grosvenor.' Eat your heart out, Honeytree Jallulah.

Dilys was escorted across the studio by Mary Jennings and Wendy, the two of them trailing her, arms slightly outstretched as though holding an invisible train. She showed no awareness of her entourage, only her eyes betraying the fact that she was less than sober. Nodding to Rolo, she made her way carefully on to the Sedgewicks' set. Mary and Wendy steered her gently across to the right one. Two firemen promptly appeared, hovering either end of the ironing board with extinguishers at the ready. Dilys eyed them curiously but made no comment.

Rolo called for silence. 'René would like us to go for a take, if that's OK, Dilys.' He tried to sound nonchalant. Dilys smiled serenely and said that was perfectly fine. Patrick gave her her cue. The actress ignored him totally and started to fiddle with the plug of the iron. The firemen rushed forward. Rolo called a halt, asked if Dilys would like a prompt, was assured that she would not, and the whole process began again. This time Dilys answered Patrick and for several moments the scene ran as directed. Sighs of relief echoed round the studio. Too soon, as it turned out, for Dilys turning to give her husband a peck on the cheek, forgot she was holding an iron. Patrick leapt back, too late to save his pyjama jacket.

Everyone watched with morbid fascination as his costume

sizzled, globules of melted nylon dripping on to the set floor. The fireman sprayed the carpet energetically. Somewhere a sprinkler was activated. The light over the studio door flashed 'RED. EMERGENCY'. In the distance a bell was ringing. An automatic tannoy message informed everyone that there was no cause for panic, but they were to evacuate the studio IMMEDIATELY. No one took the slightest bit of notice. Over his headphones Rolo was receiving frantic orders from René. 'If we could just have a bit of quiet,' he roared. 'We've still got time for another take. COSTUME.' Wendy leapt several feet in the air and landed in front of him. 'We need more pyjamas for Patrick.'

'Um . . .' said Wendy, in the full knowledge that nowhere in the building was a similar pair to be found.

'We just need to do the last couple of speeches. It was FINE up to there, René says, absolute PERFECTION.' For some reason this offended Sally.

'Jolly good,' said Jeff Wilkins, topping up Sally's glass. He had bought a crate of gassy plonk for the cast and a can of bitter each for the technicians.

'He said he had a surprise for us,' Patrick murmured as he downed his second glass. 'God, what is this stuff? It's revolting.'

'You'd think the old sod could have managed the real thing,' said Stephanie who was drinking neat whisky. 'And peanuts, for God's sake. What does he take us for? A load of monkeys?'

'Isn't this lovely?' Marley came trotting up, her cheeks fairly bulging with prawn crackers. 'I do think it's sweet of Jeff to lay on this little do for us, don't you? Much better than going up to the bar.' There was a noncommittal murmur from her colleagues.

'Where's Simon?' asked Sally to change the subject.

'He had to phone his wife,' said Marley. 'Let her know

he was going to be late. He's such a considerate man, isn't he? Oh, I do think we've been very lucky with the cast of this show. Everyone's so nice.' She tucked her arms round Patrick and Stephanie's waists and gave them an affectionate squeeze.

'I say, everyone, jolly good.' Jeff Wilkins, also drinking whisky, bore down on them. 'Excellent. Jolly pleased. Just the right note. On to a winner. Awfully sorry. Got to be off. Night sleeper and that. Keep up the good work. Don't rush off. Plenty more where that came from.'

'I'm not surprised,' muttered Patrick. 'Where're they keeping the hard stuff, Mrs Sedgewick?'

Stephanie shuddered at the reference. 'You'll have to ask the guy over there. It's René's private bottle or something. I said he wouldn't mind.' Patrick ambled off. Stephanie looked at her watch. 'Good God, have I only been here half an hour? It's no good. I'll have to go.' She grabbed at René who was passing. 'René, darling, forgive me, my sweet, but I PROMISED Frank I'd be back in time to see his bit on Inner City bus lanes.'

'Where did you get that whisky?' asked René suspiciously. Stephanie downed her glass offhandedly. 'I've no idea, darling. Did you think the bit with the photograph went OK? I was sure I muffed it up. I really thought we'd have to do it again.'

'It was fine,' said René, still eyeing her empty glass.

'You aren't just saying that?'

'No.'

'Oh, that's a weight off my mind. A huge weight. What time do you want us on Monday, or shall I wait for a call?'

'Ten o'clock,' said René.

'Me, too?' asked Stephanie, plainly put out.

'Everyone,' said René. 'What's that bastard doing?' He strode angrily away to where the barman was busily dispensing his whisky to a small queue of actors.

'René takes a while to unwind after recording,' said Rolo supportively, clutching his tumbler of mineral water. Marley beamed up at him. 'Well, I think it all went very well. What did you think, Rolo? You were on the sharp end.'

'Pretty good, considering,' said Rolo, which seemed to Sally a very fair answer.

The party began to break up. There was no more whisky and the sparkling wine was insufficient to induce anything more heady than heartburn. Despite herself, Sally half-hoped that Simon would offer her a lift. She hated late-night tubes, but when she looked for him someone said he had gone. She noted that Penny had, too. No one else was going her way as far as she knew. She said her good nights and hurried along to Reception where they ordered her a cab.

'Excuse me,' a small ferrety man in a spotted cravat was standing at her elbow. She had seen him in the Hospitality room, also drinking René's whisky, and assumed he was someone's dresser. 'Did I hear you say you were going to Charing Cross?'

'Yes,' said Sally cautiously, casting a questioning glance at the receptionist who was also eyeing the man with some concern.

'I don't suppose . . . I'm just off the Mall.'

'Yes, of course,' she said reluctantly. The last thing she wanted was to be bombarded with unsavoury details of life in the Wardrobe. She needn't have worried. The man said nothing throughout the entire journey. The silence was so pungent that Sally felt constrained to make an attempt at conversation herself.

'Did you see the recording?' she asked. The man shuffled in his seat.

'Yes,' he said and looked out of the window.

'It seemed to go quite well . . .' Sally offered. The man said nothing and continued to gaze at the passing traffic.

She gave up. Halfway down the Mall the man gave a sharp rap on the glass panel, dropped two pound coins on the seat beside Sally and with a cursory 'goodnight', opened the door and disappeared in the direction of the ICA.

'Nine pounds forty,' said the cab driver, locking the doors and fixing Sally with an immutable stare. She paid him grudgingly, thinking whoever the ferret was, that was the last time he would travel in a car with her.

5

'Sally went home with our author.' Marley, who had more antennae than a radar station, was regaling the cast with the news that Sally had been seen getting into the same cab as Wellard Kenning.

'Better keep an eye on those extra pages.' Patrick looked round solemnly. 'This could yet be *The Laura Barnes Show.*'

'Oh, come off it, darling,' drawled Stephanie. 'I don't think she's quite the type to give him a blow job in the back seat. Not like young Veeney here.' She smiled sweetly at Veeney who merely tossed her head and moved her gum to the other side of her mouth.

'Now, girls,' said Simon, pinging a paper pellet at Patrick's cup and missing by some way, 'you leave Sally alone. She's a nice girl.'

'That's what I said,' countered Stephanie.

'Still waters run deep,' said Hazel Macintosh, knitting hectically at a pullover.

'Very nice,' said Dilys. It was the first contribution she had made to cast chitchat. Marley beamed and raised her eyebrows at Patrick.

Sally heard none of this. She had broken a heel on the way to rehearsal and been forced to stop off on the way. When she arrived breathless and apologetic at ten past ten the cast were still exchanging weekend gossip and René, looking slightly less tormented than the previous week, was talking to Rolo in a corner.

'How was your weekend?' Patrick asked her, winking at Stephanie.

'Fine,' said Sally, 'thanks. Yours OK?'

Patrick shrugged. 'The usual. Do anything interesting?' Sally considered. Was defrosting the fridge interesting? Going to Kew Gardens? It was worth a try.

'I went to Kew,' she said.

'Who with?' demanded Veeney with sudden zeal.

Sally blushed. 'No one. I went by myself. I quite often do. I like the peace.'

'I met my first husband at Kew,' said Marley dreamily.

'I fell out of a tree there when I was a kid,' said Simon. 'Broke my arm.'

'Serves you right,' said Veeney. 'You're not meant to climb the trees. They're endangered species.'

'Most things are with Simon around,' said Patrick.

'Right, everyone.' René came hurrying over. 'Ready for the off? I just wanted to say I was very pleased with Saturday's show. We've got some good stuff. Few lumps and bumps but nothing I can't iron out in the editing.' Everyone stiffened at the mention of ironing. 'Now as you know,' René continued, 'time is at a premium so I'd like to get cracking straight away. Penny's coming round with a list of scenes we'll be doing this morning. Oh, just one thing – as I expect you realise, we were a tiny bit behind with Saturday's shoot. Couple of scenes need tidying up. Anyway I've had a word with Wellard and he's going to pop in a couple of fillers that will slide us over any unwanted gaps. Nothing to alter the plot lines; in fact they mostly concern Sally . . .' There was an audible hiss from Stephanie's end of the table. 'So if you could see me at the coffee break, Sally, I'll just explain what we have in mind.'

* * *

'Is Veeney annoyed with me about something?' Sally asked Marley while René ploughed through the latest of the Sedgewicks' spitting matches.

'Veeney? Goodness, no, I shouldn't think so. Why should she be?'

'I don't know. She just seemed a bit short when I asked her if I could borrow her biro.' Marley smiled. 'She's a funny little thing, isn't she? Probably boyfriend problems. You know what it's like when you're young.'

At lunch time Sally cornered Patrick and asked him why Stephanie was complaining about her accent. Patrick poured his beer very slowly into his glass. 'Sour grapes,' he said.

'But why? It's not as if I ever get to speak to her. What difference can it make what accent I'm using? Or not using.'

Patrick surveyed her intently. 'You really don't know, do you?'

'Know what? What am I supposed to know?' Patrick chuckled and shook his head. 'Young Sal, whether you like it or not, the entire cast knows you enticed our illustrious author into a cab with you on Saturday night. Now what possible reason could you have had for doing that? Don't worry,' he added as Sally's mouth fell open, 'we've all done it. Except possibly Marley. Nobody blames you. Truth were, most of them wish they'd got there first.'

'But this is ridiculous,' Sally burst out with such vehemence that most of the pub fell silent. 'You mean that nasty little man who snitched a lift in my cab and didn't even pay his share of the fare is ... was ... Oh.' She glanced round nervously and lowered her voice. 'Oh, surely not. But how could he ... I mean he couldn't even talk, let alone ... Oh, this is awful. And now René's giving me some extra lines and everyone thinks ... Oh, this is awful.'

'Don't worry about it.' Patrick was laughing. 'I'll put them straight, that's if they haven't heard already.'

Sally sat mortified. 'I bet René did. Now I won't just have extra lines, I'll probably get the sack.'

'Calm down. René's not here. He's gone to get his wipers fixed or something. I saw him driving off.'

The atmosphere lightened considerably once the other actors had learnt of their mistake. Veeney offered Sally a roll-up and Hazel asked if she could measure her pullover against her back, which she took to be a gesture of solidarity.

The rehearsals continued much as before with the same blend of crises and optimism that had coloured the first two weeks. Simon's nose was healing nicely and René had every hope of presenting him full face in the next recording. Drewe continued to come and go as though the series were built around his availability, but René, with the help of his Valium and a book on anger management was coping fairly well. 'I hope he bloody well does get a part in *Titus Andronicus*,' he was heard to mutter after Drewe's third recall. 'They all end up bloody skewered to the bloody floor.'

Dilys had reverted to her silent state and sat amongst them, gazing bleakly into the middle distance and sucking Fishermen's Friends. Her lines had been cruelly cut to prevent a repeat of Saturday, but she was the leading character's wife and as such could not be altogether consigned to the role of an extra.

Sally's new lines were walking evidence that whatever wiles she had practised on the scriptwriter during their late night dash had signally failed to excite his imagination. Coffee again figured largely, making her wonder if he was seeking sponsorship from one of the big companies. Even René was beginning to lose his place with the endless repetitions and after Patrick had broken down in utter confusion, crying, 'For God's sake, René, I'll need a bloody catheter if she gives me any more,' he had agreed to speak to Kenning about it.

Wellard Kenning was nothing if not versatile and the scripts duly came back amended to 'tea', at which point Patrick was seen to bang his head on the table.

The others had all gone by the time René dismissed them. 'Fancy a drink?' asked Patrick as they left the hall.

'Yes, all right.' Sally was feelingly particularly drained. Wendy Costume had been on at her again about having her hair cut, 'a crop – a bit like Jean's. It would give the character more body.' Rolo had saved the day by pointing out that for continuity reasons this was not feasible since, unimportant though Laura indisputably was, someone somewhere would be bound to notice if she had a French roll during one half of a conversation and a short-back-and-sides during the rest. Wendy had retreated sniffing, but Sally had a distinct feeling that this would not be the last attack in Costume's crusade to make her the ugliest woman on television.

'How do you think it's going?' asked Patrick as they settled in a corner of the Feathers. This was by now the requisite opening to any conversation between members of the cast. What it really meant was 'am I all right?'

'OK,' Sally answered wearily.

'Just OK?' Patrick's brow furrowed in anxiety. Sally pulled herself together. 'I think it's really beginning to gel,' she said earnestly. 'The scenes between you and Simon are coming on marvellously.'

'He's not bad, is he, young Simon?'

'No. I think he's excellent. He's got a lot of presence, hasn't he?' Patrick's frown deepened. 'Do you think so?' Sally realised she'd gone too far. 'A lot of it depends on you, though, of course. The interaction between the two of you is quite electric sometimes.'

Patrick relaxed somewhat. 'He's got a lot to learn. Veeney's coping very well, isn't she?'

'Yes. Has she done much acting? I know she sings.'

'None at all, as far as I can gather. Marley says she's René's love child. I can't see it myself. She's not nearly ugly enough.'

Sally laughed. 'Where does Marley get all her information from? She always seems to know more about people than they do themselves.'

Patrick chuckled. 'Darling Marley. She makes half of it up. Always has done. She can't help herself. None of it's malicious, though. She just likes to fantasise and then she can't remember what's real and what isn't. I've known her for thirty years. She hasn't changed. I think she gets a bit lonely since her old man died and it helps to make her feel part of things.'

'Hasn't she any family then?'

'We're her family.'

Sally grimaced. 'I don't think I'd pick us for relatives if I had the choice.' Patrick smiled a little sadly. 'Who said anything about choice?'

They sat on discussing René's various iniquities, Stephanie's tantrums, the neuroses of Wendy and Jean, who would play Melanie Rinseworth and Rolo's superb efficiency.

'Penny's a nice girl,' declared Sally as Patrick returned with a plate of rolls.

'Ah . . . Penny.'

'What do you mean "ah . . . Penny" like that? Don't you like her?'

Patrick shrugged. 'Of course I like her. She's very nice. A little . . .' he stopped.

Sally extracted a bit of cress from between her teeth. 'Go on. A little what?'

Patrick shook his head. 'Nothing. Are these all egg? I distinctly asked for ham.'

'Those ones are ham. Don't change the subject. What were you going to say about Penny? You can't start conversations and leave off halfway.'

'Tell that to Wellard Kenning.'

'I meant in real life. What is Penny "a little"?'

'Promiscuous.'

'PROMISCUOUS?'

The man at the next table looked up from behind his paper. Sally lowered her voice. 'How can you say that? You must be wrong. Just because she and Simon . . .'

'SIMON?' This time it was Patrick's turn to roar. Sally baulked slightly. 'Well, surely you knew . . . I mean otherwise why did you say . . .?' Patrick's expression made it perfectly clear why he had said. 'I think it's time I was on my way,' she said, searching around for her coat.

'I knew about Rolo,' said Patrick stonily. 'I put that down to pressure of work.'

'I could be wrong,' blustered Sally. 'I often get the wrong end of the stick . . .'

Patrick was staring into the distance, his eyes blank with fury. 'That jumped up little dickhead,' he muttered. 'Just catch me giving him my close-ups in future.' Sally got up. Patrick looked at her in surprise.

'Where are you going?'

'Home. I've got some things to do this evening.' Patrick reached up and grabbed her arm. 'But the night is young. How can you desert me with all these rolls to finish?' Sally detached his hand. 'There are only three. You can manage those perfectly well.'

'But they're egg,' whimpered Patrick.

'No they're not. There's a ham one there.' Sally turned the plate towards him. 'And after that I suggest you go home. You know what René's like if you don't know your lines.'

'I always know my lines,' said Patrick, drawing himself up regally. 'I shall take it very much amiss if you leave me

here by myself with all these revolting rolls.' Sally sighed
and sat down again. Patrick patted her hand. 'That's better.
Now, whose turn is it to buy the drinks?'

It was raining hard when they left. 'Where's my car?'
demanded Patrick, gazing bewilderedly around him.

'You haven't got a car, Patrick. Don't you remember you
had your licence suspended three months ago.'

'Who told you that?'

'You did. You said it was all your wife's fault for living in
Nuneaton and expecting you to drive there after a show.'

'Oh, yes. Well, it was. Where's a taxi then? We'll have
to get a taxi.'

'You will. I'm getting the tube. We're going in different
directions.'

'Nonsense. Pouring with rain. Have to have a taxi.' He
waved ineffectually at a black cab. The driver turned his
meter over and sped away.

'It must be ten years since I've been in a tube train,' Patrick
observed, gazing round at the compartment as though it
were a prehistoric find. 'What's that?' He indicated the
poster opposite.

'It's a poem,' said Sally.

'I can see that. But why? What's it doing there?'

'They have them now,' she explained. Patrick nodded.
'A very nice idea.' He now treated the entire carriage to a
full-throated rendering of the innocuous little verse. Sally
stared at her fingernails, thinking how much better it had
been when they'd stuck to advertisements.

'One for the road?' he suggested as they emerged into
the Strand.

'No, thanks. We've got to rehearse in the morning,
remember.'

'Oh, go on,' Patrick wheedled. 'There's a nice little club
round the corner.'

'I can't, Patrick. I'll miss my train.'

'No you won't. You've got ages. The last one goes at five to twelve.'

'How do you know?'

'My wife lives in New Cross.'

'I thought she lived in Nuneaton.'

'Not that one. Angie. My second wife. Five to twelve. That's the last train.'

'Well anyway, no, thanks all the same.'

'Why not?'

'Because it's late.'

'No it's not. It's all right, though. I don't blame you.'

'Blame me for what?'

'Nothing. Take no notice. Just the wanderings of an old man.' He flashed her a lopsided smile.

'You're not an old man,' said Sally firmly.

'Yes, I am,' said Patrick self-pityingly. 'I'm fifty-one. You can't get much older than that.'

'Possibly not if you sit up half the night drinking,' said Sally piously.

Patrick frowned at her. 'What's that supposed to mean? Are you saying I can't hold my drink?'

'No. But that doesn't mean you've got to prove it, does it? To be honest, I've got a thundering headache and I just want to go home to bed.'

'Spoken like a wife,' said Patrick morosely. 'I'd hoped for better things from you, Sally. You're a big disappointment to me, do you know that?'

'I'm sorry,' said Sally, unaccountably stung. 'I don't know what you do expect from me, but I'm sorry if I've let you down.'

'Now you're all upset,' Patrick snuggled up to her like a small boy. 'Don't go home all cross.'

'I'm not cross.' She pulled away.

'Yes, you are.'

'No, I'm not. Look, I'll leave you here then you can go on to this club of yours and have a drink in peace.'

'Don't want to go by myself.'

'Well, go home then.' She thumped the pedestrian crossing button. Patrick seized her hand and clasped it pathetically between his own. 'Please. Just one. You won't miss your train.'

'Oh, all right then.'

'It's gone.' They were standing on Charing Cross station. A cleaner swished past them on a motorised floor buffer. The place was nearly deserted. 'I knew this would happen. Now what am I going to do? I'll have to get a taxi.' Sally glared at Patrick who seemed blissfully unaware of the seriousness of her predicament. A taxi to Greenwich at this time would cost a fortune. *If* she could persuade one to take her there, which was pretty unlikely in itself, particularly as she was having a little trouble forming her sentences. She knew she shouldn't have had that last brandy.

'No problem.' He took her arm and draped it round his shoulder as though he had just saved her from drowning, rather than caused her to miss the last train. 'You can stay with me. I shall look after you.'

'I don't want to stay with you,' grumbled Sally. 'I want to go home.'

'No, no you don't.' Patrick began to steer her towards the exit. The floor buffer came gliding by again and she contemplated asking if it could go as far as Greenwich and if so, how much it would cost.

'Where are we going?' she wailed as he loaded her into a cab. 'Home.'

'Greenwich?'

'Fulham.'

'I don't want to go to Fulham. I live in Greenwich.' She

leaned forward and tapped ineffectually on the dividing window. 'I'm being kidnapped,' she told the driver.

'Is that a fact?' said the driver who'd promised his wife he'd be home by ten.

'Yes. Could you please drive us to Greenwich immediately.'

'I was told Fulham,' said the cabbie menacingly.

'Yes, yes,' Patrick interrupted. 'As you were. The lady's got a bit confused.'

''Cos I ain't going south of the river,' said the driver.

'No, no, of course not. Do you watch a lot of television?'

'I don't get the time,' said the man pointedly. 'I had whatsisname in the back the other week.'

'Who?' chorused Sally and Patrick.

The cabbie shook his head. 'The name's gone. Used to be a big star. Don't know what happened to him. Ask me, he was on his uppers. Still, they come and go, don't they? Here today and gone tomorrow. That's the name of the game.' They all three relapsed into silence.

Patrick's spirits had revived somewhat by the time the cab stopped outside a row of tall Victorian houses. He paid the fare and led Sally up the stone steps to an imposing oak front door.

'Is this yours?' asked Sally, impressed.

'Only the bottom half.' He ushered her in.

'It's very nice,' said Sally, gazing enviously at the enormous room with its elegant cornice and dado rails. You could have got her entire flat into the same area. Patrick put on lamps and sat her on a squashy settee. He poured two large brandies and handed her one. 'I don't want any more to drink.'

'Why not?'

'I can't stay.'

'Dear girl, of course you must stay. There's no way you can get back to Woolwich tonight.'

'Greenwich,' Sally corrected him. 'This is your fault.'

Patrick looked contrite. 'I know.' He crouched down in front of her and smiled apologetically. 'I feel terrible. It's just that I was enjoying our conversation so much I clean forgot about the time.' He gave her hand a quick squeeze. 'It makes such a change to have someone you can really talk to. Don't you find that?' Sally looked at him suspiciously. He was a much better actor than she had given him credit for.

'So I'm stuck here?'

'Stuck? Of course you're not stuck. I can call you a cab straight away if you'd prefer.'

'How much will it cost?'

'I'll check for you.'

He came back looking grave. 'How much?'

'Fifty-five pounds. It's after midnight, you see.'

'Patrick, you are the absolute end. When will it be here?'

Patrick looked visibly taken aback. 'You want me to call one?'

'Of course I do. If you think I'm going to doss down on your floor without a change of clothes and turn up for rehearsal looking like a tramp, you're quite mistaken. I'm having enough trouble with Wendy and Jean as it is. They'll probably have my head shaved to avoid contamination.'

'Sally, Sally,' Patrick laid a soothing hand on her arm, 'darling girl, how can you imagine I would let you sleep on my floor? What do you take me for? An absolute beast?' It was impossible to ignore the note of optimism.

'A rat,' said Sally fiercely. Patrick shook his head sorrowfully and led her through to the bedroom.

'That's a very big bed,' she murmured, gazing dubiously at the four-poster with its copper satin sheets and drooping canopy.

'Plenty of room for two,' said Patrick, endeavouring to find her hand amidst her stiffly folded arms.

'You planned this, didn't you?' said Sally angrily. 'You made me miss my train on purpose so that . . .'

'Sally, darling, so that what?'

'So that . . . Oh, you know damn well so that what. Well it's not on. Is that perfectly clear? I'm not Penny, you know. I have no intention of jumping into bed with every Tom, Dick or Harry who makes me miss my train. Understood?'

Patrick drew himself up very tall. 'I resent that,' he said in a sonorous voice. 'Here am I, offering you the comfort of my own bed in my own home at, though I hesitate to say it, great inconvenience to myself . . .'

'Great inconvenience to YOURself? What about the inconvenience to me? If you hadn't dragged me off to that cellar full of down-and-outs I would have been in time to catch my train.'

'Those were not down-and-outs. They were resting actors. I should have thought that as a member of the same profession you might have shown a little more sympathy.'

'I have every sympathy for resting actors. I've spent most of my career being one. It doesn't mean I have to sob into other people's drinks and witter on about how good things used to be before the wheel.'

Patrick surveyed her critically. 'You're a hard woman, Sally Grosvenor, and no mistaking. Am I to take it from this that you wish to decline the offer of my body for the night?'

'I certainly do. For God's sake, Patrick, it's nearly two o'clock. Do you think we could postpone this discussion till some other time?'

Patrick sighed. 'You are quite sure?'

Sally gave an enormous yawn. 'I have never been surer of anything in my life.'

Patrick gazed at her with a mixture of frustration and relief. 'Right. Foolish girl, you may live to regret this decision. Now, will it be Horlicks or Ovaltine, madam?' Sally began to laugh.

They slept together in the king-sized bed with a line of pillows between them. 'Tell me,' said Patrick, shortly before they fell asleep, 'what's that bloke Kenning really like?'

'Who?' Sally murmured, pulling the duvet round her.

'Kenning. Wellard Kenning. The fucking author.'

'As an author?'

'No, as a fuck.'

'About the same.'

Patrick sighed contentedly and tried to pull the duvet back.

12

'They came in together.' Marley was confiding to Hazel who was more concerned with finding the lost stitch in her tank top than hearing the latest convolution in the cast's emotional spectrum. 'And Patrick was looking very cheerful.'

'How did Sally look?'

'Oh, very happy. Fulfilled, you might almost say.' Hazel nodded and smiled. She was a Relate counsellor and knew too well what such sudden joy usually heralded. 'We'll have to wait and see.'

'Oh, yes,' Marley agreed, placing a cube of butterscotch on Hazel's pattern, 'but it would be so nice, don't you think?'

'Where is he?' René, his voice dangerously level, came striding down the hall. He had particularly instructed Drewe to be in the hall by ten o'clock that day. 'Has anyone seen Drewe?' No one had.

'Perhaps we should start with Simon and Veeney's scenes?' suggested Rolo tentatively.

'You can't do that,' put in Stephanie. 'I've got to be in Bond Street at half past eleven.'

'What for?' snapped René whose head was no longer up to smoking dope till three in the morning. Stephanie looked surprised. 'Clothes, darling. What else? You didn't think I could wear that monstrosity Wardrobe kitted me out with again, did you? Actually I'm surprised you ever gave it the go ahead in the first place. I looked a perfect fright from the back.' René began to say something and then changed his mind.

Drewe arrived a quarter of an hour late but made no apology since by his standards this could be construed as early. Penny was dragged from the security of the kitchen where she had been peacefully weeping and obliged to read an uncast policewoman which everyone agreed she did exceedingly well. 'It's such a pity she hasn't got her Equity card,' mumbled Marley who had taken it upon herself to make the coffee. 'I wonder if there are any biscuits.'

Simon was strangely subdued and seemed to be avoiding Penny, whose pale eyes followed him dolefully around the room all morning. '. . . be so nice,' Sally heard Marley confiding to Veeney as she collected her coat at lunch time. 'Are you coming down to the Feathers, dear?' Marley called.

'Yes, I think so,' said Sally. 'René wants me back at a quarter to so I can't go far.'

'Is Patrick coming?'

Sally shook her head. 'I don't think so. He's got a photo call at the studio. He said something about having lunch up there.'

'Oh dear.' Marley patted her hand solicitously. 'Never mind.'

'Has René said anything to you yet?' asked Veeney peremptorily.

'What about?'

'Your accent,' said Veeney and flounced off down the hall.

Dan Chamberlain was waiting in the hall when Sally got in that evening. She was earlier than usual, having turned down Patrick's offer of a drink, much to his amusement and Marley's consternation. He had gone off to have dinner with a grown-up son by his first marriage, the whereabouts of which wife had yet to be revealed.

Sally noticed Dan looked rather tired. Still recovering from *Clytemnestra*, probably. She noted with some relief that the planks had gone from the hall. 'Hullo,' she said. Dan nodded. 'Umm . . .' He seemed at a bit of a loss.

'Is anything the matter?'

'It's the old man,' he blurted out. 'I'm waiting for the ambulance.'

'Ambulance? Why? What's happened?'

Dan shook his head. 'He's had a bit of a fall. Seems a bit confused. He's in there,' he gestured towards his flat. Sally pushed past him. Mr Davenport was lying on the couch, an ugly bruise spreading across his bony temples and a thin slick of blood oozing from his nose. His eyes were open but he seemed unable to focus. Sally knelt beside him. 'Mr Davenport . . . Mr Davenport. It's me, Sally. Are you all right? You've had a bit of a fall. Dan's rung for an ambulance.'

A flicker of panic crossed the old man's face. 'What about . . .? Who's going to take care of . . .?'

Sally could hear the wail of the sirens turning into the road. 'Don't you worry about a thing, Mr Davenport. We'll see that everything's all right.' Mr Davenport closed his eyes.

The ambulance men were kind and efficient, lifting the frail body as though it were made of porcelain and keeping up a run of cheerful banter that was curiously soothing. Dan and Sally followed them out to the ambulance. 'What exactly happened?' Sally asked. 'Did you see him fall?'

Dan shook his head. 'I was in the back garden and I heard this sort of shout, but I didn't think anything of it. You know, he does make some strange sorts of noises when he's . . . you know . . .'

'Barking,' nodded Sally.

'Yes, well, you know. Anyway it must have been ten minutes later when I came in. The phone was ringing, and while I was talking I could hear this sort of moaning sound in the hall, so I opened the door to have a look and he was just lying there. I picked him up and brought him in here. Then I phoned the ambulance. I didn't know what else to do.' His eyes sought Sally's for reassurance.

'You did the right thing, I'm sure,' she said.

Dan looked relieved. 'Do you think he'll be all right?'

Sally shrugged. 'I expect so. It probably looks worse than it is.'

'Is that you, Sally?' Mr Davenport's wavery voice called from inside the vehicle. 'Yes, Mr Davenport. I'm here.' She leant in.

'Am I going to hospital?'

'That's right. To have your bruise looked at.'

The old man struggled to sit up. 'You won't let them put him down, will you?'

Sally shook her head violently. 'Of course I won't, Mr Davenport. Don't you worry about a thing.'

'And you'll see he gets fed?'

'I certainly will. And take him for walks. You just relax. Everything will be fine.'

The ambulance man glanced at her. 'He's worried about his dog, is it?'

Sally turned her head so that Mr Davenport couldn't hear her. 'Actually he hasn't got a dog. It's a bit complicated,' she mouthed. The man nodded understandingly.

'It wasn't his fault,' came Mr Davenport's voice again. 'I don't want you blaming him. I should've been more careful.'

Sally turned back to him. 'Of course it wasn't. It was an accident. No one's fault.'

The ambulance drew away, its blue light whirling silently

on the roof. The two of them watched until it was out of sight.

'Drink?' asked Dan, his shoulders hunched dejectedly.

'Yes please,' said Sally. 'Poor old thing. He was in such a state about this wretched non-existent dog.'

'I thought he thought he was the dog.'

'He does when he's being it, but when he's not he still thinks it's there.'

'Sounds crazy to me,' said Dan. 'Perhaps a knock on the head'll sort him out.'

Sally frowned. 'That's a bit callous.'

Dan looked chastened. 'I didn't mean it like that. Anyway, who's going to look after it while he's away?'

'I am,' said Sally ruefully. 'And there's no need to laugh.'

Dan took her arm and led her across the road to the pub. 'Look on the bright side. At least you can teach it not to pee in the hall.'

'How's your telly going?' Dan asked, setting a glass of wine in front of her.

'Oh, fine,' said Sally, hoping he would not press her on the subject. But Dan seemed as little inclined to discuss *The Firm* as Sally was. 'I hope the old boy's all right,' he said. 'That was a hell of a bump on his head.'

'Yes,' said Sally. 'He's too old really to be living on his own like that. He just can't manage since they stopped his home help.'

'Hasn't he got any family?'

'Not that I know of. There was a cousin or someone that used to call occasionally, but I haven't seen him for months.'

Dan sighed. 'Down to you and me, then.'

Sally's eyes widened. 'Oh come on. We can't possibly keep watch on him night and day. I mean I'm out a good deal, and look what happened when you were in the house. He still managed to fall over and hurt himself. It was just lucky for him you found him when you did, otherwise goodness knows . . . Is anything the matter?' Dan was leaning his head in his hand. He roused himself. 'No. It's nothing.' He hesitated. 'Well, actually, yes, there is something.' He looked at her carefully, as though trying to gauge the effect of what he was about to say.

'It's something to do with the house, isn't it?' said Sally stiffly. 'What have you turned off now?'

Dan laughed. 'You mean you didn't see the oil well?'

'Oh shut up,' said Sally, laughing too. 'That means you haven't started whatever it is yet, I suppose?'

Dan shook his head. 'It's nothing like that. It's a bit awkward . . .' he sighed. 'Actually, I shouldn't have mentioned it. It's a stupid idea. Forget I said anything.'

Sally thumped the table in frustration. 'How can I forget it now you've gone this far? You'll have to at least tell me what it was, otherwise I shall lie awake all night waiting for the pipes to burst.'

Dan grinned. 'You really don't have much faith in me, do you?'

'When did you give me any reason to? Come on, tell me what you wanted.'

'Promise not to be offended?'

'That sounds ominous.'

'Promise?'

'I promise to try not to be. I can't say fairer than that.'

Dan sighed again. 'It's a stupid idea.'

'Yes, we've had that bit,' interrupted Sally.

'Right,' said Dan, staring fixedly into his glass. 'My wife – Suzanne – rang me today. It was her I was talking to when I heard the old man in the hall.'

Sally nodded. 'And?'

'And . . . she wants to come and see me. She's worried,

you see. She feels guilty about leaving me and asking for a divorce and that.'

'She's having second thoughts?'

Dan's face creased in confusion. 'She wants a divorce. There's no doubt about that, but she's worried about me – how I'll cope.' Sally refrained from saying she wasn't surprised, given his record so far. 'Where do I come into all this?' Dan was gripping his glass so hard she was surprised it didn't break. 'This is very awkward.'

'Just tell me,' she coaxed. 'I can always refuse.'

'She's coming to see me, and I don't want her to think . . . I don't want her feeling sorry for me and thinking she can't . . . what I was wondering, but I can see now it's a daft idea . . .'

Sally began to feel a new respect for Wellard Kenning. She stood up. 'I'll get us another drink then you can tell me exactly what you have in mind. Remember, I'm an actress. We don't shock easily.' When she came back Dan had plainly got his thoughts in order.

'It's to do with you being an actress,' he said evenly. 'I thought I could invite Suzanne to dinner and you could pretend to be my girlfriend then she wouldn't worry about me any more.'

Sally stared at him in amazement. 'I see.'

Dan glanced at her quickly. 'I didn't think you'd want to. Sorry I asked.'

'You haven't asked. When you say "pretend to be your girlfriend" what exactly do you have in mind? Am I to appear in a see-through nightie, draped round your neck all evening, or do we both turn up in identical fairisle sweaters and talk about our weekend rambles in the Peak District? What exactly does your wife expect of your girlfriends?'

Dan slammed his glass down on the table. 'She doesn't expect anything. We were married eleven years.'

Sally acknowledged her insensitivity. 'I'm sorry. I didn't

mean to be flippant. I just can't see why you don't just introduce me to her as your neighbour and leave it at that. She'll see you've made new friends – surely that should ease her mind?'

'Friends aren't the same.'

'They last a darn sight longer,' said Sally before she could stop herself.

'Not always,' said Dan forcefully. 'Anyway, it's not really a starter, is it? I hope you didn't mind me asking.'

Sally recovered herself. 'Not at all.' They finished their drinks in silence then crossed back to the house.

'Good night,' Sally said, still feeling slightly shaken.

'Good night.' Dan unlocked his door. 'Who's taking the dog out tonight?'

Sally smiled. 'Perhaps we should take it in turns. Thanks for moving those planks, by the way. They were beginning to get on my nerves.' Dan stiffened slightly. 'That's OK,' he said. 'I should have done it before.'

'Good night.'

'Good night.'

The phone rang as she was getting her supper. 'Sally?'

'Yes?'

'It's Patrick.'

'Oh. Hullo.'

'My darling, don't sound so distant with me. I was wondering if you'd like to pop over and have a drink?'

'In Fulham?'

'Yes.'

'Now?'

'Yes.'

'I thought you were having dinner with your son.'

'I am. I have. He's off to a party somewhere, so I shall be all on my own. I thought you might fancy a little company?'

Sally looked at her watch. It was gone nine. 'Thanks

very much, Patrick, but not awfully this evening. I'm still recovering from last night.' There was a deep sigh from the other end. 'Sally, Sally, where is your spirit of adventure? Seize the moment, my darling, for it may never come again.'

'I shall have to take my chances with that.'

'Do I detect a note of cynicism in those mellifluous tones?' said Patrick reprovingly.

'Heaven forbid.'

'Here am I offering to rescue you from another dreary night in Woolwich.'

'Greenwich. And it's not dreary at all. It's a very attractive area. We have the park and the Maritime Museum . . .'

'Spare me the estate agent's patter, my darling. I'm sure it's the very epicentre of tourist Britain, but you are there, alone, when you could be here with me.'

'How do you know I'm alone?'

'Aren't you alone?'

Sally considered. 'Well, yes, I am . . .'

'There you are then. Into a cab. I shall put something nice in the fridge. How long do you think you'll be?'

'I'm not coming, Patrick. Thank you very much but it's too late and I'm tired and . . .'

'What sort of excuses are these? Have you no fire in your blood? No sap in your veins?'

'How much have you had to drink, Patrick?'

'Nothing at all. Practically nothing. Just a few beers with my son. Now are you coming or not?'

'Not.'

'Last chance.'

'Good night, Patrick.'

'I shan't ask again.'

'Good night, Patrick.'

'You'll regret this, Sally my sweet, as you sink into embittered spinsterhood.'

'I wish you wouldn't assume you're the only man who's prepared to come anywhere near me,' retorted Sally in a sudden fit of irritation.

'Dear girl, how can you accuse me of such a thing? I'm sure knights have fought duels over you, ships have been sunk, nations have fallen.'

'Oh shut up.'

'All I'm saying is that at your time of life you shouldn't turn your back on the promise of a little happiness, albeit transititory,' he hiccupped genteely down the phone.

'No, well I'm glad you said that,' said Sally grimly, 'because I haven't.'

'Haven't what?'

'Turned my back. And if you'll excuse me, I'd better get off the phone before he comes in and finds me talking to you.'

'Are you telling me there is someone else in your life?'

'Patrick, you're drunk. You're not in my life any more than I'm in yours.'

'Who is this man? Is he an actor?'

'No, thank God.'

'Hah!' snapped Patrick like a detective pinpointing a murderer. 'Take the advice of an expert. Mixed marriages never work. As my old granny used to say, "Never cross the footlights for a fuck". If only I'd listened to her.'

'If only you had,' said Sally wearily.

'So you're not coming over?'

'I'll see you in the morning, Patrick. Thanks for ringing.'

'Sleep well, my sweet.'

'And you.'

Patrick's hangover the following day was rather worse than usual. Marley whispered to Sally that his son was giving him a lot of trouble by wanting to drop out of university and that

Patrick was desperate for him not to blow his chances of a decent degree.

'What's he studying?' asked Sally, feeling guilty.

'Psychology,' said Marley. 'Patrick says he's terribly clever. He says he can read him like a book.' Sally smiled.

At coffee break she approached him. 'How are you feeling?'

'Like death warmed up. You couldn't ask Penny if she's got any more of those paracetamol, could you?' Sally went and got him some.

'I'm sorry if I was a bit off last night,' she said tentatively.

Patrick squinted at her. 'Were you? I can't remember. God, these taste awful.'

'I think you're meant to dissolve them in water,' said Sally, watching the foam billowing from his mouth.

'Watch out, everyone,' bellowed Simon, 'Paddy's got rabies.'

Not for the first time Sally wished he were more discerning. Patrick drank the water she had brought him and rubbed a hand across his forehead. 'Was I very rude?' he asked apologetically.

'No. Actually you were rather funny?'

'Was I?'

'Yes.'

'How?'

'Well, you said if I didn't come over I'd sink into bitter spinsterhood and things.'

'You found that funny, did you?'

'It was the way you said it.'

Patrick leant back and laid his arm across his eyes. 'I shouldn't have said it.'

'I didn't mind, honestly.' The actor reached out with his other hand and groped around for hers. She gave it to him. 'If I remember rightly you gave me the brush off in no uncertain terms.'

'Oh, well. I was a bit tired.'

'Even invented a boyfriend,' continued Patrick. Sally snatched her hand away. 'I did not.'

'It's all right. I don't blame you. I'd've done the same under the circumstances.'

'I didn't invent him,' Sally persisted.

Patrick raised his arm and opened one eye. 'He exists, does he? This paragon of the outside world?'

'He most certainly does,' Sally retorted, pink with annoyance.

'And what's his name?'

She swallowed. 'Dan. Dan Chamberlain.'

'And what does he do?'

'He's a builder,' stammered Sally, 'a construction engineer. And a teacher.'

'Brain surgeon in his spare time?' suggested Patrick.

'You don't believe me, do you?'

Patrick smiled understandingly. 'I'm just a little surprised you never mentioned him before.'

'Like you told us about your son?' Patrick turned away as though he'd been hit. Sally went to the window and stared out, hating herself.

'I'm sorry.'

'That's all right. I asked for it.'

'No, you didn't.' She suddenly felt the need to retain his affection.

'Look, come to dinner. You can meet Dan.'

Patrick smiled. 'Am I allowed to challenge him to a duel?'

Sally laughed. 'So long as it doesn't involve anything technical.'

'Hallo?' Dan sounded distinctly irritable. Sally took a breath. 'It's Sally.'

'Sally who?'

'Sally Grosvenor. From upstairs.'

'Oh yes.'

This was a good start. 'You know what you were saying last night?'

'What about?'

'About . . . your wife and if I could . . . you know, act as girlfriend for you?'

'I thought we'd agreed it was a nonstarter.'

'Well, yes we did. But what I was wondering . . . Obviously I was a little taken aback at the time, but I've been giving it a lot of thought . . .'

'And?' He really wasn't making this very easy for her.

'Well, I thought, perhaps it might be a thought, tell me if you don't agree, how would it be if we were to have a dinner party – just a small one here, in my flat, then you could invite your, er . . . Suzanne, and I could invite . . . someone else . . . a friend of mine, and we could sort of make it look, you know . . . all right?'

There was a long silence. Sally began to feel sick.

'You're sure you wouldn't mind?'

'Oh no,' said Sally rapidly. 'No. It would be fun. I love cooking.'

13

'Four three six double seven double one,' came Colin's clipped voice.

'Colin, it's Sally. I need my microwave back.'

'Sally, darling, how are you?'

'I'm fine. I need my microwave.'

'Haven't you got it?' asked Colin, gazing directly at the spot where Matthew had dumped it before walking out on him the night before.

'Of course I haven't,' said Sally with mounting frustration. 'I hope nothing's happened to it. It's past its guarantee.'

'Oh, THAT microwave,' drawled Colin as though he ran a factory for their manufacture. 'Yes, yes it's here. When do you want to pick it up?'

'I don't want to pick it up at all,' said Sally indignantly. 'I want it returned to me post haste. I'm giving a dinner party next week and it is imperative that I have it by then.'

'When are you having it?' asked Colin, reaching for his diary.

'Tuesday.'

'How many for?'

'What's that got to do with it?' asked Sally suspiciously.

'Just thought you might need a spare man. I know what it's like for you single ladies trying to balance the numbers. I'm free on Tuesday as it happens.'

'Really? Well, thank you very much but I won't have to call on you this time, Colin. Just bring me my microwave, that's all I ask.'

'What are you having?'

'I haven't decided yet.'

'I could do you a pud. That could be my contribution.'

'I don't want a contribution, Colin. All I want is my microwave. Now when can you bring it?'

'Tuesday.'

'Colin . . .'

'God's truth, my darling. I'm rehearsing all weekend and on Monday I've got to drive to Birmingham to meet my mother off the plane.'

'Where's she been this time?' Colin's mother was a Saga groupie, ostensibly in search of a second husband but Sally had long suspected she was secretly interested in European culture judging by the souvenirs of art galleries she brought back with her.

'Crete.'

'Tuesday morning, then.'

'At the very crack.'

'Thank you.'

'I could get you some lamb from that organic place off the M1?'

'No need, thank you, Colin. I'll see you on Tuesday. Early.'

They broke early on Tuesday afternoon. The Producer's Run had been unusually speedy as Jeff Wilkins, though back from his holiday, wanted to go to an exhibition of fishing tackle for which he had a free ticket.

Colin, true to form, had not materialised with her microwave, which did not greatly matter in itself but was nonetheless a source of annoyance.

There was a strange woman at the front door as she came

up the path. 'Do you live here?' the woman asked, seeing her producing keys.

'Yes,' said Sally briskly. She had no wish to be cornered by a Jehovah's Witness when she still had the flat to tidy and a lemon meringue pie to defrost.

'I'm from the Social Services,' the woman said. 'Do you know a Mr Davenport?'

'Is he all right?' asked Sally anxiously. She had been to see him on Sunday evening and thought he was looking rather well. His bruise was healing nicely and he had seemed rested. He hadn't mentioned dogs at all.

'I'm afraid I don't know about that. I understand he's in hospital after a fall.'

'That's right, but I saw him on Sunday. The nurse said he could be home by the weekend.'

'Yes.' The woman hesitated. 'I don't suppose you have a key to his flat?'

'I do, as a matter of fact,' said Sally.

'Oh good,' said the woman. 'That makes my job a lot easier.'

'What exactly is your job?' asked Sally.

The woman smiled. 'I have to assess whether Mr Davenport should be allowed to return home.'

'Allowed?' echoed Sally. 'He's not under arrest, is he?'

The woman laughed mirthlessly. 'Mr Davenport apparently has been experiencing a few problems over the past few months. You may have noticed something yourself? Do you have much contact with him, Mrs . . .?'

'He's my neighbour,' said Sally stiffly.

'Well, exactly. But here in London a lot of neighbours don't even know each other's names.'

'Really?' said Sally. She put her key in the lock and opened the front door. The woman followed her in. 'So if you could just let me have the key to Mr Davenport's flat . . .'

Sally turned to her. 'Do you have any ID?' The woman's

face clouded over but she produced a plastic card which said she was Mrs Crane from Greenwich Social Services and as such should be accorded every assistance. 'Why exactly do you want to see his flat?'

'I've told you. So that I can assess whether he should be allowed back.'

'How can you do that if you've never met him?'

Mrs Crane's lips hardened. 'I have seen his medical report. It appears he fell for no obvious reason, therefore we have to ask ourselves whether he is physically able to cope with living on his own. There also appears to be some question of a hallucinatory animal.'

'Dog,' said Sally.

'I beg your pardon.'

'It's a dog. And it's not hallucinatory. It's a joke.'

'A joke?'

'Yes. There are no animals allowed here. It's in the terms of the leaseholds so we all have pretend ones. I have a parrot.'

Mrs Crane's eyes narrowed very slightly. 'What do you call it?'

The door of Dan Chamberlain's flat opened.

'Dan,' said Sally. 'Hello, Mr Chamberlain. I was just telling Mrs Crane from THE SOCIAL SERVICES how we all have pretend pets here because we're not allowed the real thing. Like my parrot, DAN.'

Dan's face changed not a whisper. 'Oh, yes,' he agreed. 'I've got a monkey.'

'Indeed,' said Mrs Crane, small patches of red appearing through her powder. 'What do you call your monkey, Mr Chamberlain?'

Dan scratched his chin. 'I used to call it Sally,' he said, 'but then I found out it was a male.'

'What do you call it now?' asked Mrs Crane with icy calm. 'Dan,' said Dan.

They escorted Mrs Crane round Mr Davenport's flat. She marched from room to room writing on a notepad. Sally was relieved to find it much neater than she had anticipated. Perhaps she had been underestimating Mr Davenport's domestic capacities. Her heart jumped slightly as she saw the dog bowl by the back door. Mrs Crane saw it too, and wrote vociferously in her note book. 'I see he's still got that Christmas present you gave him,' said Dan, nodding ostentatiously at the bowl.

Mrs Crane's brow furrowed. 'Did you actually give him a dog bowl, Mrs . . .?' She was obviously thinking that Sally might need some care and attention herself. 'Yes,' said Sally breezily, 'and he gave me a mirror for my parrot.'

'Really?' said Mrs Crane. 'What did he give you, Mr Chamberlain? A bunch of bananas?'

Dan laughed. 'No, better than that. He gave me an instrument for detecting the sex of monkeys. I must say it's come in very handy.'

Mrs Crane pursed her lips. 'Well, as I say, I shall have to make my report. Mr Davenport is eighty-four years old. There is an argument which says people of that age should not be allowed to live alone at all. It puts an enormous strain on the council's resources.'

'In what way?' asked Sally.

'A variety of ways. Home helps, Day Centre Care, transport . . .'

'None of which has been provided for Mr Davenport for some considerable time.'

Mrs Crane sighed. 'The services are very thinly stretched.'

'In which case, we mustn't take up any more of your time,' Dan interrupted firmly and escorted her to the front door.

'I can't understand it being so tidy,' Sally remarked when Mrs Crane had gone. 'It wasn't that neat even when his wife was alive.'

'Oh well,' said Dan. 'Least I could do.'

'You? How did you get in there?'

Dan shrugged. 'Builders' tricks.'

'You mean you actually broke in and cleaned the whole place up?'

'I went in to make sure he hadn't left the gas on or anything and it was a bit of a state so I just tidied up a bit.'

'But why?'

'Does it matter?' asked Dan tersely.

'No,' said Sally, rebuffed. 'Is eight o'clock still all right for tonight?'

'Fine,' said Dan.

Patrick arrived early, laden with expensive wine which he fussed around Sally with, demanding ice buckets, openers and even temperatures, none of which she seemed able to provide. 'What sort of a corkscrew is this?' he grumbled, picking crumbs fastidiously out of the bottle. 'Haven't you got a decanter?'

'No,' said Sally who was having trouble with her potatoes.

'Well, I must have something.'

'Look in that cupboard. Not that one,' as Patrick emerged with a jelly mould, 'the one by the fridge. There might be something in there.' He finally settled for a spaghetti jar for the burgundy, and a vase full of ice cubes for his Chablis.

'This is very kind of you, Patrick,' said Sally for the third time as she struggled to get past him to oven.

'It's my pleasure, dear girl,' Patrick replied, pouring olives into a cereal bowl.

'But if you don't get out of my way in a minute I'm going to stick this knife in you.' Patrick retreated, chuckling, into the living room.

'I'm sorry about that.' Sally, sweating from her efforts

and heartily wishing she had never suggested this dinner, emerged red-faced from the kitchen.

'That's all right.'

'Yes, still, sorry. Look, I must just change. Are you all right for five minutes? There are some crisps somewhere. Help yourself.'

'I'm fine. What time's Mr Right turning up?'

'Who?'

'Lover boy, your Intended, the future Mr Grosvenor?'

'Don't start that,' said Sally hotly. 'You are not to call him that. Promise?'

'A sensitive flower, is he? I shall be on my best behaviour, trust me.'

'I don't for one moment. Please, Patrick,' she looked at him beseechingly, 'It's not serious or anything, but – you know – he's not an actor. He might not understand that you're just joking. Please, for my sake . . .'

Patrick patted her hands paternally. 'Darling Sally, I was only teasing. I shall be the perfect model of decorum, have no fear.' There was a ring at the door. 'Oh God,' screeched Sally. 'I'm not even dressed. Could you answer it, Patrick? Give them a drink . . . talk to them . . . anything.' 'Them!' she heard him mutter as he glided to the door. She fled.

The first thing Sally noticed about Suzanne Chamberlain was her prettiness. She had a torrent of red curls caught back in a pony tail and the requisite ivory skin. Her eyes were a startling turquoise but her smile, though polite, seemed a little forced to Sally's hypersensitive gaze. She looked quite a bit younger than Dan – late twenties, she surmised. Patrick, having poured them both a drink, had settled himself opposite and was telling them about the turmoils of working to Majestic's budget.

'Sorry, everyone,' Sally murmured as she joined them. 'I was running a bit late.' Dan stood up and took a step towards her. Patrick and Suzanne watched them expectantly. 'Hullo, um, Sally . . . pet,' Dan muttered self-consciously, 'this is er Suzanne.' Sally sidestepped his arms which were flapping about like a broken marionette's.

'Hullo. I'm so pleased to meet you. Dan's told me so much about you. It is nice of you to come. You've both met Patrick, I take it?' They acknowledged that they had.

'How did you two come to meet?' asked Patrick.

'In the pub.'

'At the theatre,' said Sally and Dan in unison. Patrick's eyebrows rose very slightly. 'Have you known each other long?'

'Quite a while,' said Sally.

'Not long,' said Dan in the same breath. This time both Suzanne and Patrick looked puzzled.

'I thought you met when Danny moved in?' Suzanne remarked. Her voice was flat and rather nasal.

'Well, yes we did, sort of . . . a bit.' Sally looked at Dan for support.

'We did MEET,' he said doubtfully, 'but it wasn't like meeting, if you see what I mean.'

'Danny,' said his wife in the kind of voice usually reserved for fibbing toddlers, 'you know that makes no sense. Think about it for a minute.'

Sally saw Dan's hands clench in irritation but he composed himself and said laughingly. 'No, I don't suppose it does.'

'Let me get you another drink,' said Patrick, whipping the glass from Suzanne's hand and heading for the kitchen.

'Could I have something soft this time?' she called after him.

'What would you like?' asked Sally, in the full knowledge that her fridge contained only milk and past its sell-by date apple juice.

'Oh anything, water, fruit juice . . .'

'I'll get it.' She followed Patrick, grabbing the carton from him and pouring the muddy mixture into a glass. 'You go and . . .'

'Do your boyfriends usually bring their wives?' he murmured as he took it from her. Sally cursed him and went to prod the meat.

'What's your line of business, Dan?' she heard him asking as she closed the oven.

'Danny's a Jack of all trades,' came his wife's reply.

'A Jack of all trades?' Patrick intoned like Lady Bracknell. 'How interesting.' Sally contemplated reopening the oven and placing her head beside the frizzling lamb. An earring fell down her neck and failed to appear the other end. She noticed several more bottles, presumably Dan's contribution, drawn up in battle array opposite Patrick's. Oh well, she thought, if we get through that lot we probably won't remember this evening at all. She fervently hoped they would.

'Do you need any help?' Suzanne was watching her from the doorway.

'Oh . . . No, thanks. It's all in hand,' Sally smiled unconvincingly as Suzanne's eyes took in the chaos. 'The kitchen's a bit cramped.'

Suzanne nodded. 'Small kitchens are so awful, aren't they? We had a tiny one to start with but I made Danny build me fitted units so everything had a place, and after that it was quite cosy.' Sally smiled despairingly and hid the apple juice behind the bread bin.

They rejoined the men. Dan cast an anxious glance at Sally. 'Everything all right . . . dear?' he asked.

Sally fixed him with her eyes. 'Yes thank you, treasure.'

Dan dived into the crisps.

'What are your other neighbours like?' asked Patrick.

'We've only got one,' said Sally, 'and he's in hospital.'

'Oh dear.' Suzanne looked mildly alarmed. 'What's the matter with him?'

'He had a fall,' said Sally. 'He's pretty old. I think he gets a bit disorientated from time to time.'

'Does he live on his own?' asked Patrick.

'Yes, that's the problem. In fact when I got home from rehearsal there was a woman from the Social Services snooping around.'

'Oh, I don't think they snoop,' interjected Suzanne. 'They have a very difficult job.'

'I'm sure they have,' Sally conceded, 'but there are ways and ways of going about things, and I don't think this particular one was going about them very well.'

Patrick refilled her glass. 'Why? What happened?'

'She wanted me to give her the key to Mr Davenport's flat so that she could go in and assess whether he should be let back home when he came out of hospital.'

'What was wrong with that?' asked Suzanne with genuine curiosity.

'She'd never even met the man. She was planning to decide his entire future on the basis of someone else's report. She seemed quite put out when I told her I thought it was out of order.'

Suzanne nodded thoughtfully. 'I see what you mean. Still, if he lives on his own . . . I mean you can't help wondering if some of them wouldn't be better off in a home, being looked after properly.'

'No doubt they would,' said Sally, feeling her blood pressure rise, 'but there is the question of personal choice. How would you feel if you came out of hospital to be told you were going to be placed in some sort of institution, without even being consulted?'

'I'm sure they were only thinking of your neighbour's best interests.'

'They were thinking of reducing the drain on their budget which they erroneously assumed Mr Davenport was benefiting from.'

'Bloody cheek,' said Patrick. 'They're all alike, these bureaucrats. Bloody Child Support Agency. They should line them up and shoot them. The whole lot of them.'

'I don't think that's very fair,' said Suzanne.

'I don't think that woman could find much to complain about,' Dan intercepted abruptly. 'There was nothing to make her think the old boy couldn't manage on his own. Apart from the fact that he'd fallen over. Anyone could have done that.'

'Still,' Suzanne persisted. 'If he's elderly. Some of them really don't know how to take care of themselves. It's only natural.' She smiled around.

We could be talking about retarded rabbits, Sally thought. Suzanne leant forward conspiratorially, 'If you don't mind me saying, Sally, I think I can smell burning.'

She leapt up and went to rescue her yorkshire puddings which had stuck to the roof of the oven. When she came back Suzanne was haranguing Dan about his apparent weight loss. 'That's what happens when men have to feed themselves, isn't it?' she appealed to Sally. 'They don't know the first thing about nutrients.'

'I'm sure you're right,' said Sally who thought they were something you put on plants.

'Actually,' Dan roused himself from the slough of despond into which he was rapidly descending, 'Sally's a very good cook. I've never eaten better since I met her.' Suzanne continued to smile, but a tiny flash of steel flickered through her exquisite eyes. 'That's nice,' she said. 'Hear hear,' Patrick joined in. 'She does a lovely breakfast in bed, doesn't she, Dan?'

*   *   *

At a quarter past nine, just as Sally was dishing up, the doorbell rang. Everyone looked at her expectantly. The table was only set for four.

'It'll be the social services come to check on your nutrients,' suggested Patrick.

She opened the door. 'Meals on Wheels. Make way for Meals on Wheels.' Colin, white and wheezing from his exertions, came staggering through the door with Sally's microwave in his arms. 'Where shall I put it?' he screeched, dumping it unceremoniously in the space she had cleared for her roast. 'Sakes alive, woman. Don't just stand there. Give me a drink.'

'Colin . . .' Sally gestured helplessly to her guests.

Colin fanned himself foppishly with a tea towel. 'Evening all. Sorry I'm late. I have had the most horrendous day.' Sally noticed with an icy chill that he was wearing his best shirt. 'I'll have a gin, darling. What am I thinking of?' A pale hand slapped an even paler forehead. 'One second. I will be one second only.' He retreated down the stairs returning with a carrier bag full of wine and a large cardboard box. '*Voilà.*' He set the box reverently in the middle of the coffee table and untied the coiled bow.

'What is it?' asked Sally, peering over his shoulder like a witness at an exhumation.

'It's a mousse,' said Colin, beaming round at everyone. '*Chocolat au rhum et noix de cacao* – fruit and nut to its friends.'

'Rum isn't a fruit,' muttered Sally savagely. She had a good mind to shove his face right in it. How dare he invite himself to her dinner party like this? The microwave was just a ruse to get himself in. She could see it all now. What an idiot she had been to tell him about it in the first place. Any reasonable person would have taken the hint and stayed away. But when had Colin ever been reasonable? Once again she brooded on the attraction of normal people.

'Don't worry about me.' Colin had got himself a drink and was now squeezing a spare set of cutlery between the places she had set for Suzanne and Patrick. 'I can go on the end.'

'You are the end, Colin,' she snarled sotto voce as she went to find him a plate.

'My day,' she heard him expanding, as she scraped the yorkshire puddings out of their tin, 'has been horrendous. At a quarter to eight this morning, will you believe, I was woken by the dustmen. Now the dustmen usually come on Monday round our way, but no, this week they've decided to come on Tuesday. Something to do with a Bank Holiday. Anyway I'm lying in bed and I look out of my window and there they all are. I'm on the ground floor you see. It's not so private but you get the garden. I like a bit of garden, don't you, in London? It's my contribution to the Green Party, my little patch. Not very green but lots of parties. Anyway, I look out of the window and there they all are, so I leap out of bed, and my dears, I have nothing on. Not a stitch. Well, you don't think, do you, when you've had a shock . . .?'

Sally slapped the vegetables into their dishes, turned off the gravy which was boiling, put her lamb on top of the microwave and carried in her melon boats.

'Ooh, melon. My favourite,' said Colin. 'Now I want every-body's cherries who doesn't want them.' Everyone averred politely that they loved maraschino cherries, although Sally noticed Dan chewing his like someone experiencing his first sheep's eye.

'These are different,' said Colin as she set her flattened yorkshire puddings before them.

'They weren't meant to be like that,' said Sally defensively. 'They've sort of sunk.'

'Too much bromide,' said Colin. 'What are these?'

'Peas.'

'No, not those. These sort of squidgy things with black on top.'

'*Pommes duchesse*,' said Sally, placing a chair in front of the microwave and climbing on to it.

'Are you all right up there?' asked Suzanne anxiously. 'Only more accidents happen in the home environment . . .'

'So do more murders,' said Sally under her breath. 'Yes, thank you. I'm fine.'

'What on earth are you doing?' Colin chirruped gaily.

'I'm carving the lamb,' said Sally.

'Yes, but why up there?' There was a clatter as her lost earring fell down between her legs.

'Because,' said Sally, struggling to retain her good humour, 'you put my microwave in the space I had made for the meat.'

'Oh that's right, blame me,' retorted Colin who had drunk rather too much rather too fast.

'I will,' said Sally.

'Do you want a hand, um, darling?' Dan was standing beside her. 'I can reach it more easily than you.'

'Well, if you don't mind,' said Sally with some relief. 'I'm not all that good at carving – if you remember.' Dan nodded, his eyes taking in the wodge of meat she had managed to segregate from the bone.

'This is delicious,' said Patrick, helping himself to another spoonful of the bullet-like peas. Once more Sally was forced to admire his histrionic talents. Colin, who had run through his entire repertoire of soggy vegetable jokes was now confiding in Suzanne how the love of his life had left him for a barrow boy in Gravesend only the week before.

'You must be terribly worried,' Suzanne told him.

'Oh, I am. I am. Quite desperate, in fact. It's come to the point where I may not take him back. Oh, I know I've said that before,' he shot at Sally, who was more concerned with digesting her dinner than Colin's resolutions regarding Matthew, 'but this time he's gone too far.'

'Still,' said Suzanne blithely, 'these relationships never last, do they? It's not like a real marriage.' Dan was seized with a coughing fit, while Patrick, who had spent a good deal of his working life dealing with super-egos, his own included, patted Colin's hand and hinted that it was probably Suzanne's way of dealing with a subject too painful to be discussed at the dinner table. Colin, though resentful, allowed himself to be mollified, and was soon quizzing Patrick on the possibility of a part for himself in *The Firm*.

'What did you do before you were an actor?' Suzanne asked Patrick. Patrick thought for several moments. 'I think I played with sand,' he said finally, 'and sometimes we went to the park.'

Suzanne looked at him uncomprehendingly then suddenly laughed. 'Oh I see. You mean you've always been one. I expect you're very excited, actually getting to be on TV after all this time?' There was a loud pop as Dan opened another bottle of wine.

'I have made the odd appearance in the past,' Patrick remarked.

'Have you? I don't remember your face. What have you been in? Mind you, we hardly ever watched, did we, Danny? So you mustn't mind if I haven't heard of it.'

'How about *News At Ten*?' suggested Patrick grimly. Suzanne opened her eyes wide. 'Do they use actors to do that? I always thought they were real.'

'They are,' said Dan quietly. 'He's teasing you.'

'Oh,' said Suzanne, 'is he? Oh well, I can take it,' she added, more in sorrow than in anger.

Sally closed her eyes. She would never ever give another dinner party. If she had gone out into the proverbial hedgerows and gathered together the first five people to roll out of the ditch she could hardly have picked a less compatible bunch. Suzanne was a perfect pain, Patrick was going to have the mother of all hangovers in the morning, Dan looked as though he'd rather be down a salt mine, and she herself had cooked a meal that would not have disgraced a prison kitchen. Add to that Colin . . . though hopefully his chocolate mousse might yet erase the flavour of her gravy. The lemon meringue pie was still set like concrete. She only hoped no one opted for it out of politeness. She had a sudden vision of Patrick's perfect teeth clamped symmetrically round a wedge upon his plate, gums gnashing in unspoken fury. She became aware that Dan was watching her. She tried to smile.

Shortly after eleven Patrick rose and looked at his watch. 'My darling girl,' he said, 'this evening has been wonderful, but I have to be in the crematorium by eight.'

Colin choked over his coffee. 'I've heard of some excuses,' he croaked, dabbing at his streaming eyes.

Suzanne, too, was eyeing Patrick with some concern. 'I must be going,' she said to Dan. 'Can I call a cab from your place, Danny?'

'Of course,' said Dan awkwardly, half rising.

'You can use my phone,' said Sally, delighted to speed her departure.

'Where do you have to get to?' asked Patrick.

'Forest Gate,' said Dan before she could reply. Suzanne smiled, exhibiting the smallest trace of embarrassment.

'On my way,' said Patrick, winking at Sally. She looked away.

'I don't suppose anyone's got time to call a cab for me?' said Colin, pouting furiously.

'I'll give you a lift,' said Dan.

'But he only lives round the corner,' objected Sally, who thought Colin had imposed on her guests quite enough for one night.

'I can't walk at this time of night, can I?' said Colin petulantly.

'It's no problem,' Dan assured her.

'Thank you ever so much. It has been an interesting evening.' Suzanne offered her hand. Sally shook it.

'Yes. Thank you. Good night,' she replied.

After they had gone she sat amidst the debris and scraped a spoon round the chocolate mousse bowl. She was not cut out to entertain. She couldn't cook, she couldn't carve, she couldn't even make small talk without losing her temper.

She supposed she had better clear up. At least there wasn't the problem of Mr Davenport to deal with tonight. She felt a stab of worry. What would that officious Crane woman do? What powers did she have? Probably far more than she was capable of exercising sensibly. Perhaps she should offer to adopt Mr Davenport – guarantee his welfare. Be a proper daughter to him. She shuddered. It was hard enough looking out for yourself.

There was a cough. Dan was standing in the doorway. 'Can I come in?'

'Yes, if you want. Was Colin all right?'

'Just about. He invited me in but I said I had to come and help you clear up.'

Sally smiled. 'He can't have believed that. I never clear up till the morning.'

Dan tutted. 'It's worse in the morning.'

'Says who?'

'Says Suzanne.'

'She would.'

Dan's face clouded slightly. 'Didn't you like her?'

Sally swallowed. 'She's very pretty,' she said, tactfully.

Dan grinned. 'She is, isn't she? Fabulous. And so bright. She should have gone to university.'

'What stopped her?'

Dan looked guilty. 'Me, I suppose. She was only seventeen

when we got married. I was crazy about her. So was she about me, but I should have seen, you know, that she'd sort of change over the years. Mature, whatever. Want something else.'

'No children, then?'

'Suzanne's not all that keen on children.'

'Oh no, I remember you saying. Pets?'

Dan shook his head. 'She can't stand animals.'

Sally yawned. 'Or old people, it seems. That doesn't leave much.'

Dan frowned. 'Suzanne's very shy. Sometimes she sounds a bit . . . hard. But she isn't really. She's very thoughtful. I mean, look how she was worrying about me.'

'I should think she's a lot more worried after this evening,' said Sally drily. Dan smiled and leaning forward, kissed her softly on the cheek. 'I think you're a brilliant actress,' he said. 'I'm sure she thought it was for real.'

14

Arriving at Majestic Studios Sally could not help wondering what disasters might have befallen the location crew this week. She was therefore somewhat disappointed to hear from Mary Jennings that things had gone remarkably smoothly.

'Is that what she told you?' George Bennett guffawed when she mentioned this to him as they were waiting to go into Make-up. 'I suppose it's all relative.'

'Why? What happened?'

'Nothing much. Stephanie and René had a bit of a barney and she threatened to walk off the set.'

'What about this time?'

George shrugged. 'Ask me. I think old René's finding out it's not such a good idea to cast your girlfriends in your own programmes. Not all of them together anyway.'

'You're not suggesting there's something between Stephanie and René?'

George glanced at her curiously. 'You're saying you haven't noticed?'

Sally felt silly. 'Well, I . . . Of course, I'd noticed . . . What do you mean "all of them"?'

George shook his head. 'It's probably nothing. I tell you something, It's bleeding freezing down that industrial estate. You're lucky they haven't got you roped into it. Be grateful for small mercies, I say.' He was led away to have his hair washed.

As if to test Sally's gratitude Rolo came looking for her to tell her that René had requested she should be booked for a day's filming next episode. 'Nothing specific. We may not need you. But just in case.' This sent Wendy Costume into high dudgeon since it necessitated the provision of a coat. 'I expect we can find something in Old Stock,' soothed the ever helpful Jean.

'Perhaps I could have one of Stephanie's cast-offs,' suggested Sally, but the irony was lost on them both.

René had taken the precaution of scheduling Dilys' scenes in the morning. This did not prevent her from drying three times, nor from knocking over a milk jug on her way to answer the front door. The firemen were in position early, breathing apparatus at the ready.

Sally noticed that Penny was looking more frantic than usual as she tore around the set. Simon, too, was looking strangely subdued as he sat in the snack bar fiddling with his toupé, which had been restyled to take advantage of his mended nose. She went and sat beside him, bored with the confines of her dressing room. What had seemed so compact and personal a fortnight ago had now become cramped and claustrophobic. 'How did the filming go?' she asked. Simon grimaced. 'Fine. You heard about Stephanie and the boss?'

'Well, George said something. He didn't go into any details.'

Simon laughed. 'Just as well. Not the sort of thing for a delicate creature like yourself.'

'I'm not delicate,' she objected.

'Oh yes you are. Compared to Stephanie you are, anyway. I tell you she had the camera crew blushing, and that's not an easy thing to do.'

'I miss all the fun,' Sally complained.

'That's location for you.'

'I'm coming next time,' she told him. 'René wants me to be booked for a day's filming "just in case".'

'Just in case what?'

Sally shrugged. 'Just "just in case".'

The fire doors swished open and Penny peeped through. Simon was on his feet. 'Do me a favour, old girl. If Penny comes asking for me say I've had to rush off somewhere.' He strode away. Sure enough Penny came tripping towards her. She hesitated as she came level. 'Hullo,' said Sally, not knowing what else to do.

'Hullo,' Penny echoed, her eyes fixed distractedly on Simon's retreating figure. 'You don't know . . . I don't suppose you know where Simon's gone?'

'He had to rush off somewhere,' mumbled Sally, guilt sweeping over her as Penny's eager young face contorted with disappointment. She sank down wretchedly in the seat he had just vacated. 'Are you all right?' asked Sally, feeling she had fulfilled her duty to Simon. Penny endeavoured to smile but tears were hovering in her lashless blue eyes. She wiped her arm across them. 'It's just that he – Simon, that is – it's as though he's avoiding me.'

'Why should he want to do that?'

Penny gave a shuddering sigh. 'I don't know. It must be my fault. It must be something I've done. He was so nice to me when we were on location. You know – REALLY nice – and it was all so . . . and today, since we've come back, he just . . . I don't know, every time I come near him he sort of moves away.'

'Oh, I'm sure not,' said Sally, thinking nothing could be more obvious.

'If I could only get to speak to him,' Penny continued sorrowfully, 'I could ask him what I've done. I feel so awful.'

'Look,' said Sally. 'He's probably feeling a bit tense. Actors are always like that before a show. He probably just needs a bit of time to himself.'

'He was talking to Patrick for ages just now,' said Penny accusingly. Sally reflected this might well have something to do with things.

'Yes, but it was probably about the script, their scenes together.' Penny sniffed, plainly unconvinced.

'Would you like me to have a word with him?' asked Sally, cursing herself as she spoke.

'Oh, would you?' Penny's radiance returned. 'Oh, yes please, Sally. That would be so wonderful. THANK you.' There was a buzz on her cans as Rolo enquired in icy tones whether she was still in the building. Penny leapt up and with renewed expressions of undying gratitude rushed back into the studio.

'Has she gone?' Simon came tiptoeing back from Wardrobe where he had been skulking.

'Simon, what is this?' demanded Sally.

Simon looked sheepish.

'Nothing. It's just I think she's got a bit of a crush on me and it's a bit awkward.'

'You're a married man.'

'Exactly.'

'Doesn't she know that?'

'Of course she does. It's just that . . . well, we had a few drinks after the filming the other night and I might have said something that made her think . . . well, you know. The way one does.' He flashed her a boyish smile.

Sally shook her head. 'Well, you'll have to sort it out. The poor girl's distraught.'

Simon looked anxious. 'I can't. How can I?'

'What do you mean, "how can you?" You'll have to.'

Simon sat down and looked at her appealingly. 'Oh, Sal, you know how it is. You're away from home. You have a few drinks . . . These things happen. You must know that.'

'Come on, Simon. You were only away for two nights. It's not exactly a world tour.'

'Anyone would think I'd deflowered a minor,' said Simon plaintively.

'She is very young.'

'She showed me a thing or two.'

'Well then, be bloody grateful,' Sally shot at him before she could stop herself.

Simon looked shocked. 'You feeling OK, our Sal?'

Sally nodded. 'Bit of a . . . You know . . .'

Simon nodded judiciously. 'Jenny has hell's own job.'

Sally smiled weakly. 'Anyway, you'll have to do something about Penny.'

'What?'

'How should I know what?'

'Oh come on, Sal, please help me. I know I've been a bit daft. I never meant to upset her. She's a sweet enough kid, it's just . . .' Sally reflected that on the basis of this morning's conversations either Penny or Simon could take over as scriptwriter any time they wanted.

'You'll have to do something,' she repeated.

'Yes, but what?'

She sighed. 'I suppose you could send her a bunch of flowers and say something like you will always treasure your moments together but you're far too old for her and it would be wrong for her to waste her youth on someone who can never be free to love her in the way that she deserves.'

Simon looked impressed. 'That's incredible. You're a genius, Sal. Now who can I get to nip out and buy me some flowers?'

'Penny?' suggested Sally.

'I don't think I'd better do that,' said Simon in all seriousness. 'It might upset her. On the other hand I could give her a tenner and let her choose her own.'

'And write her own card?'

Simon nodded thoughtfully. 'Point taken.'

'You can phone Interflora,' said Sally. 'There's a directory by the phone in make-up. I saw it.'

Simon beamed. 'Brilliant. You're a good girl, Sally. I owe you a drink. Speaking of which, how's our Dilys this morning?'

Sally shrugged. 'René did her scenes first. I think they were OK.'

'Funny about her and old René, isn't it?' said Simon.

Sally sat up. 'What is?'

Simon peered at her. 'You know. About them being married.'

'What?' Sally's eyes shot out of her head. 'I thought she was married to what's-his-name, the Chief Exec.?' Simon waved this aside. 'Yes, yes, she is now. But before. Didn't you know that?'

'No, of course I didn't,' said Sally, feeling that she had been living in a cave for the past two months. 'How long have you known?'

'Well, only since Wednesday really. We had a few drinks . . .'

'After the filming,' recited Sally.

'Well, you know how it is.'

'No,' said Sally, 'but I'm jolly well going to find out.'

'Marley and Patrick were reminiscing about some show they were in together, yonks ago that René directed, and Marley happened to let drop that Dilys was in the chorus, and then Patrick said "is that where he met her?" and Marley said, "Oh no, they were already married by then," so it sort of came out. Don't breathe a word to a soul, will you?'

'Of course not,' said Sally, wondering who was left that she could breathe it to.

'That's really what upset Stephanie,' Simon confided. 'Can't say I see it. I mean they've been divorced for God knows how long. I mean would you be upset if your bloke had his ex-wife in the same show?'

'It would depend on the wife,' Sally said sharply. 'Anyway I thought Stephanie was married?'

Simon sighed. 'Yes she is, but that doesn't mean . . . does it? Anyway, her old man's not even an actor.'

'So that makes it all right, does it?'

Simon stretched. 'Well, it's not the same, is it? If you ask me actors shouldn't get married at all, except to their own kind.'

'I should think that classifies you as a racist.'

Simon laughed. 'Actors *are* a race apart. "One of your own kind, stick to your oooown kind,"' he crooned, leaping from his chair and unsuccessfully attempting to pirouette round the tea trolley.

Plasters were fetched while Sally helped the furious tealady clear up the debris. Jean Make-up, who had been summoned to tend to Simon's wounds, was plainly more concerned with the damage he had done to his shirt cuffs, now thickly coated in swiss roll, than any lasting damage to his index finger. 'Keep still,' she snarled as he tried to retrieve his hand. 'If you'd kept still in the first place none of this would have happened.'

'I think there's a splinter still in,' whimpered Simon.

'No there isn't and too bad if there is,' retorted Jean, snapping shut her first aid box.

'Ooh, I love it when you're masterful,' cooed Patrick, slapping her on the rump as he passed.

Jean swung round ferociously then, seeing who it was, went an unbecoming pink and tittered. 'Oh you. You'll be next if you're not careful.'

Patrick shuddered in delicious anticipation. 'I hope that's a promise.' He plunged into the studio before Jean could take him up on it.

'That woman's got the touch of a woodchopper,' Simon

complained when she had gone. 'I suppose I'd better go and see to these flowers.' He clapped his hand over his mouth. 'Christ, I must be going round the bend. What date is it?'

'The fourteenth,' said Sally.

Simon groaned. 'It's not, is it?'

'I think so. What's the matter with the fourteenth?'

'Nothing. It's Jenny's birthday. I forgot to get her anything. What with the filming. I won't be home till midnight. What on earth am I going to do?'

'Why don't you send her some flowers?' said Sally through gritted teeth.

Simon's face brightened visibly. 'I'll tell you something, Sally. You are one whizzo kid. I can do them both at the same time.' He hurried back up the corridor in the direction of the makeup room.

'Are you all right, dear, all by yourself?' Marley came bustling along, her hair in rollers and a dressing gown over her costume.

'Yes I'm fine. I wish I'd brought a book,' said Sally.

Marley sat down. 'It can get a bit boring, can't it, if you have to hang about? Not that I'm complaining because I think René's doing a marvellous job. Did you see the tea lady, dear, by any chance?'

'I think she's gone back to the kitchen,' said Sally. 'There was a bit of an accident with the trolley.' Marley's eyes opened wide. 'Nothing serious,' Sally added hastily, 'but she had to get some replacements.'

Marley relaxed. 'Only I was hoping for a bit of that swiss roll they had last time. I know I shouldn't but I spoke to my doctor and he said there was hardly any fat in it at all, so I don't think it would matter too much, would it?'

Sally smiled. 'I'm sure it wouldn't.'

'Where's Simon gone?' Marley enquired. 'I saw the two of you chatting just now and I didn't want to, you know, butt in or anything.'

Sally laughed. 'I wish you had. He really can be very irritating sometimes.'

Marley looked anxious. 'Oh, but I'm sure that's just his way. I know he thinks the world of you.'

Sally shook her head hopelessly. 'Marley, Simon thinks the world of Simon.'

Marley chuckled and patted her hand. 'I think you're probably right, dear. But at least he's faithful.' She shivered suddenly. 'Aren't you cold out here? I find it very chilly.' She huddled her dressing gown to her.

'No,' said Sally, who thought the whole place horribly stuffy.

Marley got up. 'Well, if you'll excuse me, I think I'll pop back to my dressing room. I've got a radiator there.' She padded off.

Penny returned. 'Was it all right?' she asked. 'Did he say anything?'

'Yes, it's perfectly all right,' said Sally. Penny glowed. Sally took a breath. 'Really, Penny, I think you've got to remember that Simon is a married man.' Penny's face drained of colour. 'For your own sake don't you think it might be better, you know, to try and forget him?' To her utter horror Penny sank down in the chair opposite and clasping her hands in front of her, gazed pitifully up at her. 'But I love him,' she whispered. Sally's heart sank. 'Yes, you do now, Penny, but you won't always, will you?'

'Yes. Yes, I will. You don't understand. I know . . . I know I haven't known him long,' she looked around surreptitiously as though fearing the shades of Rolo and Patrick, 'but he's so wonderful. Do you know he told me if this series isn't a success, he's going to . . . he's going to . . .' she bit her lip agonisingly.

'Kill himself. Yes, I do know.'

Penny gawped. 'He told you, as well?'

'I was at the dress rehearsal,' said Sally brusquely. 'Well, it's up to you, Penny. It's your life. But if I were you I think I might focus my affections on someone with a better prognosis.'

Once more Penny's cans rattled to the timbre of Rolo's threats. She slipped out of her chair and raced to the studio without another word. Now I've done it, thought Sally. She'll probably wire herself up to the lights. Why do people have to confide in me all the time? It's not as though I was even interested. I just want to get on with my own life. I don't go round pouring my heart out to the first person who sits next to me on a train.

Hazel appeared. 'Good morning, Sally. I wonder if you could be a perfect angel and let me just measure this sleeve against you? It's for my niece. She's off on a guide camp and I promised she should have it before she goes.'

'Hazel,' said Sally as she stood with her arms out-stretched.

'Mmm?'

'Do people keep asking you things?'

'What sort of things?'

'Well, things about their lives and things? I mean, you're a counsellor, aren't you? Do you find that the other people in the cast keep telling you their troubles?'

Hazel took the tape measure out of her mouth. 'Goodness, no. I wouldn't let them. There's a time and place for everything and work isn't one of them. No, if people need counselling they must come to a counselling session. You have to keep things in their proper slots or you get in a frightful muddle. That's fine, dear. You can put your arms down now.'

'What were you doing posing as Jesus Christ?' asked Patrick at lunch time.

'Oh Hazel was just measuring a jersey against me.'

'It suited you.'

'What? The jersey?'

'No, the image. You have a kind of saintly quality sometimes.'

'Thanks very much.'

'It makes me long to stick arrows all over you.'

Sally nodded. 'Bless you, Patrick.'

'By the way I haven't thanked you for that lovely dinner party the other night.'

'Yes you have.'

'Not properly.'

'Properly enough.'

'I like your Dan.'

Sally looked away. 'Oh yes. Good.'

'Colin's a laugh.'

'He's a pain in the neck.'

'Yes, but funny with it. Suzanne's a nice lady, isn't she?'

Sally glanced at him. 'I don't really know her.'

Patrick shook his head quickly. 'No. Nor do I, of course. But she seemed very interesting. Intelligent, too. We had quite a chat when I was driving her home.'

'I imagine you had time to,' said Sally sharply.

Patrick raised his eyebrows. 'Oh, come on, Sal. It was the least I could do at that time of night.'

Sally shrugged. 'You don't have to make excuses to me. It's none of my concern what you do between dinner and the cemetery.'

Patrick leant forward. 'Are you all right?'

'Of course I am. Why?'

'Nothing. You're looking a bit tired, that's all.'

'Thank you.'

'Got to look after your health, you know, in a serial.'

Recording the next day began well enough, Dilys delivering her lines with a very good semblance of sobriety and mainly in the right order. René, in pure relief, came down during a

• Sarah Grazebrook

costume break to congratulate her and made the mistake of giving her a quick peck on the lips which was observed by Stephanie on a distant monitor. The next thing anyone knew was Stephanie had followed him into the Quick Change room and socked him in the side of the head. René bore this well, calling her a nicotine tart and threatening to have her cut out of the series if she so much as asked him the time of day till the recording was completed. Stephanie, satisfied that she had made her point, merely smiled and lit up a cheroot, which had the firemen careering across the studio like recruits for the Field Gunners' Run.

Nothing much more of note occurred that day and at ten thirty the lights duly dimmed on a completed episode two.

They congregated in the bar. There was no sign of Jeff Wilkins this week. Obviously having seen the first part safely into the can he felt no onus to make it a regular practice. Wellard Kenning was lurking in a corner waiting for someone to buy him a drink. Sally steered well clear of him, but was surprised to see first Patrick then Stephanie greeting him like a long lost brother and insisting on the privilege. Even Drewe, who had the greatest possible trouble remembering the lines he had got, seemed keen to make his mark on *The Firm*'s creator. He hovered around him giggling and waving his expressionless hands like a demented flapper.

Marley had a headache and wanted to get away early so Sally made a pretence of getting a cab for her her own excuse to escape. 'Oh dear,' apologised the old lady. 'I didn't mean to drag you away, dear. I can manage perfectly well. They'll phone for me at Reception.'

'I didn't want to stay,' said Sally.

'But the night is young. Surely you don't want to go home yet? Isn't Patrick giving you a lift?' Anxiety shone from her face.

'Patrick? No. Why should he?'

• 164

'Oh dear,' said Marley again. 'There's nothing wrong is there? Between the two of you? You mustn't mind him, dear. I know he can be a little . . . insensitive sometimes. But he doesn't mean it. I've known him such a long time. He really is a very kind boy.'

Sally sighed. 'Marley, believe me, there is nothing wrong between me and Patrick.' Marley beamed. 'But nor is there ANYTHING between me and Patrick, if you see what I mean. We are just good friends. Is that understood?'

Marley continued to beam. 'Of course it is, dear. Don't you worry about a thing. Your secret is perfectly safe with me.'

They said good night. On the way home Sally thought about Marley. She also thought about Patrick and Stephanie fawning over Wellard Kenning, and René being married to Dilys, and Stephanie being jealous, and Simon and Penny. They swirled around her mind like goldfish in a bowl. Their world seemed hardly any bigger. Not like hers. She could cross the threshold between fantasy and fact. She had interests far beyond *The Firm* and who was sleeping with whom, or had slept with whom, or who might be persuaded to sleep with whom. She had a proper life with all its adult anxieties of how to pay her mortgage and whether to learn to drive and what to do about Mr Davenport. And Dan Chamberlain, for that matter, who was clearly still in love with his wife.

And she wasn't sleeping with anyone. She was on the outside looking in.

15

Mr Davenport was back. Sally stared resignedly at the puddle on the floor. She was glad because it meant that supercilious female had not got her way, but worried that the old man's seeming revival in hospital had been so short-lived. Wearily she fetched her mop.

She had just finished cleaning up when the front door opened and Dan came in. He looked decidedly the worse for wear. 'Hullo,' he said, closing the door and leaning against it for support. 'He's back then?'

'Yes.'

'I could have done that,' he indicated the mop.

'That's all right. You can do it tomorrow.' She turned to go.

'Yes,' said Dan with deliberation. 'Then you can do it the next day, and I can do it the next, and you can do it the next.'

'That's right,' said Sally over her shoulder.

'For ever,' Dan shouted after her.

Sally swung round. 'Could you keep your voice down, please. Unless you want Mr Davenport to hear.'

Dan looked confused. 'He's back then?' he asked.

'Oh for God's sake,' said Sally. 'Just go and sleep it off.'

Dan advanced several paces across the hall and clutched

at the bannisters while he fumbled for his keys. 'Suzanne was right, wasn't she?' he mumbled as he tried to focus on the one he wanted.

'Right about what?' asked Sally.

Dan shrugged expansively. 'The old boy. Being in a home and that.'

Sally stalked back down the stairs. 'No she was not,' she said fiercely, ripping the keys out of his hand and opening his front door for him. 'What does she know about being old?'

Dan thought. 'Her gran's old,' he said. 'No, she's not. She's dead. I forgot.'

'Exactly,' said Sally, wondering why she was arguing with a drunk.

Dan waved a finger at her. 'She's doing a course, that's how she knows.'

'Oh,' said Sally, 'that explains it. If she's done a course she knows all there is to know.'

Dan frowned. 'I'm doing a course,' he said uncertainly.

'So you are,' said Sally blithely. 'Lucky me, surrounded by geniuses.'

'Yes.' Dan sat down heavily on the side of a chair. 'Have you done a course?'

'Not lately.'

Dan sighed. 'Do you fancy a screw?' Sally stared at him.

'No thanks,' she said icily.

'Go on.'

'You're drunk.'

'I know. Go on, come to bed with me. I'm ever so good.'

'Really?' said Sally stiffly. 'Have you done a course on that as well?' She swivelled on her heels and retreated up the stairs.

'Didn't need one,' came Dan's befuddled voice. 'I know about women now, see. All lots of it. You're all old, anyway.'

Sally shut the door. Odious man. How she wished he'd never moved in. Life had been so much more peaceful before – Mrs Davies with her charity work and Mr Davenport with his vegetable garden. Who needed a common lump of a cowboy builder stuck in the flat beneath them? And worse than that his pea-brained wife?

She caught sight of herself in the hall mirror. Her face was tight with resentment. Oh my God, she thought. Look at me, I look like a witch. She leant forward and studied the thin claw-like lines beginning to appear round her eyes. He's right, she thought. I am getting old. Old and wrinkled and bitter. She stood back. This would not do. She was thirty-three. Approaching her prime, not her dotage. Enough was enough. She'd show that carrot-haired know-all she knew what was best for Mr Davenport, and Dan Chamberlain she wasn't old, and Patrick she wasn't desperate, and Simon she wasn't delicate and, for that matter, those bloody women in Wardrobe she was entitled to her own coat.

Sally's decision to revamp her image was not much helped by the onset of a stinking cold. She took Lemsip in the morning, paracetamol with her lunch and whisky and lemon when she got home. The resultant hangover stayed with her rather longer than the cold itself.

By the weekend she was feeling better and the rest of the cast, by dint of sheer willpower or a fear of having their lines cut, had managed to remain free of infection. René had a stinker, but he could hardly blame that on Sally since he had refused to come near her, and it was already a well-known fact that Stephanie had thrown a gin over him at the Feathers the previous Thursday.

Jeff Wilkins stayed longer at the Producer's Run that week. His normally jocular face showed signs of anxiety as he watched the unfolding episode. Sally couldn't see that it was any worse than any of the others, if you set aside the fact that Dilys was paralytic and Veeney was refusing downright to continue if Stephanie was allowed to wear a fur coat.

'Not a word to anyone,' Simon confided to Sally out of the side of his mouth, 'but Wilkie's just found out it's too short.'

'What is?' asked Sally.

'The whole thing. You know the eps are forty mins each? Well, apparently the slot's for fifty including the ads.'

'What will they do?' asked Sally, a procession of coffee trays passing before her eyes.

'Well, Well's on to it now. More extra pages and they can pad a bit with the filming. Fortunately they got some super stuff at the cemetery.'

'But how do you know this?' Sally interrupted.

Simon shrugged. 'Penny mentioned something about it last night. Apparently René threw a wobbler in the office and the poor kid was there. Got the brunt of it. She was ever so upset.'

'Did the flowers work?' asked Sally pointedly. Simon looked rather startled. 'The flowers? Oh yes. Ace. Yes, everything's fine now. I just happened to bump into her last night. I had to go over to Costume for a fitting and she was there, all upset, so I just took her for a drink. You know . . . the way one does.'

'Did your wife like her flowers?' persisted Sally ruthlessly. Simon looked even more uncomfortable. 'Yes. Actually there was a bit of a mix-up with the cards.' Sally gasped. 'You didn't send her the one about being too old for her and not wanting to blight her young life?'

Simon shook his head dismissively. 'Of course I didn't. Actually I didn't put that in the end.'

'What did you put?'

'I can't remember exactly. Something about Time and Tide waiting for no man.'

'Very original.'

'It's not easy, you know. Thinking of these things.'

'Obviously,' said Sally, increasingly indignant. 'What did you say to your wife?'

Simon shrugged. 'That I'd love her for always, I think. Something like that.'

'And sent it to Penny?'

'Unfortunately yes.'

Sally gazed at him in disbelief. 'Simon, I'm beginning to wonder if you're real. What did your wife think of the Time and Tide?' Simon shuffled his feet. 'Well we had a bit of a row about it, to be honest.'

'I should think you did. Is it all sorted out now?'

'More or less,' said Simon grudgingly. 'She's asked me for a divorce.'

Sally looked at him, aghast. 'Simon! That's terrible. Can't you do something? Explain. Perhaps you could say it was a joke . . .' Simon shuffled restlessly in his seat. 'Oh, don't worry about it. She's always doing it. Every time anything like this happens.'

'Every time?'

Simon looked at Sally irritably. 'I'm an actor, for God's sake. She knows the form. She's an actress. It's not the same for us. You can't expect us to act like ordinary people.' He got up and went over to talk to Patrick. They were soon guffawing like two schoolboys.

'I think I've got your cold,' Patrick moaned as they sat huddled in the location van at seven o'clock on Wednesday morning. 'It's not my cold,' protested Sally. 'Anyway I haven't got it any more.'

'No. That's because you've given it to me. My head feels like the inside of a bell tower.'

'I don't suppose you've been drinking?' asked Sally peevishly. She was feeling particularly wretched, having been called at a quarter to six for Costume. This had entailed putting on her usual skirt and blouse and trying on a beige raincoat. No one else had turned up till half past. She could not help regarding it as an act of pure malice on Wendy's part, particularly since the taxi that had been sent to collect her had arrived ten minutes early and she had had to go without her coffee.

Patrick yawned and lay back amongst the neatly folded shirts on the seat. 'Wendy'll kill you if she sees you,' warned Sally with ill-disguised longing. Patrick smiled and closed his eyes. 'No she won't.'

He was right, of course. Wendy's first reaction on seeing Patrick was to go pink and giggle. 'Doesn't he look sweet?' she cooed. 'Just like a little baby. He's got the most gorgeous lashes I've ever seen.'

Patrick opened one eye and gazed up at her. 'My darling,' he struggled to sit up.

'Oh,' simpered Wendy, quite overcome with remorse. 'Now I've woken you up. I'm so sorry, Patrick.' Patrick reached out and kissed her hand peremptorily. 'No, no. Think nothing of it. I don't suppose there's the tiniest chance of a cup of coffee? No, don't you go. You're far too busy. I just wondered if there was any around. I can get it myself.' He struggled feebly to get up. Wendy shooed him back. 'No, don't you move. You must be exhausted. Jean will bring you one. Black with two sugars?'

'You remembered.'

Wendy's face was now resembling a victim of smallpox, so many dimples were puckering it. 'Jean,' she called. 'Could you be an utter angel and get poor Patrick a coffee?' A grunt from outside signalled Jean's compliance.

Sally stood up. 'I think I might get one too,' she said. Wendy glanced round, having clearly forgotten her existence. 'Actually I need to look at your coat. Could you just pop it on for me?' Sally obliged, although she had tried it on twice already and been passed fit. Also the fact that Wendy had brought no other rather detracted from her supposed concern.

Wendy frowned. 'I'm a bit worried about the buttons,' she murmured. Sally said nothing, knowing her opinion would not be welcome. 'What do you think, Patrick? It's not going to take away from anything, is it? If she has those buttons?' Patrick assumed a look of utmost concern. He leant forward then pulled back and screwed up his eyes as though scanning the horizon for ships. 'I think they'll be OK,' he said, his voice eloquent with doubt. Wendy read his thoughts. 'I'll get them changed,' she said with brisk decision.

'Changed?' Sally stared at them in amazement. 'The buttons?'

'They're going to reflect,' said Wendy with the air of an expert. 'It had better be navy.'

'Navy?' said Sally again. Wendy cast her a look of utter pity. 'Navy doesn't reflect,' she said patiently. 'Ah, there's Penny.'

'It may not reflect,' said Sally to Patrick as Wendy scurried after the AFM, 'but it's going to look pretty silly against beige.'

Patrick gave her a lopsided grin and winked. 'And you are an absolute poser.'

'Here we are,' Jean, wheezing a little from her efforts, climbed the steps into the van with Patrick's coffee. 'Black with sugar.'

'Two sugars,' Patrick corrected.

Jean looked mortified. 'Two?'

Patrick was all solicitude. 'No. It doesn't matter. Really. I can easily make do with one. Good for the figure.' But Jean was already on her way back to the catering truck. Wendy returned with Penny. 'Right,' she said with the air of a conquering hero, 'Penny's going to do your buttons.'

'Oh, right.' Sally took off the coat. 'Thanks, Penny.' Penny gave her a wan smile. 'In that case I think I'll go and get myself a cup of coffee.' She moved towards the door.

'Don't go,' came an anguished squawk from Wendy. 'You'll need to try it on when she's done it.' Sally sat down.

Jean returned with Patrick's extra sugar. 'I don't suppose you could do me the utmost favour and get me a cup,' asked Sally. Jean looked as though she had been punched in the stomach. 'I'm sorry,' she said stiffly. 'I really am rather busy.'

The rain started about nine o'clock. This meant the two scenes René had managed to film already had to be scrapped because they were continuous and it would look very strange for Simon to be discussing the outbuildings with Patrick on his left in sunshine and Marley on his right in the pouring rain.

They managed to get all four of the relevant shots before the sun came out again but were then faced with the problem of Marley, Patrick and Simon standing in the blazing sun, looking as though they'd just passed too close to the QE2.

Wendy was tearing around with the air of one about to have a nervous breakdown, but everyone was used to this by now so continued about their business as though there were nothing unusual in a wild-eyed woman in camouflage gear shrieking orders to no one in particular and periodically rushing at them with a pair of scissors.

Drewe turned up at lunch time and was finished by three. Sally, frozen, bored and famished, fought to smother a mounting sense of resentment as Jean ferried to and fro with little treats for Patrick 'because the poor lamb's got a cold'.

'It's my cold anyway,' she grumbled as Jean departed to warm up his coffee for the third time.

'That's not what you said this morning,' said Patrick smugly.

She was finally called at four o'clock. Rolo led her with unnatural cheerfulness to where the mud lay thickest, and trotted her up and down with increasing loads of stationery while René rained his lights on the office door as though it were the gateway to Valhalla.

They filmed her arriving at Solley's office, with her hand on the door knob, then with one foot on the step, and finally edging her way through the door, her face entirely hidden by cardboard boxes. All these actions drew such a fountain of superlatives from both Rolo and, seemingly, René, that Sally began to wonder if she mightn't be more suited to silent movies than as an exponent of the living word.

16

Sally woke late next morning, just in time to hear her agent's lugubrious voice signing off on the answerphone. She played it back to learn that there was a possibility she might be required for some filming and that she should hold herself in readiness. She sighed, thinking that Michael Snelcott must be the only agent in the world who booked his clients in retrospect.

There were a couple of letters on the mat and a small hand-written note on grey paper. She picked it up. 'Housewarming. Number One. 8.30 tonight. Dan.' Sally read it again. Was it for information only or was it an invitation? Perhaps it was just a warning that she should keep clear of Marchbank Gardens for the next twenty-four hours if she wasn't into acid.

Dan's car was parked outside the front door. He was unloading cases of beer attended, unlikely though it seemed, by Mr Davenport, who was standing on the doorstep with an armful of lettuces.

'Hullo, Mr Davenport,' called Sally, coming down the stairs. 'How are you?'

'Just giving a hand,' said Mr Davenport. 'Young man's getting married. Thought he might like a lettuce or two.' Sally turned to Dan in some shock.

He laughed. 'Not married. A housewarming. Just a few friends. You coming?'

Sally hesitated. 'I'm not sure if I'll . . .'

'Please,' said Dan.

She smiled awkwardly. 'I'll do my best.'

So this is a few friends, she thought, edging her way through a crowd that would not have disgraced a football match. There was no one she knew except Mr Davenport, who was sitting by himself on the sofa with his lead folded neatly on his lap. She sat down next to him. 'Hullo, Mr Davenport. Have you got a drink?' Mr Davenport gestured to a glass of beer on the table beside him. Dan appeared from the kitchen and spotted her. 'What can I get you?' he asked.

'Have you got any wine?'

'Somewhere. Stay there.' He retreated and returned with her drink.

'Cheers.'

'Cheers,' said Sally.

Mr Davenport picked up his beer. 'I hope you'll both be very happy,' he said. He touched Sally's arm. 'If you'll excuse me, I'm just going to look at my runner beans.'

Dan grabbed hold of a stocky young man who was passing. 'I'd like you to meet Joe,' he said. 'He's a plumber. Sally's an actress,' he told his friend. The young man pumped her hand enthusiastically. 'You known Danny long?'

'No. I live in the flat upstairs.'

Joe nodded. 'You must be the nutty one.' Before she could reply Dan reappeared with a couple whom he introduced as Meg and Freddie. They ran a market garden.

'You should talk to Mr Davenport,' Sally said. 'He grows all his own vegetables.' Freddie nodded. 'Dan's told me about him. Isn't he the nutty one?' Dan gave her a bleak smile and muttered something about getting some more ice.

Sally was mildly surprised that Suzanne was not there. This was just the sort of thing she would have considered terribly wholesome for her rejected spouse, no doubt.

'I'm glad it's working out OK for Dan,' said Meg, gazing approvingly round the room. The others nodded sagely.

'Didn't look like it for a while,' said Joe. 'I've never seen a bloke so knocked back. To tell the truth I thought he was making a mistake moving so far out. I mean he'd got no family over here or nothing. He must miss that lot.'

'I think they were half the problem,' Meg observed. 'Never out of the place.'

Joe nodded. 'Suzanne couldn't stand that, could she?' He chuckled. 'Suppose they were a bit lively.' He turned to Sally. 'Crafty old sod, never said anything about having an actress upstairs.' Sally smiled uncertainly, thinking that she probably fell far short of Joe's idea of actresses.

'I wonder how he's managing with the cooking and all that,' continued Meg. 'He never struck me as the domesticated type.'

'That's because Suzanne did it all,' interjected her husband. 'He didn't know what had hit him when she left.'

'Well, he seems to be doing all right now,' said Meg. She smiled. 'Unless he's got Sally doing it for him?'

Sally nearly choked. 'I'm afraid I'm not particularly domesticated myself,' she said. 'I've certainly got no plans to take in laundry.' The three exchanged glances.

'You mean he hasn't got you doing his ironing and baking him steak and kidney pies?' asked Joe.

'He'd only ever ask me once,' Sally said firmly. The others looked impressed.

The conversation moved on to holidays and home improvements and no more was said about Dan's previous domestic arrangements, or his current ones. Somewhere a clock struck eleven and Sally suddenly realised she had spent a whole evening talking to people who had not once mentioned being up for a film or changing their agent or refusing to wear the clothes provided for them. She hadn't thought it possible. This must be what normal people were like. She felt strangely elated that they seemed to think she was normal too. No one so far had asked her if she knew Robert Redford or what she did in the daytime. I'm just like one of them, she thought, I belong here and I belong with *The Firm*. She looked up and saw Dan watching her from across the room. She smiled and he smiled back then was caught in conversation. I'm in your world, she thought, but what would you make of mine?

At about a quarter to twelve she noticed Mr Davenport edging towards the door. She pushed her way through to Dan and jerked at his elbow. 'Mr Davenport's just going,' she hissed. Dan gazed at her blankly then followed her eyes to the door. 'Ah,' he said. 'Back in a moment.' He thrust his way through the guests and followed Mr Davenport out into the hall, closing the door behind him.

'Where's Danny going?' asked Joe, who had gone to fetch her a refill.

'Er. Just out. He'll be back in a minute,' said Sally. 'Umm, perhaps I should just go after him.'

'Is everything all right?' She was standing at the open back door peering into the invisible garden. 'Fine,' came Dan's voice out of the gloom. 'We're just checking on the lettuces.' Two shapes emerged from the bushes and moved towards her. 'There were six this morning,' came Mr Davenport's voice. 'There are only two now. What do you make of that?'

'I couldn't say,' Dan replied solemnly.

'I think I shall go to bed,' said the old man.

'Good idea.'

People were beginning to leave. 'Do you want any help clearing up?' asked Sally when the last of the guests had departed. Dan was sitting on the sofa drinking a beer. He shook his head. 'I'll do it in the morning.'

'I thought Suzanne said it should be done straight away.'

A look of blank loneliness spread across Dan's face. 'Yes, well, she's not here, is she?' he said listlessly.

'I'm sorry,' Sally said, ashamed. 'I didn't mean . . .'

Dan shook his head. 'That's all right. I asked for it.'

'No you didn't. I'm a tactless cow.' He didn't deny it.

Sally hovered. 'Well, if you're absolutely sure you don't want me to help . . .'

To her surprise Dan reached up and took hold of her hands. 'Thank you for coming tonight.'

'No,' she protested, embarrassed. 'Thank you for asking me. It was a lovely party.'

'Was it?'

'Yes. You know some jolly interesting people.'

'Do I?'

'You know you do.'

'Will you sleep with me tonight?'

Sally dragged her hands away. 'What is this?'

'What's what?'

'Why do you keep asking me to sleep with you?'

Dan looked genuinely surprised. 'I fancy you, that's why.'

Sally glared at him in exasperation. 'Only when you're drunk.'

Dan shook his head. 'That's not true. I fancy you all the time but the only time I dare to tell you is when I'm drunk.'

Sally tossed her head. 'The other thing you told me when you were drunk last time was that I was old.'

Dan looked contrite. 'Did I say that?'

'You know you did.'

'I didn't mean it like that.'

'What other way is there?'

Dan shuffled his feet. 'You don't understand,' he mumbled.

'I don't suppose I do.' She walked towards the door. A bread roll went flying past her ear. She picked it up and threw it back at him. 'DON'T throw food at me.'

'Why won't you sleep with me?' bellowed Dan.

'Why the hell should I?' Sally roared back.

'Because you're an actress.'

'Good night,' said Sally. 'I hope you feel dreadful in the morning.'

Why do I always end up rowing with him, she thought as she lay in the darkness. Just when everything seems to be all right he goes and says something really irritating. He can't really believe all that twaddle about actresses falling into bed with everyone. He just says it to annoy me. He likes annoying me. And it's not as though I provoked it in any way. I am a very easy person to get along with. Anyone could vouch for that. I've never had this sort of trouble with a neighbour before. I do wish he'd never come.

She rolled over and tried to get to sleep. Anyway, what did it matter? He was nothing to her, or she to him. Just think, in six weeks from now she might be receiving proposals of marriage from total strangers, bowled over by the way she carried her stationery. Think positive. That was the only way to survive. Look after Number One, the first law of acting. That's what people like Dan couldn't understand. They belonged to a different world, with families and regular jobs – interesting to visit but not a place to linger. Normality was all very well, but you wouldn't want too much of it.

Down below Dan lay on his bed and looked at the ceiling. She is a very odd woman, he thought. The tutor on his course had said there were only two kinds of women. He had thought it daft at the time but now he could see what the man was getting at. There were only two kinds of women, but not Matriarchs and Doormats or whatever he had called them. There were women like other women, and women like Sally.

17

'If those are for me I don't want them.'

Dan was standing in her doorway, a bunch of greenery protruding from brown paper. 'I'm sorry about last night.'

'Yes. Well, that's all right. I'd forgotten. Now, if you don't mind I'm in a bit of a rush.'

'I didn't mean it.'

'I'm sure you didn't. Anyway it doesn't matter. Couldn't matter less.'

'Can I give you these then?'

'Honestly, I do not require a peace offering.'

'No, but I'll never eat them myself. You know how I feel.' Dan placed the bag of lettuces in Sally's arms and retreated. Sally closed the door. She wondered idly what she might have got if she had agreed to sleep with him.

There was a knock on the door. It was Dan again. 'What is it this time?'

Solemnly he handed her two bottles of wine. 'I had this left over. I thought you might like it.' Sally noted that it was the same Chablis that he had praised so much to Patrick. 'Don't you want it? I thought you liked it.'

Dan shrugged. 'You like it more. Anyway, I owe you something. I was out of order last night.'

'Oh please stop going on about it,' said Sally. 'We'd both had too much to drink. It was nothing. Really. Nothing happened. No harm done. You keep the wine. Give it to Suzanne.'

'She's not very keen on alcohol,' said Dan.

'No, well you drink it then.'

'Tell you what. I could put it in the fridge and you could come down this evening and we could drink it together.'

'I really don't think . . .'

'Please.'

'Oh all right, but I can't stay long.'

Sally spent the day catching up on her housework. This involved putting some washing in, hoovering the carpet and passing two hours cross-legged on the carpet while she went through her cuttings album.

Michael Snelcott rang to say that he had just heard they definitely wanted her for filming and that she should keep herself free for the nineteenth. 'That was Wednesday.'

'Was it? Oh yes. I wonder why they said that then. I expect they meant next month. Yes, that'll be it.'

'How was your holiday?'

'Very good. It rained all the time. But you expect that, don't you?'

'In Tenerife?'

'Yes. They'd hardly had any for three years, you see, in the part where I was. So it was a blessing really.'

Sally put the phone down thinking only her agent would count the first rain for three years a blessing on his one two-week holiday of the year.

Dan was on the phone when she arrived. He opened the door and beckoned her in. 'No . . . all right . . . well, let me know what's happening . . . No . . . Right. Bye.' He put the phone down. 'Thanks for coming.'

'That's all right.' He fetched the wine. 'By the way, Joe thought you were wonderful.'

'Rubbish.'

'No, really. I saw him at work today and he was singing your praises. He thought you were very well adjusted.'

'For a nut, you mean?'

'No, for an actress?'

'Does he know a lot of actresses?'

'You're the first.'

'So what exactly is he measuring me against?'

Dan shrugged. 'The type you see in the papers, I suppose. The ones who are always having face-lifts and getting divorced.'

'In that order?'

Dan laughed. 'I should think so. I don't think I'd stay with a woman who'd had a face-lift.' He poured the wine. 'Would you have one?'

'I don't know. It'd have to be a bit radical in my case. I don't think I'd ever have the nerve. Or the money.'

Dan opened a packet of crisps. 'You don't think much of yourself, do you?'

'Oh, don't let's start that again,' said Sally, helping herself. 'If there's one thing I can't bear it's people who try to analyse other people all the time.'

Dan tipped the packet into his mouth. 'I'm sorry. You just sort of lend yourself to analysing.'

'I do not. Why do you say that?'

'Because you're so touchy. You take offence all the time.'

'No I don't,' said Sally, thoroughly unsettled. 'I get on very well with most people. You have to if you're an actress. It's only you I'm always having rows with, so how do you analyse that?' Dan sat back and looked at his glass. 'Perhaps you're in love with me,' he suggested. Sally nearly choked. 'That'll be the day,' she said.

Dan shrugged. 'Just a thought.' The phone rang again. He picked it up. 'Hullo . . . I see . . . Well, it's up to you, isn't it? . . . No, it isn't. You know how I feel . . . Yes, well, if that's what you want . . . I'm not making difficulties, Suze. I just don't see why you've got to rush everything through like this . . . OK, fine. Please your bloody self. You always did anyway.' He slammed the phone down.

Sally noticed his hand was shaking. 'Would you like me to go?' she asked.

Dan shook his head. 'No. I'd rather argue with you than her.'

Sally smiled. 'You certainly know how to flatter a woman, don't you?' Dan laughed a trifle grimly. 'I didn't mean it like that. No wonder you're always yelling at me.'

'I'm not.'

'No wonder you never yell at me.'

He emptied some more crisps into a bowl then disappeared into the kitchen and returned with a candle in a milk bottle which he placed ceremoniously centre table. 'Atmosphere,' he said. 'Cheers.'

'Cheers.'

He sat down beside her. 'Actually,' he said, 'I quite like you. As neighbours go.'

'And nuts,' she reminded him.

'And nuts. Speaking of nuts, any idea what's happening with the old boy?'

Sally shook her head. 'There's a nurse coming in at the moment but that won't last. It's an awful worry. Not that it's our responsibility,' she added quickly.

'We live in the same house.'

'Yes I know, but that still doesn't mean . . . I mean, by that reasoning I should be ironing your shirts.' Dan grinned. 'I was just getting round to that.'

'And you should be mending my overflow.'

'Ah. But to tell the truth I don't reckon he's going to make it.'

Sally stopped with a crisp halfway to her mouth. 'What do you mean?'

'Oh not that he's going to pop off or anything, but he

really is gone, you know. Last night when we were down the garden he didn't know where he was. He kept calling me Jennifer.'

'That was his wife,' said Sally, trying not to smile.

'What's so funny?' asked Dan.

'Nothing. It's just you don't look awfully like a Jennifer.'

'Well that's a load off my mind. But honestly I don't think he'll be able to manage on his own. Maybe she was right.'

'Who?'

'Suzanne.'

'Oh rubbish,' said Sally automatically, forgetting she had once thought the same thing. 'What I mean is, I'm sure she's right that in some circumstances it might be the best thing. But not for him.'

'Why not?'

Sally waved her hands frustratedly. 'Because this is his home. He belongs here. Take him away and stick him amongst a load of strangers and he'd be utterly lost. He wouldn't know where he was.'

'He doesn't now.'

'Oh for heaven's sake. You know what I'm getting at.'

Dan sighed. 'It's up to you and me then, isn't it? Perhaps you should have a word with the nurse next time she's round.'

'Me?'

'It'd be better coming from you.'

'No it wouldn't. Why would it?'

'Because you're . . .'

'An actress?' Sally suggested.

'No,' said Dan aggrievedly. 'What would that have to do with it?'

'I don't know. It seems to do for most things.'

'I was going to say "a woman".'

'That,' said Sally, 'is even worse.'

'I can't do right, can I?' grumbled Dan.

'Perhaps you try too hard.'

He glanced at her, surprised. 'That's a new one. I was under the impression I didn't try hard enough.'

Sally shrugged. 'You could try just being yourself. Not caring what other people thought.'

'Everyone cares what other people think. Fact of life.'

'Yes, but only up to a point. You can't let it rule your whole life, otherwise you'd have to keep changing to keep up.'

'Some people do.'

'Politicians, maybe. Not real people.'

'I was thinking of actors,' said Dan, emptying the bottle into her glass.

'Suppose the critics don't like your show?' he asked suddenly. 'Like that *Eldorado*? I mean would you just go on anyway or would they pull the plug on it, or what?'

'Oh they'd have to go on with it. It's been commissioned. You couldn't just stop halfway through. There'd be nothing to put in its place. And even if there were they'd still have to pay all the actors and everyone for all thirteen episodes, so it wouldn't be worth it. No, what would happen is they just wouldn't make a second series. They have this thing called an 'option', and if they think it's going to make the ratings they can book the whole cast again for the same fee, but they have to take up the option by episode ten.'

'Or what happens?'

'Or they can't make another serics. At least they can, but they'd have to renegotiate the contracts and that would cost them a fortune because they'd only do it if the show was so successful they couldn't afford not to, if you see what I mean. Which would mean the actors could ask what they liked.'

'Do you think they will?'

'What?'

'Take up the options?' Sally thought. Images of herself tramping through the mud with carbon paper, nodding into an empty phone, Veeney hallucinating, Dilys swaying over her ironing board, Simon with his bashed up nose, Patrick with his coffee ... 'No,' she said quietly. 'I don't think they will.'

Dan flicked a crisp across the table. 'You never know,' he said. 'You never know what people are going to like. Seen anything of Colin lately?'

'No,' she admitted. Truth was, she'd been avoiding him.

'I saw him down the pub the other night,' said Dan. 'He'd had a row with his boyfriend.'

'That makes a change.'

'Still it's not easy, is it?'

'What?'

'Living with someone who doesn't love you.' Sally was silent for a moment. 'I wouldn't know,' she said.

Dan went to fetch the other bottle. Sally watched him pottering around. He was perfectly self-sufficient. All that talk about him being lost without Suzanne! If they asked her it was probably the best thing that could have happened to him. Look at that stupid course he was on. Fancy believing you could change your way of thinking just to fall in with someone else's wishes. No wonder the marriage had failed. People were so odd the way they depended on other people.

Dan came back with the wine. Sally watched him surreptitiously as he poured it out. His nose was slightly wonky, she hadn't noticed that before. He had nice eyelashes – long and curling upwards – and a scar just to the side of his cheekbone as though he had been scratched by something. It wasn't deep, it might even have been a wrinkle, except that was a funny place for a wrinkle. 'How old are you?' she asked suddenly.

Dan turned. 'What? How old am I?'

Sally blushed. 'I'm sorry. I was thinking about something else. I didn't mean to say that. What I meant was how old were you when . . .' her imagination forsook her.

'When I had my first orgasm?'

'Yes. NO. When you . . . that is . . .'

'I'm thirty-six. How old are you?'

'Thirty-three.'

Dan cleared his throat. 'And your biological clock is ticking away?'

'What?'

'You want to have a baby, right? If this serial works out you'll be financially independent, but getting on a bit. So you're looking around. Quite right too.'

Sally sat bolt upright. 'I am not. How dare you! How dare you suggest anything of the sort. The last thing I want is a baby. I'm an actress, remember.'

Dan shrugged. 'That's a pity. I was about to offer myself, free and unencumbered as a sperm donor.'

'Don't be disgusting. Anyway you're not free and unencumbered.'

'Yes I am.'

'You're not, you're married.'

'Not for much longer, it seems. That's what Suzanne was telling me on the phone. Nice quick "No Blame, Clean Break" divorce. I could be a single man again in six weeks.' He smiled bitterly. 'And quite a lot richer if the sale of the house goes through.'

Sally looked out of the window. 'You're still in love with her, aren't you?' Dan sank down in his chair. 'Is it so obvious?'

'Yes.'

'I didn't think it would be like this,' he said slowly. 'I knew it would be hard. I knew I would miss her. But I didn't think it would actually hurt. It's like a pain. Here.' He put his hand on his abdomen. 'It *hurts*. They don't tell you about that, do they?' Sally continued to stare out of the window. 'They don't tell you anything that matters,' she said.

Dan roused himself. 'So. There you are. Need a father for

your baby, knock on Number One.' Sally frowned. 'I wish you wouldn't talk like that.'

'I'm sorry. Just trying to be practical. I believe that's what they advise in the circumstances. "Get out and about. See a show. Take up a hobby."'

'Yes, well I don't think sperm bank is one of the hobbies they recommend.'

'"Work from Home"? It's better than licking envelopes.'

'You're sick,' said Sally, laughing.

'Why did you become an actress?' asked Dan, lying back on the cushions.

'I love acting.'

'Simple as that?'

'I suppose so.'

'Are all your family actors?'

'No,' said Sally with feeling, remembering the blank incomprehension on her parents' faces when she had revealed she was quitting university for a tour of *The Magic Mango Leaf* and the unreliable charms of its middle-aged director. The worst of it had been that, though she had seriously irritated them, she knew in her heart she had not disappointed them. Nothing she could do could really have disappointed them by then because they had grown to expect so little of her. Even getting to university had seemed a normal thing, and it hadn't been Oxford like John.

Why do some people get born into the wrong families, she wondered, not for the first time. Still at least she had avoided the mistake of marrying into the wrong one, like Dan.

'I can see how someone would want to play football for a living, or chop people up or mess around with computers,' Dan continued musingly, 'but it's hard to understand why someone should want to spend their whole life being other people.'

'Perhaps, it's because they don't like the person they are,' Sally suggested brightly.

'Is that why you became one?'

She laughed a trifle artificially. 'Oh definitely. I should have thought your course would have told you that.' Dan smiled slightly but said nothing.

'Why did you become a builder?' Sally asked to turn the subject from herself. Dan grimaced.'My dad was one. He got me started. I didn't want to do it. I wanted to stay on at school.' He glanced at her. 'That comes as a surprise, I expect?'

'No. Why should it?'

'I just thought it might. I joined the TA for a bit. That's where I met Suzanne. You wouldn't think she was that sort, would you, to look at her?'

'No,' Sally lied, thinking nothing could be more suitable.

'We got married. I didn't want to stay in so she left as well.' He shifted on to his elbow. 'I think that's probably when our problems started, looking back. She enjoyed the life, you see. She likes organising people, being responsible for them. She'll make a marvellous teacher.'

If she can find anyone to teach, thought Sally. She put her glass down. 'I must go.'

'Why?'

'Because I've got to be in studio tomorrow.'

'What's it like "in studio"?'

Sally thought. 'Hot, tedious, and nerve-racking' hardly seemed an ideal response. 'It's interesting,' she said carefully, 'Extremely tiring. A bit of a strain.'

Dan nodded. 'What do you do?'

'Well, I . . . I get ready, into costume, and then there's make-up, and then you have to wait until it's time to do your scenes, and then you do them. And that's about it, really.'

'Sounds exhausting.'

'There are other things as well,' said Sally defensively. 'It's all a bit technical.'

'So I wouldn't understand?'

'I didn't say that.'

'You implied it.'

'No I didn't. You've got a chip the size of Ben Nevis.'

'What about?'

'Everything. Being a builder. Not being educated, whatever. It's very boring.'

Dan scooped up the last of the crisps and emptied them into his mouth. 'I'm getting an education. There are only two kinds of women – and I bet you don't even know what they are.'

'Fat and thin,' said Sally without hesitation.

Dan looked slightly phased. 'Matriarchs and slaves, actually.'

Sally burst out laughing. 'You learnt that on your course, I suppose?'

'As a matter of fact I did.'

'And they're actually charging you money for this?'

'What's that got to do with it?'

'Oh nothing. Why don't you buy a phial of the Virgin's tears while you're at it?'

Dan emptied the last of the wine into his glass. 'How much are you charging?' he asked.

18

Sally woke with a hangover. For the first time she knew how Patrick must feel having to rehearse with a platoon of drummers inside his head.

It had been late when she'd left Dan's and when she got back there had been a message from Colin saying she owed him six pounds fifty for the adaptor he'd been forced to fit to her microwave and the taxi fare to purchase it to prevent the Baptist Hall being closed by the fire inspector.

She had contemplated phoning him back and saying he had her full permission to raze the hall to the ground and the company of Resting Pieces with it, but this would only have invoked a discussion and possibly a request to call round, so she had left the answerphone on and fallen into bed with a bacon sandwich and a copy of the *Stage*, neither of which had done much to alleviate the sense of injustice which Colin's message and Dan's misplaced devotion had instilled in her.

She didn't mind Dan being in love, nor even being in love with his (soon to be ex) wife. She just minded him being in love with Suzanne. How could a reasonably intelligent, fairly attractive man, with a sense of humour and quite nice eyes be fooled by that pious, self-righteous smart ass? It was such a waste. Not that it was of any concern to her, or even interest, apart from him being a neighbour, but it was galling all the same to see someone upsetting themself over a person who really wasn't worth it. It was Colin and Matthew all over again. Why were her friends such idiots?

Pondering this enigma she had fallen asleep.

The recording was the best yet. Initial nervousness was beginning to fade and the cast was now working more as a unit and less as a bunch of hopefuls at an audition. There were the obvious exceptions of Drewe who got no better as time went on, and Dilys whose behaviour was so erratic that everyone else went into overdrive when she was around. But Stephanie had now accepted the age gap and opted for a more Joan Collins' approach and Simon, aside from his tendency to knock things over, had a definite rapport with both Marley and Patrick.

Sally saw all this and wondered how she fitted in. She had caught sight of herself once or twice on the monitor, but it was usually the back of her head, which she had never felt her most expressive feature.

René ran the filming during the coffee break to check for continuity and she was treated to a close-up of her hand on the doorknob. This left her in no doubt that she needed a decent hand cream but did very little to appease her worries about her performance.

Wellard Kenning came prowling round at the end, but as none of their previous toadying had produced results, the actors were a little more circumspect with their wallets this week.

At twenty past ten Marley burst into the bar like a belated Kissogram. 'Who wants to hear my news?' she chortled. They gathered round. 'Not a word to anyone,' said Marley, pressing her finger to her lips, 'but I know who's playing Melanie Rinseworth.'

'Who?' they all chorused.

Marley looked all round to make sure she would not be overheard. 'Vanessa Redgrave,' she breathed.

'Who?' bellowed Patrick. 'Vanessa Redgrave? You must be kidding?'

'Sssshh!' squeaked Marley, hopping from foot to foot. 'You're not to tell anyone.' The others gazed at each other incredulously.

'Where'd you get that from, Marley?' demanded George. 'I'd've thought this rubbish was a bit out of her league.'

'Speak for yourself,' said Patrick grandiosely.

'Oh, come on, Paddy. You know what I mean,' grunted George. 'She's into all that classical stuff. She's not your actual jobbing actor.'

'Well, I for one don't believe a word of it,' broke in Stephanie with the tiniest hint of panic.

'Why not?' demanded Simon who was very much taken with the prospect.

'Because René hasn't mentioned it once to me – or any of us,' she added hastily. 'Anyway, how does Marley know? Did he tell you or what? I should have thought our Dilys would know first. After all she is married to the boss man. Mind you, she probably wouldn't notice if he did tell her . . .' she stopped short. Dilys, who had not risen from the seat in which she had slumped on first arrival, looked up very slowly and focused her vacant eyes on Stephanie for a moment, then her head dropped again and she returned to contemplation of the table in front of her. Patrick glared at Stephanie who lit a cigarette and blew smoke in his face sending him into paroxysms of artificial coughing.

'Tell us how you know, Marley,' coaxed Sally.

'Well, I've been trying to persuade René to let me into the secret because, although I say it myself, I do know how to hold my tongue.' Nobody denied this. 'And I just thought it would be nice to send whoever it was a little note – you know – a sort of welcome, because it isn't easy, is it, to walk into a series where everyone knows each other and be the new face? I know I should be frightfully nervous.'

'How do you know it's her?' persisted Patrick who had recovered from his coughing fit.

'Well, I couldn't quite get René to admit it because of course it's all classified information and so on, but I hit upon the idea of me suggesting names to him and he just had to nod or shake his head, so that that way he wouldn't be giving away any trade secrets, would he?'

'And?' said Patrick with infinite patience.

'And I thought of all the actresses I thought might be right for the part and made a little list and worked my way through them while there was a tape break, and René was terribly good and kept shaking his head every time, till I came to Vanessa Redgrave. I must admit it was a bit of a long shot, but anyway I'd more or less gone through all of them by then and anyway I said it, quite casually – "Vanessa Redgrave",' she whispered like someone invoking the devil.

'He nodded his head?' demanded George in total disbelief.

Marley gave a little smile, 'He didn't actually nod, George, he did something even better. He burst out laughing. So you see, I teased it out of him in the end. But of course we must none of us let on that we know.' Everyone promised that they would not.

As they left the building Patrick caught up with Sally. 'I love Marley with all my heart, but I really do think she is down to her last marble.'

Sally smiled. 'It would serve us right if it was Vanessa Redgrave.'

Patrick grimaced. 'Have a heart. She's a foot taller than me, and she's old enough to be Drewe's grand-mother.'

'She'd guarantee an audience though, wouldn't she?' Patrick said nothing but she sensed that he was bristling slightly as they crossed the car park. At the barrier he stopped. 'Who's taking you home, Miss Mouse?'

'No one. I shall get a train. And please don't offer to give me a lift.'

'I was just about to, ingrate.'

'Well I've saved you the trouble.'

'Do I detect an air of bitterness? Not trouble on the Woolwich front, I trust?'

'Certainly not.'

'How is Dan?'

'Very well.'

'Good, good. Suzanne was telling me all about him. Apparently he's entirely self-taught.'

'She told you that, did she?'

'Yes. "A self-made man", I think was the phrase.'

'Did she say what he was made of?' Patrick looked slightly taken aback.

'Doesn't he build or something?'

'Yes,' said Sally coolly, 'the way you act or something.'

Dan knocked on her door the following morning. 'Sorry to disturb you,' he said politely, 'but she's here.'

'Who?'

'The nurse. For Mr Davenport. I wondered if we should speak to her?'

'Oh. Yes. By all means.'

'She's gone to give him his bath,' said Dan. 'I don't expect she'll be long.'

'I'll get dressed.'

She was descending the stairs as the nurse came out. 'Bye, Mr Davenport.'

'Bye, Jennifer,' came the reply. The nurse smiled at Dan and Sally. 'Nice morning.'

'Yes,' they chorused. Dan nudged Sally. 'Excuse me,' she

said, stepping forward, 'could we just talk to you a minute, please?' The nurse stopped.

'Of course.'

'It's about Mr Davenport.'

'I thought it might be.'

'We're his neighbours. I live upstairs and – he – lives opposite.' Dan indicated his flat like an air-hostess pointing to emergency exits. 'We're just a bit concerned,' Sally went on, 'you know, that he's managing all right since his fall?'

The nurse was silent for a moment. 'To be perfectly honest, I don't think he is,' she said briefly. 'He's still very disorientated. You expect it for the first couple of days or so, but he's been home a week now and it isn't getting any better. I'm going to have to put in a report to the Social Services.'

'Not that Crane woman?' Sally exploded. The nurse swallowed. 'She's not as bad as she seems. She's got a bit of an unfortunate manner.'

'Modelled on Stalin,' said Sally. The girl laughed. 'Honestly though, I don't think it's safe for him to be left on his own. I've arranged for meals on wheels but really he needs someone there all the time.'

'Does that mean he'll have to go into a home?'

The nurse looked embarrassed. 'Not necessarily.'

'He seemed so much better in hospital,' said Sally, half to herself. 'So much brighter.' The nurse nodded. 'That's probably because he had company. He's vegetating here on his own. You heard him call me Jennifer. That was his wife. He talks to her all the time when I'm there. He's lonely, that's his worst problem. A lot more people die of loneliness than of being old.' She looked at her watch. 'You must excuse me. I've got another two baths to do before lunch.' Sally stepped aside. 'Yes of course. Thank you for telling us, anyway.'

Dan closed the front door after her. 'We were right to do that.'

'What?'

'Tackle her about the old boy.'

'I didn't see you doing much tackling.'

'I said it was a woman's job. You did it brilliantly,' he added before she could protest.

'All for nothing.'

'Why do you say that?'

'Because the end result's the same. They'll assess him and cart him off to some old folks' home and he'll rot away.'

'We've done our best.'

Sally nodded forlornly. 'I suppose so.'

With a sudden gesture of fury Dan picked up a piece of loose tiling and flung it at the front door. 'Whatever are you doing?' Sally screeched. She inspected the damage to the woodwork. 'Why did you do that? You've chipped the paint.' Dan ran his hands through his hair and gave a hopeless laugh. 'I'll put it right. Don't you worry about that.'

'I still don't see what call you've got to go throwing tiles around,' grumbled Sally uncomfortably. This was a new side to her neighbour. One she didn't in the least bit welcome. Dan shook his head. 'I'm sorry. It's just sometimes things get a bit on top of me. I feel so . . .' he stopped.

'What?' demanded Sally crossly. 'What do you feel so?'

Dan looked at her for a moment then turned away. 'Oh nothing.'

She bought the Sunday papers and was gratified to see that there was a photograph of Marley on the television page with a long spiel about her career. It concluded: 'Her latest project, a thirteen part serial entitled *The Firm* for Majestic Productions, also stars Patrick Crichton (Dr Chris Merryweather in the popular sixties soap opera), and introduces Veeney Rogers as Solange.'

She read the rest of the page which spoke of fights on the set of *Coronation Street* and the decision to run an American mini-series about incest before the nine o'clock watershed. She felt vaguely proud of being mentioned in the same column as *Coronation Street* and incest. Or if not exactly her, the serial she was in, which was the same thing. She sighed. It was a bit rotten sometimes not having anyone to show things to.

John was playing golf, but Naomi, Sally's sister-in-law, said she would tell him, although they never bothered with the Sunday papers. Nobody they knew did these days.

Colin was not in. She left a message saying he must at all costs buy a copy of the *Observer* but gave no reason in the sure knowledge that he would rush out and buy three. Serves him right, she thought complacently. He can offset it against the adaptor.

Dan answered the door with a piece of toast in his hand. 'I thought you might like to see this,' said Sally rapidly, thrusting the folded newspaper into his free hand.

'What is it?'

'It's the television page. We're . . . I'm . . . There's an article . . . I just thought you might . . .' Dan took the paper and studied it. 'I never liked that Ken Barlow,' he conceded. Sally folded it even smaller. Dan peered.

'Isn't this the thing you're in?' he asked.

'Yes.'

'No, that's good,' he said when he had read it. 'Why doesn't it mention you?'

'I'm not a star.'

'Nor's this Veeney what's-her-name.'

Sally smiled a trifle glumly. 'She probably will be after this, though.'

'So might you be.'

Sally laughed. 'I doubt it. Anyway I'll leave you in peace. It was just seeing it, I wanted to tell someone. You know how it is.'

'Yes,' said Dan. 'I know.' He looked so depressed that Sally suddenly heard herself saying, 'I don't suppose you fancy going to the cinema this afternoon?' Dan looked surprised. 'I would have loved to,' he said. 'I can't. I've er . . . I've arranged to see someone. I'm sorry.'

'Never mind,' said Sally, sick with embarrassment. 'Not to worry.'

'Some other time?'

'Yes. Some other time.'

It seemed an age before Patrick answered the phone. 'This is the Crichton residence. Admirable Crichton speaking.' Sally laughed. 'You sound just like an answerphone. Have you thought of auditioning for the Speaking Clock.'

There was a pause then Patrick said, 'Who is this?'

'Sally,' said Sally, abashed.

'Sally, darling. You're very perky for this time of the morning.'

'It's a quarter to twelve.'

'Is it? My God, so it is. And I haven't even had my first fart. What can I do for you, angel?'

'I've got the *Observer* here.'

'Have you indeed? Stay perfectly calm. What would you like me to do? Phone the Bill?'

'Patrick, what on earth are you on? It's a Sunday newspaper, in case you hadn't heard of it.'

'Oh, THAT *Observer*. Why didn't you say?'

'I didn't think it would be necessary. Anyway, there's an article about *The Firm* in it. You're mentioned.'

'Me? What does it say? Is there a photo? I hope to God they haven't got hold of that death mask my agent sent to René.'

'There's a picture of Marley.'

'Marley? What on earth for? Why isn't there a picture of me?'

'I don't know,' said Sally, beginning to feel deflated. 'There isn't one of me either, if that's any consolation.' There was a silence, followed by a bark of laughter. 'Darling, Sally. I shall rush out and get a copy. The *Observer*, you said?'

'Yes.'

'Thank you, my darling. Are you having a nice day off?'

'Yes,' said Sally. 'Lovely. Patrick . . .'

'Yes?'

'I was wondering if you fancied going to the cinema this afternoon? There's a French film at the . . .'

'I would *love* to, darling, but sadly I'm a bit tied up this afternoon. Another time?'

'Yes. Fine.'

'You're not upset, are you?'

'Why should I be upset? I often go to the cinema on my own. It doesn't bother me.'

'Don't you get dirty old men with floppy willies sitting next to you?'

'You just said you couldn't come.'

Patrick snorted with laughter. 'I tell you something, young Sally. I wish you were writing the scripts.' There was a noise in the background. Someone was hoovering. 'I must go,' said Patrick. 'That's the trouble with one day off a fortnight. There's so much you have to cram in. You're sure you don't mind going on your own?'

'Of course I don't. If I get desperate I can always ring Suzanne Chamberlain. She can explain to me what it's all about.' She waited for him to laugh. There was a pause, then Patrick cleared his throat self-consciously. 'I shouldn't do that, Sally my pet.'

'Why not?' asked Sally curiously. There was another pause. 'Actually, she's here with me,' said Patrick.

'Has René told you about the press conference?' asked Simon when Sally arrived next morning.

'No,' she replied, eyes widening. 'A press conference? When?'

'Tomorrow afternoon. It's more of a photo call really, so we can hit the tabloids before transmission starts. *Radio Times* is meant to be doing something, too. My agent's sorting out *Pebble Mill* and a couple of daytimes. The trailers start tonight.'

'Trailers?'

'Oh yes. It's all stops go from now on.'

'Simon,' came Rolo's voice from the other end of the hall. 'Could we have you, please, now. René's waiting to begin.' Patrick slapped him on the back. 'Once more unto the photocopying machine, dear boy, once more.' He turned to Sally. 'Morning, my precious. You didn't mind, did you, about yesterday?'

'No,' said Sally emphatically. 'Not at all. It was a jolly good film.'

'Not the film,' said Patrick, hunting for his handkerchief. 'Suzanne.'

I wouldn't mind if you didn't go on about it, thought Sally after Patrick had referred to the matter three times over lunch, each time averring the platonic nature of his interest and the overwhelming regret he felt for having turned down her invitation to the cinema.

Everyone was excited about the press conference and this had leant a certain zip to the morning's rehearsal. René had professed himself pleased – a rare event indeed, and had backed this up by suggesting they take a shortened lunch break so as to 'hack on' while the going was good.

'You coming for a drink?' asked Patrick when they finally broke. 'No, thanks, not tonight,' said Sally airily.

'Are you still cross with me?' Patrick endeavoured to look boyish.

'Of course I'm not, but I promised to do some shopping

for the old chap downstairs on my way home. He's had a fall and he's a bit stuck for things like that at the moment.'

Patrick nodded and gave her a quick peck on the cheek. 'You're such a kind person, Sally. I only hope you're around to take care of me when I'm old and infirm.'

'Oh I'm sure Suzanne's marvellous at all that,' said Sally breezily and hurried off. On the way home she stopped off and bought a pint of milk, some tea and several tins of soup.

Mr Davenport took a long time to answer his door. 'Oh, it's you, nurse,' he said.

'It's Sally, Mr Davenport, from upstairs. I just wondered if you needed any shopping. I brought you these.' She waved the carrier bag at him.

'That's very kind,' said Mr Davenport. 'Jennifer . . . She's a little bit deaf. Jen . . . the nurse has brought you some . . .' he took the bag and peered inside, 'tins.' Slowly he pottered across the room to the kitchen. Sally followed, somewhat at a loss. She watched as he extracted the various items and lined them up along the window sill beside a wedge of cheese and some blackening bananas.

'Would you like me to open some soup for you, Mr Davenport?' she asked.

Mr Davenport smiled and patted her arm. 'No, dear, thank you. I think I'll wait till my wife gets back. She's only popped out for a minute. Will you see yourself out? Don't mind the dog. He doesn't bite.'

'Is anything the matter?' Dan Chamberlain's voice, thick with embarrassment, took Sally by surprise. She was standing in the hall, crying noisily into the sleeve of her coat. 'No.' Hurriedly she wiped it across her face and fled up the stairs. Glancing back she saw Dan's troubled face gazing after her. She closed her door and sank down, leaning her head against it. 'Bugger,' she bellowed because she didn't like people to see her crying. 'Bugger,' because Mr Davenport would have to go into a home. 'Bugger,' because she was lonely too, and she would probably end up the same way.

She was not sure how long she had been there when the piece of grey notepaper slid under the door. She picked it up and looked at it. 'Bugger, Bugger and Bugger of Flat One would like to invite you for a drink.'

The phone rang. She reached over and hoicked the receiver off its perch. 'Yes?'

'Bugger here.'

Sally began to laugh. 'Which one?'

'Oh definitely Senior. Are you coming?'

'Now?'

'Yes.'

'Well, I . . .'

'See you in five minutes.'

'Erm . . .' Sally hesitated. 'I don't usually swear, you know. Not that loudly anyway.' There was a pause. 'I don't suppose you cry all that much either, do you?' Sally looked up and caught sight of herself in the mirror. 'No,' she said blankly. 'I try not to cry all that often.'

19

'Tea and sympathy,' said Dan, handing her a whisky. Sally took a huge gulp and shivered. 'Thanks.'

'Do you want to talk about it?'

'Not really. It's nothing. Just a weak moment. I'm a bit tired. Not long now till transmission. I think we're all a bit on edge.' Dan nodded.

'There's a press conference tomorrow,' she continued, 'not that anyone will want to interview me but the tension sort of rubs off on you, I suppose.'

'They might.'

'What?'

'Want to interview you. You're in it, aren't you?'

'You don't understand. Them wanting to interview me would be like *Panorama* interviewing John Major's charlady.'

'She'd be more interesting than him,' Dan observed.

'Yes, well perhaps that was a bad example. Oh, what does it matter anyway? We'll all end up dead or mad or worse.' She took another large gulp of whisky. Dan came and sat beside her. 'Is that why you were crying?'

'Why? Because I'll be dead one day? Or mad? I'm halfway there already, I sometimes think.'

'It's the "worse" I was thinking about.'

Sally sat back. 'I don't suppose there is much worse than that.'

'There's being alive and sane and unhappy.'

'Like ninety per cent of people, you mean?'

'You're such a pessimist.'

'No I'm not.'

'Would you say your glass was half empty or half full?'

Sally drained it.

'It's completely empty.'

Dan refilled it. 'I rest my case.'

Sally took another gulp. 'Spare me the homespun philosophy, please.'

Dan raised his eyebrows. 'Would I be right in thinking whisky makes you aggressive?' Sally shrugged. 'I don't know. I don't normally drink it.'

'In that case I should slow down a bit.' He went into the kitchen and came back with some bread and cheese. 'Have some of this.'

'I'm not hungry.'

'To please me.'

Sally buttered the bread and ate it. 'There.'

'Thank you.'

'You're easily pleased.'

'Unlike you.'

She put a lump of cheese in her mouth. 'This is very nice cheese. See, I'm easily pleased, too.'

'It's very expensive cheese,' said Dan. Sally stopped eating. 'Did you buy that cheese and stuff for Mr Davenport?'

Dan grimaced. 'What's he done with it?'

'It's on his window sill,' said Sally, the effects of the whisky suddenly neutralised. 'Oh God, what's going to happen to him?'

Dan put his arm round her. 'That's what it was, isn't it?'

Sally put her head in her hands. 'I feel so awful.'

'Why?' He squeezed her shoulder slightly. 'It isn't your fault. It really isn't.'

'Yes, but . . . I took some shopping in to him, just a few bits, and the nurse was right. He does think his wife's still alive. I even offered to make some soup for him and he said no, he wanted to wait till she got back. I mean he could starve down there.'

Dan looked away. 'I don't think he'll be there much longer. At least you did do something for him. I haven't seen our Mrs Crane turning up with a bag full of groceries. What's she trying to assess? How long he can go without food? At least you made an effort.'

Sally shook her head. 'I'm a fraud. A total utter fraud.'

'No you're not.'

'I am. Do you know why I bought those things? Because I didn't want to go for a drink with Patrick after rehearsal. So I said I had to do some shopping for Mr Davenport. If it hadn't been for that I wouldn't have given him a second thought. That's the kind of perfect neighbour I am. "Like a daughter". I'm about as much like a daughter as Regan and Goneril. Not like you. You do things for him without needing any reminders.' Dan sat silent, staring at his hands.

'I'd better be going.' She rose a little unsteadily. 'Thanks.'

Dan glanced up at her vaguely. 'For what?'

'For the drink . . . and everything. For being nice.'

'I'm not nice,' he replied abruptly. 'Not at all nice.'

Sally blushed. 'I think you are.' Dan's face relaxed slightly. 'You'd do the same for me. Wouldn't you?'

'I don't know,' said Sally. 'I'd like to think I would.' Dan got up and opened the door for her. 'I expect you'll get your chance before too long,' he said.

The phone was ringing as she got back in. It was Colin to let her know he had landed a part in a revival of *The Desert Song* which was going on a tour of the Channel Islands and counties 'north of Bedford'. 'That's marvellous. When do you start?'

'Monday week. I've had to bring forward *The Decameron*. Matthew's having hysterics. He's had to take over directing. Well, the strain of it all brought on one of my migraines. I don't think people realise, do they, quite how much running a company takes out of you?'

'I'm sure they don't. How long will you be on tour?'

'Twelve weeks. Three weeks rehearsal – in Camden Town – well, naturally they would pick the furthest corner of the earth, wouldn't they? Then three days in Milton Keynes and off to glorious Guernsey.

'That'll be nice. The sea air will do you good.'

'In November? You must be joking. I'm terrified it will bring on my bronchitis.'

'Is it a good part?' asked Sally to avoid further details of Colin's health.

'Yes, excellent. I'm understudying the second lead. And a couple of the supporting roles. They would have liked me to play the lead riff but they needed a name.'

'Who have they got?' asked Sally.

'Oh I don't know. Someone from *The Bill*, I think.'

'So what are you actually playing?' There was a pause. 'Oh masses of things. I'm a sort of everyman – vagabond, nomad, merchant . . .'

Chorus, thought Sally. 'That sounds marvellous. Who's going to look after Resting Pieces while you're away?' There was another pause. This time tangible. 'I was wondering if you would be free?'

'Me? How can I, Colin? I'm working till next April.'

'Yes, but it's only television. You'll be free in the evenings most of the time. It's not like real acting, is it, television?'

Just don't ever ask me to mention your name to the director, thought Sally. 'Even so, Colin. I'm dreadfully sorry but I couldn't take it on.'

'Why not?'

'Because I lack your experience.'

Colin acknowledged the truth of this. 'Still, it would be a good opportunity for you to learn a bit about directing. Nobody would expect you to be up to my standard.'

'Why can't Matthew take over?' interrupted Sally, waiting to be informed that he had once more fled the nest.

'Matthew's coming with me,' answered Colin as though it were the silliest question in the world. 'Poor love. He needs a holiday. Anyway we wouldn't want to be parted for twelve weeks, would we?'

'You have before,' said Sally a little unkindly. Colin sniffed. 'It's hard for people like you to understand,' he said.

'What's so peculiar about me?'

'Nothing, but you've never been in love, have you?'

Sally looked at the telephone and contemplated throwing it across the room. 'I'm sorry I can't help you out,' she said and replaced the receiver.

Tuesday brought not only the vaunted press conference, but the arrival of 'Melanie Rinseworth', who turned out to be neither respected classical actress nor, as more widely anticipated, pill-popping junkie from Australian soap, but an ex-weather girl from Southern TV who had lately turned to acting via a series of games shows and a part in a children's Christmas special.

Her name was Gaby Chivers and though very friendly, it soon became clear to everyone that she was also exceedingly thick. Her acting, as Patrick described it, was of the 'postal course' variety, consisting of a long series of humming and throat-clearing, followed by an even longer discussion on motivation. René was extremely patient for the first hour, listening with a half smile as she explained why she didn't think she would be carrying a handbag to visit her lover, even though ostensibly on her way to the shops, and how she didn't see Melanie as the kind of person who would accept a cotton handkerchief from a stranger, albeit one with whom she was about to go to bed. She was forced to give way on the second issue when René explained that it was a budgetry decision, in view of the number of hankies got through per episode, that they be of the recyclable variety. The handbag, however, never appeared, causing endless problems in future episodes as Melanie's costumes were altered to conceal keys, credit cards and photos of lovers past.

Gaby was a health freak, plainly a leftover from her days on the roof of the Meteorological Office. She not only began rehearsals with a session of press-ups and cancan kicks, but seemed to be under the impression that the others would want to join her. Even Drewe who regularly attended a gym was seen to back away when she suggested he partner her in a series of backflips.

'If she put half as much energy into speaking her lines as she does into putting her feet in her mouth we might get somewhere,' growled Patrick at coffee break. On top of this Gaby was planning to get pregnant and seemed to be under the impression that the rest of the females in the cast would want to do so too. She showed them diagrams of expanding uteri with little arrows showing the way a developing foetus would turn during the course of its gestation.

'Honestly!' snorted Stephanie as she escaped into the yard for a cigarette. 'What does she think we are, brood mares?'

'She didn't half have a go at me,' Veeney complained, for once at one with her. 'Something about I'd never conceive if I smoked. I told her I didn't want to but she still kept on.'

'Do you think I could pinch one of your cigarettes, please, Veeney?' came Penny's timid voice. 'I'll pay you back at lunch time.'

René broke early for lunch. The press were due at two and it became clear fairly early in the morning that unless Stephanie could leave to have her hair done, Simon to buy a new shirt and Veeney to have a septic spot on her ear lanced the enterprise would get off to a very sticky start. Patrick disappeared to the studio to collect some photos of himself in costume which left only Marley who had scenes of any length to go through. At this point René acknowledged defeat and abandoned the rehearsal, admonishing everyone to be back at a quarter to two and on no account to mention fork lift trucks, melting pyjamas or fishing holidays to any member of the press.

'Isn't it exciting?' chortled Marley as she and Sally sat in the pub.

'Yes,' said Sally who rather wished she had been given the afternoon off.

'I'm a silly old woman,' continued Marley, patting her hand. 'I should be over all this at my age, but I can't help getting excited. I do like all these journalist people. I know people say horrid things about them, how they get their stories and so forth, but I've always found them terribly sweet. And the girls are always so pretty, don't you find? That's the thing about being an actress, isn't it? You never stop noticing other women's looks. In case there's something you can pick up on. I remember working with Sybil Thorndike and she must have been well into her fifties, but she had the prettiest nails I've ever seen. In the end I couldn't bear it any longer, I asked her what she used. 'Olive oil,' she said. 'Soak them in olive oil. You'll never have another loose cuticle.' So I took her advice and look.' She displayed a carefully manicured hand. 'Olive oil. Who'd have thought of that?'

'The old remedies are often the best,' Sally agreed, keeping her hands tucked firmly under the table.

'Oh look. There's that lovely Gaby.' Marley flapped wildly

till Gaby, who was lecturing the barman on the dangers of microwaved sausage rolls, noticed and came bouncing over to join them.

'There we are,' beamed Marley, squeezing herself up into the corner. 'Isn't this nice? How are you settling in, dear? I hope we're not too much for you?'

Gaby grinned toothily. 'Crumbs, no. I'm loving it. I'm just full of admiration for the way you all deal with your lines. You know, I mean, how do YOU feel, Sally, when you take the coffee in and John's in there, just sobbing like that?'

'I'm getting fairly used to it,' said Sally warily. 'He's been doing it for four episodes now.'

'Yes, and that's the marvellous thing. You *look* as though you're used to it. Now how do you manage to recreate that feeling of, you know, boredom, every time? I think it's incredibly clever.'

'Oh, Sally's a marvellous little actress,' Marley broke in. 'She knows how to listen, you see. Not many people can do that.'

Gaby nodded thoughtfully. 'I try never to listen to the other characters. That way it gives me a bit of extra time to internalise my thought patterns before I speak.' Even Marley was silenced by this.

They got back to find Rolo and Penny feverishly setting chairs. 'René wants it to look informal,' Rolo explained, replacing René's usual chair with one marked 'Director'.

Veeney was in the kitchen dabbing at her ear with a piece of cotton wool. 'It won't stop bleeding bleeding,' she wailed. 'What am I going to do? I'll look like something out of a bleeding horror movie.'

'Put it above your head,' said Marley solicitously.

Veeney gazed at her dubiously. 'Like cut it off, you mean?'

'I think Marley means turn your head on its side,'

Sally intervened, 'then the blood will run back towards your heart.'

'Ugh!' said Veeney, but she did as suggested, installing herself with a cushion at the head of the table where she lay slumped like a latter-day John the Baptist, much to the annoyance of Stephanie who had had an auburn rinse and clearly regarded Veeney's behaviour as a ruse to distract attention from herself.

Everyone was back, as ordered, at a quarter to two, Simon looking particularly dapper in an Aztec patterned shirt and green cravat. 'What do you think?' he asked Patrick, whose dress sense he admired. 'Very Noël Coward,' said Patrick. Simon removed the cravat.

'The Press' turned out to be two photographers and four journalists. This, George later pointed out to Sally, was a very respectable turnout for Cricklewood. One of the photographers was freelance and the other was from the *Radio Times*.

René, whose concession to the importance of the occasion had been an extra Valium with his doughnut, was chatting cheerfully to a very tall woman with *Today* attached to her lapel. When everyone was settled he raised his hand for silence. 'Ladies and Gentlemen, we're very privileged to have with us this afternoon several ladies and gentlemen of the Press, so please bear with me if I spend a few moments explaining the purpose of this little meeting. As I'm sure you all know, *The Firm* has already excited considerable interest – the *Observer*, just this week, ran a feature on one of our stars,' he gestured graciously to Marley. Marley beamed back like the winner of Pass the Parcel. 'And I don't think it would be immodest to say that when we have representatives from such hallowed journals as *Today*, the *Mail on Sunday*,' a small man with a moustache raised an acknowledging finger, 'the *Daily Mirror*,' René indicated a younger man with candid blue eyes, 'and of course,' he consulted his notes, 'the *Jewish*

Chronicle, it must be clear to everyone that *The Firm* is going to be the Big One for the autumn season and, dare I say it, for some little time to come.' He paused. The cast didn't know whether to applaud or look demure. They cleared their throats. Veeney, who had taken several painkillers, appeared to have fallen asleep on her cushion. Stephanie kicked her sharply under the table. Veeney opened one eye and closed it again. Dilys was staring stonily ahead, Hazel, next to her, was crocheting a very smart evening bag, her gold thread flashing as she worked.

The tall woman spoke. She was Australian. 'What we'd like to do now, if that's OK, is ask a few general questions, chat a bit about the individual roles, etcetera, and then Chris here can get some piccies. That suit you, Ren?'

'That's fine. Super,' said René who would normally have killed anyone who abbreviated his name.

'Right,' said the woman. 'Now I've read the press hand-out and it seems to me you've got a very interesting story running here.' They all warmed to her. 'Lots of family interest, drama, a poignant love affair and of course, you're dealing with current issues – small businesses, unemployment, the threat of bankruptcy which, let's face it, is something more and more people are facing.' They all tutted in agreement. 'So,' she smiled a feline smile, 'Patrick, if I could turn to you first, as the star,' there was a rustle from the others, 'or perhaps I should just call you "lead man"?'

'Star will do,' said Patrick. Everyone laughed. The woman smiled. 'OK. So how does it feel to be back in work after how many years is it, out of the limelight?'

Patrick's cheek twitched infinitesimally before he turned on her his most bewitching smile. 'Interesting you should ask me that,' he purred. 'Because, as I expect your colleagues know if you don't, I have never been out of work for more than six weeks during my entire career. Out of the "limelight"? Yes, I suppose I have been, if you call touring the continent of Africa with *Othello*, playing *Hamlet* to audiences of three thousand in New Delhi or directing an Ayckbourn trilogy in Japan "out of the limelight", then hands up,' his hands rose in supplication, 'I plead guilty.'

There was a pause. The man with a moustache waved his pencil. 'I have a question for Steph. May I call you Steph?' Stephanie inclined her head. 'You play a lesbian in this serial, is that right?' Stephanie opened her mouth to speak but the man continued, 'How do you feel about the rights of homosexual couples to adopt kiddies? Should they be allowed to do it, or is this carrying equal opportunities too far?'

A look of horror ravaged Stephanie's face. René leant forward. 'I think Stephanie is as open-minded as any of us when it comes to individual freedoms. The story we're dealing with here in no way impinges on the choices open to consenting adults. We would not, however, wish to convey the impression that any child would be put at risk by watching any episode of *The Firm*. This is a family show. There is something for everyone. No one need feel threatened by its content. That is why,' he continued with considerable emphasis, 'it is going out at eight o'clock in the evening. I hope that answers your question.'

The man with blue eyes had been watching Veeney for some moments. 'I'd like to ask Miss Rogers a couple of things, if I may,' he said in politely modulated tones. Stephanie again kicked Veeney but not so hard. 'It's you he wants to talk to,' she hissed, endeavouring to smile at the same time. Veeney grunted and lifted her head carefully off the cushion. The young man smiled. 'I believe you come to acting via the rock circuit?'

'That's right,' Veeney suppressed a yawn. 'How do you find the acting life? Is it harder or easier than being out on the road?'

'You gotta be joking,' said Veeney, pinching hard on her

ear. The young man laughed to show that he was not. 'It's harder,' said Veeney. 'There's more discipline. On a gig I can get up, do my stuff – long as I want, little as I want, it's my stuff, right? Here I've got to learn my lines, I've got to turn up on time, rehearse. The studio, we're in it for two days, we're filming, up to our necks in mud half the time, two days. The rest of the time it's rehearse, rehearse, rehearse.'

'So you prefer the open road? Sex, drugs and rock'n'roll?'

'No,' said Veeney. 'That's all right when you're young, but I'm twenty-three. I can't be bumming around Europe for the rest of my life. I want to settle down, go legit, you know, RCS and all that.'

'How do you feel about the starving nations?' asked the moustache. 'I feel rotten,' said Veeney, 'same as everyone else.'

'Don't you feel guilty?' put in the tall woman. 'I mean you must be earning a fortune compared, say, with a girl of your age in Mozambique.'

'Yes,' said Veeney.

'"Yes" you do feel guilty, or "yes" you're earning a fortune?'

'Both.'

'How do you reconcile your guilt with your affluence?' Veeney laid her head back on the cushion. 'I get stoned,' she said. René put his head in his hands.

It was Marley's turn next. Due, presumably, to her popularity, and also to the fact that it was impossible to get an unkind word out of her, the reporters had to content themselves with several well-worn anecdotes and a recipe for caraway seed buns which brought the first genuine look of animation into the *Jewish Chronicler*'s eyes since he had arrived.

Simon was asked if he did his own stunts which produced stifled guffaws from George and Patrick and a look of near panic from René. He bluffed his way out of it by saying he didn't want to reveal too much of the plot in advance and viewers would have to tune in and form their own opinions.

'How does your wife feel,' asked the woman from *Today*, 'about you landing a whopping great part like this? I understand she's an actress?' She consulted her notes. 'Jane Murton? Is that right?'

'Jenny,' said Simon. 'She's delighted. Naturally. My good fortune is her good fortune and the other way round.'

'Hardly,' said the journalist, smiling. 'I should think it's pretty galling to be married to someone who's about to become a household name if you haven't made it yourself. How's she going to feel if you start getting fan letters and proposals of marriage from total strangers?'

'Jenny and I have a very good relationship,' said Simon rigidly at which point Penny was seen to disappear into the kitchen.

Hazel and luckily, Dilys, did not seem to be of interest to anyone. Gaby was momentarily thrown when the man from the *Jewish Chronicle* asked if she'd forseen the hurricane of nineteen eighty-seven in which, it transpired, he had lost two greenhouses, but she pulled herself together and informed him that plants grown under glass were artificially sensitive to temperature fluctuations. The man asked no more questions.

The moustache knew George from other programmes and was more concerned in getting racing tips from him than finding out how he felt about world famine.

'Now,' the Australian woman turned to Drewe. 'Drewe, isn't it? You're a new face to our screens and a pretty sexy one at that.' Drewe curled his lip as he had seen Keanu Reeves do during interviews. 'Tell me a bit about yourself,' invited the journalist. 'How did you come to get the part of . . . let me refresh my memory . . .'

'Tholley Thedgewick,' said Drewe.

René twitched.

The woman leaned forward. 'Ah yes. And he's the foreman, am I right? A bit of a ladies' man? Tell me, was there much competition for the role? I bet there was.'

'I saw over fifty actors,' René broke in as Drewe struggled to uncurl his lip. 'There was a lot of interest in the rôle.'

'Ah yes. Didn't I hear Sean Bean mentioned at one point?' She raised a quizzical eyebrow. René met her gaze steadily. 'Certainly he was considered.' The woman smiled. 'But you opted for Drewe?'

'I did.'

'What was it that made him so right?' All three male reporters were now eyeing the actor with some disbelief. 'He has that extra something,' said René unflinching, 'as you will see when transmission begins.'

'I can hardly wait,' said the woman. Everybody smiled.

Penny brought coffee while the photographers set up.

'Who are you?' The tall woman descended upon Sally while they were consuming it.

'Oh I'm just the secretary,' she answered cautiously.

'The director's?'

'No,' Sally laughed. 'John Christie's. I dispense coffee and paper clips at times of crisis.'

'Is it true,' the woman's voice dropped conspiratorially, 'that Veeney Rogers spent six months in a drug rehabilitation centre?' Sally looked at her wide-eyed. 'Not as far as I know. Whatever gave you that idea?'

'But you know she's René Havers' stepsister?'

Sally felt her jaw dropping. She wrenched it into a cheery smile. 'Of course.'

'Doesn't it bother you?'

'Why should it? We're all family here,' she trilled unconvincingly.

The woman tried another tack. 'I expect you've heard that George Bennett did a spell in Wormwood Scrubs?'

Sally swallowed. 'Yes,' she lied unflinchingly. 'That's how he got his agent.'

'I daresay there've been quite a few quarrels amongst the members of the cast, haven't there?'

'What about?'

'Oh come on. You've got what, six main characters all vying for prime air time. Don't tell me there hasn't been a bit of bitching about who's getting all the best lines.'

'If there has I've certainly never come across it,' said Sally. 'And I've been here throughout.' The reporter moved away. Sally saw Drewe's face light up as she approached him. Her heart sank.

When they had left the cast gathered gloomily round the table. Only Marley felt that they had all been 'nice as pie'. She had given the *Jewish Chronicle* man her address and was going send him a recipe for kosher flapjacks she had got tucked away somewhere at home.

'Slaughter.' Patrick spoke for them all. 'They're going to fucking slaughter us.'

René, who had been through this sort of thing more often than most, was surprisingly phlegmatic. 'Always remember, it doesn't matter what they write so long as they write SOMETHING,' he consoled them.

'That's all right for you, darling,' drawled Stephanie, 'but I'm going to be crucified. Gay Lib, Women against Rape . . . I don't even get to look at a woman till episode six. Up till then it's all him.' She jerked her head in Drewe's direction. They no longer made any pretence of not loathing each other. 'Christ, after three weeks in the sack with him I'm surprised I don't get off with a koala bear.'

'You certainly smell like one,' responded Drewe in an unusual spurt of repartee.

'There's no point in quarreling amongst ourselves,' said

Patrick gravely. 'That's the sort of thing they'd love. The next thing there'll be a mole in our midst. How do you think they got hold of that stuff about *Coronation Street*?' There was general agreement to this. René tried to get them back to rehearsal but everyone was so dejected that he could do little more than change a few moves before dismissing them all early, with a strict injunction that there were to be no further references to the conference during rehearsal.

'By the way,' said Patrick just before they broke, 'are we doing anything on the first night?'

'Hiding under the couch?' suggested Simon.

'What like?' asked Hazel.

'Well, a celebration of some sort. We ought to do something to mark it, don't you think?'

'Let's have a party,' said Veeney whose ear was feeling much better.

'Oh yes,' enthused Marley. 'What a lovely idea. We could all get together somewhere and watch the first episode and then we could have a party. Why don't you all come to me? Yes, yes. That would be lovely. I could ask that sweet man from the *Jewish Chronicle*?'

'I think perhaps it had better be just cast,' suggested Patrick tactfully.

Simon shifted awkwardly in his chair. 'I'm afraid I won't be able to make it,' he murmured.

'Oh, go on,' Veeney agitated. 'We've got to all be there.'

'I promised Jenny we'd watch it together. You know,' he shrugged apologetically.

'Bring her,' Patrick clapped his hands. 'When I said "just cast", I didn't mean not wives and that. I just meant not outsiders.' He raised his hand. 'Yes I know he was a lovely man, Marley, my love, but so is everyone you meet. Let's just say wives, husbands and lovers. October the fifteenth. Your place, if you're sure that's OK?'

'Oh yes,' beamed Marley, excitement shining from her eyes. 'Seven thirty for eight? Would that suit everyone?'

'What about food?' asked Hazel eagerly. 'I can make a few things if you like.' Patrick shook his head. 'We should get a caterer. That's the simplest. Give me a tenner each and I'll sort it out. Better let me know the numbers, though. We don't want to run out of booze.'

'I thought I might ask Suzanne,' he murmured casually to Sally as they were putting on their coats. 'Why not?' she responded lightly, her heart sinking. She could just imagine how Suzanne would react to a party of about-to-be-slaughtered thespians. Still it was none of her business.

'Who's Sally bringing?' asked Marley, tucking an arm through each of theirs. Sally hesitated. 'I'll probably just come by myself.' Patrick's eyebrows rose. 'Dan busy that night, is he? Or don't you think he would enjoy it?'

Sally took a deep breath. 'I'll ask him. He's got quite a lot on at the moment.'

'But he wouldn't want to miss your first night, surely?'

A blast of fury swept through her. 'Actually, Patrick, I was thinking of you. He feels very responsible for Suzanne since she was discharged. He wouldn't want to think you were toying with her affections.'

'Discharged?' repeated Patrick, struggling to retain his calm.

'Oh, don't worry,' said Sally soothingly, 'so long as you haven't made any false promises I'm sure you'll be perfectly OK.'

20 ∫

The week passed. Temperatures were running high as the transmission date approached. Despite René's strictures the conversation at rehearsal scarcely left the topic of the abominable journalists. The cast's fears grew with every day that passed, firstly that they would be misrepresented and then, as the weekend approached and nothing had appeared, that they would not be represented at all. They began to see the sense in René's words 'better bad publicity than no publicity'.

No one was very happy with the photographers either. Veeney swore blind that the *Radio Times* man had taken a clandestine close-up of the blood clot on her ear, at which Stephanie, who had not been called for a close-up at all, was heard to remark that it was probably her best feature.

On Friday Marley came rushing in, panting with excitement. 'I knew they wouldn't let us down,' she gabbled, sinking into René's chair. 'Look. Come and look at this.' They gathered round. Marley turned proudly to page five of the *Jewish Chronicle*. Sure enough there, over a recipe for caraway seed buns and two lines about the transmission date of *The Firm* was a smiling picture of her, flanked by half of Patrick's torso and Simon's disembodied elbow. 'It's a start,' said George philosophically, before producing a syndicated article about his racing tips from a copy of *Sporting Life*.

On Saturday there was a whole column in the features' section of *Today*, managing to convey the impression that the entire cast had been picked from Care in the Community schemes and let loose in the graveyards of southern England. Or so Patrick interpreted it. This was not entirely fair since the woman whose name turned out to be Magda Farraday, seemed quite well disposed towards the serial on the whole, saying it was time Majestic turned out something that didn't challenge the boredom threshold of an anchorite. There was a very small photo of the whole cast grinning inanely over René's shoulder, with the caption, 'Death, Lust and Ruin in Paper Factory Saga'. 'All that's missing is the royal corgi,' said Simon cheerfully. His agent had phoned the night before to say they wanted to interview him on *Kaleidoscope*.

Sunday was even better. The *Mail* had done a half-page spread, featuring a very flattering photo of Stephanie in a cat suit and at least ten years out-of-date, and a rather nice picture of Dilys on a neurotic-looking stallion, also clearly not the work of the freelance on Monday. 'That horse is as stoned as she is,' Patrick whispered to Sally, passing her a copy of the next week's *Radio Times* which featured him and Marley on the cover, weeping over the grave of the late lamented founder.

On Tuesday Michael Snelcott rang her in great excitement to tell her that she was needed for filming the following day and that he was sorry about the short notice but that he had been most firm with them and that it would not happen again.

'The filming?' asked Sally, disappointed.

'No, no. The notice. Lack of it. How's it going, by the way?'

'Very well. You know it goes out next week?'

'Does it? Good god, when?'

'The fifteenth. Eight o'clock. It's been in all the papers.'

'Has it? That's jolly good. I see that's a Friday. I'm in Bournemouth. I'll have to tape it. Going all right, you say?'

'Yes,' said Sally, hurt by his indifference. 'It's on the front of the *Radio Times*.'

'Is it? That can't be bad, can it? Why don't you pop a copy in the post to me? I might be able to make something of it.' Sally put the phone down resolving to sack her agent if she ever got the whiff of another offer.

It was hard to decide whether it always rained on location or it always rained on Wednesdays. Either way they spent another miserable day sploshing in and out of the vans with Wendy and Jean alternately simpering and moaning as they sponged lumps of mud off everyone's costumes and powdered dripping noses between downpours.

Sally spent the day reading the new episodes. They were again unremarkable from her point of view except that it was now beginning to look as though Laura were the only sane character in *The Firm*. If he keeps it up at this rate, she thought, they'll all be dead by episode ten and the question of options won't arise. This prompted the sickening thought that this might indeed be the author's plan, but she banished it with the conclusion that even poignant silences, flashbacks and the transportation of large amounts of carbon paper could hardly keep the serial running for three further episodes without a single living character.

It appeared that Laura had now become the telephone confidante of both Dilys and Simon. Long patches of her scenes involved nodding her head into a receiver and saying 'Yes, I do understand', and 'Have you thought of speaking to him/her about it?' All of which seemed to give great comfort to the recipients who invariably finished by saying 'I'm so glad I've had a chance to talk to you about it', or 'you're such a brick, Laura', which made her feel a hundred and thirty years old.

The phone rang almost as soon as she got home. She snatched it up. It was Colin. 'Sally, my darling, how are you?'

'Fine,' said Sally suspiciously, her hand unconsciously pinning down the table.

'Not crumbling under the strain?'

'What strain?' Colin gave a tinkling laugh. 'Ah, we really are hardened now, I see. No, I've just seen the *Radio Times*. How about that! Front cover. Very impressive.'

'It's good, isn't it?' Sally enthused.

'It most certainly is. Any chance of a word in the director's ear? It sounds just the sort of thing I'd be right for, wouldn't you say?'

'In what capacity?'

'Oh, actor, actor. What do I know about television direction?'

'How's *The Desert Song* going?' she asked. 'You must be nearly through rehearsals.'

'Oh, fine, fine. Very well. Rodney, the director's a dream. So talented. Doesn't it make a change to work with a real pro?'

'Yes,' said Sally, wondering if Colin had ever heard of irony.

'I really feel he and I were meant to work together. We're on the same wavelength, you see. He hardly has to open his mouth and I know what he's going to say. That comes from being a director myself, of course. To be honest, I think he's rather glad I'm there. Sometimes some of the cast are a bit vague about what he's getting at so I have to take them aside and explain. It saves him so much time. I wouldn't be surprised if he asked me to step in while we're away on tour and just make sure things hang together OK.'

'I'm glad you're enjoying it,' said Sally.

'Yes, yes, I am. Well, I can't sit around gossiping all day. I just wondered if you'd got that cheque in the post for me yet?'

'What cheque?'

'The bill for the microwave. Eight pounds fifty or whatever it was.'

'It was six pounds fifty and I'm not paying it.'

'Why ever not? I think you'll find it was eight, by the way.'

'I won't, and since I'm not paying it it doesn't matter if it was ninety-eight.'

'It was nothing like that, I'm sure. Otherwise I'd have remembered. No, just make it a tenner and we'll call it quits.'

'Colin, I am not paying for an adaptor I don't want and don't need and incidentally, haven't got. It's nothing to do with me if the theatre's not properly wired and as for adding the taxi fare . . .'

'Resting Pieces is a co-operative, you know.'

'Only when it comes to paying the bills. In every other aspect it's a dictatorship.'

'I'm sorry you're reacting so badly.'

'I'm sorry too, Colin, but I'm afraid that's my final word.'

'I only hope you won't have cause to regret it.'

'I hope not too, Colin.'

'I might be able to squeeze you a couple of tickets for the opening night.'

'Where is it?'

'Milton Keynes. By the way, where did you find the vestal virgin?'

'What?'

'The redhead. At your dinner party.'

'Suzanne. Didn't you like her?'

'Well, she wouldn't be my choice for a desert island.'

'She's Dan's wife. I thought you realised.'

'Noooo. Really. Oh poor you. They didn't seem all that friendly.'

'They're getting divorced.'

'Oh well, that's all right then. Or weren't they before you cooked them that meal?'

'Don't be so mean,' said Sally, laughing. 'No, it's all a bit complicated. I'll tell you some other time – when I see you.'

'All right, my pet. Take care of yourself. Still doing those exercises?'

'Never a day passes.'

'Liar. And keep your eye on young Dan. Don't want him rushing off marrying another nun while your back's turned.'

'What rubbish you do talk, Colin.'

'I know. It keeps me sane. Cheque in the post?'

Sally sighed. 'Cheque in the post.'

Dan was less easy to talk to. 'Hullo?'

'It's Sally,' said Sally, feeling like a kitchen salesman.

'Oh. Hullo.'

'Hullo. Look, I know this won't interest you, and it doesn't matter a bit, but I'd said I'd ask you – knowing you wouldn't want to come, so don't worry about that— '

'I'm afraid you're losing me.'

'Yes, well, it's just we're having a bit of a first night party, on the first night – of the transmission, and Patrick and Marley, she's one of the actresses, the main one, really, – well, you saw her picture in the paper, didn't you? The one I showed you . . .'

'Marley Webb. I know who you mean.'

'Yes. Well, we're having a sort of party, but we're watching the episode first, at Marley's place. There'll be masses of actors and agents and so forth – pretty dull, really, if you're not into all that . . .'

'Why are you telling me this?' came Dan's anguished voice.

'You're invited.'

'Me? Who by?'

'Me, I suppose. But I don't think you'd like it.'

'Why not?'

'Because you've got to watch *The Firm* first.'

'How long is it?'

'Fifty minutes.'

'I could survive that.'

'Yes, but . . .'

'But what?'

Sally took a breath. This was not going according to plan. 'Then you've got to tell everyone how good it was, and how marvellous they were. I don't think it's your sort of thing. Honestly.'

There was a silence. 'You don't want me to come, do you?'

'Yes, yes, of course I do. I just don't think you'd enjoy it. And it's a Friday,' she added with some desperation.

'What's so special about Fridays?'

'Well, isn't it your class, or something?'

'Oh, that,' said Dan. 'I've given it up.'

Friday the fifteenth of October arrived. If a soothsayer had been available he would surely have been found that day on Cricklewood High Street warning its inhabitants of dire confluences in the stars.

There had been a couple more articles in the dailies, mainly about Marley, and a snippet in *Television Today* which had called them a cast of unknowns, much to the fury of Stephanie and Patrick. *Woman's Own* had run a feature on Gaby which had further incensed the females in the cast and seriously dented René's popularity, such as it was, since it was perfectly clear he had known from day one who was to play the coveted role. As if to compensate he let them go home early.

Walking along Cricklewood High Street, Sally looked around her at the shops, the people, the autumn sunshine tinged with mist. This is Before, she thought. And tomorrow is After.

'Oh!'

Mrs Crane was standing in the hall writing feverishly in a notebook. She looked up as Sally entered and the two of them gazed at each other with mutual suspicion. Mrs Crane spoke first. 'I've interviewed Mr Davenport.' Sally's eyebrows rose. 'He seems to be in some distress.' She waited, obviously expecting a reaction. Sally said nothing. Mrs Crane sighed. 'So. There it is.' She tucked her notebook into her jacket pocket and strode past Sally and out of the front door.

'Mr Davenport . . . Mr Davenport . . .' Sally tapped again at the door and waited. Eventually she heard his plodding footsteps. The door opened. Mr Davenport was dressed to go out. He had on a thick overcoat, scarf, trilby hat and gloves. 'There you are,' he said a trifle impatiently. 'I was going to go without you.'

Sally smiled uncertainly. 'Where are you off to, Mr Davenport?'

The old man shrugged irritably. 'They don't tell you anything, do they? I've got my passport.' He tapped his inside pocket.

'Mr Davenport,' Sally took his arm and tried to turn him round, 'can we just step back inside for a minute?' Mr Davenport looked at his watch. 'I haven't got long.'

'I know. Just for a minute.' The old man allowed himself

to be steered back into the flat. 'Let's sit down, shall we?' Sally sat down and waited to see what he would do. For a moment he stood uncertainly in the centre of the room then suddenly smiled and began to unbutton his coat. 'Let's have some light in here.' He pottered over and switched on a lamp. 'That's better. The evenings are really drawing in now. I'll just put my things away.' He removed his hat, scarf and gloves and hung them in a cupboard with his overcoat. 'I've had a visitor,' he said cheerfully, turning up the gas fire and warming his hands beside it.

'Who was that?' prompted Sally, watching him anxiously.

'I forget her name. Craig, Grahame . . . something like that. She was from the Welfare. Came to see how I was getting on after my accident. I banged my head, you know. Fell over in the hall. Nasty bump. Better now. Much better. Still get the odd headache. You expect it at my age. I'm forgetting my manners. Would you like a cup of tea, dear?'

'Let me make it,' said Sally, leaping up.

'You know where everything is, don't you?' called Mr Davenport. 'There are some biscuits somewhere.' Sally waited for him to mention his dead wife, but he said nothing more. When she returned he was studying the television page of the local paper. 'Tonight's the night, then?' he said briskly.

Sally frowned. 'I'm sorry?'

'Tonight. Your big night. Episode One. I shall be watching that. Planning to celebrate, are you? I hope we aren't going to be mobbed with all those reporter folk once you're famous.' He chuckled delightedly as he took the cup from her. Sally found she was laughing too, from sheer relief. 'So what did your visitor want, Mr Davenport? Or shouldn't I ask?'

Mr Davenport shrugged dismissively. 'Wanted to chuck me out as far as I could gather. Had some stupid idea I couldn't manage on my own. Just because I'd had a knock on the head. I said to her, I said, "we had a lot worse than that in the gunners. I used to crack my head on the cross beams every time we went on duty."' He leant forward conspiratorially. 'They used to say they couldn't start a shift till I'd called Hitler all the words you've never heard of.' He chuckled again.

Sally felt a wave of relief. 'Are you managing all right, though, Mr Davenport? If there's anything you need, you've only got to ask – shopping or whatever. If I'm not here I'm sure Dan – across the way, will help. You only have to say . . .'

The old man shook his head. 'That's very kind, dear, but I like to keep active. I know I get a bit confused sometimes. It's age. Can't do anything about that. I had a bit of a knock, you know. Bumped my head. Not his fault. Should have looked where I was going. Doing anything special tonight? Your big night, isn't it?'

Sally smiled. 'We're having a bit of a get together. Nothing fancy.'

Mr Davenport got up. 'Quite right too. Times are hard. I'm having soup. Soup and a bit of cheese. Can't beat it.' He looked round the room. 'Yes,' he said firmly. 'Not his fault.' Sally stood up. 'Would you like me to get the soup ready for you?'

'No, dear, no. I like to keep active. No, you get off to your party. Behave yourself, mind. Or if you can't be good, be careful.'

Sally smiled. 'I'll do my best.'

21

They arrived at Marley's to find the party in full swing. Noise and laughter were drifting down to the street from the third floor flat where someone had opened the huge bay windows and stuck a notice, 'Queue Here To Jump' on the heavy brocade curtain.

Marley greeted them, looking like a Gaiety girl in primrose silk with feather boa. 'Sally, darling, come in. Who is this?' She gazed admiringly up at Dan. Sally introduced them. Dan took her hand. 'I've seen you in lots of things,' he said.

'And I know your face from somewhere,' Marley responded, peering more closely. 'Weren't you in *Taggart*? You played the sergeant's younger brother in that one about the greyhounds.'

'I'm a builder,' said Dan.

'Yes, that's right. You'd got some shady deal going with the council.'

'Dan's not an actor,' said Sally.

'Isn't she wicked?' beamed Marley. 'I bet you don't say things like that about her.' She was swept away by René who wanted to introduce her to his own agent, a puffy-faced man drinking orange juice and not enjoying it much, by the look of him.

Sally scoured the room nervously. She had not mentioned that Patrick had invited Suzanne to Dan and was bitterly regretting it. What an idiot she was. Now she would have to brazen it out. The obvious thing would be to pretend she had known nothing about the arrangement, but if she did Patrick was sure to drop her in it, intentionally or otherwise, which would make her look more deceitful than ever. The alternative would be to behave as though Suzanne's presence were of so little consequence to her that it had gone straight out of her mind. This would require a degree of acting skill that Sally, even in her wildest dreams, was not sure she possessed.

Rolo appeared from the kitchen. 'Ah, Sally . . . ' he hesitated. Sally felt her stomach clench, waiting to hear that she'd been cut from the series altogether. 'Help yourself to drinks,' he continued, before rushing off to help Penny who was struggling with the forty-inch television that had been hired for the occasion.

They fought their way to the drinks table, past Wellard Kenning and 'friend', a nervous young woman in spectacles whom he had clearly primed to guard the alcohol with her life. She was slithering up and down in front of the glasses like a goalkeeper defending a penalty. Dan elbowed her gently out of the way and secured them both some wine.

They looked out across the sea of faces. Sally felt she should introduce him to some more people but she was too nervous at the prospect of bumping into Suzanne.

Simon was there with his wife, Jenny, a pretty woman with dark intelligent eyes and a slightly worn expression. Penny was watching the couple furtively while she and Rolo set out chairs in an arc around the television. Once a Floor Manager, thought Sally.

Drewe Atkins was leaning languidly against the marble mantelpiece talking to a fair youth in stripey waistcoat and baggy pantaloons. 'I see Drewe's brought his pageboy.' Sally leapt at the sound of Patrick's voice. There was still no sign of

Suzanne. 'Evening, Dan,' said Patrick cheerfully. 'Glad you could make it.' His lips brushed against Sally's cheek. 'You look nice, Miss Mouse.'

'Where's . . . ?' Sally squeaked in character.

'Oh, about somewhere.' Patrick smiled, passing Dan a dish of vegetarian pâté. 'Have you tried this stuff?'

'No,' said Dan, regarding it nervously.

'It's bloody awful,' said Patrick. 'Veeney insisted. Hullo, George.'

George Bennett nodded and indicated his companion. 'This is the wife, by the way. Joan. Joan, this is . . . ' he stared at Dan curiously.

'Dan,' said Dan. 'Dan Chamberlain.'

'Who do you play?' asked George. 'Sorry, mate. I haven't read the new stuff yet.'

'I'm with Sally,' said Dan. George turned to her delighted. 'So they're writing a bloke in for you now, are they? Worth sharing the cab with old Skinflint after all then. Good for you.'

'Dan's not an actor,' flustered Sally.

'Are you going to put up with this from a mere female?' demanded George. 'Next thing she'll be telling you how to play the part. By the way, has anyone seen Bendy Knees. I should have thought she'd be here organising the warm-up.'

'He means Gaby Chivers,' Sally explained to Dan. 'She joined the cast this week.'

'Didn't she used to be on the weather forecast?' asked Dan in some confusion.

'Yes. And if you ask me she should have stayed there because she knows f. all about acting,' Patrick broke in.

'She wasn't much good at weather either,' Dan confirmed.

'Hello, everyone. Sorry we're late,' came Gaby's voice, bang on cue.

'God defend me from enthusiasts,' muttered Patrick and retreated to the kitchen.

It was easy to see what he meant as Gaby and her man, who was pallid to the point of extinction, scurried round the room, she squealing at the perfection of everyone's outfits, Marley's furnishings, the colour of the curtains, the contents of the canapés, he nodding like a backseat bulldog as he trotted dutifully behind.

Sally pulled herself together and introduced Dan to Simon, and Veeney who had just arrived with the Haemorrhoids. She had spotted Jeff Wilkins in a corner, still looking pasty as he stared disconsolately into a glass of whisky. 'That's our producer,' she murmured. 'Would you like to meet him?' But Dan was not listening. He was staring over the tallest Haemorrhoid's shoulder as though he had been struck by lightning. Wretchedly Sally followed his eyes. Suzanne was standing by the window, looking undeniably stunning in a silver grey dress and long metallic earrings, her hair falling in cultured disarray around her paper-white face.

She was talking to a small fat man whose nose was only separated from her cleavage by the barrage of peanuts he was firing into his mouth. 'You didn't tell me you'd invited Suzanne,' said Dan, his eyes not moving from his wife.

'It was a surprise,' said Sally forlornly. For some reason she felt more disappointed that he wasn't angry than if he had been. 'Why don't you go and talk to her?' she added lamely. 'I need to have a word with Penny, anyway.'

She found Penny slumped in an armchair. 'I just wondered what time we have to be in on Monday?' Penny tore her eyes away from Simon and Jenny Peyter and tried to focus on what Sally had said to her. 'I'm not sure. Usual time, I think. I'll have to check with Rolo.'

'This is a very nice flat, isn't it?' Sally ploughed on.

'Edwardian, would you think?' Penny stared at her as though she were quite mad. 'I don't know. It's a bit before my time.'

'The cornices are probably more Victorian.'

'I should think she's quite a bit older than him, wouldn't you?' broke in Penny, unable to contain herself any longer.

'No, much younger. I know that for a fact. She's only twenty-eight,' sighed Sally.

'Twenty-eight!' Even someone as gullible as Penny found this a bit hard to stomach. 'I'm sure you've got that wrong. Are you sure he didn't say thirty-eight?'

'No, of course he didn't. *He's* only thirty-six.'

'He told me thirty-two,' said Penny in a wounded voice.

'I didn't know you knew Dan,' said Sally, her heart beginning to thump.

'Who?'

'Dan. The man I came with. My neighbour.'

'Oh him. No, I don't. Is he your neighbour?'

'Yes.'

'That's nice.' Sally perceived that in terms of small talk, Penny was a very poor choice. She looked around desperately, avoiding the corner where she knew Dan and Suzanne would now be rekindling their marriage. Why she cared so much she didn't know. They were the only two outsiders here. It made sense they should migrate towards each other, even setting aside the fact that they had been together for eleven years already.

There was a tap on her arm. It was Marley. 'Sally, my pet, I don't want to interfere in any way, but I wonder if you should go and rescue your Dan.'

'Oh, I don't think so, Marley,' she responded with artificial brightness. 'I'm sure he can take care of himself, and anyway he isn't MY Dan. He's just a neighbour.' Marley gave a little smile. 'Of course he is, dear, but even so . . . Stephanie can be a bit overpowering if you don't know it's just her fun.'

'Stephanie?'

George Bennett raised his eyebrows in mock alarm. 'Do you want to borrow my knuckle-duster, love?' he asked, jerking his head to where Stephanie, in a dress slit to her waist from the top and her thigh from the bottom was inviting Dan to fasten the clasp of her brooch which had inexplicably come undone. Sally watched, fascinated, as Dan's wide fingers fiddled with the pin. She knew even as she watched what the outcome would be.

Stephanie's screams were lost, however, for at the precise moment that the pin pierced her flesh Patrick called for silence and announced that it was ten to eight. There was a general gasp as everyone took in the import of his words, then an unworthy stampede as they made first for the bar and then for the best seats.

'It was an accident,' Dan repeated awkwardly as Hazel applied TCP to Stephanie's palpitating bosom. Sally tried to look severe.

'Hullo, Sally. Got the giggles? I'm so sorry I haven't had time for a word.' Suzanne, still pursued by the dwarf toad, was bearing down on her, lips stretched in a tiny smile.

'Hullo, Suzanne. Are you enjoying yourself?' mumbled Sally, her cheeks flapping uncontrollably.

'Oh yes. It's very interesting. Actors are such fun, aren't they? How are you getting on, Danny? Everything OK?'

'Yes, thanks,' said Dan darkly, his eyes wandering threateningly over the toad.

'This is Frank,' said Suzanne. 'He's a merchant banker so, of course, we have a lot in common.'

'Really?' said Sally, the argument lost on her.

'We're neither of us actors,' Suzanne explained.

'Neither am I,' said Dan abruptly. Their eyes met. Sally looked away uncomfortably.

They sat at the back, being the only people present who really didn't want to be in the front. There was an immediate stand-off between Veeney and Stephanie because Veeney had reserved two seats for the Haemorrhoids and Stephanie wanted one of them for her agent, an angular woman in black who looked a worthy contender for the Addams Family.

Wendy Costume proved uncharacteristically forceful in evicting Jenny Peyter from her place in the second row. Simon endeavoured to protest on her behalf, but since he was already installed in the centre of the front row his late concern was not viewed with any seriousness.

Dilys, who had been quietly drinking herself into a stupor on a hall chair, had to be fetched and ushered to a seat between René and Jeff Wilkins.

An expectant hush filled the room. Patrick pressed the remote control. The commercials were already in progress when Gaby Chivers squeezed herself into a space beside Patrick and then had to retreat to the side as several people cried out at the size of her head.

'And now we present the first episode of a great new serial for autumn viewing,' came an announcer's voice.

'That's Rita Green,' screeched Gaby excitedly. 'She used to be at Southern, didn't she, Phil?' The bulldog nodded.

'*The Firm*, the story of one family's struggle to stay ahead in the unforgiving nineties.' The music swelled.

'I'm surprised she's moved to Central,' continued Gaby, oblivious. 'She had a lovely little cottage just outside Salisbury. What was the name of that village, Phil?'

'Shut up,' said Patrick through clenched teeth. Gaby gave a nervous little trill. 'Oh, silly me. I never can stop talking, can I, Phil?' Phil nodded. The titles rolled over an aerial shot of the industrial estate, homing in on the muddy enclosure that constituted Christie Stationery Inc.

'They've spelt ink wrong,' came Drewe's voice from the darkness. Everyone shushed. Dan blew his nose.

The episode started prosaically with a meeting between the brothers and their accountant. This led on to Marley's entrance and the announcement of her husband's sudden death, followed by various histrionic outbursts culminating in the arrival of Veeney, covered in mud and looking more like a New Age traveller than the heir apparent to a small fortune. Sally had still to make an appearance and was beginning to wonder if René had indeed managed to edit her out completely when the office door sprang open and there she was, coffee tray at the ready.

Dan, who had been sinking gently into a coma beside her, sat bolt upright and tried to concentrate. When she had offered Patrick coffee for the third time he nudged her. 'I thought you were exaggerating.' Sally smiled uncomfortably, aware that Wellard Kenning was pacing up and down behind them like a caged rat.

Watching the whole she could not but admire René's skill with the camera. No one would know from Dilys' benign expression that she had just set fire to the studio; rather it seemed that she was a gentle and caring wife, supportive of her husband in this time of crisis. By dint of supreme editing Drewe and Stephanie seemed to be perfectly dry throughout their tempestuous rollickings, and Marley in the corridor looked as though she were walking through the Orangery at Kew rather than being crushed slowly to death between two collapsing flats.

The cast watched in nervy silence, laughing hysterically at any hint of humour, then subsiding rapidly into quiet as if fearing to miss some point in the plot. Only Gaby Chivers kept up a commentary, despite all attempts to silence her. 'Oh, look. That must be the office where I first meet Cariola. Gosh. I hope I get some wellies . . . Ah, so he, in fact, didn't know about . . . Ooh, rather you than me, Richard. Brrrh.'

After a while no one noticed her. They were too caught up in whether or not René had cut that particular line because they'd said it three times already, or because he was planning to downgrade the character in future episodes. Notes were made to ring agents. Patrick resolved never to let Jean near him with a pair of scissors again, and Marley sat happily eating Maltesers which rattled more and more ominously as she neared the bottom of the box.

Sally felt a sense of gloom creeping over her. Once or twice Dan had glanced at her and smiled almost conspiratorially, and she had smiled back, then felt disloyal to the rest for sharing his impressions.

The fifty minutes passed, the credits rolled once more and the music died away to be replaced by Rita Green, sounding horribly cheerful for one who had sold her dream home and just watched an episode of *The Firm*. 'More next week,' she informed the nation, though whether as a warning or an enticement it was difficult to decide. The set clicked off. 'Lights,' cried Simon theatrically. 'Give me some lights.'

'We'll let you know,' responded René drily which caused everyone to laugh inordinately.

The lights went on and Patrick and Marley disappeared into the kitchen, reappearing with champagne. Everyone cheered and the post mortem began in earnest.

'Darling,' Stephanie had cornered Wendy. 'I've been talking to Veronica,' the corpse nodded fervently. 'She agrees with me, that jacket is impossible.'

'But I thought that was the one you liked,' wailed Wendy, going very pale. 'That was the Ralph Lauren.'

'Yes and I was one hundred per cent wrong. I freely admit it. I should have listened to you and gone for the Calvin Klein. Never mind. I won't need it for numero seven and I'm sure we'll be able to squeeze in a shopping trip before eight gets into studio.'

'Penny's been an absolute honey,' Simon had his hand on Penny's trembling shoulder and was introducing her to his wife. 'She literally held my poor old conk together when I came off the fork lift.' Jenny Peyter smiled her weary, knowing smile.

Patrick refilled Dan's and Sally's glasses. 'What do you think?' he asked casually.

'I don't suppose there's some beer?' asked Dan.

'Not the drink. Here,' he snatched back the glass and emptied it into his own. 'The show. The serial. *The Firm*. There's some beer in the kitchen, by the way. Suzanne, my pet . . . Bring us some beer out, there's a love.' Sally saw Dan baulk, but to his surprise Suzanne trotted off like the proverbial lamb, shortly to reappear with a glass of beer. Patrick took it from her and handed it to Dan. 'Now, what I want to know is how did you, as a member of the Great British Public, feel it went?'

'Very well,' said Dan.

'A frank opinion,' persisted Patrick.

'I think a lot of people will like it.'

'You mean you hated it?'

'No, I didn't hate it.'

'What didn't you like?'

'I think it's a bit hard for someone to judge on one episode,' put in Sally.

'Darling girl, that is precisely what we will be judged on. When did your discriminating TV critic ever take into account the development of the plot? No, you have to give them the lot in the first ten minutes or they're down the pub writing their copy. Isn't that right, René?' He seized their director's arm as he hurried past in search of a drink for his agent. 'What right?' asked René, sizing up Dan. 'Have you ever played a driving instructor? There might be a small part coming up in episode nine. Who's your agent?'

'She is,' said Dan, tired of protesting his status.

'Got your Equity card?' asked René, peering at him more closely.

'No,' said Dan.

'Pity,' said René. 'Drop me a line when you have. Good bones. Can you do a Scottish accent?'

'No,' said Dan.

'That's not a problem,' said René. 'You must excuse me. Derek's going to expire if I don't get him a drink in a minute.'

'Who's he?' asked Dan.

'Our director.'

'Well, dears, that was fun, wasn't it?' Marley came bustling over with a plate of sausage rolls. 'I think we all did awfully well. And YOU looked absolutely lovely, Sally. Didn't she?' she turned to Dan.

'Yes,' said Dan.

Sally blushed. 'I wasn't on long enough for anyone to see.'

'Yes, you were,' insisted Marley. 'You should wear your hair up all the time. It really suits you,' adding hastily, 'it suits you like that, too. And you must be Simon's wife,' she told Suzanne.

'I'm Suzanne Chamberlain.'

'What a pretty name. You must be very proud of Simon.'

'Patrick,' said Suzanne looking rather coy. Dan stared straight ahead. 'Oh, yes,' Marley agreed. 'He was wonderful. I think we all deserve a pat on the back. Oh, look, there's dear young Drewe all by himself. I must just go and have a word with him.' She sailed off with her sausage rolls.

Stephanie's husband came waddling up. 'Did you enjoy it, Frank?' asked Patrick.

'Yes. Excellent. Steph's kicking up hell about those clothes of hers. Whoever chose them? She hasn't looked so fat since she played Salome. Have you ever played Salome?'

He nuzzled a little closer to Suzanne. Suzanne pouted. 'I'm afraid not. I don't act. I think life's too serious for play-acting.'

'I should say so,' said Frank. Stephanie reclaimed him at this point and dragged him off to repeat her costume criticisms to Jeff Wilkins.

'Where's Haze?' asked Patrick, looking around.

'Is that the woman in a purple dress?' asked Suzanne.

'Yes.'

'She's in the kitchen washing up. By the way, who's the woman with black hair and a long blue skirt?'

'Dilys,' everyone chorused.

'Oh,' said Suzanne. 'Well, she's sitting outside the bathroom saying she's going to slit her wrists. Of course it's only a cry for help.' Everyone rushed to see whether she had succeeded. Dilys was asleep, leaning against the laundry basket. The arrival of half the cast to feel her pulse and frisk her for cutlery was not entirely welcome to her and she let fly with a few well-chosen reminders that it was her life and she would dispose of it how and when she wanted.

Patrick fetched her another brandy and he and Dan steered her into the dining room where they thought she would be more comfortable. Any hope Dilys might have had of drinking undisturbed was quickly shattered, however, by the return of Suzanne. 'Can everyone stand a bit away, please. I'm a trained First Aider.' The cast stood respectfully back. Suzanne undid the top of Dilys' blouse. 'Get off me, you effing dyke,' roared Dilys, slapping her arm. Suzanne looked grimly satisfied with this response. 'Could someone please fetch a glass of water?' Penny was dispatched. Dilys threw the water over Suzanne's feet. Hazel had appeared, drying her hands on a tea towel, and was watching the proceedings with detached curiosity. 'I think I may need a little help from one of you gentlemen.' Suzanne looked directly at Patrick. Patrick shrugged, then leant forward and whispered something in her ear. Suzanne looked visibly shocked. 'Danny, give me a hand. I want to get her out in the fresh air.' Everyone looked at Dan. He stared uncomfortably down at his wife. 'Why?'

'Oh for heaven's sake, Danny. Isn't it obvious? Even to you? She's drunk. She needs to sober up.' Dan sighed and moved to help Suzanne prise Dilys out of her chair.

'Why?' he murmured again as they paraded her towards the death leap, but only Sally heard him.

Dilys, having made her protest, allowed herself to be suspended over the window ledge at a thirty-three degree angle as Suzanne incited her to 'Breathe and two, three. Breathe and two, three.'

'Isn't she wonderful?' declared Gaby, rotating her hips to the sound of Suzanne's chanting.

'Which one?' asked Simon who wanted to get back to talking about himself.

'There's a fearful draught coming from somewhere,' said Stephanie who was also thoroughly bored with the performance.

'I think that's enough,' said Dan forcefully as he eased Dilys back into the room and closed the window.

'Yes, that should do the trick,' Suzanne agreed. She bent low, peering up into Dilys' closed eyes. 'How do you feel now? Better, I expect.' Slowly Dilys raised her lids, smiled beatifically and was sick down the front of Suzanne's dress.

Jean and Wendy now came into their own, recommending expensive preparations and 'marvellous little men' in Bletchworth who would restore Suzanne's dress to 'better than new'.

'It is new,' Suzanne wailed, 'don't just stand there, Danny. Do something.' Dan who had gone white as a sheet waved his hands helplessly and made a bee-line for the bathroom. 'That's typical of you,' Suzanne shouted after him as Marley mopped at her with a kitchen roll.

The day was saved by Hazel who appeared noiselessly with a soda siphon and drenched Suzanne from head to foot. She was then led away to return dry but grim-faced in one of Marley's sequinned jumpers and a Stewart kilt coiled like a sari round her slender body.

Dilys, who seemed unaware of the chaos unfolding around her had retreated to a corner where she was deep in conversation with Jeff Wilkins, the two of them making considerable holes in a bottle of whisky someone had had the ill sense to leave lying around.

Sally helped Marley collect plates. She couldn't help noticing how contented the old lady looked as she pattered around, popping leftover titbits into her mouth when she thought no one was looking. Tired but happy. Genuinely happy. Marley caught her eye. She smiled mischievously. 'I know I shouldn't. I shall be back on my diet tomorrow. Promise.'

Sally smiled. 'You don't have to worry about me, Marley. I've never stuck to one longer than lunch-time.'

Marley looked pleased. 'How do you think it's gone? The party, I mean. Has it been all right? Apart from that little accident?'

Sally gave her a hug. 'It's been marvellous, Marley. You give wonderful parties. The best I've been to in years.'

Marley glowed. 'Ronald always used to say I gave the best parties in town. Of course he was predjudiced.'

'He had no reason to be. It's true. You're a brilliant hostess.'

'Well,' Marley shrugged. 'It's family, isn't it? You'd do anything for your family.' Sally smiled and looked around the room. Wendy and Jean were quarrelling like fishwives over whether the men in Bletchworth were brothers or father and son. Veeney was lying in a corner with the younger Haemorrhoid draped across her, stoned out of her mind, and Simon and Jenny were smooching as though they were the only people in the room. Penny was sitting red-eyed beside Rolo who was endeavouring to rub her back and pile up chairs at the same time. Drewe was posing like a Greek god beside a portrait of Marley's first husband in hunting gear, and Hazel was making some herb tea for Dilys and countering Stephanie's continuing moans with a long dissertation on the best way to defrost frozen pastry.

Some family, she thought.

George was taking bets as to whether René was planning to seduce Gaby before the series was done. 'The day I see him doing press-ups is the day I pay up,' Patrick affirmed. 'What do you think, young Dan?' he clapped him paternally on the shoulder. Dan shrugged. 'I shouldn't have thought he was her type.' Patrick burst out laughing. 'You're missing the point. René is the director. 'Droit du seigneur' and all that. There's a pecking order, of course. Producer – she may have by-passed him – director . . .'

'Who comes after that?' asked Dan incuriously.

'Lead actor, I should think. I think I'll forgo my rights on that one. It'd be a bit too much like hard work.'

Dan laughed but there was an edge to his voice as he asked, 'Was that how Sally got the part, do you suppose?'

Patrick looked at him to see if he was serious. 'Is that how she strikes you?'

Dan shook his head. 'I hardly know her. And you hear things, don't you, about actresses?'

Patrick put his hand on his shoulder and turned him aside from the others. 'It's not actresses, old love, it's women. Some do, some don't. You'll have to make your own mind up about Sally, but for my money, she's worth hanging on to, and there aren't many of them that are.'

'Patrick,' Suzanne attached her fine white hand to Patrick's arm and drew him gently but firmly away. 'I really think it's time we were going. I feel simply awful in these things. I'm sure everyone's laughing their heads off at me.' Patrick took both her hands and peered adoringly into her eyes. 'Of course they're not, my precious. Don't you know, you'd look gorgeous in anything? She's the belle of the ball, isn't she, Dan?'

Dan stared ostentatiously at a point above their heads. 'If you say so,' he said and moved away.

'Cinderella's off, I see,' said Patrick, nodding to where Gaby was noisily kissing everyone within reach. He took Sally's arm and steered her towards the couch. 'Come and sit by me for a bit. I haven't spoken to you all evening.'

'Yes you have,' Sally told him. 'You just can't remember.'

Patrick passed a hand across his brow. 'I think this may be one of those evenings I prefer to forget.'

'Rubbish. It's been a lovely party.'

Patrick looked at her vaguely. 'Oh, the party. Yes. I wasn't thinking about that.'

'You're not worrying about the transmission, are you?'

Patrick gave a dry guffaw. 'Wouldn't you be?'

Sally thought. This was no time for honesty. 'You were wonderful. Everyone says so. Even Wellard.'

'Does he?' Patrick's face brightened visibly. 'What did he say?'

Sally hesitated. 'You know Wellard. I think it was on the lines of "I think this calls for lunch at the Black Swan."'

Patrick burst out laughing and kissed her on the cheek. 'You're the best secretary a man could have.'

'Am I interrupting anything?' Suzanne, looking distinctly piqued, was standing in her coat glaring down at them. Patrick reached out his hand to her. 'Not at all, my darling. I'm just auditioning Sally for my harem. Come and join us, why don't you?' Suzanne started to say something then changed her mind and stalked out of the room.

'You've upset her now,' said Sally, wishing she cared.

Patrick shrugged. 'She's been asking for it all evening, silly cow. I knew it was a mistake to invite her. This is a family do.'

Sally sat up abruptly. 'Does that mean I shouldn't have brought Dan?'

Patrick cleared his throat. 'Well, if you want my honest opinion, I don't think you should.'

'Why not?'

'Because he's not one of us.'

'He's not one of you, Patrick. That's not quite the same thing.'

'And what exactly is that supposed to mean?' demanded Patrick, fixing her with an imperious stare.

'It means just because someone isn't vain and self-centred and obsessed with what other people think of them, it doesn't mean they're not fit to be seen in public.'

Patrick's eyes darkened ominously then just as quickly filled with amusement. 'Well, that's me told, young Sal. Do you know, you look just like Sigourney Weaver when you're angry?'

'Do I really?' Sally blushed delightedly.

Patrick took her hand. 'Yes, but fortunately you're not susceptible to flattery or I might have told you how good I thought you were tonight.'

'Me? Oh I was hopeless. I really looked as though I'd never poured coffee before in my life.'

'Nonsense.'

'I did in the first scene . . .' She became aware that Patrick was laughing helplessly. 'You are an absolute swine.' She thumped him in the chest.

Patrick wheezed. 'You're right, though,' he said. 'You were right to bring Dan. He's a good bloke.'

'Oh, well. So long as he meets with your approval,' said Sally, unaccountably pleased. She looked across to the door and saw Dan watching them. 'I think we're off,' she said struggling to her feet.

'Are you going, dears?' Marley popped her head out of the kitchen. 'Hasn't this been fun?'

'Very nice,' they agreed. Marley stood on her tiptoes and kissed Dan goodnight. 'I shall remember what we worked on soon,' she said. Dan smiled. 'Don't hold it against me when you do.'

The ambulance was driving away as they turned into Marchbank Gardens. Sally felt a sick throb of panic as she realised whose house it had left. The police car was still there.

Dan got out and went over to the constable. Sally sat in the car staring at the two of them. They were like characters from a cop show: the young man nodding seriously, Dan gesturing to Mr Davenport's flat. 'Interior shot', she thought. 'Old man lying by gas fire, matches in his hand. FX Hiss of gas. CUT.'

Dan came back and opened her door. She got out. 'What's happened?' she asked. They would have to shoot this again, her voice was trembling.

'Found wandering in the street,' said Dan. 'He had his coat on over his pyjamas. Apparently he thought he had to leave the flat – said his daughter was throwing him out. He must have meant that Crane woman. They've taken him to the General. We can give them a ring in the morning. Find out how things are.' Sally nodded and started towards the house. 'I'll just lock the car,' said Dan.

He followed her into the hall. Mr Davenport's door was open. Inside it looked as though a bomb had hit the place, clothes, books, crockery were scattered all across the living room. Mr Davenport's desk in which he kept his pension book and other papers had been turned on its side. For a moment Sally wondered if he'd been burgled but then she saw the suitcase, open on the bed. In it were more clothes, socks, a photograph of his wife, his pension book and passport, a dog lead.

She closed the door. Helplessly she sank down on the stairs and started to cry. Dan sat down beside her and gently pulled her towards him. 'It's all right,' he whispered. 'It'll be all right.'

Sally buried her face in his jacket. 'No it won't,' she howled. 'Nothing's ever all right. You don't understand.'

'Yes I do,' said Dan very softly. 'Believe me, I do.'

Sally sat up. 'I don't know what to do,' she said in an empty voice. Dan said nothing for a moment, then leant over and wiped the tears from her face with his finger. 'Come to bed,' he said.

22

Sally lay in bed and looked at the reviews. 'Misguided,' said one. 'Turgid,' said another. 'OBSCENE,' roared the *Sun*.

'The *Sun* says we're obscene.'

'I told you to draw the curtains.' Dan was working his way through the *Independent*. Sally giggled. The fact that the critics were united in their condemnation of *The Firm* could in no way dent her feeling of total happiness.

She studied the way Dan frowned when he was reading, the small bunch of hairs that rose and fell on his chest as he breathed, the scar on his upper arm shaped a bit like an anchor.

'Aaaagh,' she squawked as Dan suddenly threw the paper aside and rolled over on top of her.

'You were watching me,' he said. 'Confess.'

'I confess,' wheezed Sally. 'I am a spy for the Malaysian Secret Police. I can't breathe.'

Dan eased his weight slightly, 'Then you know what the punishment must be.'

'Can I confess again?' asked Sally, gazing in appalled fascination at the state of the bed.

'Not till I've got my strength back,' groaned Dan.

'Call yourself a man.' She flitted naked across the room.

'Where are you going?'

'To make some coffee.'

'Remember there are no curtains in the kitchen,' Dan muttered, sinking back on to the pillows. 'I don't want you frightening the neighbours.'

'They can't see in,' declared Sally. 'Only Mr Davenport . . .' her voice broke off. 'I'd forgotten about him. What time is it? Do you think it's too early to phone the hospital?' Dan looked at his watch. 'I'll do it. You make the coffee.'

'What did they say?' Sally, wrapped in Dan's dressing gown and quite unable to find the end of the sleeves, was endeavouring to pour coffee. 'Not much. He's under sedation. The doctor won't be in till this afternoon.'

'You mean he hasn't even seen a doctor?'

'I think he did last night. He's asleep now anyway. There's not much they can do till he wakes up.'

Sally handed him a mug. 'I feel so guilty.'

Dan frowned. 'Don't start that again. I'm running out of soothing replies.'

Sally smiled. 'That's because you're not in *The Firm*.'

They stayed in bed till noon, drinking coffee, making love, eating toast, making love, reading the reviews, laughing, making love. Sally wondered fleetingly how Suzanne could possibly have wanted to leave a man who made love like Dan but she pushed the thought from her mind. Suzanne was the kind of woman who probably held a textbook over his head while he was screwing her. 'Bit to the left, darling. Up a bit. Are we ever going to find that naughty G spot?'

At lunchtime they went to the pub and bumped into Colin who was seriously thinking of walking out of *The Desert Song* because the director had spotted Matthew meeting him after a rehearsal and offered him the understudy to the lead.

'But surely that would be ideal?' said Sally. 'I mean you were going to take him with you anyway, so if he can actually be paid to go, that makes it doubly worthwhile, surely?' Colin dismissed her suggestion furiously. 'What you're missing, Sally, is that if the main part goes AWOL Matthew will be THE STAR. How do you suppose I'm going to live with that? I mean, I do everything for him as it is. How do you suppose he'll treat me if that happens?'

Sally considered. 'Have you ever known a star go AWOL?'

Colin hesitated. 'No.'

'Well then.'

'That's not the point.'

'That is precisely the point.'

'What do you think?' Colin asked Dan.

'I think she's right,' said Dan, taking Sally's hand and squeezing it.

Colin frowned. 'You do?'

'I do.' Colin peered at him more closely. 'Are you sleeping with this woman?'

'Yes,' said Dan.

For the first time since she had known him Colin looked genuinely pleased. 'You take care of her,' he said.

'I should be learning my lines,' murmured Sally. She was lying in the darkness of Dan's room, staring up at the lights of an aeroplane blinking its way across the sky. 'Plenty of time for that,' said Dan cushioning her head with his arm. He smelled of salt and sex and damp skin. Sally snuggled closer, intoxicated. 'I have quite a lot in this episode,' she told him.

'Yes, but they're all the same, aren't they?'

'More or less. That's why they're so hard to learn.'

'Why don't you just keep saying the same thing? No one would ever notice.'

Sally switched on the lamp and propped herself up on her elbow. 'What did you really think of it?' Dan closed his eyes. 'I liked you,' he said.

'I was hardly in it. What did you think of the actual story and the acting and everything?'

'It was all right.'

'Just "all right"?' Dan opened his eyes. 'What do you want me to say? I hardly ever watch television. Not things like that, anyway?' Sally's eyes narrowed slightly. 'What d'you mean "things like that"?' Dan thrashed around for an answer. 'Soap operas, whatever you call them. I mean it's all a bit unreal, isn't it? Everyone falling in and out of bed with their relations and belting each other at funerals. It's a bit hard to take it seriously.'

'I see,' said Sally coolly. 'Ever heard of Hamlet?'

'What's that got to do with it?' Sally made a hissing noise through her teeth. She lay back and looked at the ceiling. 'So you didn't like it?'

'Look, I'm obviously the wrong person to ask. I know nothing about these things.'

'No, I can see that.'

'You were fine. Patrick was fine. That old lady was fine. So was the young bloke with the funny nose. The rest of them I thought . . .'

'Yes?'

'I thought they overdid it a bit. All that sobbing and rolling around on the ground. It didn't ring true. I liked the woman with the black hair. She was very good,' he added as though this might restore him in Sally's favour. 'She was blotto,' said Sally morosely. 'Trust you to like her.'

'Well, there you are.' Dan got out of bed and felt around for his trousers. 'I'm clearly the wrong person to ask.'

'No you're not. You're a typical member of the public.' Dan shrugged and wriggled into his trousers. 'So you keep telling me. You seem to be fairly typical of the acting profession if it comes to that.'

'What do you know about the acting profession?'

'Not a lot. From what I've seen it's mainly composed

of self-centred nutcases.' Sally sat up. 'And you think I'm one of them?' Dan pulled on his shirt. 'I didn't until five minutes ago. I don't understand you. You were laughing at the reviews this morning and they're a lot worse than anything I said. Now you're having a go at me because I don't think it's the best thing since sliced bread.'

Sally slid off the bed and went over to him. Awkwardly she threaded her arms round his waist. 'I'm sorry. You're absolutely right. It is rubbish. I always knew it was.' She laid her head longingly on his chest. 'I just wanted you to like it, that's all. I wanted you to be proud of me.' Dan leant down and kissed her hair. 'I am proud of you. You were the best thing in it.' He put his hand under her chin and turned her face to look at him. 'The reason I'm proud of you is because you're NOT like Colin and Patrick and the rest of them.'

'What am I like?'

Dan thought for a moment. 'I daresay in a bad light you might pass for a human being.'

'What's our Sally looking so pleased about?' Patrick, still suffering the results of his hangover and a day of placating Suzanne, had had to suffer the added indignity of seeing his age quoted in the *Sunday Express*. He was definitely feeling threatened. 'Nothing, really.' Sally tried to adopt an expression in keeping with the general atmosphere of the survivors of a massacre. Even Marley was subdued, although she was the only person to have been credited with bringing any life to the serial. Stephanie and Drewe had taken the worst of the savaging, being described variously as 'Goofy and the Bitch', 'The Oddest Couple', and 'Simple Solley and the Queen of Tarts'. Calamity had not united them, however, and they were positioned at opposite ends of the hall, Stephanie still complaining about her costumes and Drewe on Rolo's mobile phone, arranging an interview for a fashion show in New Delhi.

René called them all together and told them not to be despondent, that nobody took any notice of reviews, that the average viewer never even read them, that the critics were a bunch of embittered talentless old farts, that Majestic's own research was turning up very favourable reactions, that the management had been bowled over by the quality of the production and that he himself was very confident that the show would sweep all current contenders from the Jictar ratings in a matter of weeks. The important thing now was for them all to get on with rehearsal as though nothing had happened and to put everything they had into proving the bastards wrong.

The spirit of Dunkirk lasted at least until lunch time, with Veeney making coffee for everyone in lieu of Penny who, if anything, looked more shattered than the rest of them at the pasting *The Firm* had taken. 'What's the matter with her?' muttered George after she had burst into tears when he asked her to place a bet for him. 'I don't think "Simon's Darling" was the best choice,' Sally told him. George muttered something about eleven to one.

René, for the first time since she had known him, looked completely poleaxed. She had felt almost sorry for him as he sat, Prozac clenched in his palm, trying to get Drewe to look devastated. 'Show him the review in the *Mirror*,' muttered Patrick, still striving to overcome the publication of his birth date.

There was a note from Dan when Sally got home. It said he had rung the hospital again and got the same response as on Saturday. Nothing would be decided until the tests had been completed and meanwhile visitors were to be discouraged as these might tend to confuse Mr Davenport even further. 'Balls', Dan had written in brackets beside this. 'See you Saturday. Love Dan.' Saturday!

A sense of profound disappointment engulfed her. Why

did he have to go away just when she needed him? The only thing that had got her through everyone else's depression had been her own certainty of seeing Dan that night. Oh well, they were professional people. They must get used to being separated. Perhaps she would be able to behave in a more seemly fashion if she was fed up too. She must feed on her loneliness till Saturday. Hopefully by then the others would be feeling a bit more cheerful. And he was bound to ring. She moved the telephone into the bedroom.

Dan still hadn't rung by Thursday. Thoroughly wretched, she decided to visit Mr Davenport. The nurse on the ward looked uncomfortable when she said whom she wanted to see. 'He's a bit confused,' she confided. 'He's worried no one's looking after his dog.' Sally sighed. 'The dog's fine.'

She was shown to the end bed where Mr Davenport was propped halfway up the hard flat pillows, his mauve-veined fingers tucked over the sheet like clothes pegs. 'Hullo, Mr Davenport. It's Sally from upstairs. I've come to see how you're getting on.' The old man's watery eyes flickered over her. 'Good afternoon,' he said politely. 'I expect you want to see the flat.' Sally stared at him shocked. Those were exactly the words he had used when she had come to look at her flat three years before. 'It's Sally, Mr Davenport,' she repeated lamely.

'My wife will be out in a minute. She's just putting the kettle on. I daresay you might like a cup of tea? Have you come far?'

'From Wimbledon,' she responded automatically. Mr Davenport nodded.

'That's quite a journey.'

Sally's voice sank to a whisper. 'It is a bit.'

'It is a bit,' said Mr Davenport who clearly hadn't heard

her. A nurse approached. 'Ah, here's Jennifer. Jennifer, this is Miss . . .?'

Sally said nothing. 'Grosvenor. Sally Grosvenor. I've come to look at the upstairs flat.'

He was still talking as she hurried away.

23

'Where's Wellard?' Simon whispered to Sally. 'It's not like him to miss out on a free drink.'

It was Saturday night and they were gathered together in the hospitality suite down the corridor from the studio. Recording had been completed and it was while they were struggling out of their costumes that the invitation, or 'summons', as Patrick described it, had been issued. Now they sat clutching their wine glasses and pretending for all the world that they were indifferent to whatever they were about to be told.

'I'm afraid the news is not good.' William Lewis, Chief Executive for Majestic Productions, flanked by Jeff Wilkins and a very thin man with a nose like a pickaxe sat opposite them at a long table on which bowls of crisps and salted peanuts had been plonked incongruously amongst the sheets of accounts.

Lewis was a fleshy man with the kind of consuming confidence that men find intimidating and so many women find seductive. He cleared his throat. 'I would like to say here and now how sorry I am to be here at this moment.' I bet, thought Sally. You haven't come near us up till now.

Dilys sat over by the window, her hand twitching restlessly at the venetian blind. She knows, was running through everyone's minds, she's married to the man.

She must know what he's going to say. But they all knew really.

'I'm afraid it is not going to be possible to take up the options.' There was an audible hiss as the breath they didn't know they were holding escaped. 'Thank God,' said Patrick a little too loudly. 'They've offered me Santa in Bentalls again.' Bright brittle laughter filled the room.

William Lewis smiled ruefully. 'I can't tell you how sorry I am. I think it's a crying pity. Bloody critics. If they'd just given it a bit more time.'

'You mean to say,' said Patrick more sombrely, 'that you've taken this decision on the strength of the reviews for one episode?'

Lewis straightened up in his chair. 'It's not my decision, Paddy.'

'My name is Patrick.'

'Patrick. I beg your pardon. I understand your disappointment.'

'Disappointment?' Patrick gave a short sharp laugh. 'Do you? Do you know what it is to wait twenty years for a second chance and then to have it ripped away from you on the strength of fifty minutes out of – what is it? – over ten hours? You know about that, do you?'

The Chief Executive went rather red. 'I shall ask my colleague, Mr Rhys Davies to explain.'

The pickaxe looked visibly alarmed and began to shuffle the papers before him. 'Yes. Good evening. I'm Rhys Davies, Chief Accountant for Majestic Films. Now this is basically a liquidity problem as I'm sure you all recognise.'

'I expect Mr Lewis recognises it,' said Drewe with a nervous titter.

'Shut up,' said Patrick sharply. No one looked at Dilys.

'We have to look at returns and percentages for our shareholders and if it becomes apparent that these are likely to result in a downward grossage we have no alternative but to cut our losses. We cannot carry a failure.'

'And *The Firm* is a failure?' asked Stephanie sharply.

'In terms of advertising revenue it is likely to become one.'

'And in terms of quality drama?'

'That is not our concern.'

'Who'd ever have guessed?' snarled Patrick, draining his glass and slamming it down on the table. Davies recoiled slightly. He had heard that actors could be difficult.

'We're not enjoying this any more than you are, Pad . . . Patrick,' put in Lewis. Davies shook his head emphatically. 'It's simply that if we were to take up the options on a show that has been universally slated in the national press we might find ourselves in the unenviable position of being forced into substantial asset sales, simply to generate sufficient cash to fund our remaining capital expenditure programme.'

'Oh, well now you've explained it to us,' said Simon, leaning forward and staring fixedly into Davies' eyes.

The accountant studied his notes. 'We cannot afford the risk of a dividend cut at this point in time. As you are doubtless aware there have been rumours of a hostile bid and the last thing any of us would want would be for the company to fall into the hands of a rival, just when we're beginning to benefit from an upsurge.'

'To be quite frank, mate,' came George's voice from the back, 'we don't give a toss who runs the company so long as we get a fair crack of the whip with this serial, and for you to come in here bleating about shareholders' profits on the strength of a few poxy tabloids what probably no one's going to read anyway, is a bit blooming rich, if you'll pardon the pun.'

There was an awkward silence. Jeff Wilkins put his head in his hands. The pickaxe and Lewis exchanged glances.

'I know what you're thinking,' continued George after a moment. 'You're thinking, "what's the matter with him? He drops off the perch in episode twelve anyway." Well, I'll tell you something. It's principal. I don't expect you to understand that, being an accountant or bank clerk or whatever it is you are. I wouldn't expect you to understand things like "fairness" or "loyalty" or "support". We've had b. all from the pair of you so far. We've been working on this show nearly four months and this is the first time either of you have come near us. So don't come down here with your poxy wine and your poxy pink shirts and start telling us about hostile bids. If you ask me the sooner someone who knows the business takes over this company the better it'll be for everyone.'

'Hear hear.'

Everyone turned. Dilys let go of her venetian blind and very slowly clapped her hands together. Clap, one, two, clap. Clap, one, two, clap. From the other side of the room Hazel had laid down her knitting and begun to clap, too, then George, then Patrick, then all of them. The two executives gathered up their papers and silently left the room.

Jeff Wilkins stood up. 'I'm sorry, all of you,' he said desolately. 'I've let you down. Sorry.' He turned to go.

'Hang on, Jeff,' said Patrick, striding over to him. 'The bar's still open, isn't it?' Wilkins blinked at him. 'Why don't we all get down there and have a proper drink? Leave this gnat's piss for the moguls.' Wilkins smiled uncertainly.

'Yes,' said René who had been silent up till now. 'Bloody good idea.'

The barman finally got them out at half past one. A fleet of taxis was ordered and they were variously piled into them and dispatched by the night porter who, though used to doing it for the odd celebrity, had never had to organise a whole cast before.

There was a light on in Dan's flat. Sally's heart jolted as she paid off her cab and tottered up the path. She wondered whether she should let him know she was back or just creep off to bed. Half of her didn't want Dan to see her in this state, but the stronger half desperately wanted to fall into his arms and tell him all about everything that had happened that week, culminating in the scene in the hospitality room. The decision was taken from her as her keys clattered on to the steps. The light in the hall came on and Dan opened the door as she was feeling hopelessly around for them. 'What time of night do you call this?' he demanded sternly, retrieving the keys, and hauling her up. He peered more closely. 'How much have you had?'

'A lot,' moaned Sally and flopped against him. Dan steered her into his flat and on to the couch. She grinned up at him. Her legs felt suddenly weightless and her arms detached from her body. 'We went for a drink,' she enunciated carefully.

'Just one?' Dan raised an eyebrow. 'One. Or two.'

'Do you want some coffee?'

'No. Thank you.' Dan shifted her feet from the seat, sat down and replaced them on his knee. 'Is this usual after a recording?'

'What?'

'To have a drink? Or two?'

'Yes. But not so . . .' Sally flapped her hand around.

'Many?'

'Many. Yes. No.'

Dan laughed. 'I think I'd better get you to bed.'

'Bed,' said Sally, closing her eyes and making a feeble attempt to look coquettish. She could feel Dan shaking as he carried her into the bedroom. What incredible lust she must inspire in him, she thought hazily. Dan went out again. She heard the sound of running water then him coming back. He put his hand behind her head and helped her to sit up. 'Drink this or you'll feel like death in the morning.'

'Death,' she repeated, sipping unwillingly. When it was finished he let go and she sank back on to the pillow. 'Death.'

'Death,' Dan confirmed.

'Sack,' murmured Sally. 'I think we could run to a coffin,' said Dan, pulling the covers over her.

'My head,' Sally whimpered when she woke in the morning. Dan was standing by the window with a mug of coffee in his hand. He turned. 'Bad, is it?'

'Very bad.'

'Do you want a pill?'

'Ten at least.'

'Have some of this.' He handed her his coffee and went to fetch the paracetamol. Sally sat up. She appeared to have no clothes on. 'I've got no clothes on,' she called to Dan.

'Is that an invitation?' came from the kitchen.

'No. Yes. Not till I've had my aspirin.'

Dan came back with a fizzing glass. Sally gulped it down. 'That was horrible.'

'Serves you right for getting plastered.'

'I had good reason.'

'Why? Because you knew I was coming back?'

'No,' Sally caught hold of his arm. 'I've missed you like mad. By the way, did I have any clothes on when I came home?'

Dan shook his head. 'Not a stitch. The bus driver didn't know where to look.' Sally thumped him then shuddered as the movement reverberated round her skull. 'They're not going ahead with the options,' she said.

Dan looked blank. 'Who isn't?'

'Majestic. The production company. They had till episode ten to say whether they wanted to make another series, but they called us all together last night after the recording and said they weren't going to take them up.'

'What does that mean?'

Sally sighed. 'It just means I'll be out of work again after this is over and so will everyone else in the cast.'

'You'll get another job.'

'I suppose I will. Eventually. It's not even as though I had much of a part in this. It was just so nice to have regular money coming in for a while.'

Dan put his arm round her. 'You've got ages yet. Maybe they'll change their minds.' Sally shook her head. 'I don't think so. Things got a bit hairy in the end. I should think even if they did decide to do another series they'd probably recast the whole thing after last night.'

'Why? What happened?'

'We told them where to get off. At least George did. He was wonderful. Told them what we thought about having our careers written off by a jumped-up accountant.' She started to giggle. 'You should have seen their faces when he called them poxy bank clerks. It was wonderful.'

'What did they do?'

'There was nothing they could do. They just picked up their papers and left. Dilys was the best, though.'

'Is that the lady who likes a drink? The other lady, I mean?'

'Oh come on. I don't do this every day. Yes, that's her. She started a slow handclap.'

'I can't see her managing a fast one.'

'You don't understand. The Chief Executive is her husband. He was the one giving us the sack and she started the handclap.'

'Obviously takes her marriage seriously.'

'Oh, don't be such a prude. Anyway, he's having it off with some woman at the BBC. He's an absolute toad. That's probably why she drinks. I would if I were her.'

Dan was silent for a moment. 'Things aren't always the way they seem,' he said eventually.

'I know. But I think with him they are. Anyway, that's it. We're all out of work after April.'

'April's ages.'

Sally sighed again. 'I suppose it is.'

'Anything could happen before then. You might get spotted by a talent scout and whisked off to Hollywood.'

'Yes, I should think that's completely on the cards.'

'You've got to think positive. You're not very good at that, are you?'

'No,' said Sally. 'By the way, I went to see Mr Davenport in hospital.'

'And?'

'He's worse than ever. It was awful. I came away.'

Dan sighed. 'You should have waited for me. We could have gone together.'

'I would have liked to,' said Sally simply, 'but you weren't around.' Dan looked at her quickly but said nothing. Sally shivered. 'I'd better get some clothes on.'

'Why? You look nice like that.'

'I'm blue with cold.'

'Soon see about that.' He climbed into bed with her and rubbed his hands very gently over her body. 'Better?'

'A bit,' mumbled Sally. 'Don't stop.'

'How was your week?' Sally asked casually. She was eating toast, a steady stream of crumbs sliding off her plate into the bed.

'You are the messiest eater I've ever met,' grumbled Dan, sweeping them out from under him.

'Answer the question.'

'What?'

'How was your week?'

'OK,' said Dan evasively. 'Look, give me that plate. You're better off without one.'

'Don't fuss,' said Sally, wresting it back from him. The toast fell buttered side down on the sheet. 'Now look what you've done,' scolded Dan.

'It'll wash,' said Sally. 'Where did you go? Or is it a secret?' Dan hesitated. 'I'm an SAS secret agent. I have been on a mission to darkest China.'

'I can see you passing for a Chinaman.'

'I crouched.'

'Why don't you just say "it's none of your business"?' asked Sally, getting out of bed.

'All right.'

'It's none of my business?'

'It wouldn't interest you.'

'If it hadn't interested me I wouldn't have asked, but since you plainly don't want to tell me, let's leave it at that.' She went into the bathroom. Her missing clothes were on the back of a chair. She got dressed and crossed to the front door. 'Where are you going?' came Dan's voice from the bedroom. 'Home.' Dan leapt out of bed and came after her. 'Don't be angry. I . . . it was to do with the divorce. I wanted to forget about it.' Sally was all solicitude. 'I'm sorry, Dan. What a stupid cow I am.'

'No you're not.'

'I am. I'm so insensitive sometimes. Call myself an actress. I'm meant to have intuition. I should have realised. Oh, poor you. Is it all sorted now? Don't answer that. We won't talk about it any more. You're back, that's what matters. Where shall we go for lunch? I'm going to treat you. Anywhere you like. Within reason.'

Dan laughed. 'What do you call "reason"?'

'Anywhere where Colin isn't.'

'I thought Colin was your friend.'

'He is, but I just don't want him crowing over the reviews.'

'He wouldn't do that, would he?'

Sally laughed. 'You don't know much about actors, do you?'

24

If the cast of *The Firm* had been subdued by the reviews, they were a great deal more so after Majestic's decision to drop the project at the end of the first series. Even Gaby restricted herself to a solitary warm-up in the corner of the church hall where once she had sought to enlist the others in her joint-cracking exercises. She had stopped talking about prepregnancy diets, too, although still eschewing coffee in favour of pulverised prune juice.

Of them all Dilys seemed the most cheerful. She arrived on Monday morning with a new hairstyle. It was straighter and slightly boyish, which suited her. She drank coffee nonstop and chewed voraciously on Fishermen's Friends.

René behaved in his normal fashion till halfway through the morning when Patrick, who had obviously had a very heavy weekend, refused to rerun a scene which required him to leap up and rush down the hall. 'For Christ's sake, René, what the fuck does it matter anyway?' he growled. 'I might as well do the whole scene with my dick on the table, for all the people who are going to be watching it now.' René turned on him. 'When I ask you to do something, Patrick, it means I want you to do it. Not when you feel like it, not when your hangover's gone, not when you've got your fucking brain cells round the lines. NOW. All right? And stop behaving like a fucking amateur. OK? We've got another five episodes of this to get through and I am not having ANYONE screwing me up. Understood?' Patrick levered himself out of his chair and gave René a bear hug. 'Understood, Don Corleone,' he murmured and got on with the rehearsal.

When Sally opened her script that evening a little silver package dropped out. She opened it. It contained a sugared almond and a tiny card. 'Chin up, darlings. Marley.'

'Did you get one of those cyanide pills from Marley?' demanded Simon the next morning. Everyone confessed that they had. 'It nearly broke my crown,' he complained. 'Whatever is the woman playing at?'

'I thought it was very sweet of her,' said Hazel. The others agreed that it was a nice gesture, except for Stephanie who said it was childish beyond belief. 'Well, I thought it was the most beautiful thing that's ever happened to me,' asserted Gaby who was feeling unaccountably weepy. The subject was left.

On Thursday Marley was again the object of attention as she came pattering into the hall clutching a rolled up newspaper. 'Look at this. Look at this, everyone.' They gathered round. Marley solemnly unfurled her copy of the *Catholic Herald* and turned to page fourteen. '"The Acceptable Face of Soap,"' she read in the awed tones of the Annointed.

"'Majestic Productions' ambitious decision to launch a full-scale family drama in a bid to win back viewers from the BBC's newly scheduled *Mega Sports Special* on Friday nights looks like paying off if the introductory episode was anything to go by.

"'The Christie family, torn by internal quarrels, marital torment and the threat of imminent bankruptcy, managed in spite of this to come across as a warm, loving and supportive group of people. Marley Webb, as of course is to be expected, brought a dimension and dignity to her role as the widowed Rebecca Christie that one rarely finds in television today. In this she was greatly helped by that much underrated actor, Patrick Crichton, as her elder son, John, and newcomers Simon Peyter as Richard, his brother, and Veeney Rogers, who was quite superb as the errant daughter, Solange. How nice, too, to come across a really well-crafted script – pacey, intelligent and humorous. And let us spare a word for the excellent supporting cast, particularly Sally Grosvenor, as John's loyal and adoring secretary. The silent grief in her eyes as she hands him a cup of coffee on hearing of his father's sudden death put me in mind of the young Flora Robson. Three cheers for a decent family show. PS not a swearword in sight.'"

There was a silence. 'What do you think of that?' gurgled Marley, holding the magazine before her like a toreador's cape. 'Christ!' said Patrick.

René, who looked as though he were emerging from a tunnel, worked his mouth in several directions. 'Could I have a look at that?' he finally croaked. Marley gave it to him. Everyone crowded round and endeavoured to read over his shoulder. 'Christ!' he said at last, handing it back to her. 'Which one of you wrote that?' There was nervous laughter as the review was passed round.

'Where did you get it from?' asked Patrick. 'You're not a Catholic, are you?'

'She is now,' said Simon.

'My cleaning lady gave it to me,' Marley explained.

'Seems an awfully odd place to have a television review,' observed Stephanie.

'Beggars can't be choosers,' said Patrick cheerfully. 'I bet this is our Sally's doing. She's been off studying the catechism all those evenings she doesn't answer her phone.' Sally felt herself blushing.

'Well I think it's time we all got back to work,' said René. 'We can't afford to rest on our laurels.'

*   *   *

The *Catholic Herald*'s review had much the same effect on the cast as a papal bull presumably does on Catholics. They believed it absolutely. No other critics were allowed to supplant the wisdom, perception and undeniable rightness of what had been written. Indeed their recent jibes were largely forgotten in the rush to commit the article to memory. Even Sally found time to pop into Foyles on the way home and purchase Flora Robson's biography.

She had some trouble obtaining a copy of the *Catholic Herald*, but eventually found it at Charing Cross station and bought the four remaining copies. The assistant eyed her curiously as he took her money.

Dan studied his with due attentiveness. 'That's nice,' he said, putting it down and endeavouring to pull Sally on to his knee.

'Is that all?' she demanded, snatching the paper up and flattening its pages lovingly.

'What am I supposed to say?' asked Dan. 'It's jolly good. Excellent. Especially the bit about you.'

'Do I remind you of the young Flora Robson?' Sally turned her head from side to side.

'Who's she?' asked Dan.

Sally stared at him doubtfully. 'Don't tell me you don't know who Flora Robson was?'

'Should I?'

'She was only one of our greatest actresses. Look, I've bought her biography.' She thrust it at him. Dan flipped through the photographs.

'You're better looking than her,' he said. 'Much. She looks like a witch in this.'

'She's meant to,' said Sally rattily. 'If you look underneath you'll see.'

'Oh yes. I've missed you.' He hauled her on to the couch and put his tongue inside her ear. Sally squirmed with delight. 'I've missed you too.'

* * *

'I don't know about Flora whatsit,' groaned Dan. 'I think you've got a streak of Sharon Stone somewhere.'

'Well don't tell me where,' murmured Sally.

'Can I ask you something?' Dan was sitting with his back against the headboard watching her as she hunted around for her clothes.

'Of course.'

'Are you a Catholic?'

'No I'm not. Whatever made you think that?'

'Oh nothing,' said Dan gesturing casually to the four newspapers. 'That wasn't the question, anyway.

Sally sat down on the end of the bed. 'What was the question?'

'Have you slept around a lot?'

She stared at him. 'What?'

'Have you slept around a lot?'

'Why are you asking me that?'

'I want to know.'

'Do you think I have?'

'I don't know. That's why I'm asking. Actresses do, don't they? To get jobs and that.' Sally burst out laughing. 'If you think I'd sleep with René . . .'

'Not him. Not this job. But have you ever slept with a bloke just to get a job?' Sally got off the bed. 'Would it bother you if I had?'

Dan sighed. 'It's none of my business, is it?'

She went over and slid her arms round him. 'Of course it's your business. And the answer is "no".' Dan's face relaxed. 'I knew you wouldn't. I just had to ask. You didn't mind, did you?'

'No,' said Sally and laid her head on his chest. But she did.

The incident of the *Catholic Herald* might well have faded into obscurity, had it not been for the *Observer*'s decision to run a series of articles on the specialist press. Its first subject happened to be religious publications and out of this came the revelation that, despite the universal condemnation of *The Firm* by the national press, both the *Jewish Chronicle* (still regaling its readers with Marley's recipes) and the *Catholic Herald* had seen fit to describe the programme as a beacon of solace and moral rectitude in the wilderness of public entertainment. 'Family Values' and 'Back to Basics' began to rear their ridiculous heads again, and a bishop north of the border preached a sermon on Armistice Day in which he referred to the Christies' habit of 'sticking together in a crisis'. He tactfully refrained from saying that most of the sticking was done between the sheets, but his homily was much quoted in the tabloids and Patrick was asked to open the Conservative Christmas Fair in Nuneaton. He turned it down on the grounds that his second wife would undoubtedly turn up and heckle, but Marley went instead and came back with a cluster of royal blue egg cosies and the assurance that the freedom of Nuneaton could be theirs for the asking.

With true thespian sang-froid the cast took this new-found glory in its stride, Penny struggling nobly to rearrange rehearsals around requests to open bus shelters, endorse greetings cards and be interviewed by the host of women's magazines who now saw fit to present the Christies as all that family life could aspire to.

Marley was signed up to do a cookery book and a series of advertisements for Saga Holidays. Patrick received a deluge of fan mail from grandmothers who had lusted after him in the sixties and now seemed set to renew their fantasies in maturity. Simon was asked to appear on *Top of the Pops* miming to the theme tune from *The Firm*. Though eager himself, his agent drew the line, and it was finally agreed that a fresh version would be recorded with Veeney singing some hastily scribbled lyrics and the two of them girating in front of a carbon copier backdrop.

Scarcely a day went by without some new announcement from the cast. 'I'm up for the part of Harrison Ford's wife in his next film,' Stephanie let drop one morning after a protracted phone call from her agent had left Penny rehearsing Cariola Sedgewick's nervous breakdown half the morning. Penny herself was so near to the genuine thing, what with Simon's now regular forays into teenage discotheques and the actors' increasing demands on her ingenuity, that René threatened to give her the part if Stephanie wasn't back on the set in three minutes flat.

Hazel was doing a set of articles on 'Crocheting for a Christening' which was taking up most of her energies at the moment.

Drewe had mysteriously stopped applying for alternative jobs and begun to turn up punctually for rehearsal. This, no doubt, had more to do with the tendency of freelance photographers to drop in on the church hall in the hope of catching Stephanie without her make-up or Hazel in flagrante with just about anyone. The Law of Probabilities was so heavily weighted against either, however, that they had to content themselves with mug shots of whoever happened to be around at the time. More often than not this was Sally, since Penny had long since worked out that whoever else might be away opening supermarkets or talking about their broken homes to the tabloids, Sally would not.

Her face began to appear more and more regularly in the TV columns, not with any particular reference other than, 'Sally Grosvenor, who plays the long suffering Laura Barnes in *The Firm*', or 'Laura Barnes (Sally Grosvenor) answers another worried phone call from one of the Christies'. Dan would bring home the latest batch, culled from the college canteen and together they would read them, guffawing in disbelief at what a desperate reporter could read into a photograph. 'Laura Struggles with Her Childless Grief' ran one, over a picture of Sally holding up one of Hazel's cot blankets. 'When Will He Realise?' demanded another, featuring a picture of her staring blankly at a spot on the back of Patrick's neck.

The popularity of *The Firm* began to soar. Middle-class pundits confessed to staying in on Friday nights to see what dire events could still befall the family. Short of total extinction not much more remained by episode nine – the warehouse had been razed to the ground, Cariola Sedgewick's love child had been taken into care, Solange was pregnant for the third time and Richard was in danger of losing his right eye due to an accident with some chemicals in the print room. (This last had had to be hastily appended after Simon had got into a fight with a bouncer during one of his more lively guest appearances.)

Sally had never been so happy. Unlike the others no cameras had come seeking to expose the secrets of her decor, the joys of her part of London or the places she liked to shop. Hence, since no one around Marchbank Gardens expected to find a television star on their doorsteps no one noticed that they had got one. Not that she was a 'star', but she was well on the way to becoming a personality, more by dint of her silence than anything she ever said.

The only blot on her horizon was the lingering shadow of Suzanne Chamberlain. Though Patrick freely acknowledged that he had never been faithful to a woman for more than four months in his life, there was an edge to his voice when he spoke about Suzanne that worried Sally. Not that she thought he loved her. He was too self-centred for that, but it was as though he sensed that on her his hold on youth depended. If he lost Suzanne he would have to accept that the hearts that beat for him were the same generation as his own, and he wasn't quite ready for that.

Hence interviews with Patrick tended to feature his 'lovely young companion' in a startling array of 'simple' garments, poised over a Le Creuset casserole, her tip-tilted nose quivering with domesticity. 'I Could Never Marry An Actress', declared one headline, omitting the fact that he had already married three.

Sally tried to keep these articles from Dan but she knew he must have seen them. She could always tell when he had. He was quiet and vague, agreeing with everything she said and not hearing a word. She put up with it as best she could, but it hurt.

'I thought I might kill myself tomorrow,' she said jauntily one evening when he had been particularly remote. Dan grunted. 'I was thinking I'd probably throw myself under a train. Somewhere in the City. They're reasonably frequent, aren't they?'

'It's hell in the rush hour,' murmured Dan from behind a newspaper.

'I'll probably slit Suzanne's throat first,' Sally continued, her tone unaltered. The paper went down. 'I'd rather you left that to me,' said Dan coldly. Their eyes met. She didn't try it again.

Dan seemed to be working a lot in the evenings these days. When she asked him about it he muttered something about the 'pre Christmas rush' and needing to finish a conservatory for a customer. It struck her as an odd time of year to be rushing through a conservatory but his days were taken up at the college so presumably he had to fit in jobs where he could.

She, too, was busy, having decided to spend some money on her flat. Hazel had shown her how to make curtains and although that enterprise had had to be taken over by a professional, she was making cushion covers to match which took up a good proportion of her spare time as she pinned, tacked, stitched and unpicked through the dark autumn evenings. She felt cosy and domesticated as she listened for Dan to come home.

Sometimes he was very late and she had already gone to bed when she heard his key in the lock. He very rarely came up to see her on these occasions, but she was perfectly contented knowing he was back and safe. After all they were secure in each other's affections, they didn't need to be constantly together to prove it.

There was no sign of Mr Davenport and she assumed he must still be in hospital. She knew she ought to enquire but her last visit had so unnerved her that she couldn't face the thought of a repetition. She would wait till Dan was free and then they could go together.

Postcards began to arrive from Colin. He had been stung by a horse fly while pony trekking in Guernsey and had had to be rushed to casualty for anti-tetanus injections. These had resulted in an unexpected and not entirely unwelcome increase in the size of his genitalia which had caused much comment among the males of the chorus and led to a free dinner with the local head of constabulary. Not for the first time Sally wished Colin would treat himself to some envelopes when divulging the more colourful details of his daily round.

It was one morning on her way to rehearsal that she met the postman. Fearing his personal censorship she usually tried to avoid a face-to-face encounter but this morning she could not escape. Gladly she noted there was nothing from Colin. He handed her the usual collection of junk mail and bills along with a cream-coloured envelope bearing the bright bold slogan of *Television Toppers* magazine. Opening it she read,

Dear Sally Grosvenor,

Or should I say 'Laura Barnes'? We at Television Toppers are planning a new look for our Features section and it has been suggested to me that you would be the ideal person to take on our Problem Page. (In the guise of Laura, naturally). You would not be expected to deal with all the subjects on your own as we have a network of experts at our disposal, but the column requires a flagship, if you'll pardon the simile! and we feel that Laura is just the person to provide the caring face of television. What do you think?

I have taken the liberty of copying this letter to your agent, but was anxious to obtain your own reactions to the proposal as we would like to get the project off the ground as soon as possible.

Yours sincerely,
Beth Slattery
Features Editor

'You're not going to do it, are you?' Dan asked as they lay in bed that night.

'Why not?'

'You get some right nutters writing in to those things.'

'I don't think they actually want me to answer the letters. They just want to use my name over the column.'

'I thought you said it was Laura Barnes they wanted to use.'

'I am Laura Barnes.'

'No you're not. You're Sally Grosvenor. You do exist outside that serial, you know.'

'Of course I know. I just meant . . .'

Michael Snelcott rang the next day to tell her about the offer.

'I've already heard, Michael. They wrote to me too.'

'I don't think they want you to do very much. Just cast an eye over one or two of the letters. They get other people to answer them. The pay's awful but it's worth it for the publicity. I strongly recommend you accept.'

'I'm not sure I'm qualified. I mean some of these people might need professional help . . .'

'Yes, well they've got it, haven't they?'

'I don't know . . .'

'I'll tell them "yes", then, shall I? Let's face it, darling, things are not good in the business at the moment. You can't afford to be turning jobs down.'

'This came for you,' said Penny the next morning, dropping a thick brown Envopak into Sally's lap. It was addressed to 'Laura Barnes, c/o Majestic Studios' and had apparently been delivered by a man on a motorbike with the strict injunction that she be given it immediately.

'Hello,' said Stephanie, leaning directly over her and blowing smoke into her face. 'Don't tell me our Laura's being head-hunted by the opposition.'

'It's nothing like that,' muttered Sally. 'It's just something my agent wanted me to look at.' Sheets of variegated notepaper cascaded out of the Envopak. Patrick picked one up. 'Dear Madeleine,' he read. '"Madeleine"? Is this your *nom de nuit*?' He scrutinised the piece of paper. '"I am having trouble getting my meringues to set. Is my oven too high?" Well it can't be much higher than yours, can it, love? As I recall you do most of your cooking on the ceiling.'

'Look at this one,' said Simon, waving a lavender sheet at them. '"Dear Madeleine, I have been married for ten years and have just discovered my husband has been unfaithful to me three times during this period. He swears it is all over but I feel I will never be able to trust him again. What do you advise?"'

'Castration,' said Stephanie.

'Get another bloke,' said Veeney.

'Marriage guidance,' said Hazel.

'Why do they all call you Madeleine?' asked George.

'I was married to a Madeleine once,' said Patrick.

'Just what is going on?' demanded René who was too short to see over the heads of the others.

'Sally's changed her name,' Marley twittered. 'To Madeleine. Isn't that pretty? Mind you, Sally's very pretty too. And Laura.' She smiled confusedly.

'It's just the magazine wanted to know if they could use my name – Laura Barnes, that is, over their Agony Aunt column. They seemed to think it was a good idea. I don't actually have to answer the letters. At least I don't think I do.' She gazed uncertainly at the stack. 'I wonder if I could just ring my agent?'

Michael Snelcott assured her that the letters were merely an example of the kind of thing she might be asked. Beth Slattery agreed with him that it might be nice if she were to answer a few herself but that the bulk would be dealt with by their field of experts.

'How many is a few, Michael?'

'Not many.'

'How many?'

'About twenty.'

'Altogether?'

'A week.'

'I resign.'

'They've upped the money. Majestic thinks it's a brilliant idea.'

'I don't care about the money. I am not answering twenty letters a week and that is final. I'm not qualified. I know next to nothing about marriage problems and even less about meringues.'

'Yes, but they don't know that, do they? Just say anything. If they're daft enough to write in to a rag like *Television Toppers* they deserve all they get.'

'I can't take the responsibility.'

'How about fifteen?'

'Five.'

'A dozen?'

'Half a dozen.'

They compromised on nine.

'I don't know how I'm going to do it,' Sally lamented at coffee break.

'What do I know about meringues? They'll probably end up with third degree burns.'

The cast rallied round. Sewing queries were handed over to Hazel; Marley brought in her hoard of cookery books and Veeney and Stephanie gave advice on fashion. Patrick dealt with divorce litigation and George with animals. The sexual hang-ups were divided equally amongst them, which usually meant that Sally had to rewrite a more printable version when she got home. Dan vetted her efforts, adding ribald comments in the margin which she struggled to erase before faxing them through to the magazine each Tuesday morning.

The money, in keeping with everything that her agent negotiated, was indeed pathetic, but Sally could not deny a sneaking sense of pride that she, or rather Laura, had been chosen to soothe the suffering of the nation. She noticed, too, how the attitude of other people had begun to change towards her. Wendy Costume no longer looked right through her or suggested that she wear her own tights. In fact in one fleeting moment of madness she had even suggested Laura might wear a blouse with a patterned collar, though nothing ever came of it.

Penny, who had long considered her a fount of universal wisdom, brought all her troubles to her, not only regarding Simon and the teenyboppers, but also whether she should persist with contact lenses though they gave her pink eye, or go back to tinted glasses behind which she could weep with impunity.

Even Dilys, struggling manfully with the effects of withdrawal, confided to her one day that she had only got the role through her husband's insistence and that his decision to scrap the show had been like coming out of prison for her.

'I'm so glad,' she stabbed the table with her finger, 'I'm so glad he was so wrong.'

'But wouldn't you rather *The Firm* had gone on?' asked Sally. 'Surely it's better to be in work than out?'

Dilys shook her head. 'I'll get my own work from now on. Look.' She fished around in her bag and pulled out a crumpled article, adding *sotto voce*, 'I haven't shown the others yet.' It was a full page spread from *Woman's Own*. 'My Battle With Alcoholism' by Dilys Lewis. 'There,' she said defiantly. 'I'm hoping Bill will have a heart attack.'

The saddest letter that Sally received, or at least she thought so and kept it hidden from the others, said simply in the shaky handwriting of the very old, 'Dear Laura, You remind me so much of my dear wife. I am on my own now, although I still have a dog which stops me getting too lonely.' It was signed Roland Davenport, but there was no address.

25

Michael Snelcott rang in a froth of excitement one day shortly before Christmas to say that a well-known coffee company wanted her to endorse their product in a series of commercials that were worth 'a fortune, my sweet. An absolute fortune.' The advertisements were to be filmed in the summer, 'between series, my darling. They were very accommodating.'

'But there isn't going to be another series.'

'They don't know that, do they? And for God's sake don't mention it to anyone. Not even your own mother. Promise me.'

'I promise.'

'On your life.'

'On my life.' Sally uncrossed her fingers and ran to tell Dan all about it. He was downstairs planing some cupboard doors. 'Guess what!' He looked up.

'What?'

'Michael's just rung. They want me to do a series of coffee commercials. He says it's worth a fortune.' She skipped across the room and flung her arms round Dan's waist. He put the plane down and gently prised her fingers away.

'What's the matter?'

'I saw that nurse.'

'What nurse?'

'The nurse who used to come and see the old man.'

'And?'

'He died last Thursday. Had a fall. They took him to hospital but he didn't come round.'

Sally sat down. 'Why didn't you tell me?'

'I was going to.'

'When?'

'Soon. When I'd finished this.'

'The cupboard's more important, is it?'

Dan shook his head helplessly. 'I just wanted time to think. I'm not that good at breaking bad news.' Sally was ashamed of her own insensitivity. 'I'm sorry. I didn't mean it like that. When's the funeral?'

'Tomorrow afternoon. That's why the nurse came. She thought we'd want to know.'

Sally nodded. 'I'll ring Rolo.'

The funeral was brief and simple. The matron from the geriatric home where Mr Davenport had been moved and a male attendant were there. They seemed pleasant if a little jaded by the proceedings. 'They must do this all the time,' Dan muttered to Sally as they left. There was also a man in his forties who introduced himself as Mr Davenport's solicitor, stating rather firmly that there was a niece in Australia, as though he suspected Dan and Sally of hoping for some kind of windfall.

They had bought some flowers on the way and given them to a young pall bearer who laid them self-consciously on the coffin lid and hurried away before he could be asked to exceed his duties further.

The vicar had a cold and had sniffed throughout the service, giving the impression that he was crying, the oddity of which successfully took Sally's mind off her own sadness. It was only as they turned back into Marchbank Gardens that the tears overcame her. Dan put his arms round her.

'What's all this?'

'I don't know,' Sally sobbed. 'It's just he died all alone in some horrible home. We didn't even go to see him. We didn't even find out where he was. I had a letter from him. You didn't know that, did you?'

Dan looked confused. 'What sort of letter?'

'The usual sort of course. 'Dear Laura . . .' He said I reminded him of his wife. He knew she was dead, but he said . . .' she put her face in her hands. Dan fished around for a hanky. 'What did he say?' Sally blew her nose. 'Oh nothing. Just that he was lonely, but it wasn't too bad because he still had a dog.' Dan hugged her to him. 'Come on,' he said. 'Let's go in. There's something I want to tell you.'

He made coffee then changed his mind and poured them both a brandy. Sally took a deep gulp. Outside it was beginning to snow, the lead-coloured sky looked like a theatre backdrop. Dan drew the curtains and shut it out. He sat apart from her, rolling his glass between his hands. 'What were you going to tell me?' Sally asked, savouring the warmth of the brandy. Dan said nothing. 'Go on.' She reached for his hand but he made no effort to give it to her. Instead he said, 'You know that day Mr Davenport fell . . .?'

'At the home?'

'No, here. When they first took him to hospital.'

'Yes?'

'It was me.'

'What do you mean, it was you?'

'It was my fault. You know you kept on at me to move those planks out of the hall, and I kept forgetting to do it?'

'Yes.'

'He wasn't shaky on his feet at all. No more than anyone

of that age, anyway. It was my fault. I left them there and one of them slipped and he must have tripped over it. I killed the old guy, good as.'

Sally sat very still and looked at her hands. 'It was an accident,' she said at last, but her voice sound tinny and stilted. It didn't convince either of them. Dan stood up. 'I should have moved them,' he said angrily.

'I did ask you to,' said Sally, cursing herself as she spoke.

Dan swung round. 'That's why I bloody left them there. I did it to annoy you.' Sally stared at him. 'You what?'

Dan turned away. 'You heard.'

Sally got stiffly to her feet. 'I should have thought there were other ways. Still, I daresay you'd used most of them up by then.'

'Well, it wouldn't have been hard, would it?' responded Dan. 'I never met anyone who was so easy to annoy.'

'Fair game, then?' said Sally bitterly. 'Pity you had to include an old man in your tricks.'

Dan flung his hand up and for a moment she thought he was going to hit her, but he simply clenched his palm and rubbed it despairingly across his forehead. 'I'm just trying to explain. How, why it happened . . . I've been wanting to tell you for so long.'

'Why didn't you?'

'Because . . . You're so . . . I don't know. It's just so hard to get through to you.'

'Thank you very much.'

'There you go. That's it. The moment I say anything, anything that's like the truth you smack me down.'

'I don't.'

'You do. What about when you asked me about *The Firm*? That first day. I thought things were different between us then. I thought I could tell you what I thought.'

'You could. You can.'

'No I couldn't. The moment I opened my mouth you jumped down my throat.'

'I explained all that.'

'You explained and I listened.'

'What's that supposed to mean?' Dan sighed and shook his head. 'Just that, I suppose.' Sally bit her lip. 'I suppose Suzanne would have thought it was all right?'

'What?'

'To leave planks of wood lying around for the old man to fall over? After all, it would have saved a fortune in after care, wouldn't it? "Survival of the Fittest", and all that?'

Dan looked mortified. 'Suzanne's not like that,' he said shortly. Sally felt her throat constricting. 'Isn't she just?'

'You know she isn't.'

'I do not. I know nothing of the kind. In fact, if I were asked to describe your wonderful wife in words of one syllable I think "cow" would be the first I thought of.'

Dan was staring at her in total bewilderment. 'You don't like her, do you?' Sally gave a short laugh. 'Not all that much, since you ask?'

'Why? You hardly know her. What's she ever done to you?'

Sally was silent. Hurt you, she thought, but the anger was seeping out of her to be replaced with a sort of dull despair. She shook her head. 'Nothing. You're right. I just wish you'd told me all this before.'

Dan shrugged listlessly. 'What difference would it have made? He was gone. He'd lost it. He wasn't going to get well again whatever anyone did.'

'You don't know that. How do you know that? He was all right the night of the party. He was fine.' She snatched the glasses up from the table and went into the kitchen. 'At least we could have gone to see him or something. We could have done something.'

Dan followed her. 'What could we have done? You said

yourself you had a letter from him and you didn't even bother to find out where he was. Bloody Laura Barnes. You're so busy answering other people's problems you can't see the ones in front of your face.'

'That's not true.'

'Yes it is. Do you know how many times I've tried to tell you? You always put me off.'

'How can you say that? You've never once tried to tell me. You don't tell me anything. Not about you or your life or Suzanne or anyone. Every day's a one-off with you. If you're here it's fine, if you're not I don't know where you are, who you're with, what you're doing . . .'

'That's because you never ask.'

'Look what happened when I did.'

'That was different.'

'No it wasn't. If you don't want to tell me I'm not going to pry.'

'It's not prying, for Christ's sake. It's being interested. It's caring. You don't think I'm prying when I ask you how the rehearsals went, do you?'

'No, of course I don't.'

'Then why do you think I'd mind if you asked me what my day was like? You never think, do you? It's all about your life, your problems. I'm fine for that, aren't I? Come home and tell me what's gone wrong with your day. When did you ever ask me how mine went? Never. Because you don't give a stuff, that's why. You're Laura Barnes, "the caring face of bloody television". You're about as caring as the glass on the screen. You were right when you said you were Laura Barnes the other day. That's who you are. And you don't bloody exist.' He picked up his jacket and stormed out of the house.

Sally leant her head against the wall. She felt completely drained. How had she managed to get things so wrong, every single step of the way? What was it in her that said 'destroy' every time a bit of happiness came within her grasp?

When had he tried to tell her about Mr Davenport? She thought back. Right from the beginning, she realised. The looks, the silences, the care he had taken of the old man all spoke more eloquently than anything he could have said to her. But she, true to form, had noticed nothing, had missed all the cues, had offered him no support or understanding. Colin was right. She didn't know how to give. And now it was probably too late.

She cleared away the coffee cups and the brandy then sat down and wrote Dan a note. It was long and rambling and spoke much of her own needs, shortcomings and hopes for the future. She read it through, added a few lines about Dan's wellbeing and her desire to help him through current difficulties, signed it 'Laura Barnes', then took it into the kitchen and set fire to it with the gaslighter. She doused it in the sink, washed away the debris and scribbled on the back of an electricity bill, 'I'm sorry. I didn't mean to be like that. I was jealous. I love you, Sally.'

Dan came back around midnight. Five minutes later he knocked on Sally's door. 'I'm drunk,' he said as she opened it.

'Yes.' Dan's head drooped then rose again. 'I got your note.' Sally nodded. 'Can I come in?' She stood aside. Dan staggered through the door then turned and wagged the bill at her reprovingly. 'I was going to pay this tomorrow.'

Sally put him to bed then climbed in beside him. It was the first time he had slept in her bed. It was a great deal narrower than the one downstairs. She smiled as she thought about the differences between them. She was single and had a single bed. He was single and had a kingsize. She snuggled up to him and curled her leg over his. Dan grunted companionably and began to snore. This must be what being married's like, she thought. It wasn't as bad as she'd expected.

*   *   *

Dan was still asleep when she left for rehearsal next morning. Everyone was suitably solicitous, obviously suspecting the death of someone close. Sally felt a sharp prick of conscience as she realised she had felt less emotion at her father's funeral than at Mr Davenport's. The angst extended to her own insensitivity towards Dan. She cornered Patrick at lunch time. 'Can I ask you something?'

'Anything, dear child, so long as it does not revolve around the menstrual cycle.' From Patrick's tone she could only assume Suzanne had another of her migraines.

'Do you like being asked questions?'

'What sort of questions?'

'About yourself and your past and everything?'

'Only if it leads to a thumping good part.'

'Yes, but if you weren't an actor? If you were something else?'

'Like a petty criminal?'

'No. Don't be difficult. This is serious.'

Patrick frowned and peered at her closely. 'I could almost believe it was. Is this to do with young Daniel, by any chance?' Sally sighed. Patrick put a fatherly arm round her. 'What's he been up to? He's not two-timing you, is he? Because if he is . . .'

'No, no, it isn't anything like that. At least, if he is, I don't know about it and I'd prefer it to stay that way.' Patrick regarded her with some amazement. 'I shall put you down for my wife after next.'

Sally laughed. 'I don't think I'll ever be a wife.'

Patrick looked sagacious. 'Ah. I think I see what's coming. Won't commit himself, eh? Tried the old pregnancy card? That usually works. One way or the other.'

'Patrick, be serious.'

'Right.'

'Do you think I don't care about people?' Patrick looked perplexed. 'Well, you've got your column, haven't you?

How could anyone possibly say you didn't care about people? Look at the detail you went into for that poor woman with the twins.'

'You wrote that, Patrick. That was to do with custody, remember.'

'So I did. Still, you have to make sure everyone does their homework, don't you? That's the hardest part, getting all the answers in on time.'

Sally left it.

There was no one in when she got home. She was slightly disgusted to note three estate agents' letters addressed to 'The Occupier', each stating they were looking for saleable accommodation in the area and that a representative would be happy to call round at the owner's convenience. 'I bet they read the obituaries,' she grumbled to herself as she foraged in the fridge.

Dan came back late. Hearing his key in the lock Sally followed up her resolution to show more interest in his life. 'Where the hell have you been?' she screeched from the top of the stairs. Dan stopped dead. 'What time of night do you call this?' she bellowed. 'I know where you've been. You've been down that pub with those poncie friends of yours. Don't give me none of that "working" rubbish. I can smell her scent from here.'

'Bless you, darling. I knew you'd like it,' said Colin, trailing through the door.

'So why did he actually sack you?' asked Sally. Colin had been into some detail regarding his departure from *The Desert Song* and Matthew's brave decision to carry on without him in the role of the lead riff, after 'that twat from *The Bill* broke his ankle.'

'There was quite a bit of nastiness from the director about it all. I say "director". He couldn't direct a piss-up in a brewery. He blamed me, you see. Kept saying I'd sautéed when I should have spun. Well, naturally, I wasn't having any of that, so I laid my cards on the table. I told him, "either you withdraw your accusation or I leave the company." Obviously he couldn't bear the thought of losing face, so there it was. Curtains. I'm not sorry.'

'But why did Matthew agree to stay on?' persisted Sally, furious on Colin's behalf.

'He's only doing it because he can't bear to see the show suffer,' insisted Colin. 'If it had been me I'd've told them to stuff it.'

'It should have been you,' Sally pointed out. 'You were understudying.'

'Yes, but I was far too young,' said Colin, ignoring the fact that his lover was six years his junior.

'It's a bad time of year to be travelling,' said Dan tactfully.

'Exactly,' confirmed Colin. 'Who wants to be kicking their legs in Darlington with a force nine gale up your garters?'

'None of us,' they all agreed.

'I thought about writing to Auntie Laura here,' said Colin, 'but then I thought, she's got enough on her plate with that awful woman from Reigate.'

'She did go on a bit,' Sally acknowledged.

'I don't know how you put up with her. Week after week. Why didn't you just tell her to put her head back in the oven where it belonged? That's what I'd've done.'

'It probably would have been more sensible.'

Dan drove Colin home after supper. Sally was in the shower when he got back.

'Do you think we could sleep downstairs tonight?' he asked through the curtain.

'Don't you like my bed?' asked Sally.

'It's a bit cramped.'

She reached for a towel. 'It's nice, isn't it? Having two flats like this?'

Dan was silent. 'Do you think so?' he asked at last.

'Yes. Don't you?'

'I suppose so. Come on, Scarlett.' He picked her up and carried her out on to the landing.

'Wait. I'll have to lock up,' squealed Sally, nestling against him for warmth.

'What for? There's only us.'

Sally watched Dan as he lay on his side, eyes half-closed. 'Are you asleep?' she whispered.

'You know I'm not.'

'What are you thinking about?'

'Colin.'

'Colin?'

'Yes.'

'He's completely mad, isn't he? I can't help being fond of him though. Fancy that swine Matthew staying on when he'd been sacked. Not just that, taking his part as well. It's obscene. Why he doesn't kick him out, I'll never know.'

'He loves him,' said Dan. 'Anyway, relationships are like that.'

'Like Colin and Matthew? You're joking.'

'They are a bit extreme. But there's always one person loves the other more, isn't there?' He closed his eyes and turned over so that he had his back to her. Sally lay down and tucked her arm round him protectively. 'I don't think that's necessarily true,' she murmured. Dan did not respond. She lay and listened to the sound of his breathing. 'Dan,' she whispered. Dan grunted. 'How was your day? I meant to ask earlier. I just forgot. Dan . . .' But he was asleep.

26

'What are you doing for Christmas?' Patrick asked Sally one morning as they sat waiting for Stephanie to finish arguing about her hemline. She shrugged. 'I hadn't really thought. How much time do you think we'll get off?'

'Oh masses, I should think. The thing's practically running itself now, isn't it?'

Sally smiled, remembering Patrick's remarks on the first day. 'What about you?' she asked. Patrick frowned slightly. 'Not sure. I wanted to whisk Suzanne away to Prague, but she seemed to think it would be nicer if we had a family do. Offspring and that. She's very keen to meet the brood.'

'So you may yet get to play Father Christmas?' said Sally a little unkindly. Patrick looked at her reproachfully. 'No, I think it's because she likes my kitchen. She said something about her other one being a bit cramped. You know, when she and . . .'

'Yes, she did mention it,' Sally cut in.

Simon insisted they all go to a local restaurant which was doing Christmas dinner specials during the run-up to the festivities. René reluctantly agreed to let them have an extra half hour but they all returned at three o'clock, much too drunk to continue the rehearsal, so he sent them all home with the injunction to be 'prepared to stay late' the following evening.

The Christmas spirit was now fully upon them, however, and the next day saw half the morning gone in the exchange of cards and presents. Hazel had excelled herself and made them all chocolate logs, intricately iced and decorated with their character's name. George, who had won ninety pounds on the lottery, produced six bottles of champagne which René made him swear not to open before tea time.

Sally, unaccustomed to having to buy presents for so many people, bought two dozen pairs of musical socks and took home the enduring memory of Wendy and Jean arguing about the best way to wash them to avoid rust marks, plus the sight of René's increasingly irritated face as he struggled to direct above a chorus of Rudolf the Red-nosed Reindeer coming at him from every corner of the hall.

Marley had bought chocolates, plainly hoping that some-one would open theirs on the spot, and the rest of the men brought bottles which lay around the rehearsal room, mysteriously emptying as the week went by.

Dilys swore she didn't believe in Christmas but still pro-duced a sumptuous box of *marrons glacés* which Sally spotted Marley dipping into surreptitiously when she thought no one was looking.

For the first time she began to perceive what Marley meant by 'family'. It was fun being part of such a group. She tried to explain it to Dan, who had also had several celebrations with his friends, but she could tell he didn't fully understand what she was getting at. She wasn't even sure she knew herself. She just knew she felt, perhaps for the first time in her life, that she really belonged.

'What's the old lady doing at Christmas?' Dan asked one evening as they slumped in front of the television, both too lazy to move. Sally sat up. 'You know, I don't know. I expect she's going to friends or something . . .' Her voice faded as she tried to think if Marley had mentioned anyone. 'I hope she isn't going to be on her own,' she added anxiously.

'Why don't you ask her round here?' said Dan, flicking the switch on the control. Sally looked at him. 'Here?'

'Why not? It's better than being on her own, isn't it?'

'Yes, but . . . Wouldn't you mind? I mean, you hardly know her.'

'It's only for a day, isn't it? I wouldn't like to think of her being on her own.' Sally snuggled up to him. 'You really are very nice,' she said.

Dan grinned. 'You're not so bad yourself.'

'Can I ring her now?'

'Might as well.'

Sally clambered off the couch and went over to the phone. She dialled Marley's number. 'Hullo . . .?' came Marley's voice.

'Marley, hullo, it's Sally. We were just wondering – Dan and I – whether you've made any plans for Christmas Day? And if not, whether you fancied coming over to us? I know it's a long haul but Dan could come and fetch you . . . If you'd like?'

There was a pause. 'Oh, Sally, that is so sweet of you. I would have loved to come. Truly, I can't think of anything nicer, but I'm afraid I've already accepted an invitation. No, I don't mean that. I mean I'm very glad I've accepted the invitation because it was very kind and I'm looking forward to it, but it would have been very nice to come to you, too, if you see what I mean.'

'Don't worry about it,' Sally soothed. Poor Marley sounded mortified. 'It was just an idea. I thought you'd be bound to have fixed something up.'

'I feel so ungrateful.'

'Of course you're not. You can't help being the most popular person in the cast. We'll just have to wait our turn. Can I book you for nineteen ninety-nine, while you're there?' She heard Marley giggle. 'You are a silly girl, Sally, my love. Perhaps we can get together in the

New Year? I do like your Dan. Tell him I saw him in *Soldier, Soldier* the other night. He was awfully good.'

'I'll tell him.'

Patrick came up to her next day. 'Marley was telling me you invited her for Christmas?' Sally dipped her biscuit in her coffee. 'Yes, that's right, but she was already fixed up.'

'Did she tell you who she was going to?'

'No. I didn't ask. Why?' Patrick shrugged. 'No reason. I just thought perhaps she had.'

'I expect it's Hazel. She's more organised than the rest of us.'

Patrick harrumphed self-consciously. 'Actually, not that it matters or anything, but she's coming to us.'

'Oh!' Sally hoped her reaction didn't sound as ungracious as she felt. 'Oh, well, that's nice. Especially if you've got all your children. She loves children.'

'My youngest is nineteen,' Patrick reminded her.

'Marley loves everyone,' said Sally, 'and she certainly loves a crowd. She'll have a much better time with you than she would with just Dan and me.'

Patrick grinned with some relief. 'And you don't mind?' Sally shook her head. 'Why on earth should I mind?' Patrick shrugged. 'I don't know. I just thought you might. You know, that Suzanne and I had, I don't know, got in first.' Sally burst out laughing. 'I'm afraid I don't see Christmas in terms of how many people you can feed off one turkey.' Patrick chuckled. 'It's just the two of you then?'

'Looks like it.'

Patrick sighed. 'What bliss.'

Contrary to Patrick's prediction, they had only two days off for Christmas. René rehearsed them till lunch time on Christmas Eve then gave them each a bottle of wine and dismissed them till four o'clock on Boxing Day when he wanted to do a 'swift run through'. By the look on some of their faces René was in danger of being swiftly run through himself, but they were only five days from studio and two episodes from the end. This was the time when casting directors, already apprised of their potential availability, would start to watch in earnest. They must keep on their toes. With this worthy resolve they all went off to get legless.

Dan and Sally spent the afternoon shopping with the sort of hopeless disorganisation that only couples on their own can afford to indulge in. They bought a turkey in a market which was not only too big for them but too big for either of their ovens. 'Still, it was ever such a bargain,' repeated Sally for the third time as they lugged it out to Dan's car, along with crackers, a case of wine and an array of exotic vegetables which neither of them were sure they would like.

On the way home they stopped by the roadside and bought a Christmas tree. This was far too large as well and they were stopped by a police car on the edge of Greenwich and informed that they should have a warning light on it. The policeman was shining his torch into the boot as Sally hunted for their 'Glow in the Dark' star that she had assured him would fill the bill, when the man suddenly swung the beam up to her face and muttered, 'I thought so.' Sally stood stock still like a rabbit caught in a headlight, wondering what on earth she could have done to deserve such third-degree treatment. 'You're Laura Barnes,' said the constable, his voice trembling with the excitement of his discovery.

Sally smiled. 'Yes, I am.'

The young man frowned and looked at his notes. 'I've got "Sally Grosvenor" here.'

'That's my real name. Laura Barnes is the character I play,' she explained carefully. The policeman nodded. 'I hope things work out OK. You know, with the boss,' he said gravely. 'Careful as you go.'

'Happy Christmas,' said Sally.

'It's not that funny,' said Dan, casting a wary glance at Sally who was shaking like a jelly beside him. 'I know,' she gurgled, 'it's just so silly. Him thinking that was my real name.'

'I bet a lot of people do.'

'Yes, but he's a policeman. And even when I told him he still said he hoped things worked out all right with my boss.' She was off again.

They put the tree up in Dan's flat because there was more space. Sally decorated it while Dan tried to saw the turkey into a manageable shape. They had fish and chips and mince pies for supper and sang Christmas carols as they sat back to back wrapping presents. Sally wondered fleetingly what Suzanne and Patrick would be doing. Patrick had looked particularly gloomy as he set off for his 'family Christmas' that afternoon. She wondered if Dan were wondering the same, but if he was there was no sign of it in his outward demeanour as he fought her savagely for the Sellotape and topped up her glass with champagne.

On Christmas morning they opened their presents in bed. Sally lay back and gazed out over the forest of wrapping paper at the silk underwear, the jewellery, the watch, the vases, the cookery book. 'I've never had a Christmas like this,' she said.

'What do you mean?' Dan was sitting beside her with a cashmere jersey over his pyjamas.

'All these presents. I don't think I've ever had so many. Not even as a child. My parents never let us open them all at once, anyway. We used to have our stockings in the morning, then we had to wait till after the Queen's speech before we could open any more.'

'You're kidding.'

'No. We went for a long walk in the morning then my uncle and aunt would arrive and we'd have Christmas dinner, then the Queen's speech, then presents.'

'What did you do after that?'

'Play a game, usually. I always got a game of some sort. You know, Monopoly, Scrabble, something like that.'

'Sounds fun,' said Dan politely.

'It was the most boring day of the year,' said Sally.

'Ours wasn't much better. We used to wake up about five, open all our presents then spend the rest of the day fighting over them. They were mostly broken by tea time.'

'Do you miss all that?'

'Broken presents?'

'Your family? Having lots of people round?'

Dan shook his head. 'I loathed it. All I ever wanted was to be left in peace to read my *Beano* annual.'

Sally smiled and closed her eyes.

'What are you thinking about?'

'How happy I am.'

'Uh oh,' said Dan. 'That means you'll be in tears by lunch time.'

'No I won't. I'm going to be happy all day. Forever. I'm never going to be unhappy again.' Dan leant over and kissed her on the forehead. 'Here's hoping,' he said.

For a while it looked as though Sally might be right. They spent the day struggling with the complexities of her cookery book and charging up and down the stairs with trays of stuffing, bacon rolls and bread sauce.

'It's a pity we can't use Mr Davenport's cooker,' panted Sally as she prepared for yet another journey to turn the potatoes. They had got the turkey, minus its wings, into Dan's oven but there was no room for anything else.

'Why don't we?' said Dan. 'You've got the key.' Sally hesitated. 'We couldn't. Could we?'

'I don't see why not. He wouldn't have minded. Probably be only too pleased. It would save all this charging up and down the stairs.'

'Yes, but . . .'

They let themselves in. The place was cold and musty from lack of use but the cooker was still working.

'I was thinking,' said Dan as they sat over the remains of the marathon, 'what a nice house this would make.'

'How do you mean? Sally was trying to light an indoor firework which involved all her concentration. 'Look. I've done it. Oh isn't it lovely? It's a tree. Or something.' Dan watched till the flower had burnt down to the saucer. 'I'm just thinking that you own the flat upstairs and I own this one and if we could rake up enough to buy the old man's . . .' Sally glanced at him uncertainly. 'You mean, between us?'

'Yes.'

Sally felt her throat constricting with panic. 'But that would be a huge commitment, for both of us . . .'

'I know. I just wondered how you felt about it?' Sally stared at the burnt-out flower. 'I don't know. I hadn't thought about it. It's a huge commitment.'

'So you said.' She was silent. 'You don't like the idea?'

'I didn't say that. It's just you've sort of sprung it on me. Anyway, I don't know if I could raise that sort of money.'

'You could if you do your coffee advert.'

'Yes . . .'

Dan turned away and reached for the television control. 'It was just a thought. Forget it.'

Sally sat on, staring at the debris of their meal. The room seemed suddenly claustrophobic. She stood up. 'I think I'll go for a breath of air. I'll clear this up when I come back.' Dan stood up too. 'I'll come with you.'

'You don't have to. I thought you wanted to watch that film.'

'I've seen it before. I just thought you might like it.'

They walked in silence, automatically turning towards the park although it was dark and the gates would be locked. 'You're right,' said Dan at last. They were passing the model shop on the corner of the high street. The tinsel round the wafery ships looked tawdry rather than festive in this aftermath of the celebrations. 'Right about what?' It was the first time either of them had spoken. 'The house. The old man's bit. It was just I was thinking how nice it was with only the two of us. I was worried about the sort of person who might come along and buy his place, that's all.'

'You mean the sort of person who cuts off other people's water?'

Dan smiled. 'Got it. Anyway, it'll probably be empty for yonks. It needs a fair bit doing.'

Sally shook her head. 'It'd be cheap for that very reason, I should think.'

Dan shrugged. 'Well, if we don't like them we can always pee all over the bannisters.'

Sally looked up at him. His face seemed curiously empty. 'Or move,' she prompted. An expression of helpless pain shot across Dan's face, then he nodded. 'Exactly. Or move.'

'I think I'd like to sleep upstairs tonight, if that's all right,' she said casually as they turned back up the path.

'Of course. I was going to suggest the same thing,' said Dan, kicking a stone into a flowerbed.

Later, lying between her chilly sheets Sally thought, I hardly know him. He was talking long term. I'm not ready for that. Panic swept over her again. Cohabiting was one thing, co-owning was another. After all, she had her career to think about. She had waited long enough to get this far. She couldn't possibly throw it all up now. And whatever Dan said, she knew in her heart that he would want her to put him first. It wasn't his fault. That was how people like him thought. Marriage, home, family. That was what he had wanted from Suzanne and here he was looking to repeat the same set-up that had already failed him so spectacularly. So much for 'understanding the modern woman'! How could any man when their roots were set in Genesis?

She sighed and turned over. She hated this bed. It was hard and cold and empty without Dan. Her body ached for the feel of him beside her. She lay there, wondering if it was too late. Surely if she went down and tapped on his door he would let her in, take her to bed, make love to her? But if she did, would that not be tacit agreement? It would mean the end of her independence, an acknowledgement that her plans could be subjected to his. And that she could never give. Why can't it be simpler, she thought. Why can't love be all right?

Downstairs Dan switched off the television on which elderly comedians were reminiscing about landladies of their youth, and went to bed. I've blown it, was all that ran through his mind. I should never have pushed her like that. He wondered if it was too late to go up and knock on her door, say that he hadn't meant to tie her down, that he loved her way of life – the uncertainty, the strangeness of actors, the warmth and glamour and endless possibility that fuelled her world. It was all that had been missing from his life with Suzanne, who had had everything mapped out for the next forty years – new kitchen, new wallpaper, new job and now, because he had rebelled against such exactitude, new man. Well, at least she had been predictable, something Sally was definitely not. Maybe that was why he loved her.

*   *   *

They had arranged to go to the theatre on Boxing Day. Dan met her from rehearsal. He seemed distant and polite and Sally, torn between a desire to throw herself into his arms and a conviction that she must not show weakness in any shape or form, was equally restrained.

They talked about the traffic and the unseasonable warmness of the weather, taking their seats long before it was necessary in a nearly empty auditorium. This reminded Sally of their trip to *Clytemnestra* and depressed her more than ever. At least he hasn't bought chocolates, she thought, but he had. She thanked him and sat with them ostentatiously unopened on her lap while Dan studied the programme like someone swatting for an exam.

The play was long and tedious. It was supposed to be a thriller but the actors' timing, presumably due to the same resentment which had invaded Sally's own rehearsal, was badly awry.

Dan shuffled endlessly, making her want to slap him. She offered him the chocolates which he unwrapped noisily then spent ages rummaging through. 'Can't you just take one?' she hissed angrily, aware of dark looks homing in on them.

'I can't see what they are. They might be Turkish delight.'

'Well they can't all be. Take two.'

'Ssssh,' said someone behind them.

'I don't want two. I only want one.'

'Oh for God's sake.' Sally whipped the box away from him and planted a chocolate on his lap. Dan ate it sulkily.

The play was reaching its climax, the hero being alone in a mortuary with a maniac pathologist, when Dan decided to cross his legs. A loud chorus of 'Ding Dong Merrily On High' rose tinnily from his ankles, echoing remorselessly round the auditorium as Sally dragged him after her up the aisle.

'Don't ever do that to me again,' she threatened him as they plunged into the nearest bar.

'It wasn't my fault,' Dan protested. 'You gave them to me.'

'Yes, but I didn't expect you to wear them to the theatre.'

'I wanted something to remind me of you,' said Dan miserably.

'What do you mean "remind you of me"?' asked Sally, the evening suddenly cold.

Dan shrugged. 'I thought, after yesterday, it might be our last time together.' Sally looked at him, speechless, for a moment, then buried her face in his chest. 'I love you, Dan. I thought you knew that.' Dan said nothing, but pressed her head closer till she could hear his heart beating. Which one of us, she thought? Which one of us is going to give in?

27

With the new year came changes. Money, hitherto a forbidden subject in connection with *The Firm*, seemed suddenly more available. Stephanie was again taken shopping and by episode eleven two small pictures had been added to the magnolia walls of John Christie's living room.

Laura was given a new typewriter and Richard a new car (subsequently badly dented when Simon got confused between reverse and fifth gear). Wellard Kenning appeared in a new corduroy jacket and was once on the brink of buying Patrick a coffee when called away to the phone. Gaby, who had forsaken warm-ups for throwing up in the sink, coyly announced that she and the bulldog were expecting the patter of tiny feet. 'No chance,' grunted Patrick, indicating Gaby's size eight trainers.

The best news of all was that Marley had been nominated for Best Actress in a Television Serial which brought a further flurry of publicity and an offer of Volumnia from the RSC.

In all this there was no sign of Jeff Wilkins. He no longer came round after recording which was not much remarked upon, but when he failed to appear at the Producer's Run the whispers became roars. His place was taken by a beaky blonde woman in her forties who answered to the name of Pris. No one was sure of her precise function but she seemed very confident as she strutted around making notes on a spiral pad and clicking noises with her tongue which the actors found strangely intimidating. Throughout this René remained detached, giving nothing away despite the constant and ever less tactful probing of his cast.

'Who did you say Pris was working for?' queried Patrick casually after she had departed in a fast car for the studios. René smiled a weary smile. 'Oh . . . Pris,' he said. 'Can we just do that last bit of the bedroom scene again? I'm not sure if the lamp's quite right.'

'It's come to something,' Patrick remarked drily to Sally, 'when we have to rehearse for the furniture's benefit.'

Marley was not so easily put off. 'Now, René dear, I want you to sit by me at lunch today so you can tell me all about that lovely lady who was taking all the notes.' René nodded. 'I'd love to, Marley darling, but I've got to shoot up to the stills library and check the piccies for the *Radio Times*.'

Rumours once more abounded. Stephanie was of the opinion that Jeff Wilkins had been sacked, while Marley fretted that he might be ill and Patrick opined that he had drowned while drunk on a fishing trip. Drewe made mysterious noises and hinted that his agent had told him all about it, but Drewe made so many claims to the ears of the mighty that no one believed anything he said.

Dilys no longer came to the pub with them and once or twice Sally had accompanied her to the coffee bar where she now ate resolutely healthy sandwiches and consumed cup after cup of espresso. It was here that she confided that Jeff Wilkins had indeed been sacked or given 'suspended leave for health reasons' as his contract allowed it be stated.

'But why?' asked Sally, shocked. 'I mean I know he wasn't all that effective, but he was a lot nicer than some of the producers I've worked for. He didn't actually do anything wrong, did he?' Dilys gave a short sharp laugh. 'Let's say he was in the wrong place at the wrong time.' Sally waited to see if there were any more but Dilys was hunting for her

Fishermen's Friends and seemed to have forgotten all about the unfortunate Jeff Wilkins.

The others were waiting expectantly for Sally when she got back.

'Well?' demanded Simon. Sally looked at him. 'Well, what?'

'Did she say anything?'

'What about?' dithered Sally, knowing instinctively that 'Did who?' would not pass muster. 'Jeff,' put in Marley anxiously. 'We're all so worried about him, and René's being so peculiar, poor lamb. I wonder if we should get a card?'

'Go on, Sal,' said Veeney with more animation than she had shown for a long time. 'She must have said something.'

'Not really,' Sally prevaricated. 'Here she is now. Why not ask her yourself?' Dilys' timely return from the ladies gave her a reprieve. It was a fact universally acknowledged that no one ever asked Dilys anything relating to her husband or the Majestic executive, either from tact or fear of a lambasting. Sally was spared the necessity for further duplicity by the return of René in company with Dilys' husband, Bill Lewis, the accountant, Rhys Davies, and the indefatigable Pris.

The place fell silent as they walked in, striding down the hall like a vanguard of tribunes. They installed themselves at the table, setting out Majestic folders and swivelling their eyes in a precision movement towards René who was hovering, hands clenching and unclenching, at the top. 'Good afternoon, everyone,' he said stiltedly. 'If we could all just take a seat for a moment, Bill has something he'd like to say.'

They sidled over, no one wanting to sit next to or opposite the gang of three, yet too curious to be out of earshot. Only Dilys remained standing. She had been making herself more coffee and now stood leaning against the kitchen door. Her husband's eyes flickered irritably towards her. 'Come on, Dilly. This concerns you too.'

'Nothing you say concerns me,' she responded coldly. Lewis gave a nervous chuckle and exchanged glances with Pris. He turned to the others. 'What I have to say will, I think, please you in the main. There are to be one or two changes – not something that should worry you or in any way affect the marvellous work you've all been doing. And may I just say, how grateful all of us at Majestic are for this superb production. We all knew it had what it took to be a number one show, and by gosh, you've certainly more than justified our faith.' He paused, presumably expecting some kind of reaction to this volte-face, but the cast was too stupefied to respond. 'Yes,' he continued hurriedly, 'but the reason I'm here this afternoon is that, in keeping with the kind of profile we want to give *The Firm*, it has become necessary to make one or two adjustments in the production team and that is why we have brought in Pris.' He turned to her and wagged his head admiringly. She continued to survey her notes as though presiding over a prize-giving at a rather select girls' school.

'Excuse me,' Patrick raised a languid arm.

'Yes, Pad . . . Patrick?'

'What exactly is Pris . . . I'm sorry, I didn't catch your surname, 's function in the "team", as you so interestingly call it?' Bill Lewis put on his executive smile. 'Let me formally introduce Pris Evans to you all. She is your new producer.'

A flutter of surprise ran through the room. 'What happened to Jeff?' asked Veeney. Lewis sighed. 'Jeff Wilkins, as I'm sure some of you were aware, has not been well recently. Unhappily he felt that he could no longer shoulder the huge responsibilities that an important production like *The Firm* entails. He has, regretfully, decided to resign his position as producer and Pris has taken over. Some of you may be familiar with Pris' work. She was with Central for some years, working on programmes like *Haybury Corner, This Earth, Solomon's Judgement* . . .' The actors shifted uneasily in their chairs. These were the names of religious programmes.

'How do you feel about this, Ren?' asked Veeney provocatively. René shifted in his chair and ran a dry tongue round his lips. He would have to increase his dosage if this was the best it could do for him. 'I, well, naturally, I am, er . . . very disappointed for Jeff. I know how much the production meant to him. And I know that, had his health permitted, he would have very much liked to have continued as part of the team, and of course we are all very grateful to him for the enormous strengths he brought to the production, but the sad truth is that the demands of a big budget show like this,' there were stifled guffaws from the actors, 'cannot be fulfilled by anyone who is less than a hundred per cent committed to the project.' He sat down and reached for a glass of water.

Patrick leant forward on his hands, brows furrowed. 'Forgive me. I'm a little confused. You speak of *The Firm* as a "big budget" production. I have to tell you that I have worked to bigger budgets in provincial pantomime than has been evident in this show. Be that as it may. What further confuses me is your decision to let Jeff go when there are less than six weeks of production time left. Surely it causes more upheaval to have a major changeover at this late stage than to leave things as they were?' Had she not known Patrick better Sally might have believed this an innocent remark.

Bill Lewis sat back, glanced at Davies whose ferret eyes glowed, and smiled an emperor's smile. 'And that brings me to the second part of what I wanted to say. It gives me the utmost pleasure and delight to tell you that a second series of *The Firm* is in the process of being commissioned. The contracts are with your agents now.'

'That's the first I've heard of it,' snorted Patrick, triumph oozing from his pores. Lewis smiled deprecatingly. 'I know, Patrick, and I'm sorry. I'm afraid it's all had to be a bit cloak and dagger. We didn't want the papers getting hold of it before the final ep. – spoil the suspense, if you see what I mean.'

'Oi, oi,' interrupted Simon jubilantly. 'That means one of us is for the chop.' Lewis laughed noisily and nudged Davies, who was staring at Simon with unconcealed alarm. He obligingly twisted his face into a smirk.

Chattering broke out amongst the cast. Marley was wreathed in smiles of relief, Veeney was rolling a cigarette with studied indifference. Stephanie had shot off to phone her agent, Drewe hard on her heels.

'Call for a drink, does it, Bill old son?' enquired George cheerfully, though quite how he thought he could continue from beyond the grave no one was sure.

Pris Evans was murmuring to Lewis. He nodded attentively before turning to René and indicating that the cast should be called to order. René duly hushed them. 'I think this might be the moment for your new producer to introduce herself properly,' said Lewis.

Pris Evans rose, put her hands straight on the desk in front of her and stared round at them. 'It's good to be on board,' she said in a thin brittle voice. No one knew quite how to respond to this so they said nothing. 'As you know I was at the run this morning and I was more than a little impressed. It's a great privilege for me to be asked to take over a series like this and I'm going to do my best to make sure I'm worthy of it, which, I hope, with a little help from my friend up there,' her eyes rose to the smoke-stained ceiling of St Nicholas' hall, 'I shall soon be able to do.' The cast cringed with embarrassment. 'Now, I have a feeling that coming in so late in the day there may be a limit to what I can do in this series, but my aim will be to set the agenda for the next one, and this naturally will need to blend with the finish of number one. To this end I'd like to call a full cast rehearsal tomorrow morning at eight thirty to give us time to work in a few minor nuances which I think will make all the difference.' She sat down to stunned silence.

'Isn't it a bit late?' asked Patrick.

Pris smiled forgivingly. 'I was only thinking of you,' she explained. 'Eight would be fine for me. Shall we make it eight then, René? That OK for you?' René muttered that it would be absolutely fine, his eyes rooted to the table.

'Bloody hell,' said Patrick, marshalling them into the pub. 'Give me a Guinness, darling. No, forget that. Give me a triple whisky, no water.'

'What have we done to deserve her?' asked Simon, giving Penny's bottom a squeeze.

'Poor old Jeff,' said Hazel. 'That was pretty brutal.'

'René must be scared sick,' said Stephanie.

'He has every reason,' said Dilys, spraying soda water into her orange. They all looked at her expectantly. Dilys turned to Veeney. 'You warn him, love. He's walking a knife edge with those two bastards.' Nobody was sure to which two she referred, but they accepted it as the voice of the oracle and began to worry about their own positions vis-à-vis Ms Evans' planned 'nuances'.

They did not have very long to wait to find out what their new producer had in mind. She completely supplanted René during the early morning rehearsal, marching from set to set clicking like a grasshopper and arriving at the next scene long before any of the actors, who were suffering jet lag from the early start.

At the end of the run she sat them all down round the table and dismissed Penny and her tray of coffee with a 'Not now, darling. Can't you see we're working?' Penny retreated, beetroot with mortification. 'Right,' said Pris and clicked her tongue. 'Notes.'

'We usually have coffee during notes,' said Patrick menacingly. He was in a foul mood, having stayed too long in the pub and left his raincoat in a taxi.

'Did you?' Pris raised a carefully drawn eyebrow. 'Well, I promise I won't be long. Actually it's you most of these notes concern, Patrick,' she paused. Patrick regarded her politely. 'Don't you want a pencil to jot them down.'

'I don't think that will be necessary,' said Patrick with icy calm. 'I'm sure I shall remember any that are important.' The cast held its breath. Pris flipped him a tight little smile. 'As you wish. More pace, that's my first commandment. Remember your average viewer has a very short attention span. There simply isn't time for you to mull over everything the way you're doing now. Pace, pace, pace. I'm sure you've had that one thrown at you before.'

'Not since my Whitehall farce days,' responded Patrick.

'Well, there it is. More pace. Keep the thing moving, and that applies to all of you. Veeney, you were particularly at fault. What on earth did you think you were doing, slumping over the desk like that? I thought you were asleep.'

Since it was the night after one of Veeney's gigs it was a reasonable supposition. 'I was trying to decide whether to go ahead with my abortion,' said Veeney.

'Yes, and that's another thing.' Ms Evans turned to René, 'where's Wellard?'

'He's working on a few of the changes,' muttered René flatly. Pris Evans clicked. 'I particularly wanted him here. That abortion scene will have to go. That or tone it down completely. We all know these things go on but we don't have to ram it down people's throats, for heaven's sake.' They waited to see if she would cross herself. She did not.

By the time she dismissed them, for there was no other way to describe it, suicidal despair had all but engulfed them.

It was far worse than anything the early days or original reviews had engendered.

'Come back, Wilkie,' intoned Simon as he spooned sugar into his coffee. 'All is forgiven. Shut that door,' he hissed, too late, for Pris Evans was framed in it like a spectre. 'Marley, dear. Just a quick word.' She gestured with her head.

'How dare she?' said Patrick loudly. 'Take no notice, my darling. Let her come to you.'

'Oh no,' quavered Marley nervously. 'Please. I don't mind at all. I expect it's just a little secret she wants to tell me.' She shot a terrified smile round the group and hurried out of the room.

'I don't know about you lot,' said Veeney, 'but they can stuff this second series if she's going to be around.'

Simon shrugged. 'I expect she'll be all right once she calms down. Just trying to prove herself, if you ask me.'

'Don't you believe it,' said Stephanie. 'I asked Frank if he knew anything about her. He does a lot with the Central shares. He said she's been through that place like a dose of salts. That's why it's in profit. It's probably why Majestic brought her in. My agent says they're fighting like mad to keep us on the original contract terms.'

'Some jumped-up tart from the God Slot?' snarled Patrick. 'You must be joking. If she was any good she wouldn't be working on shows like that.'

'She's good with figures,' insisted Stephanie. 'She got *Solomon's Judgement* into the top twenty. That's never happened with a God Slot before.'

'What did she do?' asked Patrick. 'Cut a baby in half?'

'She would if she had to. Make no mistake about that,' said Stephanie. The door opened. Marley came back in. Her powder puff face looked quite white beneath the carefully applied makeup. 'Pris would like us to start rehearsal again now,' she whispered and sank down on to a chair.

'Marley, are you all right?' asked Sally hurrying over to her.

Marley nodded. 'Just a little tired.' She ferreted in her bag for a handkerchief. 'If I could have all those involved in the family reunion,' came Pris Evans' voice. The actors filed out.

Sally sat down beside Marley. She was horrified to see tears in the old lady's eyes. 'What's she said to upset you, Marley?' she asked softly. Marley shook her head and endeavoured to smile. 'I'm just being silly,' she said. Penny brought her coffee and some custard creams on a plate. Marley eyed them longingly. 'No, no. Pris is quite right. At my age I have to be sensible. I have been a little overindulgent lately, I realise that. But it was Christmas, and when you're on your own sometimes you get a bit lonely . . .' Her chin wobbled dangerously.

'What do you mean, "on your own",' Sally broke in. 'You went to Patrick's, didn't you?'

Marley frowned in confusion. 'Oh dear, no, dear, I didn't. Didn't I tell you? It must have slipped my mind. There was a bit of confusion. Not enough chairs or something. It didn't matter, really it didn't. I'd all but forgotten, but, you know, I think perhaps I rather overdid it. I'd bought some things to take with me and then, when I didn't go, I thought I might as well eat them myself, but it was greedy of me. I realise that. Pris is quite right . . .' a line of tears squeezed their way out and trickled down her cheeks. Sally, wondering whom she could hire to kill Patrick, put her arm round Marley as Penny prodded the biscuits nearer. Marley fought to control herself. 'She is quite right,' she repeated resolutely. 'At my age I must be sensible.'

'What did Pris say?' persisted Sally, her anger mounting.

'Nothing. Nothing at all, really. She was very nice. Just pointed out that my contract is very definite in forbidding me certain wrong sorts of food and that if . . .' she sucked in her breath in an effort to hold back the tears, 'that if I don't keep to the terms of it, there will be no place for me in series two. She's absolutely right, of course. I owe it to the rest of you to keep myself in good trim. I'm not as young as I was. I don't want to let everyone down by getting ill.'

'She said that as well, did she?' said Sally through gritted teeth.

'She's quite right,' murmured Marley distractedly. She wiped her eyes and replaced her handkerchief in her bag. Sally glimpsed the packet of Rolos at the bottom. She'll be going through her bag next, she thought. The woman has no right to live.

'Can we have Marley out here NOW,' came René's petulant voice. And we know whose side he's on, Sally reflected grimly as Marley tottered off to join the others.

Pris Evans departed at lunch time, leaving René to pick up the remnants of his production and the battered egos of his cast. Sally guessed from the way he kept them working and avoided all chance of open discussion that he was mortally afraid of the woman. The sympathy she had originally felt for him had more or less evaporated in the face of his snivelling capitulation. He deserved to have his authority eroded, his efforts denigrated, his position undermined if he were prepared to stand-by and let his cast be bullied in such a fashion. Christ, had the man got no pride? If it hadn't been for him and his peculiar casting *The Firm* might well have sunk without trace. He was the one who had kept them all going when they had wanted to sink down under the weight of the reviews, he alone had pulled them through into what was now the undoubted success (for whatever reasons) of the season. How, then, could he sit back and watch this harpy destroy everything that he had achieved?

Sally sat in the train home alternately pitying him and planning how to dispose of his body. The man opposite raised his eyes once or twice and stared meaningfully at the *Evening Standard* which she was covering with ritual stab marks from her biro.

She got off and stalked up the High Street in a veritable glow of righteous anger. Wait till she told Dan about this. He would be furious. Especially the way Marley had been treated. He liked Marley. She wouldn't be surprised if he went round and saw the Evans woman. And Patrick. That would give them a fright. Although she knew in her heart that Suzanne was probably responsible. 'Not enough chairs'! Makes better mince pies than you more like, she thought. You glossy, bossy bitch.

The two of them were standing together in the porch as she turned into Marchbank Gardens. As she approached she saw Dan reach down and take Suzanne's hand. He held it between his own as they talked. Suzanne turned away, but Dan touched her shoulder then very gently took her face in his hands and bent down to kiss her. She seemed slightly stunned, in two minds whether she should go, but eventually she pulled away from him again and walked quickly down the path and away up the road towards the bus station. Dan watched her go, then turned and went inside.

Sally stood perfectly still and waited till he had shut the door. A sick burning feeling crept through her. She walked towards the house. As she let herself in Dan came out of his flat to meet her. 'Hullo, my love. Good rehearsal?'

'Not very,' said Sally tonelessly. 'I take it the divorce is off?'

28

Sally stared at the phone. Presumably it would stop ringing eventually. She thought about putting the answering machine on but she didn't even want to hear his voice. If it went on much longer she would pull it out of the wall.

Her throat burned with trying not to cry. Somehow the enormity of her unhappiness seemed too great for so mundane a reaction. It required something deeper and more heroic. Even in her misery she could not ignore the situation's dramatic potential. She saw herself from a distance, alone, deceived, rejected – the hapless Imogen, Julia, Desdemona. Thank God for Shakespeare. He knew that men were rats. Why couldn't she have met someone like him? Not that he was all that good a husband, dumping poor Anne Hathaway while he lived it up in London. Still, he had a lovely way with words. Not like bloody Dan Chamberlain who couldn't string a sentence together when he had anything important to say and then blamed her for it – 'so hard to get through to you', 'smack me down', 'jump down my throat', floated through her mind. She looked at them and let them drift away. Her yoga teacher would have been proud of her. Her off-licence too if she continued to drink at this rate.

Looking back she could see how her life had been transformed in the past few months. She had turned from a bystander into a full-blooded participant and it had been wonderful. But now it was over. She should have known better. She should have stayed on the outside looking in. That was the safest place to be. 'Keep your emotions for the job,' a director had once told her. 'Save them up. Make them work for you.' And she had pitied him, because he was an embittered husk of a man, whose only pleasure came from rubbishing his actors' efforts. Or so she had thought. Now she saw that he had been right. Better far to keep your feelings for an audience. Let them take the burden of your hopes and disappointments on their shoulders; there were more of them, they could spread the load. Let them do the crying.

But it was too late now. She would have to do her own.

Over and over again as she sat crouched by the gin bottle she went over what she had seen. Every movement, every gesture, every wave of Suzanne's revolting hair. The way he had taken her hand between his, touched her shoulder, kissed her – not with any savage passion or passing flash of lust, but gently, kindly – as though there were an understanding between them, a knowledge of each other, an intimacy beyond anything she had known, born of long years of companionship. Which, of course, was what it was.

How could she have hoped in the space of a few months, to replace the woman he had loved for eleven years? Pitiful even to imagine she might have. And Suzanne's fling with Patrick clearly meant no more to her than it had to him. So now they were back together again, as good as. And she was back where she had always been. The eternal onlooker. But this time she would keep her eyes firmly shut.

She topped up her glass. How could he? How could he have used her like that? Why? When she had given him everything? Her love, her trust . . . that was the worst . . . That he should have betrayed her trust when she had never trusted anyone so completely before. Her mind strayed back to the conversation with Patrick. 'He's not two-timing you, is he?' The irony was not lost on her. Well, she had been right about one thing. She'd certainly never be anyone's wife.

'You never ask me about my day,' Dan had complained. Just as well or she'd have had to listen to the lies even longer. How many times had he 'worked late' and she'd never suspected a thing? But what on earth was the point of it all? Surely he couldn't be so sex-starved that he needed a woman on tap, no matter whom? It would have served him right if *she*'d been the one to drop dead and he'd had to make do with Mrs Davies. This struck her as inordinately funny till she remembered that he had once called her old. Maybe there wasn't that much difference between thirty-three and eighty if you didn't have red hair and big tits.

The phone stopped.

Sally refilled her glass. She leant her head against the wall and pictured once more the dreadful sight of Suzanne and Dan embracing. If only she hadn't come round the corner when she had. If only she'd been five minutes later, Suzanne would have been gone. She could have had one more evening's happiness at least. Trust bloody British Rail to run the train on time. Was there nothing you could depend on?

The tears began to slither down her face. She gulped at the gin. The room was beginning to move.

And what had been Dan's reaction to her challenge? 'There's something I think you should know.' As if she didn't know it already. She might not be an expert in these matters, but she did know a husband and wife groping each other didn't usually signify good times ahead for the lover.

The phone started to ring again. 'Shut up,' she yelled. 'Shut up. Shut up. Shut up.' It stopped. She heard Dan's door open down below and his relentless tread on the stair.

Outside her door he stopped. Sally braced herself for the knock. There was none, however, and after a few minutes she heard him turn and go back down the stairs. She lay down on the couch and watched the ceiling spinning above her. I wish I was dead, she thought. I wish I was dead and Mr Davenport was still alive and that Dan Chamberlain had never been born.

When she awoke the following morning she wondered if she had been the victim of a hit-and-run accident. Her stomach ached, her throat was sore, her head felt as though a brigade of cavalry were practicing manoeuvres inside it. Agonisingly she pulled herself up off the couch. It was nine o'clock. For one dreadful moment she thought she was supposed to be at rehearsal, then remembered that that had been yesterday. René had not dared to suggest a repetition. But she was still going to be late.

Slowly the events of yesterday came flooding back to her. Dan, Suzanne, Pris Evans, death by gin.

My life is over, she thought as she searched for the aspirins. I have nothing. Her eye fell on the jar of coffee next to the bread bin. Yes, I have, she told herself grimly. I'm going to make a fortune. We're doing a second series, maybe a third, maybe a hundred. Maybe *The Firm* will run like *The Mousetrap* and I'll end up playing my own grandmother. I will not be destroyed by that bastard downstairs. He's only a man. There are plenty of others. What matters is my career. I am an actress. That is all that matters. It could never have worked with Dan anyway. He doesn't understand. He thinks a job's a job. She gave a short laugh. Her throat cracked angrily under the strain. She winced and felt her way towards the bathroom.

On her way out she caught sight of a sheet of the familiar grey notepaper on the mat. Oh no, she thought. You don't get me that way. She snatched it up intending to throw it in the bin, but curiosity was too strong. 'I must talk to you. It's urgent. Dan.' The hell it is, she thought bitterly, crumpling the note into a ball and aiming it unsuccessfully at the wastepaper basket.

There was no sign of life as she crept down the stairs and out into the cold morning air. Like a thief she scurried down the path and away from the house.

'How did you feel when you heard the news, Miss Barnes?' a microphone snaked its way towards her. St Nicholas' Church Hall was under siege. Sally gazed uncomprehendingly at the Outside Broadcast van, the reels of cable, the popping lights. Surely not even the news of a second series could elicit this kind of response from the media? And what had all that 'cloak and dagger' and not revealing anything till episode thirteen been about? There had obviously been a leak. 'Miss Barnes, look this way.' A bulb flashed. 'Miss Barnes, when did you first . . .'

'My name is Grosvenor, Sally Grosvenor,' she burst out in frustration. 'Please let me through. I'm late for rehearsal.' She banged on the door. A bolt slid noisily aside and Rolo peeped out and admitted her before rapidly relocking the door.

Inside the cast sat huddled at the far end. They looked up as Sally entered but no one spoke. The blinds were all drawn to keep out the curious eyes of reporters who were now endeavouring to climb up on the window ledges to focus their lenses on the inhabitants. 'What is it? What's going on?' Sally asked, bewildered. Rolo led her silently to a chair. Sally scanned the wretched faces for some sort of answer.

'You mean you don't know,' demanded Stephanie incredulously, dragging on a cigarette. 'It was on all the news bulletins last night.'

'What? I . . . I didn't see any television last night.'

'Oh for Christ's sake,' snorted Stephanie. Patrick gestured to her to calm down. 'It's Marley,' he said quietly. 'She's been arrested for shoplifting.'

Sally stared at him, at all of them, waiting for one of them to crack. For the first sign that this was a wind-up because she was late to creep into someone's eyes. For the joke to be over. Surely René who had no sense of humour at all would not allow this to interrupt his rehearsals much longer? 'René?' she turned to him, willing him to snap them all back into reality. René shrugged. 'I'm afraid it's true,' he said.

'But where? When? Oh I can't believe it. There must be some mistake. Where is she now? She's not . . .'

'No, no,' said Rolo quickly. 'Miss Webb is at home. The police did not feel there was a need for custody.'

'For custody? Oh for Christ's sake,' erupted Sally. 'You're talking as though she was an armed robber. What's she supposed to have taken anyway? It was obviously a mistake. You know how vague she is sometimes.'

'You really didn't see the box last night, did you?' said Patrick.

'What's that got to do with it?'

'They caught her on camera. Some bastard store manager passed it on to ITN. It was all over the news. Marley putting these – I don't know what – chocolates into her bag. It was completely damning. She looked all around before she did it. There was no chance of a mistake whatsoever. Of course it'll never come to court. They'd never get a jury after that, but it's disaster for Marley. Pure disaster. She'll never work again.' He shook his head. 'How could she be so stupid? She needed this job. She's got no savings, you know. This will finish her.'

'Who's with her now?' Sally cut across him. Everyone looked surprised.

'No one, as far as we know,' said Simon swiftly. 'It's best we all keep our distance. That way it may all blow over.

Wellard's writing her out of the last two eps. now. She has a heart attack. Perfectly logical. It should work.'

Sally gazed at him disbelievingly. She stood up. 'How could you leave her alone at a time like this? How could you?'

René cleared his throat. 'Actually, Sally, we need to get on with rehearsal. There've been quite a few changes, what with Pris' input and so forth and we really can't afford to spend any more time on this latest . . . development.'

Sally looked at him. He wasn't a director; he was a crumpled, self-abasing, gutless creep. She wondered that she had ever valued his good opinion. She looked at the others. 'Hazel?'

Hazel coughed and folded up her crochet. 'I was planning to go over at the weekend,' she murmured. 'I've got rather a cold at the moment. I don't want to pass it on.'

'Veeney?'

'I wouldn't know what to say,' said Veeney honestly. 'I've got nothing against thieving, you understand, but I'm no good at chitchat. Give her my love, though. Tell her "pecker up". There're some nice screws in Holloway, anyway. She might enjoy it.'

Sally turned and walked away from them.

'Erm . . . I won't be getting to you till about two o'clock,' came René's conciliatory bleat.

As she reached the door a hand grabbed her arm. 'Hang on. I'll get my coat. Strength in numbers.'

Sally nodded. 'Thanks.'

She and Dilys went out of the door together.

The reporters at St Nicholas' Hall were nothing compared to those outside Marley Webb's flat. They were lining the stone steps up to the old house like a peasants' army, tattered leather jackets vying for space with shoulder-padded hustlers. Sally and Dilys debated whether to look for a way in round the back but there were more photographers there than at the front so they retraced their steps and ploughed their way up to the entryphone. Sally pressed Marley's button. 'She won't answer, love,' said one of the reporters. 'We've been trying to get her to open the door for hours.' Sally pressed again. There was a crackle and Marley's quavering voice came over the intercom. 'Please leave me alone. I'm very tired. Please go away.'

'Marley, it's Sally. Dilys and I have come to see you. Please let us in.'

There was a pause. 'I don't really think . . .'

'Marley, let us in. Please.' They waited. There was a click as the lock opened. The reporters surged forward. 'Let us in with you, love. Just one piccie and I'll be gone. Promise.' Dilys and Sally squeezed through the crack. 'There's money in it for you,' came the cry.

'Isn't that the lush?' asked one of the females as they slammed the door and hurried up the curving stairway to the third floor.

Marley looked dreadful. She was dressed, but that was all. She had made no attempt to comb her hair and it sprouted out in tufts, exposing patches of crinkled pink scalp amongst the fluffy curls. Her face, bereft of make-up, looked old and baggy. Standing in her doorway she gazed out at them with hopeless childlike eyes. Sally stepped forward and hugged her, feeling the frail joints clicking as she did so. 'Let's go inside,' she said, guiding her back into the flat. It was stiflingly hot. Sally sat her down while Dilys went to make tea.

'Whatever came over you, Marley?' she asked at last. Marley's shoulders started to shake. Sally put her arm round her. She felt strangely protective, as though Marley were a small child, not a woman in her seventies. 'Only tell me if you want to,' she whispered.

Marley nodded. 'I've never done anything like that before. You must believe me.'

'I do,' said Sally.

'It was just I was so worried and upset by what Pris had said to me. And I don't know why it happens, but the more worried I am the more I want to eat sweet things. I know it's ridiculous, but that's how I am. And I was in Oxford Street. I sometimes go there late night shopping. I rather like it. The stores are so beautiful and warm, and I like just looking at all the things and being warm, and seeing all the faces. I do like being with people, you see. It's dreadfully important to me, being on my own at home and everything. And sometimes someone recognises me and we have a little chat, and I do so enjoy that. I know it's vain and silly, but I don't think it does any harm really, does it?' Her anxious eyes pleaded with Sally for approval. 'Of course it doesn't. It gives people a lot of pleasure. More than it does you, even, I expect.'

Marley shook her head. 'Oh, no, but it is fun, and then last night, it was only about six o'clock because René had kindly let us off early, hadn't he, after our early start, but I don't know why, I was awfully hungry. I thought I'd get myself a cup of tea and some bread and marg. I'm allowed that. But the queue was so long and I felt quite weak with tiredness so I thought perhaps one tiny bar of chocolate wouldn't hurt.' She paused and Sally felt her shoulders sagging.

'What happened,' she coaxed.

'I was going up to the till when a lady stopped me and asked me for my autograph. Naturally I was only too pleased and we chatted for a few minutes and then she went on her way and, I don't know what came over me – maybe it was the tiredness and the excitement of all the changes and everything, but I suddenly thought, supposing Pris finds out that I've gone straight out and bought a bar of chocolate the very day she warned me about not eating it any more? And to start with I thought I should put it back, but it's a long way home from Oxford Street and sometimes you can't find a taxi, and it was such a cold night . . .' Her head sank. 'I always meant to pay for it. I did really.' Sally gave her a squeeze. 'I know you did.'

'And now I've caused such trouble for everyone.'

'You haven't at all,' said Sally through gritted teeth. 'Everyone was very worried about you. They all send their love.'

Marley's face brightened momentarily. 'Bless them. They're such good people. You all are. I'm so lucky. It's all the family I've got, you know, really, but I couldn't have chosen better if I'd picked each one of you myself. And now I've let you all down. I shall never forgive myself. It was such a terrible thing to do,' she began to cry. 'I deserve everything that's happened to me. I'm so sorry. Please tell everyone in the cast. I'm so sorry.'

Dilys brought the tea. At first Marley refused it but gradually they got her to take a few sips. 'You've put sugar in it,' she said, gazing at Dilys in alarm. Dilys nodded. 'For shock. You've had a shock. You need sugar.'

'But I'm not allowed it,' Marley whimpered.

'Yes you are,' said Dilys crisply. 'And now I'm going to make you something to eat. What would you like?'

Marley shook her head. 'Nothing.'

'I'm going to do an omelette,' said Dilys purposefully. 'Wait there.' She returned to the kitchen. Marley raised frightened eyes to Sally. 'Dilys is looking much better,' she whispered. Despite herself Sally burst out laughing. 'Yes,' she agreed. 'She is.'

They stayed with Marley all morning, in which time Sally had arranged for a solicitor to call round, fended off telephone enquiries, contacted Marley's doctor and tucked her up in bed with pile of recipe books and strict instructions that she was to have sorted out her answers for Laura's problem page by the following morning.

'You've both been so very kind,' mumbled Marley as they prepared to go. 'I'm sorry to have been such a nuisance.'

Sally sat on her bed. 'You're not a nuisance, Marley. You're a friend. And you'd do the same for us.'

'I hope I never have to,' muttered Marley with the nearest she'd come to a smile.

The cast were unnaturally perky when the two women rejoined them after lunch. The reporters had dispersed and there was a definite atmosphere of 'let's all pull together' about the way the actors tore in with suggestions for improved moves and possible explanations for Kenning's ever more convoluted plot lines.

No one mentioned Marley at all. From the way they behaved it would be possible to believe that Rebecca Christie had never even appeared in the serial, let alone been its mainstay for eleven episodes.

There were quite a few jokes made at Pris Evans' expense. She had been designated 'Pope Pris' by Patrick which in normal circumstances would have been quite amusing, but under the current ones just made Sally more angry.

'I've got a horse here called Holy Orders,' George informed them at tea break. 'What say we all put a quid on it?' There was general assent and Penny took a plate round collecting. When she got to Sally she shook her head. 'No thanks.'

'Oh come on, Sal,' said George. 'It's only a quid. I'll lend it to you if you're short.'

'Course she's not short,' laughed Patrick. 'She's going to be on double what she's earning now in a couple of months.'

'I doubt it,' put in Stephanie. 'You're with Michael Snelcott, aren't you, love? Frank says he's the only agent who actually gets his clients' fees reduced the more successful they are.'

'That settles it, then,' said George. 'This one's on me.'

'I said no,' said Sally sharply. 'Thank you.' There was an awkward pause.

'Please yourself,' said George, raising his eyebrows to the rest of them.

Rolo approached her soon after. 'René says you can go home early if you like, Sally. He won't be needing you again today.'

'When's that ever stopped him keeping me till the last knockings?' snapped Sally. Rolo recoiled slightly. 'He just thought you looked a bit tired,' he said apologetically. Sally swept up her script and thrust it into her bag. 'Oh yes,' she said savagely. 'I am very very tired.'

There was a message from Michael Snelcott on the answerphone. Stephanie had not been far wrong. He managed to make a rise of three per cent an episode sound like the winner of the lottery. 'Roadsweepers get more than that,' she grumbled to herself, reflecting that they probably did a more useful job.

There was no sign of Dan, for which she was grateful. She didn't suppose she could avoid him forever but she certainly didn't feel up to an encounter now. She wondered about ringing Marley to see if she was still all right, but then remembered she had told her not to answer the phone. Instead she rang her agent and said she thought three per cent was feeble and she knew for a fact that Patrick Crichton's fee had been doubled. There was a silence then Snelcott said, more in sorrow than in anger, that Patrick was in a different category. 'You're right about that,' snapped Sally.

She was more upset by Patrick's behaviour than any of the others'. No one would expect someone like Drewe to put his head on the line for anyone, or Stephanie – there had never been any doubt whose interests they had in mind, and Simon was such an out-and-out coward that she was not all that surprised about him. But Patrick had been a friend of Marley's for over twenty years. How could he sit back and ignore her at a time like this? She'd always suspected he was a bit of a bastard, but not this kind of bastard. There were no two ways about it, actors had the moral fibre of slugs.

The phone rang. It was a young man. 'Is that Sally Grosvenor's number?'

'It is.'

'Er, my name's Christopher Crichton.' He paused, plainly hoping for some encouragement. Sally said nothing. 'I'm, er, my dad's asked me . . . Are you still there?'

'I take it you're Patrick Crichton's son?' said Sally coldly. She heard the young man swallow. Poor sod, she thought, it's not his fault, then she remembered the misery he was causing Patrick and warmed towards him. 'Why are you ringing me?'

'It's my dad,' the young man gabbled. 'He was wondering if he could have a word with you?'

'Why couldn't he ring me himself?'

The youth's voice sank. 'He's shit-scared of what you'll say to him. Shall I put him on?'

'To be honest, you could put him on a conductor rail for all I care.'

Christopher laughed. 'You sound like my mum. Will you speak to him, though?'

Sally sighed. 'If I must.' There was a thud as of the receiver being dropped and the sound of arguing in the background. After a few moments Patrick's voice came down the line. 'Sally?'

'I'm here.'

'Good. Sally . . . about this afternoon . . . Are you still there?'

'Not for much longer,' said Sally who was getting sick of the whole performance.

'It's just you seemed awfully upset . . .'

'I was.'

'I thought so . . . George's horse won by the way. I've got six pounds fifty for you. We did put the bet on, you see. We thought you'd have wanted us to.'

'I didn't. You'll have to excuse me, Patrick. I've got a lot to do this evening.'

'I rang Marley,' Patrick blurted out.

'You what?'

'Yes. When I got back from rehearsals. There was no answer.'

'No. I told her not to answer the phone. She was being pestered by reporters.'

'I am terribly sorry about it all, you know.'

'I'm sure you are.'

'I felt even worse when you and Dilys marched out like that. I did so admire you both.'

'Not enough to join us, obviously.'

There was a pause. 'Sally, you won't understand this but I'll tell you anyway. I can't lose this now. I've spent twenty years in the wilderness. I need this part. I need to be a name again. You don't know what it's like, drinking cups of tea out of plastic cups and listening to senile old crones telling you how good they were in *Pygmalion*. Spending half your life touring places where they've never even heard of Shakespeare, let alone you. I'm fifty-one years old, for Christ's sake. I can't go back to that.'

Sally pursed her lips. 'Well, it looks as though you won't have to. Perhaps you should give Marley the name of your agent?'

'You bloody little cow,' shouted Patrick down the 'phone. 'Do you think I'm going to let her starve? I'm going to look after her. What do you take me for? Don't answer that. I just cannot be seen to be involved from a public point of view. Surely you understand that?'

Sally sat down and leant her head against the wall. 'I think I do.'

'It's different for you. You're young. This bloody serial's not for you. Passing coffee cups to and fro. You should be out with a proper company, playing some decent parts. You've got it all to come. This is just a step on the way for you, unless you give it all up to spawn, of course. By the way, how is the Ex, as the lovely Suzanne insists on calling him?'

'I can't think why,' said Sally, a shattering emptiness sweeping over her. 'I don't know, actually. We're finished.'

Patrick sounded strangely subdued when he spoke again. 'I'm sorry. I didn't know. As a matter of fact Suzanne and I have decided, you know . . . it wasn't really for us.'

Sally smiled grimly. 'Your granny was obviously right.'

'What?'

'About mixed marriages.'

'Oh. Yes. Actually it was the bloody Christmas that settled it for me.'

Sally sat up indignantly. 'Yes. What happened about that? Marley said you cancelled her invitation because there weren't enough chairs.'

Patrick snorted. 'Bloody Suzanne couldn't cope, that's why. She was the one who wanted everyone round. Not me. I wanted to go to Prague, if you recall. I knew what it would be like. It's always the same when that lot get together. All of them slagging each other off, then their mothers, then all the mums ring up in tears because they miss their little darlings, and then the whole lot of them turn round and start on me. Add to it all the fucking turkey was raw in the middle. Lucky we didn't end up in hospital. I tell you, Marley was well out of it. If I'd known what it was going to be like I'd've gone round there and joined her.'

'Pity you didn't,' said Sally viciously.

'How was yours?' asked Patrick. 'Oh, sorry.'

Sally closed her eyes to stifle the tears. 'It was OK.'

Patrick cleared his throat. 'And it's really all off with the tall guy?'

'Oh yes.'

'I'm very sorry.'

'Just one of those things.'

'Yes. Of course.'

'So from now on I shall be concentrating on my career.'

Patrick's voice sounded suddenly very weary. 'Yes. The play's the thing. Word of advice. Keep away from Nairobi.'

29

The letter stating that Daniel Mark Chamberlain of Flat One, Number Five Marchbank Gardens, Greenwich, intended to apply for the freehold of the above-mentioned property arrived a few days later.

It was a shock. Sally had spent much of the week, aided by an understanding doctor and social worker, persuading Marley to come to terms with the situation. René had consistently let her off rehearsals, presumably for fear that if he did not she would go anyway and he would lose even more face.

Colin had rung one night, ostensibly to tell her about his new production, but really to moan, and squeeze what he could from her about the scandal. 'What does Dan say?' he had persisted when she had refused to indulge his nosiness.

'I really wouldn't know.'

'Oh come on, Sal. "Flesh of my flesh" and all that. Don't tell me you haven't discussed it.'

Sally took a breath. 'Dan and I aren't together any more.' She waited for the deluge – the advice, the solicitations, the thirst for details, but Colin, perhaps for the only time in his life, offered no panacea. 'Oh, Sally,' was all he said.

The dreaded Pris Evans continued to put in unannounced appearances, striking fear and paranoia in the hearts of all but Sally and Dilys, who pursued their daily visits unaffected by any dread of having their parts reduced or their contracts revised. Dilys had been offered a sitcom with the BBC and had taken great delight in refusing her husband's blandishments to get her to stay. 'They'll just have to bump me off,' she had announced blithely in the hearing of the dreaded new producer. This, naturally, was not at all what the company had in mind, since the threat of annihilation was the Damocletian sword with which they sought to hold the actors in check. The last thing they wanted was a minor character hogging the 'coffin columns', as the terminology had it. It was decided that Lesley Christie would be sent to visit her sister in Australia.

Pris Evans, who had so far skirted round Sally, unsettled her by asking her to remain behind on the afternoon of the Producer's Run. She consented coldly. When everyone except René had gone Pris treated Sally to one of her rare smiles and asked, 'How did you think it went this afternoon?'

'How did what go?' enquired Sally.

'The run.'

Sally looked surprised. 'As well as ever, I suppose.'

Pris Evans permitted herself a brief laugh. 'Ever the diplomat, our Laura.'

'My name is Sally,' said Sally.

'Yes. I'll come straight to the point, Sally. We here at Majestic can see Laura going places.' I'm being sacked, thought Sally, the adrenalin beginning to bubble. 'René, here, has been full of praise for you. He's . . . we're all amazed at what you've managed to do with, let's face it, what started off as a very small part.' That's how it ended up, too, reflected Sally. She did not respond. Pris Evans looked very slightly harassed. 'I'm going to be perfectly frank with you. I think it's the best way . . .' Still Sally said nothing. 'We've been talking to Bill, and Wellard, and of course, Rhys, our accountant, and they would be perfectly happy to see you taking over where Lesley leaves off, if you see what I mean.'

Sally glanced across at René who nodded enthusiastically. 'I'm not sure that I do,' she said slowly. Pris Evans gave a deprecating little smile.

'Perhaps you're too modest for your own good,' she suggested. 'What we're saying is that with the departure of John's wife, a new love interest will have to be found for him. We'd like that woman to be Laura.' A bolt of excitement shot through Sally. She wasn't sure if she had heard aright.

'Me?' she murmured.

'That's right. How does the idea appeal to you?'

'Well . . .' she looked from one to other of them. 'A lot, actually . . . I'm . . .'

René and Pris both laughed. 'I can see we've taken you by surprise. Hopefully we can take that as a "yes"? Someone will be in touch with your agent as soon as the details have been worked out. Obviously this will mean a lot more work for you in terms of study, etcetera, but I'm sure that will present no problems to you . . . I'm right in thinking you don't have a family, aren't I?'

Despite her excitement Sally felt a slight sting as she replied. 'No immediate family, no.' Pris Evans positively glowed. 'It's just such a problem with small children running around and that sort of thing.' Sally's thoughts flashed to the hapless Gaby. Surely she had been lined up as Christie's potential mistress? 'I expect now you're going to tell me you have five Alsatians that need four hours' exercise a day?' continued Pris chattily. Sally smiled. She felt strangely ungracious. Their new producer was not so bad after all. She was obviously going to take a far greater

interest than poor old Jeff had ever done, and it was good to
have a woman on the team. It added perspective. She might
even get Wellard Kenning to finish some of his sentences.
Though if the end were half as bad as the beginning it
might be better not to try. After all Laura had risen to
her present eminence through her silences rather than her
speeches.

René leant across and tapped her kindly on the shoulder.
'Well done, Hon . . . Sally,' he said. Pris Evans rose. 'Well,
we mustn't take up any more of your day. It's been a long
week, one way and another.' She turned to pick up her
coat. 'By the way, René, did you mention that other little
matter to Sally?'

René went rather pale. 'I . . . No . . . the thing was I rather
thought you . . .' Pris threw him a look of impatience. 'Oh
very well. Just a small point, Sally my dear. In view of the
prominence Laura will be receiving in our forthcoming
publicity promos, we'd prefer it if you didn't see too much
of Marley Webb. At least until things have blown over. I'm
sure you understand.'

The two women faced each other, as René fiddled hopelessly with the clasp of his briefcase. 'What do you mean
by "too much"?' asked Sally. Pris shrugged and pulled on
an immaculate kid glove. 'Anything at all for the time
being. It might cause unnecessary problems. Ones which
we would rather not have to face at the moment, just
when things are going so well – for you in particular. It
never does to be associated with unpleasantness when
one's in public life. I'm sure you've seen it yourself –
how totally innocent people can be, how shall I say
it, "tarred with the same brush". It would be such a
shame if that were to happen to you. Goodness, is that
the time? I'm meant to be in a meeting at five. Come
on, René. We must dash.' She pressed Sally's hand with
the soft slimy palm of her glove. 'Thank you so much

for giving me the chance of this little talk. As I say, someone will be in touch with your agent, probably next week.'

Sally sat in front of the television. She was watching the BAFTA Awards. Best Actor, Best Actress, Best Supporting Actor, Best Supporting Actress, Best Character Actor, Best Character Actress, Best Actor in a Television Serial, Best Actress in a Television Serial. 'And the contestants are: Rita Frank, Claire Bevan, Lucy Dahl, and Cassie Bartholomew.' She reached across and flicked the button. The screen went dead. It doesn't take long, she thought, never to have existed.

The phone rang. She picked it up. 'It's Dan.'

'Oh.'

'How are you?'

'Fine.'

'Good. I wanted to say . . . about Marley . . .'

'What?'

'I'm very sorry.'

'Yes. Thank you.'

'Sally . . .'

'Yes?'

'Can we talk?'

'I thought we were.'

'You know what I mean.'

'I'd rather not.'

'Why won't you let me explain?'

'Because I don't want to hear.'

'You never did, did you?'

'What?'

'Want to hear. Listening's not a big thing with you, is it? Except to the sound of your own voice.'

'If you mean, do I prefer truth to filthy lies, you're probably right.'

'What do you know about the truth?' Dan suddenly exploded. 'Your whole world is made up of lies and make believe. Bloody actors. You wouldn't know the truth if it came up and hit you in the face.'

'Oh wouldn't I?' countered Sally, unnerved by his vehemence. 'Well, it came pretty damn close last Friday night, I can tell you. I suppose you're going to tell me that was just a social call? Does Suzanne often pop in on you like that?'

'No.'

'No, I imagined not.'

'She came to ask if we could get back together.' Sally's heart gave an uncontrollable jolt. She struggled to compose herself. 'Oh, I see. Patrick's kitchen not up to scratch?'

Dan, when he spoke, sounded subdued. 'I think Patrick was the problem, not his kitchen.'

'Yes, well, I suppose his flat was a bit small for two egos that size.'

'The Taj Mahal would have been too small.'

'But Marchbank Gardens isn't? I got the letter, by the way.'

There was a silence. 'That's what I wanted to talk to you about.'

Sally suddenly felt sick. 'Don't talk to me about anything, Dan. I've done enough talking to last me a lifetime, and at the end of it I'm no further on.'

'That's because you don't listen.'

'So you keep telling me. But I do listen sometimes and I do remember what people say. And I remember you saying to me once that I didn't even exist. What you should have said was that I didn't exist for you.' She put the 'phone down. She had a pain in her stomach. Sinking down on to the floor she rocked slowly to and fro, waiting for it to go away.

There is a special kind of awe reserved for people with terminal illnesses and actors who have blown their careers. Such was the reverence which greeted Sally Grosvenor after the appearance of her column the following week.

Dear Readers,

It has been my privilege over the past few months to share with you some of the problems and anxieties that have been troubling you and to offer you some suggestions as to how these might best be tackled.

I hope, therefore, you will forgive me if this week I ask for your help and understanding in a matter which has touched me deeply, namely the arrest of Marley Webb (Rebecca Christie in *The Firm*) on a charge of shoplifting.

Let me give you the background. Marley Webb is seventy-four years old. Widowed, she lives alone in a third floor flat in North London. Those of you who live in the capital will know that rents are not cheap. Why else, you may ask yourself, would a seventy-four-year-old woman be working a fifty-two-hour week? "Yes," I hear you say, "but she's an actress. Surely that's a glamorous life?" Is it glamorous to be called at six in the morning to be filmed in the rain and the wind in a cemetery forty miles from your home? Is it glamorous to work till ten o'clock at night in a hot stifling studio? Is it glamorous to crawl into bed at midnight, knowing you have to be back at work at eight in the morning, because some new producer wants to replot all the moves you have taken a fortnight to learn, three days before recording? Above all, is it glamorous to be old and alone and be told that the little pleasures you allow yourself – a biscuit with your elevenses, a piece of cake with your afternoon tea, a cup of cocoa at bedtime – are forbidden, on pain of dismissal? Is this the kind of contract Mel Gibson and Madonna sign their names to? Is this what you would want your loved ones to submit to in order to live? If it is, fine. If it is *not*, write to Majestic Studios, write to the press which has villified her, write to the judges who will sentence her. Write and say, "if my mother, my grandmother, any old person I loved, was so hungry and frightened that she stole a bar of chocolate," and make no mistake, Marley Webb did steal that sixty-five pence bar of Toblerone from a department store on January 4th this year, "because she was tired and cold and hungry, and she was afraid of being caught in default of her contract and sacked, then who, in God's name, are we to condemn her?"

What sort of world do we live in where people who have given their whole lives to entertaining and cheering up others, and helping them through their hard times, are cast out like lepers the moment they transgress? Was it not Shakespeare who said, and here at *Television Toppers* we pride ourselves on preserving the great culture of our dramatic heritage, "The weight of this sad time we must obey, Speak what we feel, not what we ought to say. The *oldest* hath borne most; we that are young Shall never see so much, nor live so long."

The response was unprecedented. Temps were hired to write 'Yea' or 'Nay' on sacks of mail which were sorted and stockpiled against the walls of unused offices in the Majestic Studios' complex. The 'Nays' were so outnumbered that disaffected sorters took to stapling 'Yea' to everything that came in.

MPs called for an Early Day Motion about heating for the elderly. Selfridges endowed Help The Aged with twelve-thousand-pounds' worth of cardigans and chocolate. Marley was booked to turn on the Christmas lights in Regent Street at the end of the year.

In the last episode of *The Firm* Laura Barnes, while driving to work, on the way from taking her deaf and dumb neighbour to speech therapy, was struck by a runaway fuel tanker and fell into a coma from which she was not expected to recover.

30

The coast of Norfolk was cold. It was the wrong time of the year and the wrong sort of play, but it was the set book so there were coachloads of disgruntled fifth formers who sat in the audience flicking pellets at each other and farting during the soliloquies.

Their numbers were augmented by chilly pensioners who could get in for a pound on matinée days and found the fug of the theatre more comforting than a one-bar electric fire at home. Also *Much Ado About Nothing* sounded like a farce of some kind, and they had always enjoyed those Brian Rix things on their organised trips to London. Having discovered their mistake they accepted it with equanimity and fell peacefully asleep till the interval.

Sally had rented a small cottage. They were cheap out of season. No one had been to see her Beatrice, Michael Snelcott having all but struck her from his ledgers, such was the depth of his despair.

She could still hear his voice down the phone on publication of her appeal on Marley's behalf. 'Are you quite mad? Have you completely taken leave of your senses? After all I've done for you. How could you do this to me, Sally? How could you treat me this way after the effort I have put in to building up your career? Is it something you've got against me personally? Because if it is I'd like to know.'

'No, of course it isn't, Michael. Don't be so melodramatic. It just seemed to me Marley was being unfairly treated and that something should be done.'

'SHE was being unfairly treated? What about me? No one's been on the phone asking ME to turn the Christmas lights on, I can assure you of that.'

'Well, perhaps next year . . .' retorted Sally, suddenly sick of them all.

'Oh ha ha. I'm glad you can see the funny side of it. By the way the coffee deal's off. They're going to use that weather woman. If her coffee's anything like her forecasting she probably won't even get it in the cup.'

Normally Sally would have laughed, particularly since her agent was entirely serious, but the reminder that Gaby had been rebooked, complete with pregnancy storyline, to star opposite Patrick for a further two series still stung with unbearable intensity.

She knew now she had done the wrong thing. She had made the wrong choice. She had underestimated the power of her column and overestimated her position in the cast.

Why couldn't she have done what Patrick had done? Laid low and helped Marley privately?

Because she had laid low once too often. She had turned her back on a few too many people in order to preserve her famous independence. And where had it got her? Her own relations ignored her; Mr Davenport had died alone and unvisited; Colin, whose gullibility she had so often condemned, pitied her, and Dan, whom she had loved with all her heart, had finally been repelled by her obsessive fear of commitment.

It was too little and too late, but it was a start.

The part of Beatrice had come about almost by accident. Snelcott had happened to let drop that the actress originally engaged for the part had been offered a role in a children's serial. He had intended the information as a goad rather than a tip, but as soon as he was off the 'phone Sally had rung the director and asked if it was true he was looking for a new Beatrice. 'Have you done any Shakespeare?' he had asked with a desperation that said knowing the man's first name would have got her the part. She had left for Norfolk the next day.

She had enjoyed rehearsals. It was good to walk around a stage without being confined by filing cabinets and the shadow of the boom. The cast, though inexperienced, brought an exuberance to the play that she now realised had been missing from *The Firm*. None of them appeared to have watched it. They were still too full of ideals.

Benedick was played by an actor in his forties called Edward Garth. Watching him Sally thought about Patrick and his years in the wilderness. This was exactly the kind of life he had talked about, touring the provinces, giving good but not startling performances in theatres where no one came, always waiting for the 'main chance'.

One more week and the run would be over. What next? Somehow she doubted Michael Snelcott would have anything lined up for her when she returned. He had been very prim about her taking this part. Plainly he didn't believe her fecklessness merited work of any kind. He had not been slow to remind her, however, that he was still entitled to his twelve and a half per cent.

She walked home. The cottage was on the seafront, set back from the coastal path by a little garden. It was flint and extremely pretty. Extremely draughty, too, and possibly a little bit daunting for anyone unused to being alone. But Sally had been used to being alone, and would learn to be again, so this was as good a place as any to practice.

Dan was a million miles away. So were Patrick and Marley and the shamefaced cast presenting her with Olivier's biography and a bottle of brandy in her dressing room, before rushing off to the last night party to which she had not been invited.

She made herself some cocoa and took herself to bed. It was cold in the wide iron bed, between the mothballed sheets and the crush of utility blankets. It was a bed for a spinster. One who yearned for the coming of the dawn.

Dawn brought very little, barring mist and a renewal of the rain that had persisted for most of her stay. The afternoon matinée, however, brought a rather severe shock. There in the front row, in mauve shirt and purple tie, sat Michael Snelcott, surrounded by Patrick Crichton, Marley beaming like someone newly released from Bedlam, and Pris Evans, who looked as though she would rather be pumping an Aids victim's stomach than sitting through a play by William Shakespeare.

'Max says there're agents out front,' confided the young man playing Claudio. 'He says they're looking for someone to play Margaret Thatcher in a film about her life.' Sally smiled. Max, the stage doorkeeper, was obsessed with Margaret Thatcher. It was therefore more of a shock to her to spot her agent's raddled profile in the front row than if no one had said anything in the first place. Him she could have understood – in a fit of remorse or the need to complete some business with Anglia – but Patrick, Marley and PRIS! It was positively sinister.

Notes were delivered in the interval. Could they come round after the show? Could they buy her tea? They were all very excited by the production. Weren't the provinces marvellous?

The five of them sat at a table in the tea shop across the road. 'You were wonderful,' said Patrick, pressing her hand. 'You were born to play Beatrice, wasn't she, Marley?'

'Oh yes,' chirrupped Marley who looked ten years younger than when Sally had last seen her.

'I wonder if I could have lemon with my tea?' Michael Snelcott asked the waitress who had recognised Patrick and Marley and was working up the courage to ask them for an autograph.

'Don't you find it terribly cold?' asked Pris Evans as though the two of them had never met.

'I wear a vest,' said Sally.

'I found it very slow,' said Pris. 'Tremendous lack of pace. I think I might have disposed with some of the subplot.'

'Oh no,' said Patrick with forced jocularity. 'You mustn't tamper with the Bard. Not even you, Pris.' They exchanged unfriendly smiles.

The waitress brought the tea. Pris wanted a fork for her macaroon. 'Aren't you eating anything?' asked Patrick as he delved into a slice of fudge cake. Sally shook her head. She was amused to see that Marley was consuming a cream cake and that Pris had not so far batted an eyelash. 'I have to be back in town by eight,' fretted her agent, looking at his watch. Pris Evans frowned. 'Perhaps we'd better get straight to the point then.' Sally waited. From the look of the two of them it was not something they relished. Snelcott was nibbling round his scone like a rabbit. I'm being sued, she thought, and he's afraid he'll have to stand surety.

Pris took a deep breath, dusted an invisible crumb from her lapel, and said, 'We've decided to give you another chance.'

Sally stared. Snelcott's nose was deep in his teacup. 'Yes,' Pris continued, 'we recognise that what you did, though badly mistaken, was from the best of intentions. We are prepared, therefore, to let the matter slide. I've spoken to Michael here, and we can offer you a second series at the same rate as the first which, I think you'll agree, is very generous under the circumstances.'

There was a silence round the table. Snelcott was nodding at her vigorously from behind Pris Evans' head, Marley was smiling delightedly and even Patrick was raising a quizzical eyebrow in encouragement. Sally finished her tea. 'I see,' she said. 'Thank you. Naturally I'll have to think about it.'

Michael Snelcott looked as though he might be in the first stages of apoplexy. 'What is there to think about?' he spluttered. 'Majestic has been extremely fair – more than fair. I don't think there's anything to think about. Filming starts in five weeks' time. They can't be expected to hang about.'

'I appreciate that,' said Sally, also looking at her watch. 'You'll have to excuse me. It takes me hours to get my make-up on. Thank you all so much for coming. I'm glad you enjoyed the performance.' She shook Pris' hand, kissed Marley and Patrick and nodded to her agent.

On the way out the waitress asked if she thought Patrick and Marley would sign a napkin for her. 'I'm sure they will,' said Sally. 'They don't mind what they sign.'

Patrick caught up with her as she crossed the road. 'You were good,' he said and she sensed a slight envy in his voice. 'I love that play. I played Benedick once – in Hong Kong. Those were the days.'

'The days you don't want to come back,' she reminded him.

Patrick grinned. 'Maybe you're right. Look, Sal, what I wanted to say is, don't turn them down. I know they've stitched you up on this contract, but it's only for one series and the thing's set to run forever. Don't let your pride get in the way.'

'What pride?' asked Sally gloomily.

Patrick clicked his tongue. 'The pride that's screwing up your life in all directions.'

'I don't know what you're talking about,' said Sally

haughtily. 'Anyway, what brought about this sudden change of heart?'

Patrick laughed. 'You are out in the wilds, aren't you? Don't you get newspapers down this way?'

'What do you mean?'

'My darling, OUTRAGE! A tiny bird told the editor of the *Sun* that Laura Barnes had been sacrificed because of what she'd said about Majestic and the public went mad. There was a march to Trafalgar Square last Sunday. 'Spare Laura Barnes'. 'Let Laura Live'. You must have seen it on television?'

Sally looked at Patrick carefully. 'You are a liar,' she said. Patrick shrugged cheerfully. 'You're right,' he said, 'but the thing was someone pointed out to our lovely new producer that what had happened for Marley might yet happen for you, and she didn't awfully fancy the prospect.'

Sally grinned at him incredulously. 'Was it you?' Patrick shook his head. 'I wish it had been. But you know me, no balls. No, it was someone they had to believe. Someone who had nothing to lose – and quite a lot to gain from a personal point of view.'

'Dilys?'

'That's the one.'

'Dilys. I should have known.'

'So you will do it? Gaby won't last more than a series, take my word for it. She's got Full-Time Mum stamped all over her.'

Sally nodded. 'I think you're probably right there.'

Patrick kissed her. 'Then perhaps we may get to see the famous Barnes body in all its pubescent loveliness.'

'It's a bit late for that.'

'It's never too late.'

Michael Snelcott came wheezing across the road. 'Sally, I must have a word. I've got to go. I'm supposed to be at the Gielgud —'

'By eight,' finished Sally.

'Yes. Exactly.'

'I've left my umbrella,' said Patrick tactfully and hurried off.

'Sally . . . Dear . . .' Snelcott struggled, 'Don't be silly about this, will you? Don't do anything you'll regret.'

'What do you mean?'

'You know bloody well what I mean,' exploded her agent, then restrained himself. 'Sally, please believe me, I'm saying this for your own good. I have your best interests at heart. I've just had a word with Pris. They'll keep the offer open till two o'clock tomorrow. The afternoon, that is. After that they'll scrap the whole idea.'

'Are you sure about that?'

'Absolutely. The woman is adamant. Oh, she knows the score – that that dipsomaniac wife of Bill Lewis is threatening to blow the gaff, but she doesn't care. Between you and me the woman's a monster. Shouldn't be put in charge of a herd of buffaloes, let alone a troupe of actors. I don't know what the business is coming to, I really don't. But there it is. Do you want to accept now, Sally? I really think it might be best.'

Sally put a soothing hand on his arm. 'I'll ring you tomorrow, Michael. Trust me.'

'Before two o'clock. It's got to be before two or the whole deal's blown.'

'Before two.'

There was a toot from the car park. Michael Snelcott jumped. 'Oh that's me. I'll have to go. Don't let me down over this, Sally. Don't forget to ring.' He scurried off.

'What did you think of the play?' Sally shouted after him. Snelcott turned distractedly. 'What? Oh, yes. The play. All right. Very good. I couldn't hear Leonato at all.' And he was gone.

*   *   *

Just before the half Edward Garth knocked on her dressing-room door.

'May I come in?'

'Of course.'

'How did it go?'

'What?'

'Well, I couldn't help noticing you had a party in this afternoon. Annie in the tea room said they were from TV. Some series she was going on about?'

'Oh, yes. *The Firm*. That's the thing I was in before I came here.'

'Oh.' Edward looked slightly disappointed. 'I thought it might be something new they were doing. I was going to ask you for the director's name.'

'It's René Havers,' said Sally, 'but if I were you, Edward, I think I'd give it a miss.'

'Not too good, eh? I expect you're right. Still, I might just drop him a line, if you've no objection?'

'None in the world.'

Edward brightened a little. 'Any chance I could mention your name, just in passing?'

Sally sighed. 'You can if you like. I don't think it will be much help somehow.'

Edward nodded. 'I'd better get changed. Annie said she got your friends to sign a tablecloth for her. She's never asked me for my autograph. Has she you?'

'No,' said Sally. 'Never.'

'Ah well. Our day will come.'

'Let's hope so.'

'I don't know, gal,' said Max in his permanently lugubrious voice. 'It's like Piccadilly Circus round here today.' Sally raised an enquiring eyebrow since, with the best will in the world, it was difficult to see why he should think so. 'Four of them after the matinée,' chuntered the doorkeeper, 'and now another one tonight. What'll it be tomorrow? A coach party, I reckon.'

Sally smiled uncertainly. 'What do you mean "another one"?' Max jerked his head. 'He's outside. I said he could wait in here with me but he said he didn't want to be in the way, so he's outside.' Sally opened the stage door and stepped out into the alley that ran along the back of the theatre. 'Oh my God.'

'Hullo.' Dan stepped out of the shadows.

'What are you doing here?'

'I came to see you.'

'Why? How did you know where I was?'

'I phoned your agent.'

'He had no right to tell you.'

'He had no reason not to.'

'If this is about the freehold . . .'

'It's about you and me.'

'There is no "you and me". I thought you understood that.' She started to walk away. Dan caught up with her. 'Sally, just give me half an hour. I've driven all this way. It's not too much to ask, is it?'

'I thought you came to see the play.'

'No, I came to see you.'

'Half an hour then. I'm rather tired.'

Dan nodded. 'The pub?' Sally shook her head. 'Everyone's in there. If we're going to have a row I'd rather it wasn't in front of my friends.'

'Where then?'

'You can come to my digs. It's only ten minutes away.'

They walked in silence. The wind had got up and was whipping little flurries of sand across the footpath. It stung their faces as they pushed along. Sally unlocked the door and the draught swirled through the house taking the letters she had forgotten to post down the hall.

'Quick.' She shut the door and hurried to put a match to

the fire. 'Take your coat off. There's some wine in the fridge. I'm afraid I haven't got anything else. I wasn't expecting visitors.'

'That's all right.' The fire was sparking and blowing bits of paper back into the room. 'You need a guard for that.' Sally stood up, flushed from her efforts. 'Do you have to start criticising the moment you arrive?'

'I'm sorry.' Dan poured the wine and handed her a glass. 'Cheers.' Sally nodded curtly but did not respond. 'Is it all right if I sit down?'

'Of course.'

They sat either side of the fire and stared into it. 'About the house,' Dan began. Sally got up. 'Would you like a sandwich? I'm going to have one.'

'Yes, all right. Thank you.'

'I've only got marmalade.'

'Marmalade is fine.'

She went out into the kitchen. When she came back she noticed that Dan had rearranged some of the logs with the poker. The fire was now blazing brightly. 'Here you are.'

Dan took the plate. 'I assume,' he said formally, 'that you have no objection to me buying the freehold?'

Sally feigned surprise. 'Would it matter if I had?'

Dan sighed. 'Probably not. The point is I also plan to buy Mr Davenport's flat.'

Sally's mouth dropped. 'Oh. I see.'

'Is that a problem?'

She pulled herself together. 'Why should it be?'

'Because that only leaves your flat, if you see what I mean.'

'I'm not sure that I do.' Dan kicked a loose coal back towards the grate.

'I was wondering if you'd like to sell that to me too?' Sally choked on her wine. Dan put his plate down and came and patted her on the back. She waved him away. 'How will you manage that?' she croaked. 'I mean, won't it all be rather expensive?'

Dan shrugged. 'I've got a bit put by.'

'You'll need more than a bit.'

'I know. I can raise the capital. What I wanted to know was, would you be willing to sell?' Sally sat back in her chair. Her head was spinning. 'But a little while ago you were asking me, before . . .'

'If you wanted to come in on it with me. I can see now that was a mistake. I didn't realise, you see . . .' for a moment his voice faltered but he quickly continued. 'I didn't know how much all this acting stuff meant to you. How involved you got. For me, a job's a job. But it's not like that for you, is it?'

Sally shook her head. 'It's my life.'

Dan nodded. 'And I was in the way.'

Sally looked up sharply. 'No you weren't. How can you say that? You were a part of it. The most important part of all, if you must know. If you knew the dreams I had . . .'

'Yes, but that was it, wasn't it?' Dan broke in angrily. 'It was all dreams with you. There was no room for reality.'

'If you mean like standing in for your wife . . .'

'You were not standing in for Suzanne. You never let me explain. Not once did you let me tell you my side of it. You just jumped to conclusions. You worked out the story line, or whatever you call it, and I had to fit in with the details. That's how you live your life. I tell you something, you laugh at the public for believing in soap operas. At least they wake up from time to time. That's more than you'll ever do.'

'Oh shut up,' said Sally wretchedly. 'I came home and found the two of you slobbering over each other on the doorstep. The next thing you tell me is she wants to come back to you. You're right, it is out of a soap opera. But you're the one who's living it, not me.' Dan put his head in his hands. 'I know how it must have looked to you.'

'It looked the way it was.'

'We were saying good bye.'

Sally stared at him uncertainly. 'What do you mean? You said she wanted a reconciliation . . .'

'Yes. She did.'

'But . . .'

But I didn't.'

'YOU didn't. You've been in love with her from the day I met you. I realise that now.' She hesitated, then said quietly, 'I didn't at the time.'

Dan put his hand out to silence her. 'I thought I was. I really did. And I thought it was my fault that we'd drifted apart. That's why I went to those stupid classes and the Marriage Guidance counselling and all that.'

'Marriage Guidance? When did you go to that?'

'Twice a week. All those evenings you thought I was building that conservatory.'

Sally felt herself flushing hot and cold. 'So,' she said with deliberate calm, 'while you and I were having an affair you were spending two evenings a week trying to put your marriage back together?'

Dan dug his fingernails into the side of the chair. 'It wasn't the way it sounds. I wanted to make sure. . . We'd been married for eleven years. I wanted to be sure that the things I felt for you weren't just a reaction – a way of getting back at her. I didn't want to make the same mistake again.'

Sally leant back in her chair and closed her eyes. 'What "things" did you ever feel for me, apart from an overwhelming desire to ruin my life?' Dan reached out and tried to take her hand. She pulled it away. 'I didn't ruin your life, Sally,' he said softly. 'You'd never have let me.'

They sat for a while in silence. 'You can buy my flat,' said Sally at last. Dan looked up. His eyes were full of pain. 'I was afraid you'd say that.'

'Why? Can't you afford it really?'

'Oh yes. Once the divorce is through. That was the other thing Suzanne was telling me. We've had a firm offer on the flat. The mortgage was nothing, so I'll have more than enough for the deposit.'

'What about Suzanne?'

'Suzanne will be all right. Her type always land on their feet.'

Listening to him Sally thought, he could be talking about anyone. 'A matriarch, then?' she murmured reflectively. To her surprise this made Dan laugh. 'Something like. She'll survive. Best thing for both of us, really. A clean break.'

'That's what I need,' said Sally. 'I wouldn't have wanted to go on living there under the circumstances.'

'Under what circumstances?'

'You buying up all round me.' She looked at him. 'Let's face it, you wouldn't be doing it just for you, would you? You're not the type to stay single.'

Dan smiled sadly. 'And you're not the type to get married, I suppose?'

Sally shivered slightly. 'It seems not.' Dan reached across and gripped her hands. 'I suppose you're not prepared to try?' Sally closed her eyes. 'It wouldn't work, Dan. I couldn't stay at home and keep house.'

'I wouldn't ask you to.'

'Not to start with, maybe, but after a while you'd get sick of me hanging over the phone and charging off all over the country at a moment's notice. You'd want children and things and I'm just not like that. It's impossible to explain. Actors are different. We're gypsies. We can't stand still.'

Dan let go of her hands. 'No,' he said. 'I suppose I knew that all along. I thought I could fit into it, but it's not so easy, is it?'

Sally smiled. 'It's not so easy for the people who are in it already.'

Dan nodded. 'Still, at least here you're doing what you really care about. Not that television rubbish.'

Sally gave a wry laugh. 'Not for much longer. This finishes next week.'

'What then?'

'Flat-hunting by the sound of it.' She got up. 'Actually I've been offered another series of "that television rubbish".'

Dan looked up at her. 'Are you going to do it?'

Sally stared into the fire. 'I'd be a fool not to, as my agent spared no effort in telling me this afternoon. It's just . . .'

'What?'

'Oh nothing. Too many dreams, I suppose.' She glanced at him and smiled. 'But I'm learning.'

Dan watched as she emptied the crumbs into the flames. He seemed about to say something then changed his mind. He stood up. 'I'm glad I've seen you.'

'So am I.'

'I'd better be off. It's a long drive.'

'Yes . . . Dan . . . '

'Yes?'

'You can stay if you want. On the couch, I mean.'

Dan smiled. 'I don't think so. But thanks anyway.' He touched her face with the back of his hand. 'You should have more faith,' he said. As he turned to pick up his coat Sally flung her arms round him and hugged him to her. 'I do love you, Dan,' she whispered. Dan put his jacket down and gently detached her hands. 'I know,' he said. 'I know you do.'

Sally watched him struggling back up the path towards the distant lights of the town.

Annie set the poached egg in front of her. 'Fancy you knowing the Christies, like that,' she said admiringly. 'He's a real gentleman, isn't he?'

'Yes,' said Sally, reaching for the pepper. It was half past one and she had still to ring Michael Snelcott.

'And she's a real lady. I never believed a word of what they said about her, you know. You've only got to look at her to see she'd never go thieving. It's a wicked lie. She was lucky she had Laura Barnes to speak up for her. You look a bit like her, you know. Only your hair's different and you're not so tall. Has anyone ever told you that?'

'I don't think they have,' said Sally. Annie left her to eat her lunch.

'Mrs Shaw says you look like Laura, too,' Annie indicated an elderly woman who was eating a pancake as Sally rose to pay her bill. Sally smiled. The elderly customer swivelled to get a closer look at her. 'Her nose is different,' she observed critically. 'Isn't it dreadful what's happened to the poor girl? And her never done anyone any harm in all her life. It's not right, is it? Why couldn't it have been that Richard? He's no better than he ought to be. Or that Careeriola. I can't stand her. Do you know we're offering up prayers for Laura in church this Sunday. The vicar's promised to make a special mention.'

'I'll be along to that,' came a voice from the other side of the tea-room.

'It's wonderful what they can do these days,' said someone else.

'Stoke Manderville, that's where she should be,' suggested a local farmer.

'I think they should take her to Lourdes,' said Mrs Shaw. 'They should take her on a pilgrimage.'

'That would be beautiful,' whispered Annie, her eyes filling with tears. 'What do you think, Miss? This lady knows the Christies. They were here only yesterday. In here, having tea and cakes. She's a friend of theirs.' The company regarded her with silent awe. 'Laura will get better, won't she?' pleaded Annie. Sally looked at the anxious faces all around her. An enormous sense of power invaded her being. It's up to me, she thought. I can decide. It all depends on me.

'This is excellent news, Sally.' Michael Snelcott sounded like someone who has been snatched from the jaws of death. That was probably how it felt to him, Sally reflected.

'There is a condition.' She heard him wheeze.

'I'm not sure I can push them too far on the contract, Sally, my love. It's all been a little bit hairy, to tell the truth. I might as well let you know, they wanted to drop the fee in view of all this . . . Well, you know what I mean. Oh, not that I would have allowed them to, of course. You know me. But I don't think any other agent would have got you the terms I have.'

'I think you're probably right,' Sally acknowledged.

'I'm so glad you've seen sense. I always knew you would. By the way, I can tell you now. I wasn't going to till you'd agreed. At least I would have if you hadn't so that you would have had to, if you see what I mean . . .'

'Not really.' Sally looked at her watch. 'I'm going to have to go, Michael.'

'Oh, yes, of course. No, the good news is I've had a drugs company on to me.'

'That's good?'

'For you, Sally. Don't you see? With Laura in a coma and everything, they thought you might be just the person to advertise their latest product.'

'What is it? A Life Support System?'

'Not as such. It's some sort of migraine pills or something. I mean the poor woman's bound to have a few headaches, isn't she? You would if you'd been hit by a lorry . . .'

'I really don't think . . .'

'It's worth a fortune. The coffee was peanuts compared.

And if it's a success, there's no knowing where it might lead . . . arthritis, that's very common after accidents; dizzy spells – amnesia, even. I'm not sure if they do anything for that . . . Still, with time.'

Sally cut across his flow. 'I want some new clothes.'

'What? Oh I should get yourself some. It must be dreadful there when the wind blows. I hate the east coast. Always have done.'

'For *The Firm*. That is the condition. I must have some new clothes.'

There was a pause. 'I really don't think . . .'

'It's off then.'

'Salleeegh . . .'

Sally was silent.

'What sort of clothes?'

'Nice clothes. Like Cariola's.'

'I really don't think . . .'

'Goodbye, Michael.'

'How many?' came an anguished gurgle. Sally considered. Better not overdo it. She didn't want to strain her newfound muscle. 'I want a spare skirt. One that fits.'

'I should think that might be arranged.'

'And two new blouses.' Snelcott groaned. 'And a coat.'

'What on earth do you need a coat for? You're always in the office. I might be able to manage the blouses.'

'No coat. No contract.'

'You're being very demanding, Sally, if you don't mind my saying. I hope all this . . . business . . . isn't going to go to your head.'

'I hope not too, Michael.'

'I'll see what I can do. What colour do you want?'

'I don't mind at all.'

'Thank goodness for that.'

'So long as it's mink.'

* * *

Dan was a long time answering the 'phone. When he did he sounded tired and depressed. 'Yes?'

'Dan?'

'Sally?'

'Yes.'

Dan cleared his throat. 'I'm afraid I haven't had time to get hold of the solicitors yet.'

'Good.'

'Eh?'

'Don't, Dan.'

'What do you mean?'

'I've changed my mind. I don't want to sell my flat to you. I want to stay.'

There was a silence. 'Does that mean you want me to move out?'

Sally shook the receiver in frustration. Outside a young couple were arguing as they waited, frozen, for her to finish. The phone card clicked remorselessly through her credits.

She took a deep breath. 'It means I want to marry you.' She heard Dan gasp. 'Dan . . . Are you still there?'

'Only just.' He was laughing. 'Oh God, Sally . . .'

'Yes?'

'You're a very pushy woman.'

'You'll get used to it.'

'It might take a long time.'

'We've got a long time.'

The line went dead. The phone card slid noiselessly out of its slot and lay glinting up at her. She picked it up, kissed it three times and threw it in the air.

The young couple eyed her curiously as she left the kiosk. 'It IS,' hissed the girl.

'Nah,' said the man authoritatively. 'It inna.'

'Ask her,' prodded the girl. The man shrugged. ''Scuse

me,' he sniggered to show his scepticism. 'You bin in a coma lately?'

Sally smiled beatifically at their critical young faces. 'I've been in a coma most of my life,' she said airily. 'But I'm out of it now.'

A Summer Affair
AMANDA BROOKFIELD

Nicholas and Kate Latimer have a lovely cottage, three healthy children and twenty successful years of marriage to their credit. Then their lives are thrown into confusion by a crisis of the most insidious kind.

Nicholas suddenly finds himself staring into a dark future that seems to offer nothing better than a modest pension and the burden of caring for aged parents. His elegant, vibrant wife has more time for her new career and the problems of her dashing bachelor brother than for her husband, which does little to bolster Nicholas' disintegrating sense of self-worth.

Kate still cherishes her marriage but can't help relishing the almost forgotten luxury of having time to herself – and, increasingly, time away from her husband's relentless bad moods. The arrival in the village of the darkly enigmatic Max Urquart adds a fresh twist to Kate's predicament, providing a welcome but potentially fatal distraction to the problems she faces at home.

Amanda Brookfield's other novels, *Walls of Glass*, *Alice Alone* and *A Cast of Smiles*, are also available from Sceptre.

SCEPTRE

The Love Letter
CATHLEEN SCHINE

Smart, Independent and sexy, Helen MacFarquhar owns a tiny bookshop in an idyllic seaside town, where her life is exactly as she planned it, comfortable and full. But then an anonymous letter arrives in her mail one steamy summer morning. Written by an unknown lover to a mysterious beloved, the letter becomes Helen's obsession.

'How do you fall in love?' the letter asks. To her dismay, Helen finds out, when the letter propels her into a fiercely tender love affair with Johnny, a student working in her shop.

Cathleen Schine's delicious comedy of manners is a sparkling and sophisticated ode to the seductions of modern love and old-fashioned letters.

'This is the kind of novel that can make your own life feel pedestrian, but you'll be having too much fun reading it to notice'
The New Yorker

'An irresistible treat, light as a soufflé, rich as a sundae and as satisfying as love'
San Francisco Chronicle

'A sophisticated and witty valentine of a novel'
People

'Delicious romantic fantasy'
Cosmopolitan

SCEPTRE

The Dancing Stones
CATHERINE FEENY

An aristocratic family and an ancient stained-glass window would be quite enough of fame and heritage for Wyley. Unfortunately, the village was built within a circle of standing stones. Over a thousand years later this fact still has the power to surprise, and to irritate.

As far as seventeen-year-old Melanie Flowerdew is concerned, the stones are the only redeeming feature of a place where it's bad enough to have to spend a Sunday afternoon, let alone millennia. For Melanie, the stones confirm something that it's easy to forget: not everywhere has the same values as Wyley. And though, so far, the circle has failed to deliver, Melanie still trusts in its power to open a door to somewhere else.

For the stones have been restless lately. The summer solstice is approaching. A group of travellers is following a ley line towards the stone circle, and nothing in Wyley will ever be quite the same again.

'*The Dancing Stones* is a witty debut from a new writer providing an affectionate but satirical view of the new age world of travellers and their impact on a quiet English village'
                                    Fiona Pitt-Kethley

'A funny and perceptive first novel'
                                    Northern Echo

SCEPTRE